Farewell the Dragon

Lee Barckmann

authorHOUSE®

AuthorHouse™
1663 Liberty Drive
Bloomington, IN 47403
www.authorhouse.com
Phone: 1 (800) 839-8640

Published by AuthorHouse 01/26/2017

ISBN: 978-1-4343-1351-5 (sc)
ISBN: 978-1-4520-4132-2 (e)

Library of Congress Control Number: 2007904093

Dedicated to **Qi Xinghua** – 亓兴华 **(1951–2006)** – my teacher and mentor, but most of all, my friend. I still miss him. Qi came to Eugene Oregon in 1983-84 and I was his student, in his Mandarin Chinese 101 class. On his return to China he invited me to teach English at the Xian Medical University, where he was the Vice Chairman of the English Language Training program. We remained close friends afterward, marveling together at the changes being wrought in his country. His death from pancreatic cancer in 2006 was a painful shock, and I think about him often.

Introduction to the Second Edition

I wrote *Farewell the Dragon* in 2006, while my memory of my time in China was reasonably fresh and I could still find my letters and diaries. Now ten years later, I am reminded how poorly I grasped the craft of writing, how rushed I was to publish, and how little time I had to devote to the task because I was making a living. But I did believe that I had the germ of a decent book, and was told so by more than a few readers. But I was also told by by some readers, that it was full of errors, both technical and logical, even though I had trouble admitting it to myself in the beginning

Now retired from the IT profession, I decided that it was worth the effort to re-write the novel, seek professional editorial guidance, and to release a second edition. This is the result.

The story is basically unchanged from the first edition. I am relieved to at least finally finish it, and I hope you like it.

Lee
11/27/2016

Part 1

Chapter One

Oct 21 1987

I was a guest of the PLO, living in an apartment at the embassy "guest house," an ugly, concrete, rectangular building with tiny windows that served as a safe house for "Friends of Palestine" traveling through Asia. It was 7 AM and I was reading a two-week-old *International Herald Tribune*, drinking tea, and waiting for the Beijing cops to pick me up. Yasir Arafat's portrait looked down, smiling from above the couch, dominating the bare room. There was a bad odor, sweet, rotten and pervasive, maybe coming from the grease-covered electric stove or the contents of cupboards in the kitchenette or maybe from the cigarette-burnt, ominously dark-stained couch.

The guest house was not even on Embassy grounds, but a block away on the street. An older Middle Eastern guy, wearing thin gray slacks, a khaki shirt and a black and white keffiyeh, was stationed out front, leaning on or sitting in a green Toyota Celica, under the aegis of the Chinese *Gong An* (公安, Public Safety, i.e., the Cops).

The Guest House had no thick oriental rugs on either the walls or on the floor (as did the main part of the embassy), just bare cracked concrete. The PLO "Embassy" wasn't even an embassy, but just a mission, but everyone pretended otherwise.

I was nearly broke, had a change of clothes that could stand washing, and about a week left on my visa. Chinese police were watching me, but I was safe, at least for the time being. If it wasn't for Ibrahim, using his influence as the chargé d'affaires at the PLO embassy (I mean the mission), I'd still be sleeping on the cot in the police station, in their "guest" room. I was not much better off here, but, for tonight at least, I lay in bed, alone with the illusion of freedom.

I tried to dream about sex, to forget and escape. I had blown up my prospects, spent almost all of my money and now was a suspect in a Chinese murder investigation. A half mile away, in my (USA) embassy, I had a serious and well placed enemy. And those sexy dreams weren't ending too well either, because I couldn't keep Erika and Sandor out of them. Their bullet-shattered heads leaked like sepia images onto the back of my retinas, haunting my wide-eyed half-awake dreams, and they were not always dead either.

All last night I was interrogated by the Beijing police. What did I tell them? They recorded everything I said, transcribed it while I slept, and then asked the same things so many times that I couldn't remember what I said. It wasn't over. What did I say? Some of it was lies and they knew it.

I didn't walk the shortest way, which would have led me past the door to my old apartment. I walked around the back by the work unit's restaurant, which was still open. I lowered my head; I tried to walk "Chinese" with mincing steps, so my normal looping stride wouldn't give me away. I didn't want to meet my old neighbors tonight, and fortunately no one seemed to notice me, or at least no one stopped or greeted me, actions which normally I expected every time I was on the campus. Had everyone already heard I was gone and been told to ignore me?

I had to cross a small plot of hard, uneven, dried mud to get to Erika's porch. Vacant land seems especially cursed in China, and I felt like a solitary, noxious weed growing through the cracks in the mud.

The lights were out and the curtain across the sliding glass door window was drawn. I climbed over the rail and nudged the slightly opened door wider, let myself in, and then closed it.

I found the light switch in the kitchen and flicked it on. The couch faced away from the kitchen and I saw the back of Erika's head lolling. Even before I was sure, I began to get queasy, and as I walked closer it was clear that she was dead. Her eyes and mouth were wide open, and her tongue was jutting just past her front teeth. She was still flaunting her arrogant beauty, looking down her nose at me while somehow, laughing at me for finding her.

She had been full of schmaltzy *schadenfreude* and was a mean bitch to boot, a stone-cold Fraulein with big, clear blue eyes and a button nose that made her seem much more open and friendly than she really was. But still – dead? A bullet in her head? No, this was too real, yet I wasn't sure I wasn't hallucinating. I hadn't exactly liked Erika, but my ex-girlfriend did, and well, she wasn't all bad.

Next to her on the couch, leaning over to the side against the armrest – at first I didn't recognize him. He had a big-barreled gun in his right hand, and a big, bloody, black and blue hole in his head just above his right ear. I slowly walked around the couch not taking my eyes off of that bloody spot.

Sandor was wearing tight, white under-shorts, with the elastic band ripped away about two inches in the front. How pathetic, caught dead in raggedy, torn underpants. His eyes were closed, very tightly. I realized then that I never really knew Sandor very well. I had watched him from across the table in the crowded cafeteria, and thought him witty, droll, melancholy and wary. His tightly closed eyes had been limpid and slightly sad, and something about them told me he didn't kill her or himself. But it sure did look like that.

I looked at Erika's face. She had a neat little hole in her forehead, and a tiny stream of dried blood dripped down between her wide open eyes. The blood stopped just at the bridge of her nose. She was wearing a pair of white nylon panties – bigger than what I imagined she would wear, about two inches wide on the side of the hips, and a low-cut white bra. She was a beautiful woman, in a severe, antiseptic sort of way, but still, I had never imagined her in white underwear. And I did imagine.

I walked around the couch again and could not find an exit wound. I came around again and looked at the gun in Sandor's right hand, lying between them, a Luger-style, fat-barreled semi-automatic. His finger was through the trigger guard. It was a funny looking gun, with a long, thick and unadorned gray barrel. Where the hell did he get that, here in Beijing?

I picked up his left hand and dropped it. It fell in slow-motion. I leaned down and smelled the faint whiff of nitrates from the nose of the gun. The answers were right in front of me, I thought. They had been dead for more than a couple hours – at least that's what it seemed like to me.

He shot her in the head, then shot himself. That's what it looked like. Right?

Right. I knew better but I couldn't tell the cops. I was sure I knew who really killed them – I had just been face-to-face with him five minutes ago.

I looked at Sandor's face and his arms. No scratches or bruises. The same with Erika, completely unmarked, except for the little Brahman bindi, her third eye, a Hindu beauty mark, crying red tears. I looked at her top to bottom and just stared. Nearly naked and completely dead, she was still beautiful. Her fingernails were unbroken and clean.

Dressed in their underwear – it didn't seem sexual, but it wasn't normal either. Was it a pact, some kind of weird ritual? No. I knew both of them well enough to realize that couldn't be – could it?

I looked around the room. Packed suitcases were by the door. Erika's frilly green dress, the one she wore that night in September, dancing at the Youyi (友谊), was folded neatly on a chair. They hadn't packed everything, but surely she would have packed that dress? Sandor's pants and shirt piled on the floor next to the couch. Food all put away in the kitchen, dishes washed. In the bedroom, the bed made, but the closets and dressers open. Nothing pulled out or out of order. A pile of stuff, some books, an old towel, a small radio with a broken antenna; all of it looked like it was to be thrown away.

It smelled like shit. Oh yeah – I was too scared to look any further than that. My mind was suddenly frozen.

I went out the way I came in, and walked fast to the guard station in front of the campus. I stayed there while one called the *Gong An* and the other ran to the apartment. The Public Safety car showed up fifteen minutes later, by which time the guard who ran to the apartment had come back.

"Shuang zisha(双自杀)" he told the two *Gong An* cops. Double suicide.

I guess it might look like that if you didn't know them – or if you didn't know what I knew.

I rode in the back of a Datsun squad car through the campus. The squawking police radio, unmounted on the passenger side floor, was turned up so loud that it acted like a siren attracting my old neighbors who came out of Xilou into the narrow alley to see what the fuss was about.

That's about what I told them. They didn't tell me what they found. They took me back to the police station in Haidian (the northwest section of Beijing where the universities are), and covered my forearms with wax, let it dry and peeled it off. They fingerprinted me and took a sample of my blood. In the States, the first rule is to shut up and ask for a lawyer, but it doesn't work that way here. I told them I was staying at the PLO Embassy, so they drove me back here to sleep rather than put me in a cell.

I am a red-haired American, and red hair is considered a sinister trait in European culture, a prejudice came over with the Mayflower. Western Europeans and their descendants around the world have an instinctual distrust of redheads. Every redhead knows what I am talking about. This subtle, suspicious distrust of gingers does not compare in kind or degree to racist KKK or Nazi ethnic hatred, or even to that smug, American WASP kind of prejudice. It is almost a subconscious tic and even we redheads feel it when we meet other carrot-tops.

China is self-contained and completely self-confident about race, at least their Han race (汉族), and no one who has ever been in a Chinese city will ever associate the word "minority" with them. They have many prejudices of course, but you feel it comes from a completely different historical point of view. Sometimes I feel like I am always admired from afar, sometimes like a rock star, sometimes like an exotic animal in a zoo, and it is largely because of the way I look, i.e., my red hair. I feel there is genuine warmth and friendliness toward me here. For what it's worth, I like living in China and don't want to have to leave.

But that didn't change the fact that I felt like suspect number one in a double murder, and they shoot violent criminals here, about a month after a quick trial.

I looked around my PLO hideaway - white walls, cheap Western style kitchen utensils. I looked in the refrigerator - oh the smell could gag a maggot! I guess I could have cleaned out the rotten food from the last tenants. I slammed the door shut. Maybe tomorrow, I thought.

Why am I here? Maybe the Chinese let me stay here to give me a false sense of security. In an ancient Chinese story, an ambassador brings a refusal to his king's enemy and is told he must give up a limb to satisfy the enemy's outrage and honor. Then he could return home missing an arm but a rich man. The stump heals and he is told no, he must give up one more limb but the reward is doubled. The scene repeats two more times and he is sent back to his king in a basket filled with gold coins, a stark raving insane quadruple amputee. I looked in the cupboard vainly hoping to find something to drink, any booze would do. Nothing.

The interrogation room seemed homey compared to the PLO apartment in some ways. Ibrahim told me the last tenants were a couple of PLO soldiers coming to China as a reward for something that he didn't specify. Future martyrs, getting their earthly reward (a trip to the Great Wall, a tour of the Forbidden City, maybe Ibrahim could arrange something a little more sensual...), before flying off to a mission that would probably lead to virgins and grapes in a heavenly oasis. Hopefully they would eat better there than they did here judging by the remains in the fridge.

The police interrogation room that I had spent the day in wasn't a medieval torture chamber. I sat at a solid, square, tea-stained table covered with files and reports, hot water thermos always within reach, comfortable wooden chairs that didn't hurt my back. Along the wall, saggy, cushioned chairs with shabby embroidered doilies on the arms reminded me of something from a Tennessee Williams drawing room. When I got restless and wanted to break away from the questions for a while, I would move over to one of those cushy seats and it was somehow recognized that those chairs were my refuge. The interrogators were polite, solicitous. They called me professor or doctor, read aloud from the personal files of the Chinese colleges where I taught, noting what a wonderful teacher I was, and how helpful I had been, etc., etc.

But the threat was delivered with whispers that hung out of earshot as we walked to the interrogation room. There was an occasional scream, of coercion or pain, quick intense, off-stage tortures that my interrogators ignored by raising the volume of their own voices.

I had heard of only one American in recent years who went to jail in China, a businessman in the north who allegedly burned down the hotel when a cigarette fell out of the corner of his lips as he slept. He survived the fire but others didn't. But this was a different kind of crime altogether. It seemed to have my inquisitors confused. They were constantly being interrupted to consult with unseen superiors. They continued to tell me that they "had full power to investigate wherever the crime might lead," and that foreigners were subject to the "full protection" of Chinese law.

I suppose I could have solved this whole thing for them, then and there. They wanted it to be a suicide pact or at worst murder-suicide, just some unfortunate circumstance, but not really involving China. I could have led them down that road easily. Sandor's adoration of Erika – and Erika's contempt for him – I could have pulled plenty of events out of all the times I had seen them together to confirm that. Unrequited love and depression – I could tell stories that showed that they both suffered from that. But I was afraid I would not be able to explain everything else nor the other things that I knew they would probably discover without me.

I was innocent. I hung onto that. I was scared of Chinese prison. Malaysia had recently hanged an Australian for drug smuggling and China published a very prominent article supporting Asia's right to execute anyone who broke their laws, including Westerners. In Louyang I had often seen flatbed trucks file by with condemned prisoners, thieves, breakers of the peace, and various other criminals, trussed up in the "airplane" position, wearing signs around their necks that described their crimes, on their way to the execution grounds, a local gravel pit, to get a bullet in the back of their head.

If I said nothing, it would be almost the same as a confession. I needed to tell them everything, the complete truth. Well, everything except for the one thing I knew that would change the whole investigation. Otherwise I would be hopelessly entangled in my own stories.

"Tell me again," said Qi, who was young, maybe thirty to thirty-five, dressed in a sweater and nice slacks, and who spoke wonderful English. (Qi always spoke in English. And Lang, the other detective, about fifty, spoke with a heavy Beijing accent that sounded like gravel being crushed, and knew only a little English as far as I could tell.) "Please, just one more time, explain, Dr. Schuett, why did you go to the German woman's apartment that night?"

"We were going to have a party – a farewell party for myself actually – and I wanted her to come."

"Was she a friend of yours?"

"Yes – I suppose." Good Christ what else did I tell them? And what really happened? How could I possibly keep it straight? What did I know and what did I tell them I knew? I knew the one thing that could help them and that was the one thing I couldn't say.

The day before yesterday, before I found the bodies, I was sure my life had hit bottom and that things couldn't possibly get worse. Little did I know...

***

Two days ago seems like a lifetime. No one was dead yet and I had never seen the inside of a Chinese police station, yet it seemed as though my life had fallen to a point the idea of "below which" did not exist. I didn't fall asleep until the sun was almost up and then finally I slept until almost noon, vainly hoping that Molly would come by and crawl into bed with me. All morning I would start to wake up and then allow myself to go back to sleep rather than get up and face it.

When I got up, I saw the note. When did she leave it there? She must have let herself in that morning while I was sleeping.

I read it.

I quickly dressed and walked down to Embassy Row. I didn't know what else to do. I was standing across from the American Embassy. I didn't believe, at least I didn't want to believe, that Molly was gone. When I read her note, I couldn't tell if she had left it this morning or last night. I didn't even go into the kitchen last night. She didn't come by while I was sleeping; that is ridiculous. She would have woken me. She is not that sneaky and certainly wouldn't be afraid to face me. She must have come back yesterday, probably while I was at the US Embassy trying to get that asshole clerk to tell me where they had gone and when they had left. I wanted to rub that useless piece-of-shit's face into the wall. It seemed as if everyone was in on it, hiding the truth from me.

Did Molly come to see me then in order to tell me to my face? She had the key to the apartment in the compound and the note is in her handwriting. Then I found the open notebook over on the counter. She had torn a page out it so she could write it there. She must have written it at the table in the kitchen. She had to have been in the apartment for a while, at least as long as it took to write it.

Nate,

No sense sugar coating this – I am leaving you – for Dexter! We are leaving for Thailand and after a couple of weeks there, I think he will be posted somewhere else or he will resign and we will raise horses. You must know that is really what I want. I am still mad at you for telling me not to bring my cowboy boots to China. We both want to leave Beijing. Either way it doesn't matter to me. We are getting married sometime during all of that. I am very happy and excited, and so is Dexter.

I know you think that it is because you lost your job and have made a mess of things – at least that it is what you probably tell yourself. But under it all you must know that I know about all of the women when I was gone.

Is there a woman anywhere within the radius of all the people you and I know who you did not FUCK? You ripped my heart out so many times I don't know how it beats! My heart isn't beating for you anymore that's for sure – you are just a memory already. Someday, maybe, it will be a fond memory but now it is too fucking painful.

You son of a bitch – I know there are others – probably that Chinese cello player and all of the Chinese women at the Friendship Hotel. And probably half the tourists that passed through this summer too. And I think you probably fucked Erika. I know you fucked that slutty East German – Erika herself told me that. You see there is nothing I wouldn't believe about you now Nate. There can be nothing between us anymore. ~~BASTARD! YOU MADE ME! – YOU FORCED ME! I HATE YOU!~~

I don't hate you. When I was with you alone, it still seemed so unimportant. I was starting to get over that. I thought in time I could forget all of that. Even when you forced me – so creepy! But I could forgive even that!

I have a lot of reasons to leave you. But none of them really are true. I am leaving you for Dexter. That is really the only reason. Dexter likes horses and he loves me – he so loves me Nate! Have you ever bought me flowers? Dexter does almost every day. Let's face it something was missing. You know that as much as I do!

I will miss *** with you. But Dexter is leaving his career – for ME! It seems like you were ready to throw me over for a career. <u>Until you fucked that up.</u>

You made me follow my own star – I never learned how to be independent until I met you. So thank you for that. I'll write you in care of your parents when I am settled. We probably have other issues to settle but they can wait.

Molly

"<u>Until you fucked that up</u>." Yeah it's funny how she underlined that at the end. As soon as I lost my job and my visa, I am sure that was just a "minor" reason for finding a CIA douche bag to replace me. But then she probably doesn't know what it is he does. Or that he is not even very good at what it is he "does."

Still – if she was there long enough to write all of that, then maybe she would have stayed long enough for me to talk her out of this. Maybe she didn't leave last night. Maybe when she was looking for me here and I was at the Embassy, maybe no one there told her I was looking for her. I was positive that fucker Dexter didn't tell her I was there looking for her. I was suddenly sure of that.

I started thinking about it and realized I have capable friends who would be quite happy to kill him for me. Just a nod from me and he'd be dead. That is how far I had sunk, which would be just what I needed now to add to the other two dead Europeans. I just wanted to jump out of my skin. I could not believe that this was happening to me. Everything had fallen in on me at once.

***

Anyway that was all two days ago, before I discovered Erika and Sandor dead in their underwear. Qi and Lang said they would pick me up at 7:30 AM and they were right on time. I put the note away, having read it again for the fiftieth time, as I heard their voices outside. No sense worrying, I thought; if I come back, I can gather my stuff up and if I don't, I won't need it. It's funny, the only person I trusted in the world was Ibrahim. For some reason (many reasons really), I had no doubts about him.

I sat in the back of their Datsun, Lang driving and Qi reading a report of some kind. Lang was commenting on the traffic, the weather, the number of foreigners on the street, anything to distract me. The trip was all the way across town, and I was actually sleeping when we pulled up to the Haidian police station. We got out and walked in. I followed Qi up the stairs and we ignored all of the activity around the front desk and in the various alcove-like rooms that seemed to take up all the wall space around the main processing room. All steel and concrete, the Haidian station smelled somewhere between a hospital and a zoo.

At the top of the stairs was a thick door and it was a different world, quieter, cleaner, fresher. No screams this morning, that all seemed like a distant nightmare. We went into a fairly large room and I sat at the table. Qi poured me a cup of hot water and indicated for me to help myself to the loose leaf tea in front of me, black tea, red tea, green tea. I dropped a few black leaves into my water and watched the fast-darkening rust-colored cloud leach into the hot water. I sat and drank tea. The minutes ticked by as if it were a scene in a Swedish movie.

Lang walked in and nodded to Qi.

Qi turned on the tape player and asked, "Tell us about the events that led up to you discovering the bodies."

I walked around the block on Embassy Row for two hours like a rabid dog, trying to find something to bite. My girlfriend had just left me and I didn't know where she was and I saw her and her boyfriend in every building behind every door. I am sure that the Chinese security must have wondered about me, but no one approached me.

It was chilly and the sky was clear, a beautiful autumn day. To a homesick Westerner, Guanghua Lu (光华路 Brilliantly Glowing Road) is the most beautiful part of Beijing, with its full deciduous trees at the point of turning, elegant lawns, well-crafted stone walls, and almost no people on the street. Chinese don't go there unless they are trying to get a visa, which was usually a last-ditch effort after official channels failed and was quite frowned upon by the government. But I don't need to tell you that do I?

This was the first time I had ever walked around Guanghua when I wasn't in a hurry and preoccupied with business. It was the first time I ever noticed it looked like a very high end neighborhood, the embassies all different, behind fences surrounded by green, well-tended lawns.

I was going to miss her, but the idea that I was free was beginning to creep into my consciousness. Life with her hadn't been much fun lately, at least not since the night after she came back from Montana in early September, and then the wild night of dancing and drinking on the roof of the Friendship Hotel. The night she met Dexter. I introduced them. It had not been much fun since then and now I was free. That is what I told myself to keep from thinking about her with someone else, or never...I tried to think about more immediate problems, like that fact that my visa was expiring in a couple of days. I was going to have to leave very soon if I couldn't get an extension.

I was standing on the sidewalk across from the Indian embassy, with its broad manicured lawn and Bengali-Victorian architecture, thinking about all of this when Ibrahim and

Rashid drove up and pulled next to me in the PLO mission's staff car.

Rashid vacated the front seat and got in the back, leaving the door open. I got in. Ibrahim was worried about me. I could see it in his face and hear it in his voice.

We drove in silence for a minute or so. "How many times has Mikku left you," I asked. He laughed. Rashid asked Ibrahim something in Arabic and they started talking fast, animated and laughing.

"Five times. Rashid says it is seven times. Twice I didn't even know she left me. He might be right."

I forgot that Rashid doesn't speak English sometimes. But I am pretty sure he understands most of it. It is his electric blue, Circassian eyes – reflecting a Western awareness but yet so Eastern, focused in on not being focused – more Eastern than most of the Chinese I know, more mysterious, yet in the end Western and familiar.

Rashid looked at me with a leering contempt.

"Rashid – I saw you looking at Mikku. When they argue do you comfort her," I asked, in Chinese of course, trying to start a hassle between them, to take my mind off of my problems.

"Of course I do. So do many men. I am surprised that you don't."

Ibrahim shrugged in resignation. "Mikku is a complicated woman. All families have their problems," he said. When he didn't say, "You see Nate these things happen, they blow over, and there is no need to become miserable over it," I knew then that this was his way of telling me I should probably forget about Molly...Rashid smiled at me, friendly and yet...even in our common language, Chinese, I still had no idea what he was thinking. The ancient and timeless Circassians, probably Herodotus's Scythians, are a mystery to history, but not to themselves. Rashid knew exactly who he was, even though his people have been displaced by history more times than he could count. Nothing seemed to bother him. Live or die, he could take it or leave it. In other words, sometimes he scared the shit out of me.

I envied Rashid's attitude at that moment, because I couldn't get Molly out of my mind. Someday, as she said, it will be a "fond memory," but right now, the feeling of loss is just too bitter. I'll probably just remember her as the greatest piece of my life, and that will be that. Does everything come down to sex? No. Well…maybe. I just wasn't ready to accept the fact I would never sleep with her again.

They were on their way to dinner and it was understood that I was coming with them. We went out to eat at a simple Korean restaurant, a little hole-in-the-wall near the Worker's Stadium. Mikku met us there, a Japanese Audrey Hepburn in a round, wide-brimmed hat and a simple white cotton dress. She was very nice to me, laughing at my jokes, while keeping my plate filled with radishes and kimchi, like the Chinese do at banquets and in their home. Mikku showed me and Rashid the pictures of Boris and Yevgeny, with their hard dicks in the vodka glasses. It embarrassed Rashid, even as he laughed hysterically. Ibrahim would not even look.

"In socialist solidarity with my Soviet brothers, I condemn this outrageous capitalist conspiracy, this barbaric trick!"

That got us all cracking up. We laughed and it felt so good, the first sense of relief I had felt in days.

Ibrahim was drinking more than usual and practicing his not-too-bad Korean with the daughter of the owner of the place. Rashid was giving me the signal to make my play with Mikku, who was ignoring Ibrahim's flirting, as if she didn't even care.

We cooked the meat right on the table in a little charcoal hibachi grill. I put the first sizzling piece of meat on her plate and she smiled. We ate kimchi and drank Korean sake. As the sliced beef sibilated on the grill, I thought of the last time…no it wasn't the last time, but it was very long ago. Maybe before we came to China? I was so confused.

"I have a treat for you, Nate," said Ibrahim. "I have discovered a nightclub that you will love."

I must have not looked too enthusiastic. I had had my fill of whorehouses for a while.

"It is a night club out by the Great Wall. I have told my friends that we will be there and we'd better go – these are not the usual people as you will see – it is unlike anything you have ever seen in Beijing. I guarantee that you will find something to change your mood. You will come?"

"Yes."

"Good. Maybe we do that tomorrow. Tonight let's go to the Youyi. You must see your friends. They will help you through this."

"Molly is a great woman you know," I said, unable to stop myself from blathering.

"Sometimes the great ones are not meant for each other." I looked at Ibrahim closely and saw the hint of a smile, but quickly forgave him for mocking me. I think this was his way of showing me how stupid I sounded by saying something stupid in reply.

We had to stop at the school for Mikku to change clothes, no doubt from Holly Golightly into a latex-clad comic book super-villain. We drove through the front gate, onto the dirt-covered square, a mini-Tiananmen, nothing on the ground, all dirt, just ancient Beijing dirt. Thirty meters across the square we drove past the Institute's administration building. Ibrahim let me out and then turned right and drove over to park in front of the foreign student dorms, where Mikku lived. Now that I think of it, when I was living here, I don't remember the guards coming on duty until later. The gates were left open at night sometimes, although I remember guards being there in the middle of the day sometimes too. But tonight we just drove through without stopping.

I said, "I am going to walk over and see Erika – see if she wants to come." I don't know why. I guess I just wanted to talk to…where did Molly get the idea I was sleeping with Erika anyway? And why not, I thought, as I got out of the Mitsubishi hatchback, maybe she will inspect me in my underwear before allowing me to…OK…I was thinking that, I can't deny that. Molly and I used to joke about Erika inspecting her lovers in their underwear as she snapped a riding crop against her bare thigh while barking orders.

Ibrahim let me out and then parked in front of the student dorm. I assumed he and Rashid would go upstairs with Mikku and talk to some of her friends while she changed. I said I would meet them later at the Youyi if I wasn't back in ten minutes. I walked across the campus and came around the old shower building. I had only been gone a week and it didn't seem familiar anymore. The crickets were almost gone. In September they had been loud, and now I thought I heard one, but wasn't really sure.

The campus is on the northwest edge of Beijing, and is bordered by an old canal that drains Kunming Lake next to Cixi's Summer Palace. On the east side of the ring road, where the Chinese students lived, the buildings were old – some of the buildings on the east side were fifty years old. They made me think of the old black and gray pictures of turn-of-the-century tenements in eastern American cities.

The senior faculty and foreigners, both students and teachers, lived on the west side of the ring road, and to the west beyond that was nothing but farmland.

I turned left and walked toward the communal shower building, then on to Xilou and eventually to the apartment building where Erika lived. It was dark – the moon was only a sliver in the sky. I turned the corner right by the shower building and I saw him. He walked past me, and I didn't recognize him, and I was sure he didn't recognize me.

A shiny, bald dome crowned the top of the new American teacher, but the hair on the sides and back of his head was thick, dark, and meticulously groomed. Obviously, his most recent haircut had not been in Beijing. He had taken my job about a week ago and now lived in Xilou (The West Building) – in the same apartment that Molly and I had shared. I stopped to tie my shoe in the doorway of the shower building and he walked by me. He was a big guy and he kept walking without turning to look at me, not out of overt rudeness or a lack of curiosity but mostly because he probably thought I was just another Chinese person bending down and staring at him in the dark as he passed.

Chapter Two

The interrogation room was like other meeting rooms in China; it had the Chinese style that is so peculiar, like the rooms in the news reports that Deng Xiaoping uses to meet foreign leaders, where Mao greeted Nixon, old soft chairs around the wall, the arms covered with embroidered doilies, lots of open space in front of the chairs, the same milieu as the meeting rooms for factories, ministries, universities. The motif occurs and recurs. The only difference was the small but thick wooden table in the middle of the room. So maybe it wasn't really an interrogation room. Maybe I was not a suspect. Maybe we were just having a meeting, exchanging information as representatives of our respective cultures. The two cops kept apologizing for my inconvenience and the pain I must be feeling at discovering the bodies of my friends.

We had been going at it for almost two hours, and I had taken Qi and Lang from my Korean dinner with Mikku, Ibrahim and Rashid to the drive to the Institute, to me getting out of the car in front of the administration building and walking toward Erika's apartment and turning the corner by the communal shower building and seeing...

"So this man who startled you – an American?"

"I don't know. I didn't speak to him – I don't think he saw me as he walked by. It was dark. But he just seemed like a European – American something – a big white guy. Come to think – definitely American. Maybe. It is just a sense I had, I know my own kind."

"Why do you think that?"

The way his clothes fit, the way he walked...little things like that. Americans carry themselves differently than anyone else."

"Had you seen him before?" asked Lang in English.

I looked at Lang again. "Do you speak English," I asked. He ignored me.

"Did you recognize him?" Qi asked, as if I hadn't heard correctly.

"No. I just saw him from behind," I said, holding my hands behind my head like I was surrendering. They said nothing, but continued looking at me expressionlessly, sitting at the square wooden table in the middle of the room, drinking black tea. My first lie. Why did I say that I saw him or anyone? I looked at Lang, a little unsettled.

"And he just walked past you."

"No – he was already behind me. He must have come out of the shower building."

"Did you hear him come out?"

"No – well, I don't know..."

"You don't know?"

"I might have heard him, I might have just felt him come out. You know how you can feel someone behind you sometimes? I sensed his qi." That was good, I thought. Qi had a good laugh and Lang was still pissed off at me for mocking his English. I didn't look at them to see if they believed me. Fuck'em, I believed it.

"Did you greet him? Did he greet you?"

"No." I gave Lang and Qi a "Give me a break!" glare. It worked! We all were quiet for an uncomfortably long time, which was fine with me.

"Perhaps you would prefer to sit in a more comfortable chair," suggested Lang, pointing to one of the cushioned chairs set against the wall behind me. I took my tea and moved there. Qi pulled his wooden chair away from the table and moved it over to where I sat. He sat backwards, leaning his chin against the back of the chair, and stared in a weird cold way that was bizarre for someone in that posture. Lang sat next to me, cornering me, scooting in close to me, obviously pissed off, letting me know that they give the glares, I don't.

"OK. How did you enter the apartment," asked Lang.

"From the outside entrance. I climbed over her porch wall and knocked on the sliding glass window."

"I don't understand," said Qi. "Before you said you didn't knock?"

"Right – I didn't knock – I usually did..."

"So why didn't you knock?"

"The lights were on and it was too quiet – it was just a feeling..."

"Why didn't you just go in the front door?" Qi was just calmly asking questions, with his disembodied head on top of the chair back, but it was Lang who was scaring me, sitting dead still with his eyes focused on me.

"I told you..."

"Tell us again."

"It was shorter. She lived on the corner of the building and I didn't have to walk as far."

Actually that was true. The hallway leading to her apartment door was foul smelling to the point of regurgitatious gagging. So I almost always came via her back porch when I went over to Erika's house, although it wasn't the reason I went that way on that night.

I turned and looked at Lang who was smiling at me. "So, tell us about Erika. What was she like?" He said it in Chinese.

I didn't know where to start, but then everything seemed to be coming back to the day after Molly got back from the States, in early September, the afternoon before we went out to celebrate her return at the bar on the roof of the Friendship Hotel.

Six weeks ago – Sept 8

I was trying to figure out if it would be OK if I turned on the TV. Last year, when Erika came over it was accepted that when they started talking I could ignore them. But since I haven't seen Erika since – well since Dagmar left and...

"...Molly! That is so wonderful. I want to visit Montana someday."

"Well, it's not all that exciting, but it is big and pretty. I think Nate and I needed a little time away from each other."

"Um," Erika said. I nodded. Erika nodded too. I was starting to get a little antsy sitting next to her…"I have some good news. You won't believe it is true! I have a new boyfriend!"

Normally she had good posture but now she straightened up even more, putting her head up and looking out at the future like a young German woman in the crowd in the Riefenstahl propaganda movie, *Triumph of the Will.*

"And guess what? You'll never guess? He's a Chew!"

I thought I heard the theme from a song I had forgotten, but it was only her neighbor's tea kettle starting to boil.

"That is marvelous, Erika! Where did you meet?"

"Of course, where does anyone meet anyone here in Beijing – while eating at the Youyi Bingguan dining room! I was sitting by myself having those awful pork chops and mashed potatoes. Why can't they make decent food here? Then he crossed the room, straight toward me as if he had known me all his life. I sat looking at him and he said – to me! 'I won't live with myself if I don't talk to you tonight. You are so beautiful. The most beautiful woman I have ever seen!' No – he said - 'you are beyond beautiful!' Something like that. He was so *verwundbar*! His black eyes burned right through my soul. Can you believe it? I am in love, Molly!"

Molly and Erika hugged. Erika was almost crying. I remember Molly rolling her eyes as she looked at me over Erika's shoulder.

***

Later that day -

I don't want to go," I said.

"Please? Erika wants to introduce her new boyfriend to us and I have been away for two months. Please be normal for heaven's sake." Molly hugged me, very tightly. She shivered even though it was 80° with the windows opened. "Just be normal for me OK. That is all I want."

"Don't you think it's a little early to be doing the 'couple thing' with Erika?"

"She likes this guy, Nate. Can't you tell? We should do this for her. She had been a good friend. She can't help being so German." Molly was rubbing me with her hands, hips and chest.

"OK." What choice did I have? I had a boner that wouldn't quit. Again. Just be cool I thought. I looked at my watch then at Molly. She went a little dreamy and unlatched the top button of her shorts. She had just returned from the States last night after six weeks away and this was…but who's counting? I don't know where my energy came from.

Afterward, I remember sitting on the side of the bed pretty happy with myself. I put on a clean tee-shirt and shorts and Molly dolled up with a slinky blue dress and semi-whorish make-up. She was suddenly way too beautiful, too sexy – people will say, "Why is she with him?" Even I thought that. We went off like that to Erika's apartment.

The foreign PhD's live in a drafty prefab apartment building with leaky plumbing and heat that only works in the summer. Erika's apartment was much like that, only shoddier. She lived on the bottom floor with a walled patio, and a sliding glass door on the outside. When she moved in, she lived on the top floor, but she complained about that, so they moved her to the ground floor, and now she didn't like the bottom floor because it didn't have a view, and the lock on the sliding glass door didn't work. I told her to put a broom handle or something in the rails where it slid to lock it but she just shrugged. "They should just fix it," she exclaimed, with an overdone resolute look that said she would never compromise her principles. Erika was difficult to please, and I think she was jealous of the apartment where Molly and I lived. I didn't blame her for that.

I wanted to walk in through the back and just climb over the patio wall, but Molly wouldn't hear of it. "I've got a dress on!" she said. "Besides, it's not polite."

So we walked in through the front. The hallway stank; it seemed as if everyone's kitchen and bathroom ventilation was piped out into the corridor. Erika answered the door and she had a party dress on too. *"Qing jin, qing jin.* (请进)" She was giddy and I had never heard her use Chinese greetings before. Molly and Erika hugged and the apartment was filled with the odor of sizzling meat.

"Hello." It was Sandor the Hungarian. Lately, I had seen him around Xilou, in fact, I had seen him twice either coming or going up the stairs of my apartment building. He told me he was visiting my neighbor Bing, who I had introduced to him about ten days previously. He came out and thanked me for the introduction, that it was such a pleasure to work with such a curious, eager student. He said he was teaching Bing the Torah and the meaning of the Bar Mitzvah.

But what was most surprising was that here was Sandor, who displayed his Jewish faith in a most obvious and peculiar way, and now he was Erika's lover? He was the son of a prominent Hungarian Communist official after all. I thought to myself, what a turn-around. Sandor is the only foreigner other than me who almost never came out to socialize at the Youyi with the other foreigners. Erika and Gregor had always treated him like a punch bowl turd, and Sandor always seemed to act sheepishly resentful. I tried to smile and let him know that, at the time, I remember thinking to myself, it was great that Sandor was putting it to the Teutonic bitch.

"So were the Hungarian and the German woman...did they..." Qi seemed a little embarrassed to ask me, so Lang just popped out with it in Chinese.

"Were they fucking?"

"I don't know," I said honestly.

"And you say that the Hungarian was always walking up and down the stairs of your apartment to meet Bing?" Qi looked at Lang.

"Tell us about that," said Lang.

"Yes, please, explain what the Hungarian was doing in Bing's apartment," said Qi. "And what was that you said he was teaching Bing?"

I wanted to continue telling them about how Molly and I met Erika and her new boyfriend and what happened that night. That was the night she met Dexter. Looking back, it is clear to me that the events of that day and that night changed things, and I am still not clear exactly how and why. When I walked in the door of Erika's apartment and saw Sandor, at that moment, I still misunderstood Sandor's relationship with Erika.

But Qi and Lang didn't seem interested in pursuing it. I wasn't going to argue with the way they questioned me. As I thought, they were really focused on Bing, at least at first. Of course he is Chinese; that was much easier for them to deal with, less dangerous for them.

"When was this, what date, do you remember?"

Qi had his notebook out, tapping his pen impatiently.

"About a week before school started," I said. "It was a Saturday, I think."

Qi, flipped back, apparently to a calendar in his notebook. "Saturday August 29?"

I nodded – that was about right.

I introduced Bing to Sandor. But it was really Gregor who made that happen, so I better explain him first.

I ate lunch with Gregor that day at the "Red House," the Hong Lou Café,(红楼菜馆) about a kilometer south of the Zoo. Hong Lou was a bit of a pun, because Red House could also mean a brothel, something the Chengdu Brothers who ran the place enjoyed pretending they didn't understand.

Beijing, as Chinese cities go, is not a great food town. The Manchurian Qing never took to southern food. "Peking" roast duck is OK, and hot pot mutton can get you through a cold night once in a while, but beyond game food and sheep, Beijing is a barbarian town, where the hunter and butcher dominate the kitchen with a meat cleaver. Oddly, that sort of cuisine often

25

meets more favorably with the Western palate than the food of other regions.

There were great restaurants based on the cuisine of other regions in the '20s and '30s after the fabulous Forbidden City chefs were turned out of the palace and had to make a living in the city. I've heard that some of those restaurants stayed open through the '50s, but Mao's madness pretty much ended dining out in style. At least that's what I've been told.

So I eat, once a week at least, at the "Red House" *a Sichuan (四川) caiguan* owned and operated by a couple of brothers from Chengdu. Earlier that day Gregor had accosted me in the courtyard where I was returning from buying tomatoes, corn and a Hami Melon (honeydew) in the vegetable market outside the walls of the school. I was planning on buying a pot of *jiaozi (饺子)* at the campus cafeteria and that was to be my dinner, but he wanted me to go with him over to the Youyi.

His main idea for dinner was to sit in the downstairs Youyi bar with other foreigners, eat smoked sausage and deep fried chicken and smoke cigarettes. I turned him down and he gave me that familiar hurt look. So I invited him to come with me to the Hong Lou instead.

It was a twenty-minute bike ride, and he was pretty drunk when we started. Gregor borrowed Molly's bike and I was seriously concerned it would break in two from the weight of the fat Croat. But we made it, and parked the bikes and walked down the alley to the front of the *canting*. There was no sign outside; the only advertisement was the rich odor of Sichuan food wafting from the open doors and of the *caiguan's* rice steamer, which was just outside in the courtyard in front of the restaurant. Wicker baskets full of rice were pulled out of the steamers by a system of bamboo pulleys and levers connected along a flimsy elevated track that flowed through a hole in the wall just a couple of millimeters wider than the baskets. Each time a basket came through the hole, billows of steam exploded out of the porous wicker, raising the humidity and fogging all of the glass. The steaming rice slid down the track to the center of the dining room perfectly fluffy and light. As much rice as you wanted to eat.

I had fish-flavored pork on rice. The hot and sweet plum sauce isn't really fishy, just often used on catfish. The owners were foreigners in Beijing, from Sichuan. The locals, the Beijingers who eat there, shared the secret of the place with me like conspirators. We had seen each other before.

Gregor ordered a quart of ice-cold Five Star beer. He spat on the floor and was studiedly ignored by the Chengdu brothers. I glared at him. He spat again.

"I don't understand how the English drink warm beer, do you?" I looked at him with wonder. How he could be drunk this early in the day? I got up and went over to one of the owners.

"My friend is drunk," I said. "I am sorry."

"No matter," he said. He smiled. He looked the cement. "The floor is dirty anyway."

Fucking Croat. I was very angry and I let him know it.

"You are right...I am a pig!" He looked away from me with a tragic, blank stare. He might have seemed like a bad actor, but I knew he was being sincere. "We are all pigs, we Croats. You don't understand us!"

I fired up my lighter and held the tips of my chopsticks over it for about ten seconds as I stared at him.

He looked down at his chopped chicken and with the assurance of Minnesota Fats, opened a small leather case and pulled out his fork and started picking at the gongbao chicken (宫保鸡丁).

"You can't understand us!" he was muttering, with his mouth full.

I had stayed to myself, all last year, almost never going out, and my only friends were Molly and my Chinese neighbors in Xilou. Lately though, I had been hanging out with the foreigners at the Youyi once in a while. So I had heard quite a bit of Gregor's story. As I endured another lecture on the tragic history of the western branch of the southern Slavs, I remembered why I had avoided the Friendship Hotel foreigners all last year. And, as I thought this, I heard something about saving Western civilization in front of the gates of Vienna, holding off the Turks even as the Croat nation and their women lay in the clutches of the cruel invaders. Get over it, Gregor! He kept saying that it isn't over yet...

***

The beer from lunch had made me sleepy so I took a late afternoon nap. The rays of the setting sun woke me, and I sat up half asleep on the couch and after a quick pee, I continued from where I was in Graham Greene's *A Burnt Out Case*. The main character, Querry, burnt out on life, can't believe in God, can't avoid his own fatal attractiveness to women, and can't stand the pain he causes, so he tries to hide from the world in a leper hospital. Even in the heart of darkest Africa he couldn't hide from the world.

That's where I was when I heard Bing knock and I let him in, reluctantly. I wasn't happy to see him, because at that moment I was trying to hide from the world, but still, I asked him three times to have a cup of tea with me and he finally relented.

We made small talk for a while. Then he told me his father was sick and in the hospital and that his sister wanted to marry. If his father died, he was determined to leave and let his sister have the apartment.

"Would you be allowed to leave the work unit?"

"I don't know."

I didn't ask him what he was thinking about doing, but I didn't want to change the subject. I am usually the one to fill the awkward silences with some banality or a joke, but I just let the silence lie between us. I couldn't imagine what it must be like for Bing to continue living here after what he had done.

"I want to study and teach, if I can," he said finally.

"But they will never let me teach in China, at least they won't let me teach here at the Foreign Language Institute."

Another knock. I opened the door and there, bushy-browed and obsequiously posturing behind wide arrogant eyes stood Gregor. Again. It had only been four hours since we got back from lunch. I forced a smile, and thought about Querry and whether it is possible to hide. Maybe not.

"Look what I bring!" Sandor, the Hungarian, tall and skinny with brownish blond hair and sloping eyes, a long face and a long nose – Sandor looked almost fearful to be at my door in the company of Gregor the Croat.

Because he brought someone else, Gregor knew I couldn't turn him away. I felt lost at the time, unable to decide what to do. I didn't know if Molly was coming back or not. Dagmar had just left, forced to return to East Germany by her government. I tried not to think about her but was not succeeding.

And Zhang, who was in Xian, had told me she would "always be my lover."

I was going to have to quit teaching as soon as my apartment came through for my other job. I hadn't told anyone about that.

Only three days ago, at the train station, I had been choked into unconsciousness by East German secret police, who kept me from kissing Dagmar goodbye. Sandor must have seen me throttled at the train station. I saw him. He could hardly have missed me after what happened to me on the platform. Did he know I saw him? I don't think so. I knew I was going to have to tell these cops about that day at the train station, because they surely already knew about it.

But I wasn't going to do it now. Not unless they asked me.

"So this was the first time that Sandor came to your apartment?" asked Qi.

"And the last time. After that, when he came to Xilou, it was always to visit Bing."

At the mention of Bing, both Qi and Lang looked visibly uncomfortable. It was clear they did not want to bring him into this.

29

But cops everywhere have a need to know the truth and that seemed to override whatever reluctance they had. Lang pushed the recorder back on and Qi continued to take notes.

Gregor and Sandor came into my apartment and I introduced them both to Bing, and then had to beg Bing, again three times, like some crowing cock, not to leave, but to join us. Before that, I hadn't shared what I knew about Bing with any of the other foreigners.

I should have let him go.

"Are you a student, Bing?" I could see that Sandor was immediately curious about Bing, although I didn't know how much he had heard about him.

"No." Bing tried to hide his embarrassment. "But I spend most days in the library. So yes, I suppose I am a self-taught student."

I was amazed how quickly Sandor came to understand Bing's situation, undoubtedly because of their common experience of living under communism, with the busybody informers, neighborhood committees, work unit boards, unions, and the police, all of which submitted to a Party "discipline" that rewarded conformity and submission. Although the Cultural Revolution was a Chinese phenomenon, the Party's punishment for ideological heresy and the work unit's reaction to the crime and the punishment for that heresy were not unique in the Communist world. Bing's exile in his own neighborhood, his invisible prison, was something that Sandor seemed to grasp and understand in a way that I don't think I ever could, even though I witnessed it every day.

Gregor brought out four glasses and a pitcher filled with an icy yellowy-blue concoction.

"It is a lychee vodka martini. Tell me, isn't it good?" he asked. I had almost a liter of lychee juice in the fridge and of course a half-drunk bottle of Stolichnaya.

Both Bing and Sandor drank their lychee sweet martinis down like soda pop. Gregor lit up with happiness.

"The Russians are celebrating Boris's birthday." Gregor sat down to catch his breath. "They will be very drunk in a few hours. We should go and join their celebration."

"Not me," said Sandor. "I don't love the Russians."

"What do you think? I love them? No, no, I will celebrate to taunt them. They are afraid of all Croats, because you know Nate, Tito was a Croat and he beat them at their own game! Right, Sandor? They didn't dare invade us like they did Budapest!" Gregor held a tight smile and shifted his eyes toward Sandor mischievously.

Sandor ignored the jibe. "You hate Russians," Sandor said, "because they help Serbs. Croat politics is very easy to understand."

"Yes!" His eyes lit up. "They love the Serbs too much! Too much!"

"You southern Slavs are the most psychologically damaged people in the world. You make us Jews seem quite well adjusted. At least we know who we are."

Gregor waved him off in faux anger.

Bing looked at Sandor in surprise. "You are a Jew?"

"Yes," said Sandor, eying Bing with a sudden intensity.

"The Jews in Hungary, I thought they were all killed by Eichmann. I know this because I did research after reading a translation of *The House on Garibaldi Street*, how the Israelis captured Eichmann in Buenos Aires. I wondered why Israelis would capture him."

"Yes," said Sandor. "It happened in 1944, when the war was almost over."

"I don't understand why it happened though," Bing continued, "If Jews were often powerful outsiders, how did it happen? This clearly did not help Germany fight the war."

Sandor was visibly taken aback. Then he smiled, and said, "Yes it is true. I still don't really understand why. Perhaps we are hated because we kept our faith. If Jesus was a Jew, and the Jews didn't accept him...this contradiction meant that either they were wrong or we were. Generation to generation...our faith..." he stopped and thought. "We had to conform to keep our faith. Often we joined the very people who despised us. Which is what our enemies, like Gregor..." he smiled at his Croat friend, who nodded in appreciation back, "...always say about us." He stopped and seemed to understand that Bing really had no preconceived ideas or feelings about Judaism, none of Western civilization's murderous baggage toward the Jews. Sandor, clearly uncomfortable with the discussion, looked at me.

"Nathan, that is really your name?"

"Yes."

"Do you know what Nathan said?"

I didn't understand his question and looked at him perplexedly.

"When David had the affair with Bathsheba, who was Uriah's wife, Nathan, the prophet, told David, in front of everyone, "Because you have despised me, and have taken the wife of Uriah to be your wife, I will raise up trouble against you from within your own house; and I will take your wives, and before your eyes give them to your neighbor. He will lie with your wives in the full light of day. You did it secretly, but I will do this thing in front of all Israel, and in the full light of day."

"The prophet Nathan said that?" Gregor spoke with mock profundity, looking at me with wide-eyed minstrel show horror.

"Yes." Sandor, ignoring Gregor, looked at me blankly. I got a funny feeling in my stomach. It was like he knew what I was really thinking and worrying about. Did everyone on campus know how I had spent my summer? I was suddenly angry at him, wondering who the fuck he thought he was coming into my apartment and judging me like that. But I said nothing.

"What do you believe?" asked Bing, probably not knowing Nathan was a minor Hebrew prophet.

"First," Sandor seemed to shrug, as if to say, I tried to get out of this, "it is said that Jews rejected Christ in order to survive as a people, as a nation. But I don't think so, because you have to consider something in order to reject it. As Christianity developed and built up a mythology around Jesus in order to legitimize him, it was found in your Gospels..." He turned to Gregor and pointed at him, "...all manner of references in the Hebrew sacred texts foretelling Jesus. Almost in every case this kind of logical reduction was dismissed and laughed at. But as Christians took power we discovered it was not a wise thing to laugh too loud." Sandor stopped and took a sip of his lychee martini. Gregor smiled at me as if he expected congratulations for bringing this discussion into my apartment. It made me uncomfortable, but Gregor loved any kind of religious or ethnic dispute.

"We have had many prophets who said many things," Sandor continued. "Our history in exile is a history of the Mishna, which is what we thought the old prophets meant. The great Rabbinic commentaries easily showed that Jesus could not have fulfilled the prophecies. In those times with the Romans all around, there were many of us who were calling for rapprochement, to come to some kind of arrangement with the Romans. But the Romans wanted to destroy us root and branch like they did Carthage, for we were as much a threat to them as Carthage if not more. We weren't just another barbarian tribe, looking for more pasture. We had a history and a sense of purpose as a people, a national destiny, and it didn't require the Romans, or anybody else. This was our crime. And it hasn't really changed for the last two thousand years. That is the only explanation I have for why." Sandor looked at Bing, who was dead lost in thought.

But my mind was still on what my namesake said about David and Bathsheba. I will take your wives and give them to your neighbor? And they will lie with them in the full light of day? What the fuck does that mean, I thought. And more importantly, I thought, what was Sandor doing at the train station that day?

"Wait," said Qi. "Who was at the train station?"

"Sandor," said Lang. "He just said that. But why do you say it? We know what happened to you there. What did he have to do with it?"

"I don't know why he was there, and now I'll never find out. I should have asked him, but I didn't." What a stupid idiot I am. I can't seem to keep my mouth shut about anything. It just flew into my brain and out of my mouth.

Qi and Lang turned off the Sony tape player and walked to the corner to talk. Qi then left and Lang came back and started the Sony again and stared at me with a dark look.

Sandor continued to explain Judaism and by now it was clear that his audience was Bing, who was visibly enthralled by Sandor's sermon.

"Have you ever heard of the Khazars? They were a people who lived in the Caucasus – they were related to the Xiongnu, (匈奴)the Huns. In the eighth century they swept in from the steppes and were very powerful and had a great king. This king invited teachers from the two great religions, as well as Greek philosophers, to instruct him on the true path to follow. Both the Christians and Muslims said they got their core beliefs from the Torah, so he sent for a Jew to instruct him. After listening to this Jewish teacher, the Khazar king became a Jew and so did his people. They ruled the great overland trade routes for more than a hundred years. Our greatest poet, Judah Halevi, wrote about this conversion in Arabic, the *Kurzari*. It is a point by point explanation of our history, laws and customs. In the poem, as in history, the Khazar king converts to Judaism. It too gave us faith and kept us on the true path.

"So you see, you didn't need to be a Jew to become a Jew. Your mother doesn't need to be a Jew. No Jew denies that the Khazars were really Jews, yet they were not descended from Jacob. The only people who really insisted that Judaism is hereditary were the Nazis. They defined rules – half Jew, quarter Jew – rules which doomed so many. Those are not our rules."

Sandor took another long sip from his lychee martini. "My mother was a Jew and my father a Magyar. I am a Jew."

"Did your family go to Auschwitz?" asked Bing.

"I think so," Sandor said. "My grandparents and aunt. Yes."

"Eichmann killed them."

"Yes. He was a very good organizer. Efficient," said Sandor.

We were very quiet for maybe a minute.

Gregor got up and stretched. "I think we should go over and wish Boris happy birthday before the vodka is gone," he said.

"I won't go," said Sandor, suddenly very pensive and withdrawn.

"Sandor, please continue your talk!" Bing was sitting on the edge of his chair, clearly excited by what he had just heard. "I am very interested in the Jewish things. Perhaps, if you don't want to visit the Russians you would come up and have tea with me. I have so many more questions!"

Sandor nodded to Bing, put his glass down and stood up awkwardly and stared at Gregor.

"We can meet later perhaps?" he asked Gregor. He didn't look at me.

Sandor nodded goodbye and I walked them out, but Bing was questioning Sandor about the book of Genesis before they were out the door.

"So that is how Sandor met Bing," said Qi.

"Yes." I felt very sorry for Bing, because the last thing he needed was to be involved in this investigation. Not with his record. "I suppose you have arrested him."

Qi ignored my comment. "So then you went to see the Russians."

"Yes," I said. "The Russians were my friends until - that night."

Lang said something to Qi. I didn't quite catch it but it was something about the smell of bears.

"So you left your apartment and went to the dorm, to embarrass the Russians. Tell us about that."

"Come – we should go to the Youyi," Gregor said after Sandor and Bing left. I finished my lychee martini.

"I thought you wanted to visit the Russians at the dorm," I asked.

"You don't want the skinny-arsed Chinese tonight...?" Sometimes Gregor used British-isms.

"You mean Zhou? No." I glared at Gregor the Pimp, letting him know it was best he drop it.

"I understand." Gregor seemed to relax a bit, smiled at me as if to warn me not to play him false, that he knows too much. "Come," he said, seeing that I wasn't ready to understand him yet, "We go torment the Russians."

***

"Checkpoint Charley," the entrance to the foreign students' dormitory, requires that an attendant open the door, which was otherwise always locked from the outside. The attendants were sleepy, dull Chinese girls who didn't want to talk, but seemed to enjoy pushing the buzzer to open the door. I was with Gregor and well known on campus so we just breezed in. There were curfews and lights out times, but as with most rules in Beijing, everyone ignored them. The only problem was getting the girls to wake up if you came in too late, even though their beds were partially visible from the checkpoint window.

The second floor was the women's dorm, and the third was for men. The door was open, so we walked through the women's area on our way upstairs. Almost all the room doors were open. I saw Mikku, sitting on the side of her bed, sewing. She went to school here and when she was fighting with Ibrahim she would stay here; otherwise she was driven here every day from the PLO embassy for her classes. There were four or five North Korean girls and three or four from the East Euro bloc along with a couple of Russians, a black Cuban volleyball player and the French girl, Monique.

We walked up one more flight to the men's section and were greeted by the singing of drunken Russians. Everybody else seemed to have been driven out by the Slavic opera. Boris watched us walk toward them with an enigmatic glare. Blond, tall, solid, deep-set eyes and a square flat face, he didn't look all that drunk as he sat with a half-smile, watching. He waved at me, ignoring Gregor as we approached where they were sitting.

"Why are all the whores in Russia Ukrainian?" he asked Yevgeny, while still looking at me, proud of his English. Yevgeny was darker and not quite as tall. His sad eyes made him seem older, yet both he and Boris were in their early twenties.

"Your mother was a whore who practiced the spirit of Socialist fraternity with monkeys and Muslims, but she was not Ukrainian, was she? So your theory is shit." Yevgeny said it impassively with a slight smile.

They sat in shorts and muscle shirts, on chairs pulled out in the lobby, playing cards and drinking straight vodka. There were three empty bottles on the floor. Two other Russians I didn't know threw down their cards and seemed embarrassed to not be as drunk as Yevgeny and Boris.

About six North Koreans were packed into one of their rooms, listening to a taped speech from their "Great Leader."

One of them poked his head out - "Erika – tell hello – Erika." Gregor nodded to them gravely.

Gregor greeted the Russians in their own language. They invited us into their room and we went in with only Gregor and Yevgeny. We grabbed some glasses, poured and drank. Glassy-eyed smiles and nods and "happy birthday" greetings.

"Where are you from, Nate?" Boris was slowly accentuating the word "Nate," as if trying to hide his astonishment that I had suddenly replicated myself a couple of times right in front of him.

"New Jersey."

"New Jersey." He nodded knowingly. "Princeton University – no?"

"Yes. Where are you from, Boris?"

"I am from Zheleznogorsk! It is near Kursk."

"Oh." I couldn't tell if he was slurring the pronunciation of his hometown or not. I suddenly thought that perhaps it was vodka that made Russian sound the way it does.

"We make nuclear processing material. For peace."

"Of course, for peace." I said. He nodded. So did I. "Yevgeny, where are you from?" I asked.

"I am from Kiev." He spoke carefully and softly.

"He is not Russian," said Boris.

"I am Russian. My father is Russian. Kiev is Ukraine. It is Russian. Russia is Kiev. At one time in middle ages, Kiev was Russia."

"But all women in Kiev get fucked by Mongols, so now they not Russian," said Boris.

"No," said Yevgeny shaking his head smiling. "No."

"Boris, we came over to wish you a happy birthday," I said, loudly and slowly, as if I were talking to an eighty-year-old man.

Boris snickered and gave a dark look to Gregor.

"We miss Dagmar," said Yevgeny, with a slight leer.

"Yes," said Boris. "She was good girl. We all miss her no?" His eyes went up and down with some laughing. Yevgeny stopped laughing.

"We Russians, and you Americans – our fathers – they took Germany and we continue the family tradition," said Boris.

I smiled and nodded as they laughed. Boris looked at me knowingly to make sure that I understood what he meant.

Gregor said something in Russian.

"Your Russian – it is very bad," said Boris. "When you speak English I understand you much better."

"Yes," said Gregor, pausing, a better actor now. "You are correct. I am ashamed. Russian is the mother tongue for all of us Slavs."

Thoughtful serious looks.

"Another drink for our friends!"

"To the great Russian writers – may they be forever read," I saluted. Gregor poured Russian style from his bottle.

"Of course the great ones are always Red! All great writers are socialist, deep down, in their soul," said Boris.

"To Dostoyevsky, Tolstoy and Gogol," I toasted, skipping Chekhov, Pasternak and Bulgakov, for reasons of drunken diplomacy. "And Pushkin!" I added, although I really hadn't read anything by him.

"To Lermontov!" said Yevgeny. "He is our best, or would have been if he not shot so young. A hero for all time!" We drank and filled the glasses. "Dostoyevsky..." Yevgeny was off on a lecture about the Inevitable Convergence of Soviet Thought with the Emerging Russian Nationalism. After a rather long preamble and overwrought premise, Yevgeny said, "...his best characters were psychotic. Gogol's were fools and Tolstoy..." Yevgeny shook his head, not even wanting to get started with Tolstoy. "But Lermontov – he wrote about reality. The people – the soldiers – on the front – the frontier – fighting in Asia – the Russian burden! Lermontov is my hero – and there is nothing else to say!"

"I was a soldier last year," said Boris. "I translate American technical books. My English is not good."

"Yes, it is very good."

"My leaders want me continue language study so I am sent from Zheleznogorsk. I grew up from child and I miss it very much," he said sadly.

"Where were you, Yevgeny?"

I study in my town too. In Kiev."

"Oh," I said – getting an idea.

"What," asked Boris. "What is oh?"

Gregor looked at me. I shook my head very, very slightly.

"What?" Yevgeny's voice was voice rising in suspicious anger. "You two keep secrets?"

"Give me your glass." I held the bottle.

"No. I not drink if you keep secrets."

I gave him a long, painful look. "We met a Finnish doctor today at the Sichuan restaurant," I said. Gregor and I looked at each other with great seriousness.

"A doctor? Are you sick?"

"No. I am not sick." The two Russians waited, looking at me as I hesitated. "It is just…Chernobyl," I said.

Both Yevgeny and Boris went a little pale.

"What about it?" Boris asked.

"They have discovered a side effect recently. Last month…"

"You mean a health side effect," asked Boris.

"Yes."

"You must tell us," Yevgeny demanded.

"I know, I know!" I looked down. I had no idea where I was going with this, when Gregor jumped in.

"It is crazy. It makes no sense! I don't understand it – do you, Nathan? I think that Finn is full of shit. In Hiroshima they found nothing like it!" Gregor looked away in the distance, his dark brow worried for his Slavic comrades.

"But," Boris said quickly, understanding without prompting the gravity of the situation. "You know the level of radiation was much higher around Chernobyl than in the

Japanese cities. For a period of time it was higher by a hundred times."

"What is side effect?" asked Yevgeny.

"They have discovered that the tip of some men's penises becomes radiated – the skin is so sensitive that it – they have to remove them in some cases." I fought not to burst into laughter.

"Oh my God," said Yevgeny fearfully, undoubtedly thinking of Lenin.

"Yes," said Gregor. "You know that iodine is released with radiation."

"Of course," said Boris.

"Well, the sex organ, it absorbs the radiated iodine in the air. Like a flower." Gregor and I looked darkly at each other trying to hide our twinkling eyes.

"But the good news is," I said, slowly, "It can be easily detected – if you are affected. Iodine dissolves easily in alcohol. The tip of your penis begins to glow when it is emerged in iodine and alcohol. If you are..."

"Yes – apparently the solution draws the radiated iodine to the surface of the tip," said Gregor. Gregor and I again looked at each other with sad, serious expressions. I was struggling not to explode.

"It makes sense," said Yevgeny. He took another long drink, and poured more for the rest of us.

"It must be approximately a 5% iodine solution in alcohol," I said.

"I will calculate," said Boris, "50 proof, this equals 25% of 4 ounces – 5% of one ounce..."

"The Finn said at least 5% of the alcohol," I said. "It can be more with no problem."

"I believe approximately 25 milliliters each should be enough," said Boris, underlining the number with a pencil.

"Good," I said. "We can do this. Let's drink up now, we will need the glasses."

They laughed, and stared at their vodka glasses. Boris and Yevgeny were smiling bravely but real fear was in their eyes.

"They have some iodine in the first aid kit downstairs," said Gregor. "I will get it. You two should know right away. The Finn said as soon as you know you can begin the treatments."

"Oh yes, there is one more thing. I know how we can do this. The other thing that is required for the test…remember him reminding us of this?" I shook my head with disappointment at Gregor. "The penis must be fully engorged with blood in order for the radiated iodine to be drawn to the surface."

"Yes," said Gregor, almost too enthusiastically. "I forgot the most important part of the procedure. You must be hard. Do you understand?" Boris laughed and nodded. Yevgeny rubbed his crotch absentmindedly.

"If it glows after about a minute then we will go find the doctor. He is staying at the Youyi. They are developing treatments that can save your manhood in Sweden. They have discovered over a hundred cases already."

We both nodded seriously. The two Russians now looked stunned. The reality of life without dicks was beginning to dawn on them.

"Of course," said Yevgeny. "Sweden."

"I know that the first cloud passed right over Zheleznogorsk when I was there. I think about it every day. I was afraid to sex with the Russian woman – to bear the horrible child."

"Kiev is downstream from Chernobyl – on the Dnieper," said Yevgeny morosely.

"Let's get this over with. I am sure neither of you is affected," I said, with weak cheerfulness.

"Yes," said Gregor. "But it is much better to be safe than sorry."

"I will turn the lights out. You will need privacy to make your penis hard. Then when Gregor comes back with the iodine I will put them in the vodka and then you can – you know – soak your penises in the vodka and then we can see if they glow."

Just we were leaving Boris said, "Gregor, I tell you lie. You speak the Russian very good."

Gregor turned and looked at him with heavy "Slavic" emotion, barely controlling his laughter while tears seemed to well up as he walked out the door.

I stood by the door in the perfectly dark room listening to them breathe hard. About a minute later Gregor knocked. I cracked the door open and Yevgeny and Boris both turned around so we could not see them jerking off.

"OK – the solution has been placed in the test glasses of vodka. Here are the glasses – Yevgeny here – Boris. OK – have you started the procedure?"

"Oh – it burns – yes."

"Yes."

"Good. Turn around so we can see if it glows." I heard them turn to face us.

Gregor turned on the light. Monique and the black Cuban girl and two of the Euro women from the second floor were in the room, smiling and pointing. Mikku was taking pictures. Gregor and I, laughing hysterically, ran as fast as we could out of the building.

***

Gregor and I practically skipped to the Youyi; it seemed like we were flying. We arrived and continued to drink. I had never seen Gregor so happy. He told everybody the story five times at least, and it got better each time. I allowed everyone to buy me drinks and barely remember walking home. I hadn't drunk like that in weeks! But I do remember trying to unlock my door. I stood outside trying each of my several keys, none of which worked. After a minute of fumbling, I gave up and started hammering the door with my fist while shouting obscenities in English.

I was still pounding and cursing when Dr. Lü opened the door. Wrong door! Her entrance looked like mine and was right next door. I stared at her in horror.

Dr. Lü was the head of the Communist Party on campus. I'd never talked to her except for the night of the beginning of the semester banquet.

But I did know that she was the cousin of Rennie's former fiancée, Rennie being the idiot American who gave up his job teaching here at the Institute and then recommended me, so technically it was Dr. Lü who got me this job. Rennie's former fiancée had asked Dr. Lü to save him the teaching job, but he decided at the last minute that teaching was too much work and that is how I ended up here. But that is another story. The situation has always been a little awkward because Rennie and Dr. Lü's cousin broke off their engagement last year. Rennie was of course a regular at the Youyi bar and was very rich.

Anyway, I stood in the doorway and looked down at Dr. Lü, who was about five feet tall and maybe fifty-five years old. She looked at me, frozen in supreme embarrassment, and smiled. She invited me in. I couldn't refuse.

We sat in her kitchen and she made me a cup of tea. She told me about the early days. I had to sit and listen to her for as long as she wanted to talk. She told me what it was like to stand in Tiananmen Square on October 1 1949. She repeated Mao's opening line – "Today, the Chinese People's Republic has been established." She said, "Everyone thinks he said, 'the people of China have stood up!' But he didn't, he said that at an earlier Party meeting."

"Really? I have always been told he said 中国人民站起来 on the podium."

"Well, he didn't. He said he 'established the Government' which is much less dramatic than 'the Chinese people have stood up!'. It would be like your President Reagan saying at his speech at the Berlin Wall last month, 'Mr. Gorbachev, allow free travel between the two Germanys!' We Chinese have a way of fooling ourselves, of rewriting history if it is convenient. It's a little thing, but, little lies become big ones eventually."

She told me that I was always welcome to visit her. She told me she enjoyed "our chat." I apologized as profusely as I could for banging on her door. She asked about Rennie and I told her he was dating another Chinese woman. She smiled. She said she was happy that they decided not to marry. She didn't say why, but I suspect that just knowing Rennie was reason enough, even though she must have known how rich he was, because his family is world famous.

She was very nice and said it was no trouble that I mistakenly woke her in the middle of the night in a drunken stupor. I had sobered up very fast, because I clearly remember all that happened in her apartment. Then she said, "Please don't talk to Bing. Since you've talked to him he has been smiling. Please. His happiness mocks all of us."

I didn't answer her.

"I know you feel sorry for him," she said.

"You think it is unfair, don't you?" I still didn't say anything. She stood up and walked over to a lamp table and picked up a photograph of a laughing man looking sideways at the camera, in a Mao suit, leaning against a parapet on the Great Wall. He had a cigarette hanging out of the side of his mouth like Humphrey Bogart. I have never seen a Chinese person pose like that, at least not in a Mao suit. He was so at ease with the world, while so disdainful, of what wasn't clear, but of course I could guess. The photo had an unreal quality. She looked at it for a minute and then set it down. "He would still be here if it wasn't for..." She and I sat in silence. I don't know how long we sat, but I remember listening to the pipes creak.

I should have come by with a gift to thank her for giving me the job a year ago. If I hadn't drunk so much, I would have had trouble sleeping.

Chapter Three

"She didn't want you to talk to Bing." I nodded slightly. Qi and Lang were silent for a moment and Qi pretended to write something.

"Did you like your job? Your teaching job I mean," Lang asked.

"Yes. I really like teaching. I am good at it and I love it."

"Your students liked you. Dr. Lü said you were one of the best foreign experts that the school had ever had. So why did you leave?" asked Qi.

"Well, I guess it was the money," I said. They both smiled and nodded.

"Yes, China is a poor country," said Lang. "But tell us about it."

"What do you mean?" I asked.

"Just give us an idea how you did your job. For example, what was your first day like when you started teaching in September?"

The first day of class, the first week in September: I had butterflies in my stomach. The first class was my hardest, English Writing.

I was excited and I know my students were excited too, wired up tighter than a drunken violin. It was starting to get easier for me though, because this was the beginning of my third year teaching in China and I was finally starting to get good at it.

I stood waiting patiently for the buzz to stop, and I didn't make any faces or gestures to hush the class. Beijing was exploding with political discussion. Something happened this summer, maybe it was Hu Yaobang losing his party Chairman's job or maybe it was all of the people like me who were teaching (and being to encouraged to teach) "non-socialist reality," but there was a serious and rebellious buzz in the air that everyone felt.

The party was talking and acting like it was going to crack down and get tough. Everyone (at least the foreign community) expected mass arrests, but when very little happened it was like somebody had shaken China like a bottle of Coca Cola. Here it was right in front of me, and I had my thumb on the end of the bottle. Oh why was I quitting teaching now? Earth Shattering Events loomed – it is not the time to walk away!

Listening to the buzz before classes started, I heard students loudly and in English arguing about the merits of political freedom and democracy. Freedom is more efficient than Communism they said. Their approach was totally utilitarian. How much productivity is lost because people don't like their jobs? What else could we invest in if we didn't pay people to do useless work? Arguments in English were raging and from a teaching perspective we were off to a good start.

The women, about a quarter of the big M-W-F 9:00-1100 AM lecture class, in their thirties, mid-career at manufacturing plants, food processing, a metallurgical institute, mining, petroleum refineries, etc., were different than any of my previous Chinese women students. They were hard edged, not tied to a University, and were looking to make big changes. They were all party members of course, and women party members are generally very loyal to socialism, but not these ladies. They were right back in men's faces, demanding that this "democracy" needed to give them real jobs with real responsibility that paid real money, otherwise it was as worthless as communism.

I raised my head just a little and the room became quiet. "What do you want to learn?"

"How can we pass the TOEFL?" someone said and everyone laughed a little nervously.

I nodded. I could do this. The key to passing the TOEFL (Test of English as a Foreign Language) is to work your ass off. So I assigned twenty difficult vocabulary words every night, two original sentences for each word, every night, and on Friday they had to write sentences for fifty words. Weekly writing assignments, three in-class tests a week, and a daily grammar sheet that took probably an hour to complete. And I topped it off with about an hour of reading. It was hard for me to keep up with what I was assigning even if I only graded a fraction of it. I had my lesson plans from last year and that helped. I kept them up every night until three in the morning.

I told them I would do all this. "Do it and you will pass the TOEFL," I said.

I told them that the key to writing TOEFL essays is understanding old-style rhetoric. "Tell the audience what you are going to say, say it, and then tell them what you said." Beginning, middle and end, written with a thesis and antithesis.

Chopsticks or knife and fork? Which is better?

Thesis: Chopsticks, traditional, Chinese food is designed for it, develops dexterity in children, they are cheap to produce and dispose. (But if they are wooden not so easy to wash as they age and they encourage the destruction of trees.)

Antithesis: Knife and fork – works with all kinds of food, more sanitary, accepted internationally. (But require manufacturing, which breaks down traditional values and life.)

Explain the arguments for each in general.

Make the case for your antithesis. Make the case against your own idea better than any argument you've ever heard. Tear your own idea apart in front of your audience. That is the key; convince your reader you really do understand your enemy and why he believes what he does.

Then destroy that case and destroy your enemy. Explain why your thesis is the best idea. Sum it up.

Think of a snappy title.

Chinese Food is Chopped for Sticks.

The key, I tell them, is to understand your opponent's argument and be able to counter it. It is warfare – the most fundamental kind, a war for the beliefs of the people reading your writing. If you make your opponent's argument better than your opponent can, and can still dismantle it, then you are the master and your idea (and TOEFL essay) will prevail.

Under Mao, you never made your opponent's argument. The idea that capitalism would have any merits at all was absurd. Examining opposing ideas was new for this generation even though it had been one of the principles of Sunzi's (孙子, Sun Tzu's) Art of War.

We wrote an essay on the blackboard, with loud enthusiastic input from the class. They criticized it and edited it and I was writing furiously, drawing lines linking ideas, arbitrarily assigning students to rewrite the paragraphs from my blackboard notes, then assigning others to recompile what they wrote, then have someone else read aloud those results. The classes were loud and chaotic and generally over too soon.

I passed out example columns – George Will, Russell Baker, WF Buckley, Molly Ivins, Murray Kempton, Alexander Cockburn, etc. For two women technicians, both in their mid to late thirties and very conservative, I could tell by their disapproval of my slightly risqué jokes and innuendos that I needed to find something that talked directly to them. So I hit them with Ellen Goodman columns and her "The personal is the political" style, because they have undoubtedly been hosed over by their male colleagues.

Basically, politics is everything. I tried to give them something that resonated, and it really wasn't hard, because in spite of forty years of propaganda by each of our governments, there really isn't much difference between us as people. It is the same principle as my other job, selling software. Find a hook, something that resonates.

Because, and this is difficult for me to confess, I have to tell you, officers, that the worst thing I did was start teaching in September, knowing I probably would not finish the term.

Lang looked at me hard. "Excuse us." They both left the room.

I sat there in the interrogation room wishing none of this had ever happened and that I was still teaching. Teaching was the one thing I was good at and that I liked and I threw it away. Somehow if I had just focused on that, I have a feeling that none of this would have happened. I know if I had been on campus yesterday maybe Sandor and Erika would still be alive.

Qi came back into the room together, his expression giving almost nothing away. Qi warmed up my tea and brought it to me with a wan smile. I struggled very hard to keep my interrogators at a distance. I was determined not to become infected by the Stockholm syndrome. Of course, Sweden. I laughed out loud remembering Yevgeny, remembering those two holding their hard dicks in glasses of vodka. Mikku's pictures – she framed their erect dicks and mortified faces perfectly.

I was beginning to realize that the best I could hope for was to be expelled from China at the end of all of this. I didn't know how I was going to adjust to going back to Reagan's America. I guess I've known that for a while really, but I've never admitted it to myself until now. I wanted to stay, but it was looking less and less possible. The possibility of jail in China – or worse – I couldn't bring myself to think about that. I was under no illusions – if you get on the wrong side of the government in China – it is essentially over. You are erased from life. One bad thing could happen internationally – and I end up being the poster boy for all the evils of America. I was scared, even though I was innocent. We had gone over the same thing about five times. I don't think I tripped up. I told them the truth only leaving out the one fact that was uncheckable – well – if the guard at the gate remembers the exact time I came into campus and any witnesses saw me and remember when I entered Erika's apartment – it is likely to be about a twenty-minute gap. Ibrahim and Rashid can say I stayed talking to them at Mikku's dorm. I have to get back to the embassy and get the story right. And quit saying whatever flies into my head!

Lang came back into the room.

"You must be very tired," said Qi, reading my mind with disturbing prescience.

I smiled. "Perhaps I can return tomorrow..."

"We really have not come close to finishing our talk. This is an important case as you must know."

"We can't allow you to leave yet," said Lang with alarming frankness. I nodded nonchalantly, yawned and waited. "The investigation is about to become much, much wider." Of course it is, now they are wondering about the train station, the East Germans, stolen artifacts and the CIA. I looked at Lang as he looked at his notebook, flipping back to something and making a note. Qi whispered something to him and he nodded.

"Would you accept an invitation to have dinner at my home and spend the night there?" asked Lang.

I looked at Qi. Coming from Lang, it seemed a strange request. Qi and I were nearly the same age and he was a bachelor. Lang had a family. (Talk about Stockholm syndrome? I even knew the age of his daughter!) I am sure that the possibility that I was somehow involved – that I was the murderer – is something that they have not completely discounted. I have never heard of a cop taking a murder suspect home to meet the wife and kid. We walked downstairs to get in the car.

We were quiet on our drive over to Lang's apartment and I thought about the last time I had been happy with Molly, right after she got back from the States, after she had been away from China and me for two months. But it also was right after I got back from my weekend trip to Xian, after I saw Zhang for probably the last time, at least in that way. It was the beginning of the end, when it all started spinning out of control.

Six weeks ago – The first week in September

We spent the day in and out of bed. When we met in Taylor's, a Eugene, Oregon, college bar, Molly told me that she was looking for love. No beating around the bush, right to the point. I had never met a girl that out front who wasn't drunk or desperate. Beautiful, with luminous brown eyes, nacreous skin, iridescent brown hair and big ruby lips – she looked right at me and dared me. I took her up on it, not a second thought.

And oddly enough it didn't end that night either – it just kept going – even when I got offered the teaching job in China, she just kind of tagged along; any hint of permanence in the relationship was completely unspoken. She didn't require much maintenance. Last year in Louyang, she was in the depth of depression, yet she didn't take it out on me. She smiled when she thought I was getting concerned or worried. She entertained herself reading, or watching TV even when it was unintelligible as most Chinese TV was to her. We were comfortable together, and we just let it ride. Maybe that was the problem.

Molly had a boyfriend back in Montana, a cowboy like her dad, but she wanted something a "little different," which I guess was me. That was all I ever got from her on the subject. All she had to do was give me that "Sorry, it's something you'll never understand" smile, and that would shut me up. I never learned how to see beyond that smile. She was, in some ways, more mysterious than any of the Chinese women I knew.

That afternoon we stayed in bed trying our damnedest to wear each other out and we lay exhausted with the window shades half open and the afternoon sun wrapped around our naked bodies. I watched the dust dance in the warm rays.

"You want a beer?" Of course I did and she jumped out of bed and ran naked toward the kitchen. My brain caught her in a moment of perfect motion and beauty, her back flexed, her hair flying, her fanny in perfect proportion to the rest of her, like a Michelangelo sculpture that he never dared to carve out of fear it would profane nature's perfection. It was a timeless event, frozen forever, like watching a prelapsarian mare at the moment she broke from the Garden gate. I don't think I've ever in my entire life been so transfixed with awe. No Dutch painter has come close to depicting the perfection in that all too quick movement of her all too beautiful ass. She brought back the beer and I floated off to sleep in contentment.

The next day

I opened my eyes to the "ta-ta-ta-ta" of Mrs. Liu's garlic knife. Molly was curled up, snoring through her nose. She kept a syncopated beat with the garlic chopping. I got up, put on some sweat pants and went for a walk. The day was just starting to break and looking back now I know that it was the beginning of the day that would be the beginning of the end of all this.

The campus is divided in two: the west side of the Western Ring road was where the higher faculty and foreigners lived, and across the road on the east side was the junior faculty and student quarters. I wandered among the bleak student dorms, the buildings very poorly maintained, and I know it is even worse on the inside.

Some students saw me out their window and waved. Everybody knew me. I was a celebrity on campus. Classes at the English Training Center started the next day and I suddenly realized that I love teaching and I really don't like selling software that much. I had to tell Molly – what? Where do I start? I kept hoping that things would play out – what – naturally? Is there a natural order for when an unspoken, uncomfortable truth becomes a betrayal? How would I do it?

In a dream – I saw a man die, I couldn't see his face but I knew that I knew him, and then he returned, then died again. The same man – everywhere I went I saw him dying. Gagging, coughing, smashed head, falling, splat – then later fit to tap dance. Then he was dead again. I couldn't get away from him and I couldn't clearly see his face, but I knew that I knew him. I needed to quit drinking. I needed to straighten out. I needed some kind of redemption. I remembered thinking all of that. It was a strange feeling because I thought I was so happy. I don't remember if the face of the dying man was Sandor's, but I don't think so for some reason.

Everybody knows about me and Dagmar. For a week we were inseparable, arm and arm at the dining room, on our bikes together. At least Erika was traveling that week, but she knew about Dagmar too. I needed a strategy. I was at the point in life where I could finally hold two conflicting ideas in my head at the same time. It was either maturity or jadedness, I wasn't sure which. But it didn't feel at all odd for me to think of Dagmar the way I did, even after spending the night having sex over and over with Molly. And in the very back of my mind, I felt that it was really Zhang, my secret Beijing beauty, whom I loved. But I knew I had irredeemably lost her, even then on that September morning. And with Dagmar on a train heading across Siberia toward Berlin... what a joke I had become.

I came back across the street and saw Molly bargaining with a vegetable vendor. She was dressed like a Polish peasant, wearing a scarf over her head with an oversized sweatshirt and baggy pants.

"Why did you get up?" I fingered the scarf.

"Stop it! My hair is a mess!" I laughed at her and she gave me the evil eye. "I want to cook. I am starving, aren't you? I haven't been in my own kitchen in so long! So I thought I'd buy some eggs and we could have omelets." I really was hungry, and the Chinese word for breakfast translated as "early food." Going out to have breakfast was always a bad idea in Beijing where breakfast meant snacking on leftovers until lunch.

"I've got cheese in the fridge..."

"I saw that."

We carried the groceries back across campus. Campus was busier than it had been all summer as school was starting the next day. We passed faculty and neighbors out and about, lots of friendly hellos and nods. Molly took my arm.

"I really love this campus. Oh, I haven't told you yet. I met the head of the Beijing International School on the plane! I told him what I am doing and he said come on down. I could have a job."

"What?"

"A job, Nate! It pays twenty-five thousand US dollars. I don't even think they take taxes out."

"Doing what?"

"Teaching of course. I am going to teach the kids of the embassy people. Americans mostly, but lots of other Westerners, third grade." I tried to remember third grade but I couldn't. "Nate, you don't even have to work. You can just teach here. You see the catch is, the Embassy can't provide me housing so I need to stay here with you. So as long as I have a visa as your wife..." She gave me a look.

"If we say we're married then we are; the Chinese don't care."

"Oh." Her sad puppy dog eyes looked at me as if I completely missed the point. "Anyway, I can make some money and you can work twelve hours a week teaching English, and sell software if you want. Or not, I don't care. We'll be doing pretty good, don't you think?" She leaned on my arm and put her head on my shoulder.

"Yeah. Pretty good." Of course it would work out, I thought. The joint venture was getting us a nice apartment, so no problem. Tai promised me that. There shouldn't be any visa issues. We discussed that too; the joint venture would do whatever had to be done to get her a visa. It was a done deal, agreed outside a Chinese whorehouse with my Taiwanese boss. I'll tell her I am quitting teaching later. Later, the most dangerous word in the language.

Then just as we were about to enter the door to our apartment...

"Molly! Molly!"

...we ran into Erika.

Chapter Four

Lang's wife cooked a delicious dinner. She was about ten to twelve years younger than Lang, spoke very good English and made me laugh when she poked fun at Lang's officious gruffness. Now I saw what was going on: bring a foreigner home for his wife to practice her English. Lang was completely under her thumb. When we got there, dinner was almost ready to serve.

They lived in a high-rise just west of the first Ring road, two bedrooms, a small living room and an even smaller kitchen which connected to the porch that overlooked an unfinished four-lane highway below. Lang's wife was grilling pork and garlic on the narrow balcony and was steaming rice and a tomato and greens mélange on top of the rice just in the kitchen. It smelled wonderful.

"Would you like a beer, or perhaps something stronger?" Lang's wife asked me.

"Beer is fine." Lang's five-year-old daughter provided entertainment by reciting a children's song about a red rooster. It went something like this.

Red rooster, kok kok kok,
Scratching its face and laughing at me.
Laughing at me for not learning,
Laughing at me for not working,
Only knowing to hold out my hand for food,
shameful and selfish!

We clapped at her recitation. Lang's daughter looked down, shy, and carefully isolated the tomato chunks on her plate. Lang's wife kept up the chatter and I smiled and talked about life in the US and we both steered the conversation away from the murder investigation. Lang watched me as I chatted with his wife in English.

I nursed my beer through dinner and still had half a glass left. Lang's wife kept trying to fill my glass and she was draining hers, having a merry time. I was being careful. I knew that the interrogation wasn't finished.

After dinner, Lang lit up a couple of Marlboros for himself and me. His wife cleaned up and then disappeared with their young daughter into the bedroom.

"Do you want to continue our discussion of the deaths?" I asked.

I felt strange since I had accepted his hospitality. The only thing I had to offer in return was my story. We were speaking completely in Chinese and I was afraid of saying something that I didn't exactly mean.

"Your wife returned to America in August," he said.

"Yes, she came back just before school started, in early September."

"And she left you...your wife left you...three or four days ago."

"Actually, for the last month we have not..."

"And you think she plans to leave China with the American from the Embassy?"

"Yes. I guess so. I haven't seen her since then. That's what she said she was going to do, but I don't know if it's true. She might have said that just so I wouldn't go looking for her. I don't know for sure. You would know better than..." He stopped to write something. There was no tape player and he didn't take notes as dexterously as Qi.

"You know," he said looking up, "Americans are a mystery to us Chinese...to me anyway. Your lives are so...adventurous. We Chinese are more settled in our lives."

"You mean personal lives - relations between men and women, marriage, family."

"Yes," Lang said. "Perhaps you could tell me what happened. We are trying to understand the cause of the death of the German and the Hungarian. Western customs between men and women are confusing. You were friends with both of the dead people. Your wife left with another man. Her leaving and they dying so close together...I am a policeman and we have to decide how to investigate from incomplete information sometimes." He stopped and took a drag off of his cigarette. The ash on his butt was a half inch long, but he made no move to the ashtray. "I don't speak English very well. We have not talked to the other foreigners yet. After your wife returned to America, back in August I mean..." He paused and tapped his pen on the table. He looked up at me and smiled.

"Perhaps you can tell me about your life? I mean your relationships with the other foreigners in Beijing. You have said that you didn't socialize with the foreigners in Beijing. Your Chinese is very good, so that is easy to believe. I am sure you had many Chinese friends. Yet, you must admit that you did socialize with foreigners. We have many reports, from the Chinese who work at the Friendship Hotel and from the University, and from piecing together what you have told us, of course from your friend, Ibrahim Abu Ghazaleh, the Chargé d' Affaires at the PLO Mission, he has helped immensely as I am sure you know." Lang looked at me a second longer than necessary. I nodded. He hesitated before beginning again. Finally he flicked his ash, but he missed the ashtray and half of it hit the table and half went on a bare spot on the floor. He noticed that I saw this and stooped to clean it up. I took advantage of the pause to take one more dope-smoker's drag of my butt and stubbed out the rest.

"We know that you formed attachments to several foreigners during this period. As well as other attachments. We are pretty sure of that too!" he smiled at me and I stared back. "Wait. I just remembered... my wife has a recorder. Excuse me." He went into his bedroom and returned with a portable Sanyo cassette recorder and turned it on. "Tell me something about that month when your wife was in America. Speak English and if I have questions I'll ask them. I understand English better than I speak it."

Early August 1987

Chop, chop, chop – I knew it was still pretty early, even though the sunrise was beginning to light up the white walls of my bedroom. In the apartment above, I could hear Liu Taitai still chopping up garlic. She usually finished the chopping and cutting before daybreak. Chop, chop, chop – China's heartbeat.

As I lay in bed, I remember thinking that I was going to stay in China, at least for another year. Chop, chop, chop...I can remember turning over on my side and the noise from the cast iron bed springs drowning out the chopping. Everything in Xilou was so solid; the steam radiator against the window must weigh a ton. The red brick building called Xilou, West Hall, was constructed by Russian engineers and Chinese labor in 1957. It was one of the first buildings in Beijing specifically designed not to collapse in an earthquake.

Xilou: each apartment was designed with socialist equality and utilitarianism in mind, two big rooms, a kitchen, bathroom, high ceilings and lead-framed windows with the view of the courtyard to the sunny south. The living room is the same size as the bedroom. We moved in almost a year ago to the day in August. In the winter, the apartment had been luxuriously warm, hot if you wanted. It was a long way from our cold, dank apartment in Louyang.

Molly and I were the only foreigners in Xilou. Nearly all of the men there were teachers, authors, or language researchers, as were several of the women. All had been exiled for ten years during the Cultural Revolution. Some did not come back. My next-door neighbor, the Party leader Dr. Lü – her husband did not come back. Those that survived returned in 1977, and were told by the Party to sweep it all under the rug, for everyone to just go back to the way they were, and forget about the ten lost years. Like the morning vegetable chopping, it was part of the rhythm of this place.

"Please," said Lang, stopping the tape player to get up and bring me another beer. His face looked very pained. "We don't need to talk about that. I am pretty sure that the Cultural Revolution had nothing to do with the deaths of the two foreigners."

I didn't argue, but I wasn't sure he was right.

I had another five weeks before I had to start teaching again. If Molly decided not to come back from the States, then I would have that huge apartment to myself. Molly left three weeks earlier and said she'd be back when school started in September. She didn't know I saw the other letter that her sister had stuffed into the envelope. She didn't know I read that letter, from her old boyfriend in Montana. Then in bed, she did what he wrote about to her with me. The bumping was pretty wild and I didn't say anything about her new technique, and she seemed fine not talking about it either. But it was then that I realized I didn't want to be a victim. I didn't want to be the guy who waited up in vain for his beautiful girlfriend to come home. I did love fucking with her. I did love that. Sex has a powerful pull, with me anyway, and in this case anyway, it made a lot of other crap seem not so important.

So Molly went home to see her family, or so she said. Also said she'd be back in six to seven weeks, gave me a peck on the cheek and headed down to Hong Kong by train and flew back to the States from there. I got a postcard from HK. "See you in September!" Right I thought.

It was August and school wouldn't start for a month. Then I would start teaching English writing and conversation again, about twelve hours of class a week. The Foreign Language Institute also housed foreigners trying to learn Chinese. College-aged students from Japan, North Korea, and the Soviet Union are the majority, followed by a mélange of Europeans from both sides of the Berlin Wall. There were two or three young Americans too, although to be honest, I didn't even know them. Most of the other foreign teachers at this Institute were academics who lived in their own building on the other side of campus. They were mostly older, in their fifties, and either on sabbatical or recovering from a divorce or loss of tenure back home. I almost never saw them except at the dinners the school threw for all of us at the beginning of the semester.

For some reason, I remember watching a documentary that morning about the artificial insemination of cows. The picture showed a smiling Chinese technician with his arm up to his elbow into a cow's lady parts. The pleasant sounding voice of a young woman narrated, explaining something, but I only understood about half of it, because I don't know the technical animal husbandry vocabulary.

After watching that, I decided I needed to take a shower, before they turned off the hot water at 9:30 AM. I grabbed a towel and my razor, with the blade I hadn't changed in a couple of months. Since starting my "other job," I've been shaving regularly and even with my light beard, the blade was beginning to hurt. Someone recently said that they had begun selling Gillette disposables at the Friendship Store. I hated going to the Friendship Store, because I would always run into some lonely American trying to latch onto me, someone who wants to be Marco Polo, but they would only be in town for two days so they needed to find a guide fast!

"Please," they would seem to say, "show me the secrets of the Middle Kingdom, I've been planning this trip for five years and all I've seen is the lobby of the Marriott, the Great Wall and a lot of museums. Take me to the real China. All I am doing is giving English lessons to tour guides. And the food is so terrible," continued their plea, "I've never had worse Chinese food – EVER! PLEASE HELP ME!"

So I would dress "touristy" and try to act lost whenever I made the trip downtown to the Friendship Store, but somehow they would still smell me out as an American who "knows." That's the trouble of course; I really don't have a clue about this place. One thing I've noticed is that the people who have lived in China for only a couple of months speak much louder about their China expertise than those who have lived here for years. The longer you stay, the more confusing it gets and the less willing you are to brag about your "China-hand-iness."

I put on my green terrycloth robe and flip-flops and headed for the shower building. I walked out into the dirty, dark vestibule and then into the alley that runs along the north side of the building, the same alley-way that I walked up two nights ago on my way to Erika's apartment, when I found her and Sandor. Two workers, whom I didn't recognize, stood in front of the still half-finished construction site. The work stopped just after Molly and I moved in, and these two guys lived in a room with a small "window" (no glass) that faced the alley. At first they had eyed me ominously, but now I took the hard blank stares for granted and didn't think twice. These workers, who lived on the construction site, slept on boards supported by sawhorses, had one set of clothes and looked forty years old at twenty, were probably the only Chinese people on campus who knew Molly was gone. Her comings and goings were the highlight of their days and I think they blamed me for her absence.

Last winter, I began to get to know the foreign students in the early morning after a cold night. They would come shivering in their robes out of the dorm across the common area toward the concrete block house shower building, desperately seeking hot water. No hot showers in any of the residential buildings, nor in the faculty buildings like mine – Xilou – or in the dorm. Socialism in action I guess. There was a big, concrete, communal shower that sat in the middle of the west side of the campus. The communal shower was my only contact with most of the "foreign community," but I usually took mine when nobody else was there, generally just before it closed at 9:30 AM. Molly, however, spent quite a bit of time with the Western Devils and kept me up on their gossip.

For example, I knew two things about a mysterious East German woman whom I had never met. She never took hot or even warm showers in the winter, and she had fucked almost every guy in the dorm over the last year. I bring this up because that I heard Deutsch-speaking Frauleins across the partition that divides the men and women showers. I took a cold shower, at least that day...

Voltaire said German was only fit for talking to horses, but any language sounds beautiful when spoken among young women when they think they are alone. I love to listen to peasant Chinese girls chitchatting as they washed clothes or shucked corn...their pure Beijing tonality echoed like the songs of wild goldfinches.

German can sound nice too especially when spoken by pretty, naked, young women taking a shower together, a nipple-hardening cold shower, if rumors be true.

I heard "Amerikan" and laughter. Did they know it was me across the wall? They probably guessed it was. I timed my departure with theirs.

"Ah, it's you!" said the mysterious East German. Of course she undoubtedly knew all about me. Erika walked behind her, drying her hair. Erika was a West German, from Stuttgart, Molly's best friend and probably her spy as well. She looked a bit like the American actress Susan Dey from the TV show *The Partridge Family*. She had told Molly and me that she despised East German women for reasons that "transcend" political ideology. I wasn't sure what she meant by that so I asked her.

"They are sluts," she said. I distinctly remember Erika saying that while sitting at lunch last spring in the student dorm cafeteria. "They will fuck anybody. Berlin of course has always been like that, even before the Communists." And now in the communal shower at nearly 9:30 in the morning, she was chirping away with Dagmar, Queen of the Valkyrie-whores.

Erika had rosy cheeks on alabaster skin, and medium length blond hair, with a pouty mouth and starry vacant eyes that seemed like windows to nowhere. She was almost too healthy and grossly wholesome. Her posture was too good and she always lifted up her head when she spoke, as if she was pretending she hadn't just farted. She carried herself with what appeared to be an "I am above you" attitude, and dressed very fashionably and wholesomely yet remained antiseptically sexy. She didn't like me very much either.

She told the English language department that her native language was more English than German, that her mother was English and she spent her summers as a child in Cornwall, all of which was a lie, but they still hired her to teach English, probably because she was good looking.

Molly told me that Erika had a thing for the North Korean boys, students who lived in the dorm across the campus, and wore Kim Il Sung lapel pins. They all looked like they just stepped out of a 1930s Comintern propaganda poster. Apparently, according the gossip Molly told me, Erika liked more than one North Korean boy at a time.

Molly and I did lie in bed once laughing about it, imagining her lining up young Korean men in their tight white jockey shorts, inspecting them while wearing a black bra and panties herself, slapping her riding crop against the furniture, barking orders at them.

Anyway, that time I had breakfast at the student cafeteria brings something else to mind. The big topic for Erika that day was Sandor had put a small menorah in the window that sits right above the main entrance to the student dorm, so you can't help but see it as you come in the front door. Erika spied Sandor in line getting food just as she was telling us about it.

"I don't care that Sandor is a Chew, but why does he put that candle holder in the window?" she said. "He would be the first to complain if I put a cross there."

I remember thinking that students in Erika's English class would associate the People of Abraham with mastication.

"Remember the movie *Annie Hall*, when Woody Allen thought they were talking about him?" said Molly. I could tell she was egging me on to do a Woody impression.

"Did you hear that," I said, picking up her thread, with my thickest Jersey accent, "she said 'Chew'. Not 'Did you?' but 'Chew.' She's talking about me!"

My Jersey-Woody had Molly in hysterics, and Erika looked amused, if confused. Then, like a fly to a flame, Sandor came over and sat down at our table. Erika and Molly continued laughing and following the joke without acknowledging him.

"Be sure to chew your food!" Molly barked at Erika.

"My feet hurt – I can't wear these chews!" Erika oddly pronounced everything correctly.

"Why don't chew shut up?" They went back and forth, laughing like a couple of drunken whores at two in the morning, entertaining each other immensely.

Sandor sat quietly and I attempted to joke about something else, but Erika and Molly would not let it go. It wasn't my fault, but I could see he was hurt. The next time I talked to him was when Gregor brought him to my apartment and I introduced him to Bing. I already told you about that.

Lang stopped the tape and just looked at me.

"Sorry." I said. "I am talking for myself as much as for you. We treated Sandor very poorly."

"I don't understand. Chew?"

"Yao," I said in Chinese using the word for "to chew." "When Germans speak English, it sounds like the word for 'youtai ren.'" Youtai (犹太) means Jewish in Chinese.

Lang shook his head. "I thought we were talking about the East German woman? Let's keep going and review it later," he said and he restarted the tape recorder.

The three of us were in our bathrobes, in the brick shower "outhouse," Erika, the East German and me. She introduced herself to me as Dagmar. Erika apologized for "forgetting her manners" but I could see she was not happy to see me talking to Dagmar.

Dagmar was tall and lanky, seemingly unpretentious, with open, active, yet sad aqua blue eyes, an upturned nose and severely cut dark blond hair that hung to her shoulders. She walked with a slow lope, like a tired athlete, wearing her carelessly tied robe and a lopsided, sexy smile.

"Your wife is gone, no?" Dagmar surprised me with that question.

"Well – she isn't my wife, actually..."

"Oh, what is she then," asked Erika as she combed her hair. "She is coming back, isn't she?"

"Yes, of course she is," I said. Erika eyed me closely to see if I was lying.

"The Chinese must think she is your wife, otherwise why do you get such a nice apartment?" Dagmar smiled, like a friendly inquisitor. "Don't single people have apartments in your building?" she asked Erika.

Erika shrugged.

"Yes, the Chinese think we are married. She went back to the States for a while, visiting her family. Her father is getting older and..."

"It must be hard for you," said Dagmar.

"I am sure it is very hard, right, Nate?" deadpanned Erika, overly proud of her English pun. I tightened the belt on my robe.

"It is sometimes difficult, yes. But being alone is nice once in a while also." I smiled at Dagmar, ignoring Erika.

"It is...I feel that way too, sometimes," said Dagmar. "But you should come out and visit with everyone sometime." By everyone Dagmar means the foreigners. "Since your Cossack Dance last year everyone wants to see you. Can I ask you something...?"

"What?"

"No, it is none of my business." Dagmar shook her head.

"Yes, you must come out more." Erika broke the awkward silence. "Since Molly returned to the States no one has seen you. What are you doing?"

I shrugged at Erika. She smirked.

"Maybe I will pay you a call," Dagmar said noncommittally.

"Good. I'll see you later." I gave them a polite wave, smirked at Erika.

After that, walking back to my apartment I saw a black Hongqi (红旗) or "Red Flag" parked in front of my door. The Hongqi was China's national car, one of the only brands available in China before Deng Xiaoping's opening to the West in the early '80s. It was then that Japan had flooded Beijing with quality-control-rejected Datsuns and Hondas. But the big, plush "Red Flag" limos are the status symbols of the young disaffected children of high officials of the party.

In the back seat of this Hongqi sat Pan Honghua. Pan's father was the Party "Ganbu" (干部) or Cadre assigned to the joint venture I work for, my other job. I had never actually seen Pan's father, but Pan was the executive secretary of the organization. She spoke a little English and traveled to Hong Kong every three months or so to shop.

She got out of the car to greet me. In my bathrobe and flip-flops, I thought of flashing her...

"Where were you? I knock off the door." I saw her driver, Lin, watching me through the rear view mirror.

"What's up, Pan?"

"Up?" Pan looked confused for a couple of seconds. "We need you in the office. Ling Ye sent me to give you the message."

I switched to Chinese. "What message?"

"Because we have a big customer coming to buy the software, Ling Ye needs you for Quick Rabbit software display."

"Big customer?"

"Ling Ye receive a call..." she slipped back into Chinese. I was not going to be her English teacher. "...He wants to buy a large quantity of the Quick Rabbit system. Ling wants you there to demonstrate it. The customer is an American like you."

"OK. When?"

"1 PM this afternoon."

"That is in three hours. Go back and tell Ling I'll be there at 1 PM. I'll take the bus."

"The bus? Why do you want to take the bus? We have the work unit's car here!"…English again…"You should not drive the bus."

I stayed in Chinese. "It's not for three hours. I need to do something first. I'll be there on time."

"Oh. I will return to the office then." She pursed her lips and looked away from me.

"Would you and Lin like to come in and have some tea?"

"No, no. We won't bother you then."

"It's a short bus ride and subway too, but quick just the same."

She didn't seem to believe me.

"Pan, I need to get dressed and I have my computer here. I will work on the demonstration for the American customer."

"OK. Please tell Ling that I tried to get you."

"I will."

She returned to the back seat and was arguing with Lin as they drove away.

I went back inside and sat on the side of my bed watching the bright rays of light shimmer through the cracks in the incompletely closed curtains. I put on a white short-sleeve shirt and brown slacks. I wore a tie too, for the "big customer." I would have to lug my Compaq 286 on the bus. I could afford a taxi, but time was one thing I had a lot of and the bus wasn't crowded in the middle of the day.

My Compaq was a rocket, a 40-lb suitcase with a 9-inch green monochrome monitor, a 40 meg hard drive, an 80286 CPU, 128K RAM, and a 5.25-inch floppy disk drive. Technology like that gave me a real edge. I was the first person to ever use direct mail commercially in China and it was cheap and quick communication with the 600 or so Western commercial offices in Beijing. I mailed out a newsletter every month and I always picked up new customers right after sending it.

As I was locking up to leave, I heard laughter coming into the vestibule and I saw Mr. Liu, my upstairs neighbor, carrying a bag of groceries while Mrs. Lü opened her door. They both seemed embarrassed. Mr. Liu invited me to come up for tea very soon. Mrs. Lü, a widow, the Party leader who got me the job at the Institute, smiled at me.

It was Mr. Liu's wife who woke me every morning with her garlic chopping. Mr. Liu and I visited together about once a month and talked about literature and life. That morning though we did the minimal required friendly greetings, and then they both quickly went into Mrs. Lü's apartment.

It was very hot outside. Noontime was when Chinese couples have sex, first a noon lunch and then a "nap." The work unit's kindergarten kept the little kids over lunch hour, so people took advantage of the free babysitting to "make love." Most of the old people were outside, sitting in various nooks and crannies of shade talking to each other or just sleeping. In crowded apartments, the early afternoon was the only time that couples were alone. From the corner of my eye, I saw shades being drawn by half-dressed men and women in the apartment building across from Xilou.

It was going to be a hot day and I was already sweating. I started across the main courtyard and Dagmar came ambling over. We met in the middle of the dusty, dirt-covered deserted courtyard, the central point of the west side of the campus, just in front of the shower. She wore knee-length brown shorts and a green tee-shirt imprinted with the Albrecht Durer engraving "Melancholia" - two winged angels, a Cupid-like baby and an "adult" Archangel, sitting next to a filthy trash-covered backyard outside a workshop. The Archangel and Cupid were obviously depressed, with their heads in their hands. A grungy dog lay at their feet.

"Nice shirt," I said.

"It's my political statement," she said, with a wry, lopsided smile. Her English was resonant and clear, and I remember Gregor saying she spoke Japanese and that her Russian was "like Moscow prostitute."

"Innocence lost in the worker's paradise?" I was staring at the Durer woodcut imprinted on her tee-shirt. I noticed she wasn't wearing a bra.

"I hadn't thought of that," she said. "Perhaps they are Asian factory workers taking a rest from making sports shoes or tennis rackets."

I laughed. We stood there.

"So."

"So."

"Take me back to your apartment. I believe that brick buildings stay cool in the afternoon, and it is so hot." She theatrically wiped sweat from her forehead.

I'm not sure why, but I flinched.

"I have to meet someone right now," I said. I lifted my Compaq. "Business. What about later?"

"Later." A pout like I've never seen before, an end-of-the-world pout. "Who knows?"

She turned around and headed back to the dorm.

I was in shock at my pusillanimity. It didn't really hit me until I got on the bus. I had just lost a sure opportunity to get laid, and I was in agony. If this big customer was calling us, he would have waited. I felt completely stupid and worthless.

I got to Gongzhufen traffic circle, (公主坟, *was the burial mound of an adopted Princess of Emperor Qianlong*) and jumped on the subway – got off two stops later at the Military Museum and hustled across the street. I was sweating but walked into the Joint Venture office exactly at 1 PM.

A red plastic banner with black characters hung above the window that looked out across Fuxing Lu at the Chinese Army Military Museum. In smaller type the English read "International Tectonic Measurement Systems." The company (ITMS) made earthquake detection software. KuaiTu(快兔), the Chinese word processing software that I sold, was a small part of the bigger operation, but lately it had been generating much needed cash.

Pan, dressed in a black and red plaid skirt and a white blouse, was sitting in her glass-enclosed office, holding a tiny mirror up to her face while she pulled on her eyelashes. The bell on the door had announced me, but she hadn't looked up. Most of the tech staff were gone except for the two guys who lived off-site. They had their heads on their desks, napping next to their greasy tin lunch boxes and chopsticks covered with noodle residue. Ling was in his office and motioned me in.

"I received a fax. I think we have a big opportunity," he said. Ling, in his fucking Mao suit, was always trying to insert himself into my sales.

"Can I see the fax?" I asked.

"Of course. I'll have Pan make you a copy." I knew that asking Pan to do anything was like asking a cat to bark. Since I was responsible for all of the English language advertising, it was my lead if the prospect heard about us through my mailing. Otherwise I split the commission with the joint venture.

"Oh, by the way, I have a letter for you." Ling walked into his office and gave me an envelope. From the Beijing Music Conservatory, it was the announcement of a recital this coming Thursday. I only saw one line, "Zhang Xi, to play erhu," well that needs to be explained...but I don't really understand it myself. I put the announcement in my pocket.

"This American," says Ling, "he sounds like a sure thing. I think he will be placing many orders."

"Really?" I have no reason to doubt it. The product is great and perfectly positioned. My biggest worry lately was keeping the inventory in stock. "Sure, I'll go and meet him."

"He is at the Friendship Hotel."

I had to squeeze my hands to keep them from punching Ling and bit my lip to keep from screaming. I had dragged my ass in this heat down to Fuxing Lu when my customer was practically next door to my Institute at the Youyi Binguan?

I thought about what it would have been like to put Dagmar's legs up over my shoulders while I piled into her.

"So how did he find out about us?" I asked with a bit of an edge to my voice I think.

"We think it might have been through our advertisement in *China Daily*." The other part of our agreement was that I was responsible for coordinating the marketing to the foreign community. Since *China Daily* was published in English, it stood to reason I should have designed and placed the ad. Ling had written it with Pan.

"Quick Rabbit writes Chinese fast! Please purchase Quick Rabbit. fax 362208," the same fax number I advertised.

"So how do you know he answered your ad and not mine?"

"Let's not worry about that. Until you sell we have no money right?" He slipped into English, "Don't count your cocks before they break the eggs!" Good advice in general. I laughed. I would get another shot at Dagmar.

"OK, we'll discuss that later," I said. Since I was meeting the client, I was in control anyway.

I stopped to take a sip of beer and Lang jumped at the chance to turn off the tape recorder. He addressed me in Chinese – "So are you telling us anything important?"

"I don't know," I said. He made a face. He was bored.

"It was very nice of you to come to our home tonight," he said.

I looked at him hard. It was late and I was tired and I didn't want to play Mandarin charades tonight.

"We just want you to talk. For a cop like me to understand you foreigners, it is almost impossible, even when we translate what you say. For example, what did your desire for sex with the German from the Democratic Republic have to do with...I don't understand..."

I started to say "Forget it, Jake – it's Chinatown," but something stopped me.

"Your partner should have come then," I said. "He could have asked me questions and translated for you." Lang gave me a hurt look. Me and my big mouth – I didn't want to go down that road again.

"Anyway," I continued, "You really don't think that it was a suicide pact or murder-suicide, do you? When I saw the bodies that night," I stopped. I suddenly lost my breath or something like that. It wasn't the thought of corpses that made me pause, but the face of the man I met coming around the shower that night. Was it his face that I saw dying earlier? Lang sat up slowly like an old wolf watching a weakened animal. "When I first saw the bodies," I continued, struggling to take back control of my thoughts, "I thought 'He shot her, then shot himself.'"

Lang sat back, and the light slowly dimmed in his eyes. He got up and opened two more beers and turned on the tape player.

"Please," he said in English, "Dagmar – the East German..."

"Yeah – I'll get to her. Just – let me tell the story."

I called the guy from my desk.

"Hello." He had a southern accent, maybe Texas.

"Yes – I'm Nathan Schuett," I said. "I represent International Tectonic Measuring Systems, the company that sells the Quick Rabbit word processing."

Preston Newhouse lived in one of the newer buildings on the Friendship Hotel compound. He was very anxious to see me, so I called a taxi, because it was easier than asking Pan to do it.

The Friendship Hotel,(友谊宾馆) aka the Youyi, pronounced "yo-ee," is the social center for foreigners from the University district of Beijing. Its broad lawns separate many offices and apartment buildings. It is somewhat like a college campus. The main building, the "hotel," was built in the 1950s and has an interesting Sino-Stalinist quality, rectangular and monolithic with a sloped curving roof and upturned eaves. A huge dining room on the "mezzanine" floor is accompanied by a bar that stays open pretty late, sometimes past midnight.

The main attraction, the rooftop bar, was the best place in town on summer nights.

Preston lived in a new, yet dilapidated prefab concrete building on the north side and had a noisy, jerky Czechoslovakian elevator that managed to get me to the third floor. I rang the doorbell.

A shriveled and pinched gray-haired white lady wearing a white dress with little blue polka dots opened the door and quickly turned and walked away calling, "Preston!"

From the right, just out of my sight, I heard "Come in, come in!" The owner of the voice came into view and as soon as I closed the door he came up and shook my hand. Preston was medium tall, fat, and balding, with scraggly white hair hanging slightly over his ears and collar. His jaw hung a little off center to the left and he had a slight wheeze when he breathed. The apartment smelled strangely familiar, comforting and disturbing all at the same time. I had been away from the States for two and a half years, and had not smelled the grandmother smell since…whiffs of lilac, apothecary, old hard candies in glass dishes, dust and mothballs. The dust danced in the afternoon sunlight filtering through the drawn shades, casting slanting shadows on the straight-backed imitation Chippendale chairs and table. A glass-covered, brown-stained antique cupboard stood next to the door like an ill-tempered butler, holding painted, upright gold trimmed plates on the middle shelf. On the upper shelf were two framed pictures of Preston standing amongst large groups of other old white men. Spread out on the table, as well as on the window sills, across most of the chairs and even scattered on the floor were piles of white paper, each about a foot high: reports, letters and contracts.

Two Chinese, a man and a woman, sat amongst the stacks of paper at the dining room table. The woman was about forty and the man twenty-five. Both were unattractive and neither of them smiled at me, which is very rare for Chinese when greeting guests whom they haven't met.

"These are my interpreters, Paul and Hanna." Preston waved his hand over them. I smiled and introduced myself. They looked up quickly as if afraid their pay would get docked for the interruption.

He motioned me to sit down and offered to have his wife get me a ginger ale. I declined and he said he would have a glass. He didn't offer any to his interpreters.

Preston pulled a stack of stapled paper out of one of the disheveled piles and handed it to me. It was a document, a five- or six-page contract in Chinese on thin, rough paper, the printing smeared and broken up. The characters were not lined up straight.

"The Chinese respect the written word," Preston said very authoritatively. I disliked him immediately. "They've been keeping records for thousands of years." He took a drink of his ginger ale and looked closely at me. "I need documents to do business with these people." He was looking at me but he wasn't really talking to me. I just happened to be the only one in the auditorium of his mind. He slowly walked over to a different side of the room and dug out what appeared to be a contract printed on watermarked heavy stock off-white paper, tastefully arranged with different fonts, in English. A quick look showed it was American legal boilerplate for leasing a piece of land. I started to read it, but quickly got bogged down. It was full of phrases such as - "...stipulated that the party of the second part retains control of the income that would otherwise be collected by the party of the first part unless the party of the third part agrees to pay a penalty clause, to be deferred until the lease is executed…"

It went on like that for at least twenty pages.

"I'm going to build a modern office building from which to run an interlocking group of joint ventures dealing with oil, natural gas, and high tech manufacturing. I represent a consortium of businesses and individuals who are ready to commit to China for the long haul. I am talking about hundreds of millions of dollars, right up front." Out of the corner of my eye I saw his ghostly wife standing by the kitchen doorway. As I turned to look, she slipped out of sight like a flaw on the edge of my eye.

He paused and frowned. "Most Americans can't take it here. I don't like it much, but I feel I have to be here. It is where I am supposed to be." He smiled at his two interpreters, who both laughed a little. "Opportunity is about to explode in this country. Every company I know of is waiting for the conditions to change just a little bit. The legal system needs to protect property better, and the currency system needs to be reformed. Nevertheless, China can handle the industry of the whole world and still have workers looking to work for almost nothing." I noticed the smiles on the interpreters disappeared. "Skilled, educated Westerners such as yourself will soon be highly demanded," he said as he smiled at me. I said nothing. He looked at me for a few seconds and then continued his oration.

"A man like you should be making a very high salary." He paused and again smiled at me. "But I don't want to start my offer too high." He moved his eyebrows up and down and I laughed nervously. I have to admit, I took the hook. I was willing to smile and act cute if a big check was waved at me. I was a salesman after all.

"Anyway, to our business at hand? I have hundreds of pages of documents that I need translated and more importantly formatted and attractively printed. Here look at this."

He showed me another thick document in English, this one discussing non-disclosure of "technology transfer" for what appeared to be computer chips. "Did you know most of the computer chips that IBM uses are not made in the US?" I shrugged ignorance. "The real cost for most computer products is the specialty chips that are needed for all of the other components besides the main, what do they call it, the main part…?"

"The Central Processing Unit, CPU."

"The CPU!" He smiled as if I had just solved a profound mystery. "You see – You really know about this…and you speak the language?" He shook his head and smiled. "So we will need to train hundreds of workers to be able to program special chips and then manufacture them. I am talking about clean rooms, serious security, on-site apartments for the workers."

"Here in Beijing?"

"Of course here in Bejing. Or we can negotiate to move to another city."

"So this agreement here is…?"

"I've been talking to several very highly placed officials in the central government. In principle, everything is agreed to. Next week after my certified check comes in from the consortium, I hope to be breaking ground in a month." Now he deliberately looked away from me.

"What certified check?"

He smiled, but still looked away. "Are you from Missouri?" He smiled at Paul and put his arm on Hanna's shoulder while nodding his head. "Where's the money? Yes, that is the right question!" He laughed, as if to himself. "Here." He picked up a piece of paper lying at his fingertips, turned and dramatically passed me the letterhead from the "First Liberty Bank" of Bartlesville, Oklahoma. In part it read,

> "This is to assure you that all necessary instruments have been properly drawn up and executed as prescribed by the laws

of Oklahoma and the United States of America. The transfer of $704,526.00 to Mr. Preston Newhouse of Beijing, China, has been approved. Please inform us within ten days of this date as to the manner of transfer of said funds."

I looked at him. I noticed he wasn't wheezing now.

"So when can you deliver the software?"

"As soon as…I am assuming you are waiting for funds from the bank to arrive?"

"I will have the funds at my disposal in the Bank of China by the end of the week."

"I can come back then and…"

"Listen, Nate…"

Nate? That didn't sound quite right, I remember thinking.

"…Time is working against me." He stood up and looked grim faced at Paul and Hanna. They looked grim too. "Have you heard of IG Farben?"

"Of course I have," I said. I wasn't sure though. It's some German company, something to do with war crimes or something.

"Well, let's just say, I am competing with them," continued Preston as though I had asked him. "IG Farben has a man here in Beijing working on this project. This is the project that they hope will revitalize their company. But we can't let them, Nate. I have the jump on him now, but I am going to lose it if I can't deliver the documents this week." His eyes, rummy and red until now, suddenly burned with concentration.

I had retrieved the complete list of West German companies working in China from their Embassy last spring and I distinctly remembered that IG Farben was not on the list.

"I didn't know they had an office in Beijing?" I said.

"They don't. Their operation is being run secretly out of a Chinese hotel. Just like my operation here." He moved his eyebrows up and down roguishly again. "I know about them, but I don't think they know about me."

"So, is this your computer?" The Packard Bell *500 XT* was up against the corner on a tiny table. It didn't add up, but at least I knew where the guy lived. Something smelled in the apartment and I couldn't put my finger on it but it was familiar.

"Yes. Can you install it today, so that my staff," and he again nodded to Paul and Hanna, "can learn it and produce the documents?" He pulled another piece of paper off one of the stacks on the floor and handed it to me. It was an agreement for five (5) units of software at $700 each, dated today, with the first unit to be delivered today, and the other four (4) to be delivered in two weeks, with full payment to be made in one week. My name was spelled correctly.

$1,000 profit for me.

"How did you get all of this information?"

He smiles. "We'll continue our discussions. I think we can learn a lot from each other." At this he got up and stuck out his hand. We shook, and without another word he walked out of the room.

I always carried a packaged copy of KuaiTu with me for the occasional easy sale. I installed it, tested it and it worked fine. Preston had one of those new EGA monitors, so I saw it in 16-bit color for the first time – it was pretty impressive. I showed Paul and Hanna how to start it, write a sentence, and save. They acted as though they understood but I had my doubts.

I typed, "Jintian tianqi hen hao." It instantly converted it into 今天 天气 很 好. I tested the printer and handed Paul the page. He showed it to Hanna, who smiled.

"The weather is very fine today," she translated.

I looked out the window at the circle driveway in front of the main building of the Friendship Hotel and noticed the shadow had almost reached the front gate. It was 4 PM and I was tired of the stuffy apartment. With the software installed and payment to be made later, I guessed I was done. I packed up and left. No one showed me the door.

I was suddenly very pissed at myself for leaving $600 worth of software in his machine without getting any money. I had this silly promissory note which had the value of a grade school IOU and that was it.

***

I got out of the shaky Czech elevator, walked around the back of the hotel building and over to the swimming pool, and pulled up a lounge chair in the far corner, sliding it over to the shade. I made eye contact with the bar waiter and eventually ordered a vodka tonic with a glass of ice on the side.

The Russians had established air and sea power in the pool. One after the other flew off the high dive, gliding or spinning before entering the pool splashlessly, as if being swallowed up by a warp in space. The Russians and a couple of other Europeans, plus a couple Chinese guys, formed a constant procession up the high dive ladder. Dagmar, Erika and the snotty French girl, Monique, sat on the edge of the pool, dangling their feet and holding up fingers to signify scores. Sandor sat down the fence from me, also by himself in the shade.

Two dark-haired, attractive young women whom I had never seen before were lounging on the other side. They appeared to be recent college graduates from their age and demeanor, one looking like Marlo Thomas in *That Girl* and the other wearing a Che Guevara tee-shirt, torn blue jean shorts, frizzy long hair and a pair of round gold-rimmed glasses. Oddly matched friends, they were taking in the scene with flirtatious friendliness.

I took off my shirt, stooped by the pool and splashed water on my chest and armpits, and kept at the splashing until my pants were soaked. I wanted to kill my white collar funkiness before going over to talk to them. Dagmar came over.

"How's business?"

I shook my head and smiled.

"Oh well." She smiled too.

At that moment one of the Russians breached the surface from his high dive and butterflied like a speedboat toward us. His wake splashed me a little on arrival.

"Come – we are having the battle now!" He waved his hand toward the other side. Erika and the French girl jumped in. Erika climbed up on Boris's shoulders.

"I am too sore for that, Yevgeny." Dagmar rubbed her thighs and smiled knowingly.

"Oh," he said knowingly, "of course." He looked at me smirking. "How about you? Come join us."

"Thanks," I said. "No swimming today."

I got up and retrieved my drink and really didn't care how sore Dagmar's thighs were and started talking to the waiter, who was picking up empty glasses. I gulped my V&T.

Without me to torment, Dagmar apparently changed her mind, and overcoming the pain in her crotch, climbed up on Yevgeny's shoulders and joined in the chicken fight. There were six couples mounted up in the shallow end, girls on the boys.

Refreshed from my little birdbath, I joined the two women on the other side of the pool.

"Are you here for the Moscow Olympics?" I asked indicating the pool competition.

"Ohhhh. Is that what this is?" answered the Marlo Thomas girl. She gave me a big smile. Longgg Island already, by her accent.

"What are you drinking?" I asked. I felt the Marco Polo syndrome coming on. I introduced myself and they did the same – Judy was "That Girl" and Margie was "Grace Slick," both from Ronkonkoma, NY.

"I'll have what you're having," said Margie. Her perky tits pushed Che out, exhorting us on to battle imperialism. I smiled at Margie, but out of the corner of my eye I saw "The

Look" that Judy gave her, which did not seem to encourage fraternization. Undeterred for the moment, I pushed on, and made the "V"-"T" finger sign to the bar waiter, and then shook my drink and held up three fingers. He smiled and nodded. I walked over and brought my 40-lb suitcase Compaq and shirt closer to where I was sitting.

Most of the foreigners who teach in China have to bum drinks from tourists, but I had money from selling software, so I didn't worry about covering a few rounds of drinks.

I talked to the two touristas from Ronkonkoma and learned that Reagan was still president, a fact which seemed to still have them pissed off. I didn't give a shit, and they were pissed off a bit at my apathy, so I had to tell them why I was here in the first place.

I had been a "Democratic Activist" and political junkie right up until I left in 1984, just after the election. In fact, I had been a "senior strategist" in fucking Mondale's campaign in Oregon, as if any strategy other than intergalactic voter fraud would have helped. Reagan got 56% of the vote in Oregon. It was so fucking embarrassing, to lose to that B actor, even if he was the incumbent. 1984 was a bad year all around. Orwell warned us.

Anyway that was the main reason I decided to go into exile, in the People's Republic of China, and stop giving a shit about politics. This was more or less my story to the two Ronkonkoma girls. I felt like I could take my pick between them, if I didn't mind – well – giving a shit. But I knew I didn't have the patience. I just had no shit to give, I am sure part of it had to do with letting that creep Preston, a Reaganite if there ever was one, talk me into giving him the software on the come. But I didn't mention any of that to the Ronkonkoma girls, or anything about Molly either. They were fascinated by my laconic ennui, but I knew from experience that it probably wouldn't last.

So I let them tell me what American media told them was really going on in the world. Living here in China made the context of the American daily chatter about Iran Contra and Ollie North seem like foolish noise. Judy gave me a blow by blow account of the hearings and how the press had made North out to be a big hero. Judy was vitriolic to the core in her hatred of what America was doing in the world, particularly in Central America. She was all slogans and clichés. There was never any danger that she would veer off into originality with her insights, nothing I hadn't read before, except that she just prefaced everything with "Those fucking bastards..." I found myself wondering if I was going to have to listen to polemics until nightfall, and even began to wonder if getting laid that night would be worth it.

Margie was the intellectual, and gave off zero "come hither" vibes, so naturally, me being the masochist that I am, she was the one I wanted.

Margie filled in the color, describing inner workings of the whole sickening charade, the corporate tie-ins, the historical continuity of American Imperialism going back to WW2. Margie was very unemotional, and a little shy, but clearly her hatred for Reagan and Republicans was cold and almost pathologically clear, even though she never called them "fucking bastards" like Judy.

Margie almost got me caring about politics again, even if she was a cold fish. Listening to the details of how we subverted Nicaragua, and supported mass murder and worse, how the American people just let them get away with it, did begin to piss me off. But I had been isolated in China for the last two years, with nothing but an occasional *International Herald Tribune* to read, and that made it all seem almost imaginary. Margie said that the people Reagan appointed were no different than Pinochet's henchmen. She said that there were American Fascists who would happily round us all up into college football stadiums and shoot us if they had the chance. I knew she was right, but I didn't come all the way to Communist China to sit around a swimming pool listening to American radicals bitch about the US. I could have gotten that experience at home, talking to my fellow "campaign strategists."

Reagan was a sappy, wooden, B-minus actor, but for some reason the American people thought he was a political genius. He was right about one thing: Communism sucks for the great mass of people who live under it. I could see that even as I sat here poolside, as an honored guest of Deng Xiaoping's regime. America's faults were clear and the meaningless striving, middle-class existence that waited for me at home whenever I finished my sabbatical scared me more than Communism. I swore I would drink myself to death rather than submit to it! But, even with that, having been away from it all for a while, and having seen "the communist menace" up close, I was never completely sure I wasn't missing something as far as Reagan and living in the United States was concerned. He was actually funny sometimes, and as it says in *Reader's Digest*, isn't laughter the best medicine? We'll all be dead eventually anyway, so why stress over it?

"Anyway," I said, changing the subject, "the best thing going around here is the bar right up there." I pointed up to the roof. "Not now, but at night, in the summer, when it's not raining, it is the best place to be in China."

I was starting to get sunburned, so I put my shirt back on. It was nice to be with Americans again, who were not consumed with the minutia of China. There was an easiness to the conversation that I hadn't had for a while and I have to admit I liked that too. We were all from the New York City area and I was enjoying myself talking to Margie and Judy. The chicken fights were familiar from the Parks and Rec pools back home. It appeared that two couples were dominating the competition: Erika atop tall and broad-shouldered Boris, and a smaller, cat-quick Chinese springboard diver supporting a woman they called "The General's Daughter." The General's

Daughter's best friend, a willowy, oval-faced Chinese beauty, pulled herself up on the side of the pool and sat near us. She gave me a little wave, with just the top of her fingers, as if we had a secret, and I signaled her over to sit with us. Across the pool, I noticed irritation in Dagmar's expression. Yevgeny pretended not to notice. I had myself a little three-girl harem.

"Hello," she greeted me in English.

"Hello," I said in Chinese, "Your name, I am sorry, it's…"

"Zhou Jinghua."

"Of course," I said expressing confoundedness with my stupidity in forgetting. Zhou Jinghua and the General's daughter were two of maybe ten to fifteen Chinese people, all of them under thirty years old, who hung out at the Youyi – the Friendship Hotel – and socialized with us foreigners. Maybe they were the only ones with the courage to do it or the only ones who cared to, like I said, I don't know the rules. I know that it is generally considered forbidden for "regular" Chinese people to be on the hotel grounds unless it was business or a direct official invitation. I had no idea what Zhou's "guanxi"(关系, juice, power) was unless it was simply that she was a friend of the General's daughter. The moniker "General's Daughter" was pretty much self-explanatory.

"Zhou, this is Margie and Judy." Cheers all around.

We turned our attention to the pool and the spirited chicken fight. Erika was quite strong as well as beautiful, and easily dispatched most of her opposition. Although the majority of the attention focused on the women topside, the men struggling to maintain balance was where the real action was. Suddenly after several minutes of awkward ballet it was down to two teams – Boris and Erika, and the Chinese diver carrying the General's daughter. The General's daughter was big, especially for a Chinese woman. She and Erika grappled desperately; Erika was hanging off to the side of Boris and about to go in the drink, when the Chinese diver – took a dive.

It was almost as if he got a signal not to beat the foreigners (even a Russian).

After displays of bonhomie commie solidarity and congratulations, the General's daughter swam over and joined us. We cheered the fallen athlete and I ordered her a Havana Club Rum and Coke as she dried off.

"You should have won," said Margie. The General's daughter smiled but didn't seem to understand a word.

I sat in the sun enjoying the company of four attractive women. I let them talk and helped interpret. I couldn't figure out which one I wanted, and I knew from past experience that you can't just wait it out and take who was most available. My Dad took me duck hunting when I was a kid and he told me something I have always remembered. You have to aim at a particular duck and don't just shoot at the flock or the covey or gaggle, whatever the hell you call a bunch of flying ducks.

Most of the foreign women at the Youyi didn't talk to the Chinese women who hung out there, whether they thought they were there to steal the few foreign men or not, I wasn't sure. But Judy and Margie didn't seem to know the score and were having a good time figuring it out.

The General's daughter, Chen Renmei, was athletic, cute, and had kind of a chubby sexiness. She downed her first drink in one gulp.

"Another drink?" She shook her head enthusiastically to my question. Cuban Rum and Coke is the popular drink for the Chinese this summer. I stuck to V&T, but the Long Islanders switched – I think they liked the Cuban thing. Zhou, practicing her English, entertained Judy and Margie, talking about work and school and boy-girl stuff, etc.

"You know," Zhou said as if she had just remembered something, "Chen is waiting very eagerly for GeGe'er to return from holiday." Gege is Chinese for big brother so I was a little confused.

"Where did your brother go?" I asked Chen, translating for the two Americans as well.

"No, no," said Zhou, "Not brother (哥哥, brother). The Yugoslavian (革革, revolution doubled)."

"He is Croatian," said Chen in English. I looked at her closely and she smiled and shrugged her shoulders. Oh, that guy. Yeah, now I realized I had seen her with Gregor.

At that time, I only knew Gregor by sight and reputation, and I had instinctively avoided him. Chen had a sly, sybaritic look about her and I suddenly saw her and Gregor as very compatible item.

"So why didn't you go on holiday?" asked Zhou.

"Work."

"You are a teacher though."

"I have another job." I signaled for another drink, and asked with my hand if they would like refills. Zhou and Chen put their hands on their glasses and Judy and Margie both held out their glasses. Good, I could buy them another drink and leave. The Ronkonkoma girls lost interest in me once they started talking to Chen and Zhou and I didn't have the energy to keep up. Girl to girl, West to East, something to talk about back home. Erika and Sandor were sitting in the back in the shade. When the drinks arrived I said, "I need to get out of the sun," and retreated to the shady table toward the back, next to Sandor and Erika.

As I pulled up a chaise longue, Erika was smiling at what she took to be my failed attempt to seduce a couple of traveling students.

"Americans?" I nodded at Erika as I gulped my drink and signaled for another.

"Jews?" Sandor spoke with a bit of sour condescension in his voice.

"I suppose so," I said. "They look vaguely Mediterranean, and they don't talk like Gypsies or truck drivers. And they are from Long Island." Sandor, who was almost impossible to typecast himself, looked puzzled, but then he smiled at Erika, like he had won a bet.

"Look at Dagmar," Erika said. Dagmar was sitting on Yevgeny's lap. "She is giving him a bump in his bathing trunks," she said.

I couldn't see the bump from my angle. They were kissing sporadically too. Dagmar looked over at me and smirked.

I was pissed off that she went from me to Yevgeny this afternoon, but even more pissed that I gave a shit.

"Dagmar is very nice and smart, but this is what is wrong with Communism. They don't learn the old values. She has no self-respect. That why she is a slut," said Erika, surprisingly without sounding personal about the whole thing.

"So you…" I started…

"No, I am not." Erika smiled and seemed to know where I was going even if I wasn't sure exactly. "She can't control herself. That is a slut. She allows her desires and emotions to rule her. She ends up where she shouldn't be or doesn't want to be. That is a slut. You are not a slut if you are in control."

I looked at her over the top of my sunglasses and shook the ice in my glass. She smiled and Sandor's sad puppy dog eyes narrowed. I put my drink down.

"There he is. I told you," Sandor said. A tall red-haired guy came walking into the front gate of the pool. He was wearing a BBC baseball cap and red Speedos. Oh fuck, not him.

"You are right," Erika said. The tall, thin redhead sat next to Zhou. She touched his arm and he shook hands with Judy and Margie. He looked over at me and we stared at each other. He waved, I nodded and then he looked away.

"There is your brother, Nate," Erika said. Sandor chuckled.

He even sat like me. It was Rennie, the guy I owe everything to, the guy who gave me his job so he could be a part-time student, and now part-time actor. I sat up straight and just as I did, so did he. I was suddenly very angry. Erika and Sandor were both laughing hysterically and I ordered another long-distance V&T.

I watched him for a while from behind my shades. Erika was prattling about the East German chaperon at the Institute, a razor-faced woman in her mid-forties, who gave off a cold, butch Marlene Dietrich vibe. Definitely a Stasi agent, Sandor whispered.

I looked over at my double, Rennie. Dostoyevsky and Gogol both wrote about doubles from the point of view of a man slowly going crazy. My drink arrived and I gulped it.

Zhou was sitting close to him now, listening, while he talked to Judy and Margie. Rennie was saying he didn't care that he came from a rich and powerful family, and that he knew such and such and that, oh yeah, he was spending most of his days as Peter O'Toole's stand-in at the shoot of Bertolucci's film about the end of the Qin Empire. Apparently he was an heir or the heir to the DuPont fortune. His last name was DuPont, but aside from that, I've heard different stories. Apparently he had told different people different things. He was nice to me and I was polite in return. I guess it was Zhou. If she saw something in him, other than all that money at the end of the rainbow, maybe he wasn't all bad.

All that said, judging from the bored sideways glances Margie and Judy were throwing at each other, Rennie was boring them. The two Long Island girls got up to go. Judy looked over, waved and pointed to the roof. I raised my glass.

Chapter Five

I woke up on Lang's couch and his wife, fully dressed, and tiptoeing, was quietly putting food in little bags and packing them into a brightly colored school backpack. Lang's daughter came out of the bathroom and her mother gave her a very harsh look, along with a signal to be quiet. They were almost finished, so I closed my eyes to avoid any embarrassment.

After Lang's daughter was hustled out the door to school, Lang came out wearing his work pants and a muscle shirt. I opened my eyes.

"Awake?" I sat up and pulled on my clothes. "I will drive you to the Palestine guest house," he said. "You rest up there and we can start up again in the afternoon. Qi and I will be in meetings all morning."

The drive over was quiet. Lang was troubled by something. "This businessman who bought your software...?"

"I didn't say he bought it. He promised to buy it. He signed a contract to buy it." Lang looked at me as if I had told him a very profound and important secret. We didn't talk again until we pulled up to the PLO apartments and he was letting me out of the car. "Don't discuss any of this. I'll have a driver pick you up at 1 PM."

When I got back to the embassy apartment, I didn't want to do anything else but sleep, but Ibrahim was waiting there for me, sitting reading an Arabic newspaper. I hadn't talked to him alone since just before I discovered the bodies.

"Nate – my friend!" He got up and quickly walked to me and grabbed my shoulders and held them, while looking at me closely. "You look tired. Did they abuse you?"

"No." Ibrahim continued to look closely at me, so I got to the point. "I told them that I saw some Westerner, but that I didn't recognize him. I think that was a mistake because if they find out..."

"No. That is good. They won't find out. That is perfect. It could have been a Russian, German or American – perfect. They will waste time trying to figure that out."

"There were guards at the gate and they never saw him come out. So they must know I'm lying or..."

"...or that he drove out with us," said Ibrahim.

"Or it was someone who was already there and probably still is. Like the American teacher who took my job. So how...?" I was confused. "What do you want them to believe? If he drove out with you, then they know I'm lying. If..."

"Why? You didn't come with us."

"But I arrived with you," I said.

Ibrahim shrugged. "No – tell them everything. Don't lie. Tell them everything. They don't care about anything except these two European bodies they have to explain. So give them everything – except..."

I nodded. "I want to sleep some more," I said. "I think this afternoon is going to be tiring."

"Don't worry – it is going to be fine. Just try and sleep," he said as he left.

But I didn't sleep. At 2 PM, a *Gong An* cop picked me up and we drove across Beijing in silence. I walked into the Haidian police station and was already part of the scenery. Several of the desk cops who had ignored me yesterday now greeted me like I was an old colleague. Qi came down to get me and told me a joke as we walked upstairs.

"A panda bear walks into a restaurant, sits down and asks the waiter to bring him a platter of bamboo. After eating it, the panda takes a gun out and kills the waiter. The restaurant owner is horrified.

He asks the panda, 'Why did you do this?' The panda says, 'That is what I am supposed to do - go look in a dictionary.' So the restaurant owner gets an English dictionary and looks up panda. 'panda: giant mammal indigenous to China. Eats bamboo and shoots.'"

I smiled and chuckled. Qi seemed a little disappointed.

"Isn't that funny?"

"Yeah. It would have been funnier if the panda took the gun out of his pouch and instead of calling him a mammal you called him a marsupial - because they have pouches - he could have kept the gun there..." I made a little imaginary pouch with my hands. Qi apparently didn't like me editing his joke, because his smile disappeared and as soon as I sat down he got down to business.

"Pandas are not kangaroos, they are related to bears. Everyone in China knows that. So your wife went back to America and you thought she was going back to see her old lover..."

"Well actually she wasn't my wife..."

"OK. You worked for the Canadian joint venture selling software. Software that writes Chinese on a computer. You made money, but paid no taxes to China? OK?"

Qi looked up at me as if he were my accountant. "OK. You met with the two victims at the pool in August, the Hungarian and the German woman. I don't understand - you say that the German woman was against the Hungarian because he believes in the Jewish religion. This is related to the massacre of Jews by Germans in World War II?"

"It is very complicated..."

"Yes. But they sit together and seem to be friends?"

"They are European. Europeans are friends when facing Americans. They don't really like us. Like I said, the Europeans are complicated. I don't understand them either."

Qi looked closely at me. "Marsupial? A marsupial is a mammal, isn't it?"

"I am not even sure, to be honest. Now that I think about it, it is funnier the way you told it."

Qi's face remained completely blank. "So continue," he said. "I've listened to your recording from last night. The American women tourists left the pool and then what?"

The sun and the vodka had their way with me when I returned to my apartment from the pool and I fell into a coma on the couch. I must have set some kind of alarm in my brain because I opened my eyes suddenly with a fear that I was late for something. It was almost 10:30 PM. I missed dinner. Did I have a date to eat with the Long Island girls? I couldn't remember. I had been dreaming about the one with the long frizzy hair, Margie, and felt like I had missed an opportunity at the pool early. I stood in the bathroom, rubbed my face with a washcloth, and then rode my bike back to the Youyi. It was just about 11 PM, and the sky was clear with a bright crescent moon.

I walked up the three flights of stairs, poorly lit, all brown stained wood, and came out into the open sky and drunken laughter. It was a full house. The rooftop bar is a big space and when you open the door and come out onto the roof, the noise level suddenly rises. Of course when I stepped into the place it went up even higher.

The scene that unfolded was like a tableau in a passion play. Nearest the door, Zhou and Chen were holding court with Jorge, an Argentine long-haired chain smoker, and Harold, a fat English homosexual, who gave me a quick, but deep look. They were all half-listening to my so-called double Rennie, who was talking to Harold very closely and very seriously. Neither Chen nor Jorge spoke English too well, but both were nodding gravely while Zhou was staring at Rennie as he talked to Harold and she took her eyes off of him, just for a second, gave me a little smile and a tiny half-wave with her fingers, then turned back to Rennie who was going on and on oblivious to whether Harold was listening or not.

How did he get "The Job"?

Rennie is Peter O'Toole's stand-in on the big movie they are making about the last Qing Emperor over at the Forbidden City. He's making tons of money he doesn't need, and to top it off he spends his evenings with Zhou. I wanted to ask him about his ex-fiancée, my boss's niece, but I had to be nice because I owed him my job. He had never mentioned the favor he gave me, even obliquely. In fact he had been nice to me. In fact, as far as I could tell, he was nice to everyone. But still, I couldn't stand him, and every time I heard him open his mouth I wanted to strangle him because he was so unaware of his own stupidity. And now that I think of it, he was probably the reason why I didn't like coming over here to the Youyi in the first place.

The General's daughter, Chen, simply stared at me with a catbird grin. I addressed her in Chinese and put my hand on their table as if to bless it and tilted my head, kind of like Ronald Reagan does, as if to say I'm not ignoring you even though I am walking away. I started to look around again when...

"Have some drink!" Boris was standing right in front of me holding out a small glass like you find in cheap motel bathrooms, half filled with something as clear as water and no ice. I drank it in a quick gulp. The men at his table all stood and cheered like I just won the Soviet Clean and Jerk championship. Dagmar rolled her eyes. Boris ushered me to a chair and I couldn't give them the Gipper brush-off because it would look like I was mad at Dagmar, and I'd be damned if I was going to let her know I gave a shit...

"We think you are the best American!" Yevgeny was standing unsteadily. I was toasted as the "Best American" all around. I drank again with good cheer. Dagmar gave me a glassy-eyed look that said, "Please break into the castle and save me." It was strange to be the sober one, but I quickly began to fix that problem.

"You know," said Boris, "we will be friends soon." He stopped and looked around for approval then went on, "The

Muslim!" He spat, but it ran down his chin. This got everyone laughing for probably a minute. Boris wiped himself off, took another drink and continued..."You will be sorry you give them rockets in Afghanistan." He looked deep into my eyes and shared a "Slavic Moment of Transcendence" with me, something deep and profound and based completely on vodka. I did my little Gipper head tilt. As I sat down, I saw the two traveling American girls from Long Island, sitting with Ibrahim and a couple of his Arab buddies. I waved.

"Nathan – you don't travel?" Boris was a big guy, handsome in a Russian way, with pretty good English. I had another shot of vodka. The Russians don't let you get to know them. They always traveled in threes. If two of them were together it looked conspiratorial and one Russian walking alone was probably an escaped lunatic. But sitting publicly at a table with three or four Russians, drinking vodka was OK. Even in Stalin's time Americans had done that.

"I'm working for a Canadian company. I had business, so I stayed in town."

"Who assigned you to that?" asked a little guy with a squashed face and a blond flattop.

"No one needs to assign, Demetri – it is free enterprise," said Yevgeny, his Clark Gable mustache and slicked black hair groomed straight back. He smiled at me, sad eyed and ironically as though I were complicit in something that only he and I were aware of. Dagmar sat next to him, drinking quickly and pouring herself another.

"Yes," I said. "Hired. Fired, that's how it works. It's just a job."

"Just a job," repeated Yevgeny and for some reason it was funny to everybody at the table. Dagmar made a face, stood up and excused herself with a forced smile and walked over to sit with Erika, at a table with Sandor and Monique the French girl.

Yevgeny's face reddened. He pushed the chair that Dagmar had been sitting in out to the middle of the floor and scooted in next to Demetri the Flattop. Yevgeny was an amazing diver, and his body was sculpted like a Greek statue, but now he looked cramped and twisted, as he took a cigarette without asking from Flattop's package and waited for his comrade to fumble and find a lighter. "Look around, Nathan – tell me – who are the spies here?"

"You mean other than you guys?"

Guffawing and nervous mumbling rippled down the table.

"Really. You all work for the state, right?"

I had their serious attention now. "Yes," said Boris.

"Aren't you supposed to report what you know?"

"You've lived here how long now?" asked Yevgeny. He started coughing and it turned into a small fit.

"You sound like Myshkin's consumptive friend Ippolit," I said, name dropping characters from Dostoyevsky's *The Idiot*. This got them all to smile. "I've lived here a little more than two years," I said.

"Are all of the Chinese spies?" he asked.

"All of the Russians aren't spies in Moscow. But you are in Beijing. That is different," I said.

"And you…?"

"Yes, but I don't work for the United States. I'm…" I stopped, not sure what I wanted to say. Oddly, no one pushed me to finish, they were looking out at their own thoughts.

"Who else is a spy?" asked Boris after a second.

"Well, Sandor. Probably. Maybe," I said, for some reason. I wish I hadn't.

"Yes. Definitely," said Yevgeny. "Hungarians. And Jewish, yes? The question is – for which side?"

"His father was a very important ally," said Demetri the Slavic Flattop, "he supported the anti-imperialist faction during…"

"Yes of course," said Boris. "But what about from your side?"

"My side?" I asked, feigning surprise. I smiled but Boris kept looking and waiting. "Well, perhaps…?" I said nodding at

Rennie, my double. They looked at me with silent puzzlement. They obviously knew he was an idiot too.

"What about the fat English?" said Slavic Flattop.

"Harold? Don't you guys own the British Secret Service? MI6? You should ask Kim Philby."

The laughter at the table drowned out everything else. They toasted me and Philby.

"Nate, my friend!" A pair of lumpy, hairy hands wrapped around my shoulders from behind. The hands' owner spun me around, looked me in the eye, then hugged me.

When I met Ibrahim, it had been strange and auspicious. It was at the Baiyun Hotel in Guangzhou during Spring Festival the year before last. I was with my parents, who had brought Molly to China, which is another story completely. Mom and Molly were in the room and Dad and I were having drinks in the bar. I went to take a piss and this fat bearded Arab in a polo shirt and dress slacks came up and stood next to me. He began staring at me until I looked at him, then he turned away. I finished up and was washing my hands and I noticed he was holding his hands next to the stream of water but not in it. I looked up from his hands and he was staring at me again.

"Is something wrong?"

"No! Nothing..." Then, "Yes, yes! Something is wrong." He took a deep breath and smiled. "I'm sorry. My girlfriend stole my money." He pulled his wallet out and showed me it was empty. "She is Japanese," he added meaningfully. "We were staying here and this morning I wake up and – it is gone. She is gone." He smiled again. "I thought, no problem, I have a friend in Guangzhou, but, it's just..."

"Just what?" Something put me at ease. His smile, I don't know – but I believed him. Japanese girlfriend? Nobody would make that up. Normally I'm pretty standoffish, but this time something about him made me stay to see what he wanted.

"My friend doesn't answer the phone."

I invited him for a drink – easy to do, my Dad was paying. I always got on better with Dad if we had a third person around and we had a great two hours trading stories.

Ibrahim was PLO and had been in Lebanon in 1982. In spite of the horrors of the war, he told funny stories about pretending to be Israeli, using captured papers and speaking bad Hebrew while sneaking his little unit in good order through the Israeli lines that had beaten him to Beirut. My Dad told funny stories about Vietnam and World War II, about stumbling drunk off of a floating bar in the middle of the Mekong River just as it blew up behind him, or shooting at a cousin in the Luftwaffe. I had never been in a war, so I told what I thought was a funny story about trashing a cop car in front of the ROTC building on my college campus in 1970 right after Kent State.

My Dad gave Ibrahim thirty dollars to buy a train ticket to Chengdu and I left him my address in Louyang. When I got back to Louyang the money was waiting for me (I never did get around to sending back it to Dad), along with a beautiful tiny jade statue of Buddha for Molly, even though Ibrahim hadn't met her and obviously wasn't a Buddhist himself. I wrote him, thank you for the Buddha, etc., but we lost touch after that. Then we both showed up in Beijing last year and here we were.

"We waited for you..." said Judy, pushing between Ibrahim and me.

"Was I supposed to meet you?"

"Yes!" She put her arm through mine to make sure I didn't get away. "We were in the dining room downstairs when Rashid and Nasser and Ibrahim sat at our table..." Judy moved close to my ear so she didn't need to shout. "Well, one thing led to another and...then when we saw you come in, Ibrahim said 'That is my friend!' and we said, 'He's our friend too!' Isn't that funny?"

I agreed it was funny and Judy then leaned even closer and whispered to me – she smelled of perfume and Cuban rum - "Look at Margie."

She dragged me arm in arm to their table and Margie was forehead to forehead with a startling-looking young man – that was the first time I had ever met or even seen Rashid. He looked up at me as we got to the table and his eyes looked like sapphires, bluer than any eyes I had ever seen. His hair was golden, not blond, not red, but golden. The more I looked at him the more I realized I was staring. His eyes looked way too blue for his face, way too blue for anyone's face, so blue that they looked completely stoned yet behind those eyes was intentness and clarity that was the opposite of stoned, almost unworldly.

He looked at Ibrahim and asked him something in Arabic. Margie couldn't take her eyes off of him. "His name is Rashid," she said. "His friend is Nasser..." As if on cue, a very tall, taller than me, very Arab-looking young man with close-cropped hair, wearing an Izod knockoff golf shirt, stood glaring nervously at me.

"Nate, let me introduce you to my friend, this is Nasser." Ibrahim said something in Arabic and Nasser smiled. He suddenly looked like a teenager with an innocent disarming smile. We shook hands and Ibrahim said something else to jewel-eyed Rashid. He looked away from Margie only long enough to smile and nod at me.

Rashid spoke no English, but he did speak Margie's high school French, so they got by with whispers and giggles.

"Rashid," said Ibrahim smiling mischievously, followed by a stream of Arabic. Both Rashid and Nasser started laughing. "Circassians were favorites of the Turks for their beauty," said Ibrahim to us in English. He struggled not to laugh. "You saw the film *Lawrence of Arabia*?"

"With Peter O'Toole," said Judy. "I've seen it three times."

"Remember when the Turk Colonel did that to Lawrence." Ibrahim made a face of painful disgust. "Lawrence was pretending to be Circassian – when the Turk did it." More rapid-fire Arabic from Nasser and Rashid leaned over and punched Nasser in the chest so hard it knocked him to the floor. Nasser lay next to the table laughing hysterically and even Ibrahim could not stop. Even Rashid started laughing now. He stood up and shouted above the din on the rooftop – "P'tar Oh Tooo! - P'tar Oh Tooo!" Everyone turned and Ibrahim and Nasser laughed uncontrollably, contagiously, and soon we were all laughing although I wasn't sure at what.

"I work with Peter O'Toole every day. What is so funny?" My double, Rennie, spoke up loudly, as if he were demanding satisfaction from a gentleman, but was ignored. He walked over to our table with trepidation.

"Peter is a great guy you know. I bet I could get him to come over and drink with us. He stays downtown mostly, but I know he would really like it here."

Ibrahim nodded diplomatically. He shot me a look that said, "What the fuck is wrong with this guy?"

Rashid said something in Arabic. "He wants to know if O'Toole enjoyed being a Circassian." Now everybody was bending over laughing. Rennie still didn't get it, which was now what was so funny.

"Rennie is Peter O'Toole's stand-in. They are making a movie about Puyi, who was the Last Emperor of China," Zhou said quietly in Chinese. She stopped the laughing, even though only about half of us understood what she said. Ibrahim looked at Rennie and then at me.

"You two should go stand in front of a mirror so you don't get confused as to which is which!" Ibrahim spoke in Chinese with a pure Beijing accent.

"Americans and Europeans all look like eggs in a basket," said Rashid.

"Eggs are eggs," said Ibrahim. "They rot, they are white, brown, big or small and can have any kind of animal inside – an eagle or a snake!" Both Rashid and Ibrahim's Chinese was indistinguishable from that of a native speaker.

"East meets West," said Rennie, suddenly seeming to understand the joke. "It's always an interesting story." He nodded and laughed and put his hand on my shoulder like a good sport. He of course had not understood a word of what was said. I smiled tightly and excused myself.

I walked over to the deserted west side of the bar. I looked over the parapet and out into the night. Nothing was out of place. I traced Orion's belt to the Little Dipper. It was all familiar. I am getting older. The same sky, the same stars. Even on the other side of the world.

Then an obviously Japanese woman walked in wearing a short, shiny, tight, plastic blue skirt. She looked like she just got back from a David Bowie concert, with Twiggy-style short hair, blue lipstick, and plastic boots up to her thighs. Dagmar stood up, hugged her and guided her to the Russian table. She stopped and turned and looked at Ibrahim. It was a face-off at the DMZ.

"Mikku!" Ibrahim's voice went up an octave and he looked as if he had just been shot. She looked at him with no change in expression and then turned back to Dagmar and laughed, much too quickly to have been told a joke. Dagmar spoke to her a bit loudly, showing off her drunken Japanese.

"Mikku!" Ibrahim was almost pleading.

She turned to him again and looked at him as if she were waiting for something that she could take or leave. Ibrahim went to her.

"Let's join the tables," said Dagmar.

"Yes..." Ibrahim said although he didn't take his eyes off of Mikku. "Yes. This is China. We are all from the same country anyway." He touched her elbow and she pulled away, but went with him anyway.

"Waiguo," I said, getting a big laugh even from Rennie. Two Chinese girlfriends and over a year in Beijing, and Rennie still could not speak much beyond "Ni hao." But even he knew "waiguo" (外国) can mean something foreign or foreign country. How long had it been since we'd been home to the green hills of Waiguo! In China, we were all compatriots.

"Everyone! From now on!" I pulled out a $100 bill – an enormous sum - "We drink until it is gone!"

Dagmar jumped up, ignoring the Russian edginess to my suggestion. "Here! Give it to me." She came over and relieved me of the money. "I'll negotiate. We need food too, right? Erika, come and help." Erika, smoking cigarettes with Sandor, the Argentine longhair, Monique and Harold, had been trying to settle the Falklands War peace treaty, without success, so she joined Dagmar.

I suddenly recognized Mikku. She was the mousy Japanese school "girl" who always wore pigtails, usually with a pleated skirt and white knee socks and who studied by herself in the courtyard at my Institute.

"So," said Boris to Nasser, "You are Arab – from where?"

"I was born in Bethlehem."

"Of course you were!" Now everyone was laughing.

"It's true – just like the Christ. And like him, I am sure the Israelis will kill me eventually."

"No!" shouted Judy authoritatively, leaning over and kissing him. "It was the Romans."

"You see? They won't kill you right away! First they torture you," said Yevgeny. Boris stood on his chair with his arms out, hanging his neck slack. Most of the other Russians looked mortified at Boris's mock crucifixion, but the rest of us were laughing our asses off. Judy climbed on Bethlehem-born Nasser's lap, and straddled his waist. Nasser really did look like he was being tortured and everyone was in hysterics laughing.

"No," he said suddenly picking up Judy as if she were a loaf of bread, and standing up. "First I go to Afghanistan and kill all the Russians for Allah!"

Silence. "No, no," said Ibrahim, "the Russians are our brothers. To Kalashnikov!" He stood up and toasted. The Russians held up their glasses. Mine stayed on the table.

"Let's stop killing," said Judy, grabbing Ibrahim and pulling him back into his seat. "Don't you all understand how rare this is? This could be like a Peace Conference! We could settle it! We all could settle everything here tonight!" Judy looked at Margie, who rolled her eyes and went back to kissing Rashid. "In America this would be big news." Judy turned back at us. "Everybody is here. I've never met a Palestinian before. Why can't we change things? How do we stop the fighting? All of it?" She turned to Nasser and now straddled his lap again, and kissed him long and full on the lips to the cheers of everybody. "You and me! We'll make Peace!"

"To peace!" I toasted, holding up my glass. Everyone lifted their glasses.

"Is that what it's called in America?" said Yevgeny, with a stage-whisper. "If you really want peace, then stop giving the religious crazies the Stingers," he said. "It will come back to haunt you."

"My mother, God rest her great soul, was a Maronite Christian," said Ibrahim. "She married my father, Mohmet Abdullah. He was Sunni and I was raised in a Shiite village after the Israelis took my grandfather's orchard outside Jaffa. That orchard is my religion."

"What if we became one people? We know what happened wasn't fair," Margie said. "But in 1945…it was desperate for so many…"

"…But maybe," said Judy, "maybe we can…"

The thought hung out there. I thought to myself, maybe you can fuck for peace. I had the feeling that this had all been played out long before, and maybe before that. It didn't work then either.

"The problem is it's a sex thing – a male-female thing. Isn't it just tribes – my tribe and your tribe – keeping women under control?" asked Judy, pulling away from Nasser.

"That's the problem. Sexual envy. Men will die rather than lose that control," said Margie.

Ibrahim said, "It is more than that. Even though Sharon killed thousands of us in Lebanon, I do understand him."

"He's a mass murderer," said Margie.

"No, he's a soldier. He was born on the land and can't go back to America. I know that we will win eventually, and so does Sharon. He is just trying to claim as much as he can. I don't think the sex interests him. He is too fat." Mikku patted Ibrahim's stomach lovingly.

He looked at Judy and Margie, "You don't need to be afraid of it when we win. During the Crusades, the Arab who finally captured Jerusalem was Saladin."

"He was a Kurd," said Nasser, kissing Judy.

"Yes, yes, Kurd. He killed no one, well, he killed some but not for sport. He destroyed no churches, let the Crusaders who had farms keep the farms. Moses Maimonides, the greatest Jew of his time, was his physician. He preferred to live under the Muslim rather than live in Europe with the Christians. Jews were always safe in the Muslim world until…"

"So you think that sex is the answer to the problem between cultures," asked Chen, interrupting Ibrahim, in Chinese. I translated for Judy and Margie.

"Yes," said Judy.

"We Chinese have always thought so too," said Zhou in English. "We had a policy called 'huanqin'(换亲) which is exchanging daughters for marriage. The Princess was sent to the wild men. How do you say, Xiongnu?"

"The Huns, the barbarians…"

"Yes," added Zhou, "and the Huns would send their Princess to China. In order to keep the peace, the Chinese Princess had to go. It was terrible. She lived in the round tent and wrote many beautiful poems about the difficulty."

Everyone was quiet. "But now it is different. To go live in a foreign land as a bride is not bad." She looked down and reached across the table to put some food on my double's plate.

"Communism succeeded in some places, Vietnam perhaps, Cuba definitely, because of sex," said Harold.

"Why?" asked Dagmar. She looked at Yevgeny impassively.

"Because Americans or French could come in and buy girls cheaply," said Harold. "If I had seen my little sister have to go off with some fat American for a few dollars, I would have joined Castro. Besides, he was actually pretty cute back then."

"What if the American wasn't fat?" asked Chen.

"You would have joined Castro, because his cause was the correct one," said Boris.

"Yes – of course," agreed Rennie, looking at me, nodding seriously, as if he knew that I understood.

"No, my Russian friend," said Sandor. "Communism is dead, or will end very soon. It is almost gone here in China. The 'dictatorship of the Proletariat' will of course continue, but the Capitalists will take over." He stopped to take a drink and looked a long time at Erika. Boris just stared at Sandor.

"I see it on the movie set," said Rennie. At that moment I understood why I disliked him so much. "Everybody from the West is highly paid, and they live separate, but the girls..." he stopped.

Zhou stared off with a blank look. He looked at her and it was the first time it seemed as if he might have a hint of self-awareness, but it quickly passed. "...Men from the West can be big stars here," he held his hands up as if to demonstrate his point.

Wow, I thought. Of course, he is right.

"But then I am rich," he continued. "My family is anyway. I could have any girl I wanted. But here, I'm not just a rich boy, because Socialism makes us all equal. Here I am myself. And I feel free because of it." Rennie looked around, then at Zhou, who appeared vaguely unsettled. Flattop toasted his drink to him, while laughing. Everyone else tried to avoid looking at each other.

Ibrahim laughed. "Free – yes – free to find a mate! That is as old as life. Male wolves are kicked out of their pack and leave to find female wolves. Chasing a mate is what we all have to do – it is as free as we'll ever be – and then we find them and we lose everything – most of all our freedom! That's the way it is supposed to be – to spread seeds around. Peasants have always known that. Royalty stays in the family and look what happens to them – hemophilia, insanity…"

"Prince Charles," said Harold.

"No," said Dagmar. "Sex outside your class or tribe ends up being exploitative. Women are still property, in fact they are the only valuable property still allowed everywhere. Love is not a bargain, is it? We still are no different than wolves or barbarians. Most of the time, it's just rape." Dagmar looked harshly now at Yevgeny.

Rennie excused himself saying that he had to be on the set early. He came over and offered me seventy dollars to help pay for the food and booze, which I quickly took. He pulled Zhou away for a private talk. I went for a piss and Dagmar followed me down and threw herself around me, clearly drunker than she looked. "So what shall we do?"

"We still haven't finished the vodka," I said.

"Of course – we are Germans – we can never waste anything!" I noticed I was suddenly a German in her eyes. My immigrant grandfather is smiling, somewhere.

Zhou came up behind her and innocently interrupted us with a little two-fingered wave for me to come over to her. I nodded to Dagmar and then walked over to Zhou.

"I need someone to see me home. Rennie is angry at me and I don't want to see him anymore tonight."

"OK." As I left, Dagmar smiled at me with a shrug – no anger and no hurt look. She was pretty drunk.

"Can you get home?" I asked her. "Zhou lives on the other side of the Zoo and it's pretty late."

"Boris is getting a taxi for us all – I was just hoping you could come and pay for it!" She held out the change (about sixty dollars) from the $100 I had given her earlier. I took it.

"Well, send me a bill."

"Oh – you will get a bill!"

My bike, a well-oiled, fat-tired, solid machine, pedaled easily. Zhou rode on the handlebars, fearlessly, expertly. The night was beautiful as we rode away from the hotel.

Recently I had been taking my bike to an old street tinker who oiled and adjusted it. He worked off of a blanket where his well-used tools were laid out clean and straight. He never set up in the same place, and he fit his shelter and tools on his bike with intricately designed baskets and bars. The tune-up cost me fifty mao, half a yuan, about a nickel in dollar value. I paid him twice that, a whole kuai, and refused the change. I remember the old street vendor gave me a smile that promised something extra for the tip.

The night air was cool and the crescent moon was suddenly very close. I leaned back and my well-oiled machine took off for the stars and soared above the earth. My bike handled perfectly, banking from one side to another, seeming to lose all attachment to gravity as we flew into and then out of a cloud bank. I looked down and could see the Great Wall at Badaling to the north and the Forbidden City to the southeast. We dropped down to flying at treetop level and Zhou relaxed and leaned back on my handlebars and I stood and pedaled hard, and we were riding fast, almost cheek to cheek; the thick-framed, fat-tired bike was a magic carpet, sailing us through all time and space with ease. The night had cooled off after the hot day and I knew she wasn't thinking about Rennie. I made her laugh somehow as we breezed down The Western Gate Road and past the Beijing Zoo. The moon was still bright, bright in the clear open sky, and a little breeze picked up, making the temperature so comfortable that it seemed like a crime to go inside even for sleep. We turned at a little hutong (胡同) and went down a construction road past a half-finished apartment complex. Just beyond that there was an old wall that looked to be half torn down. The wall was hundreds of years old and would soon be bulldozed. Time stood still and we stood at the edge of her hutong village, next to that crumbling wall. We kissed, just kissed. It was so nice in the summer breeze under the splintered moon. I said good night and rode home.

Chapter Six

"That is very interesting," said Qi, as he stopped the tape player. His blank expression seemed to say that he didn't believe that my bike had actually left the ground. "You told the Russians that you thought the Hungarian was a spy. That is a serious charge!"

"No one took it very seriously."

"Are you sure? The Hungarian who said that Communism is dead. Where is he now?"

I thought about it. Ibrahim said that the killer wasn't the guy I met coming around the corner of the shower the night I found the bodies – and if he wasn't the killer, then Qi's guess was as good as mine. Maybe the Russians did kill them. Maybe it was my big mouth that got them killed.

I sat quietly for another minute, watching Qi take notes. After a few minutes he stopped and we looked at each other. Then he smiled and waved off the thought.

"They wouldn't dare, not here in Beijing. We threw them out once and they don't want to have to leave again." He pushed the button on the Sony tape player and I continued.

When I arrived in Beijing from Louyang it was as if I had just been cured of deafness. Everyone spoke Chinese like it was taught, the way it sounded on my language tapes, the way the announcers spoke on TV, the way Gong Li speaks in most of her movies. Spoken Mandarin in Shaanxi province is like

111

English in Kingston, Jamaica, or Bombay, India, or Shithole, Texas, or any of the many places where accents and pidgins and Creoles make English familiar, but not really completely understandable to an outsider. Beijing is the best environment to learn Chinese. That's why I moved here from Louyang with Molly, about a year ago. Of course it was dumb luck I met Rennie just when he was looking for a teacher to replace himself; it wouldn't have happened if I hadn't tried.

Later, another lucky tip led me to an afternoon job at Kone Instruments. I didn't teach in the afternoon, so I was able to grab the noon bus down to the Minzu Hotel, where Kone had its office. Kone marketed medical equipment and its customers were bankrolled by the World Health Organization. The WHO had given huge loans to the Chinese National Health department, and Kone was after that money. Serena, an attractive American woman in her late twenties, married to a Chinese-American, ran the Kone office in Beijing. A graduate of Smith College, she spoke good Chinese, much better than me. I showed up and said I heard they needed help and went to work the next day.

My main job, although it was never exactly spelled out, was to take meetings with people who claimed to have access to WHO money, and wanted to broker deals for medical equipment. Chinese mid-level health officials tried to cut themselves into the WHO bonanza by asking for meetings with Kone. Ostensibly these meetings were about business, but actually they were shakedown sessions to get free trips, relatives jobs or into college in the US. My job was to filter these people out so that they wouldn't waste Serena's time or clout. I was a "buffer."

"So the only purpose to your job was to distract and mislead Chinese officials?"

"No. It wasn't the only thing I did. I took care of the computer database and wrote programs to extract information from it." I looked at

Qi. "Maybe you just want to ask me questions and then I'll answer them? If I am not talking about what you want, then you have to ask me."

"No – no – no." Qi was smiling now.

"My colleague is very inexperienced in these matters," said Lang. He turned to Qi and gave him a horrid tongue lashing. I could barely follow it, but it included the proverb about a farmer trying to make crops grow faster by pulling on them when they are only shoots – meaning you just have to let things take their natural course (拔苗助长 – don't pull on new sprouts to make them grow faster). Then he asked me if I understood what he was saying. I smiled.

"Listen if you want me to tell you the truth, you can't become offended, Qi. I thought you were a cop?" I said the last sentence emphatically and in English. Qi nodded. Lang laughed.

"A cop," he said nodding.

I intuitively understood my assignment and that made me a welcomed addition to the office. Serena let me spend money, and I entertained the clients at the Minzu Hotel's fancy restaurant. On such days, I was pretty tipsy by three in the afternoon, and that was never a problem for Serena. My title was "Special Assistant to the Vice President." I landed one good-sized contract that way and I guess, that is really what this is all about.

Qi looked at me quizzically and stopped the tape recorder. We stared at each other.

"I think you will be interested," I said. "I don't even know why, or if it has anything to do with the murders, but Lang wanted to understand how we foreigners live, and what we did." I didn't know if I was doing it to lead them to the truth or away from it.

He shrugged and turned on the tape player.

Mr. Ding, a middle-aged cadre from the National Health Department, wanted to talk to Serena, but she pawned him off on me, so I took him to the Minzu dining room. He told me the story of his nephew, a graduate of Beijing Medical School, who was driving a cab. If only he could get advanced training in the US. It was a pity to see such talent go to waste, didn't I agree?

He launched into a tale that took him to the end of a long lunch, and three or four rounds of expensive Maotai jiu (茅台酒, the highest quality Chinese "White Lightning"). Wanting to show me how much power he really had, this "Health Official" told me how he used his personal power that is based on who he knows, his guanxi, to get his nephew out of his low-paying work in the hospital operating room and into a glamorous, highly rewarding career of picking up foreigners at the airport. But now, however, his nephew was tired of driving a cab and wanted to get back into medicine and use that to go study in America. I acted impressed, and said I wanted to meet the young man, just to keep him talking. It sounded like a deal was in the works.

"I know of several teaching hospitals in the interior that will need X-ray equipment soon. They recently received a large grant from WHO," he told me.

I took down the name and number of the nephew and told him I would call him. He gave me the name of the purchasing agent for Hunan Health Department.

The name led to a half-million-dollar sale. Serena was happy with me, and stopped looking at me funny when I would come back from lunch only half sober.

The nephew led to something completely different.

Anyway, I did that and as I said, I also took care of the customer computer database.

"Computers?" asked Qi. "You work with computers?"

"Yes." I said. "Didn't I explain that? Do you know software?" (I used the Chinese word for software, 软体, ruanti, and Qi nodded.). "The brains of the computer?"

Qi translated for Lang, who looked up from reading the *People's Daily* and nodded, unimpressed.

As I said, I worked at Kone in the afternoon, after I was finished teaching for the day. I usually rode my bike down to the Minzu, but sometimes, such as if I was meeting important Chinese guests, I'd take the bus so I wouldn't be all sweaty. Otherwise I spent most of my time with a Chinese version of dBase III, which was where we kept our customer lists.

The office employed two other people besides Serena, a thirty-year-old Ivy League snot, and an overweight, overworked, and very unhappy product technician, who was never in the office because the medical equipment we sold often broke as soon as it was installed. The snot was Andy, a Brown graduate who was married to a trade specialist at the US embassy. His job, as far as I could tell, was keeping Serena up to date on rumors from the embassy.

Serena paid me in US dollars once a week. The dining room was always open and since I had my White Card (license to use Chinese currency as a foreigner), I would use People's money to entertain customers rather than foreign currency. My expense account also paid US dollars, so I was able to seriously augment my salary.

"Explain again, how did you add to your salary?" asked Qi.

"You know better than I do. Do you not want me to detail it? Is it a state secret?"

"You keep alluding to things you do that are illegal in China. There is a limit to what we can ignore."

"The two-currency policy is stupid for China, unless it is done so that party members can get rich. I am just taking advantage of what everyone else does and you know it. Dollars trade to Renminbi at about 7 to 1 on the black market. The official rate is 3 to 1. Normally foreigners were required to use the currency traded at the official rate. Because I was a teacher, and got my teacher's salary in People's money, the school gave me the White Card, which allowed me to spend Renminbi (人民币) anywhere in the country.

"So I change my dollars for Renminbi at the black market rate and use that money to live well. In essence I doubled my salary, plus got to keep the equivalent of whatever I spend as expenses." I smiled because if there was one thing that Beijing cops would understand it was currency manipulation. Nevertheless Qi started to explain it to Lang but he waved him off, so Qi restarted the tape player.

The job at Kone lasted through the fall until the Christmas party last December at the embassy. Andy, the Brown boy, was the source of that disaster. He was always asking about all the Commies I socialized with at the school or at the infamous Friendship Hotel. I invited him a couple of times to have a drink with me at the Friendship (Youyi, 友谊) and get an eyeful himself, but that was an unthinkable act, beyond the pale for the spouse of an embassy employee. The fact that I was on speaking terms with North Koreans, East Germans and Russians gave him a nervous flutter I think. He lived a sheltered life in Ol' Peking, shut up in the foreign legation, worried about the next Boxer Rebellion.

Since I invited him more than once to my world, some sort of Yankee code of retribution forced him to invite me to the American Embassy Christmas party. Serena would be there, and I think because of that, he was sure that I would decline the invitation. He obviously overestimated my intelligence, and clearly displayed his disappointment when I said sure, I'd go.

The invitation to the embassy Christmas party included Molly of course, but that night Molly came down with a flu bug. This didn't disappoint me, but it started the dominoes falling. Molly liked to play the hard-talking cowgirl when she was not flirting and while men generally find her charming and stimulating company, mostly because she is gorgeous, she tends to put off and piss off office-bound women who want to be measured by their brains and capacity for hard work, women like Serena.

So I thought, good, she is sick. At least we won't have a scene that would get me fired. That is what I was thinking at the time, but if she had come to the Christmas party, I probably wouldn't have been such a jerk myself or at least she would have been introduced to Dexter in his native habitat and seen what a jerk he is, which would have changed things, one way or another I think.

I rode my bike to the US embassy, five or six miles from the Institute. It was icy cold that December night. Riding my bike was another mistake because I immediately got into a hassle with the Chinese guards who stood outside the embassy. They were cold and cranky, and I think they thought I was one of those New Age vagabonds the Chinese had recently been throwing out of Tibet. I couldn't park my bike outside the gate and the Marines didn't want it inside the gate for security reasons. So I left it a couple of blocks away chained to a tree, out of sight.

When I finally got in (I had to show my blue passport at the door), I grabbed a drink, without even looking at the gross grease-fried crap on crackers. It was immediately clear that I didn't belong there, but I needed to get warm and eat something before riding back. My heavy, somewhat worn clothes made me look like a Russian peasant at the Czar's coronation.

I tried to mingle, another mistake. I stood on the outside of a group listening to the Ambassador, Winston Lord (who wrote the Shanghai Communiqué with Kissinger) explain why a technical loophole in the SALT treaty didn't matter. His wife Bette, a brassy little Chinese lady, had all of the ambitious women in tow and was otherwise really running this show. Serena placed herself in the front of the group following her around as they moved from wall painting to painting, acting totally enthralled with the Ambassador's wife's lecture on the inferiority of Ming landscapes to that of the Song. If Molly had been there I am certain she would have been standing in front of Serena, pissing off my boss.

I wasn't sure if it was the party or me that was boring. There was a lot of ass-kissing going on that didn't completely register with me, and I barely passed on delivering any sarcastic comments.

Andy came up, "See that guy," pointing to a medium height man wearing a leather vest over a tight buttoned-down powder blue shirt, jeans and cowboy boots, built like a very lean wrestler, nervously playing with his pocket watch. He completed the dickhead look with a mock turtleneck that rolled up out of his button-down shirt like a foreskin.

"I think you should meet him." I looked at Andy blankly. He lip-synced the word "spook" and then put his index finger to his lips. "But please, please don't say or act like you know that. OK?" I wasn't sure why Andy was telling me this, but I acted interested. "You want to meet him?" At that point I didn't have much choice because he and Andy smiled at each other like they had some kind of prearranged play worked out, probably because Andy had told the spook about my Commie terrorist friends over at the Youyi.

We sidled up to his conversation, which was about the Buddhist statues at Longmen Caves. I spent a year in Louyang and had been to the site several times and knew more than most people if only because it was part of my locale at the time. The dickhead spook in the dickey was younger than he looked, probably a couple of years older than me, in pretty good shape, solid, yet thin in the middle. He had dark hair, not particularly short, at least on the sides, with a Nixon-like baldness creeping up his forehead and wire-framed glasses pushed down his nose.

"Longmen shiku," (龙门石窟) I said. "A crazy place, built by some crazy monks. The China never got Buddhism quite right, did they?" I had no idea what I meant by that.

"What do you mean?" The spook's name was Dexter, and he gave me a smoldering look that said he didn't like his conversation being hijacked and that he didn't like me.

"First of all," I pompously lectured, "Chinese Buddhism ain't Indian Buddhism. Xi You Ji (西游记)– The Journey to the West and the Monkey King? Come on. The meditation and contemplation was a just a sideshow. The Chinese are too rational, too mischievous for Buddhism, don't you think?" Dexter shook his head with a mild look of contempt. "That stuff was just for old ladies being fashionable in the Chinese way, and aristocrats trying to avoid responsibility. The Qing, northern barbarians, couldn't handle the weight and moral clarity of Confucius or the profound absurdity of the Dao (道). The Commies don't like Buddhism and that is why they hate Tibet. I think the Qing used it as a counter weight to the ideas of the native Mandarins..."

He began to speak, but I interrupted him. "Anyway, most Americans think of Kwai Chang Caine as the ultimate Buddhist."

"Who?"

"You know, on the TV show *Kung Fu*. "I am – Caine." The Shaolin (少林). Buddhists or Zen or Chanzong (禅宗), whatever, all that is metaphysical like a motherfucker! Meditation! Concentration! That stuff is no more Chinese than Charlie Chan. It's like trying to understand America by reading Marvel Comics. Saturday morning cartoons don't define our culture, do they? Chinese aren't the way people in the West think they are. We all know that, don't we?" I stopped and looked around but everyone looked away from me. Fuck'em, I thought. "The Chinese are grounded in the five senses. See it, hear it, touch it, taste it, smell it, that's the way they are, as far as I can tell. They are not all that superstitious."

Dexter looked at me for a good five seconds before saying anything.

"Buddhism is a quiet way of life for millions, hundreds of millions of Chinese who probably never think about martial arts in relation to their religion. Buddhism has been in China as long as Christianity has been in Europe."

"I kind of liked that show though, didn't you?" I said. "Before I came over here my girlfriend and I used to sit up late watching *Kung Fu* reruns. It got her in the mood I think."

Dexter looked for a minute as though he was going to have the Marines throw me in the cellar. I stared back at him with a look that said, "Suck my dick, you dickey-wearing dick."

"The need to believe is universal." He paused like he was letting something heavy sink in. "And I don't believe that the East is predestined to authoritarianism ether."

He looked at me with a smug and superior stare. I took a deep breath and counted to one.

"China is like Europe would have been if Rome had never fallen. But Europe broke up, and had genocidal wars. China stayed united and yet it is more diverse than Europe. We have to homogenize our culture to be a 'democracy.' They did it differently, staying politically united but not mono-cultural. I think that the Mandate of Heaven has finally been repealed over here." Fuck it, I thought, I am going to end up defending Maoist socialism.

"Well, I don't know exactly what you are talking about," said Dexter. Which made two of us. "But Buddhists don't make good Communists; maybe that is why I like them." Dexter let that one hang in the air like a silent fart.

"So what is it that you believe?" Qi translated the gist of what I just said and Lang brightened up. "We are different, huh? We don't have a spirit? Can't meditate on the meaning of life?"

"So sorry big number one American – please help us understand who we are?" He said it in Chinese of course, so it had the flavor of a Mandarin flatterer rather than a guy who owns a laundry. Both he and Qi were laughing with an introspective sort of chuckle that was hard to read.

"What I meant was –".

"Please – it is all we Chinese talk about. How do we stay Chinese, when our culture is so feudal? Maybe it is not your problem," said Lang.

"You are right," I acknowledged.

Qi and Lang began to talk rapidly to each other and even though I couldn't understand them completely, the fact that I was listening made them nervous so they walked out of earshot. I suddenly realized that I had confirmed to agents of the Chinese government that an American official in the embassy was CIA.

"OK – continue," said Lang, sitting down across from me. "We don't care about American embassy business. Please – continue."

I wonder if the Americans could have bugged this place. For all their stupid fuckups, the CIA is good at that kind of shit.

I went outside on the back porch of the Embassy, even though it was pretty cold, just to get away from the Spook-in-the-dickey and Andy. I sat at a picnic table next to an older guy, some Down Under Commonwealth type about my age (New Zealander, I think), who was just lighting up a hashish pipe. He quickly let me know he was on his way home in a couple of days, tired of the "foreign service shit." He was going to get into the tour guide business. He was quite drunk too. "Working for an embassy is like being a concierge in a shabbily run hotel, except no tips, no rich divorcées on the run looking for fun, just boring clerical work. If I'm going to do that I might as well make more money and enjoy myself."

I really wasn't looking for trouble that night, but I can't claim complete innocence, because I did take one very shallow hit off the pipe, just to be polite, and nobody saw me inhale.

I was in the process of exhaling, however, when Serena walked by with Bette Lord, the ambassador's wife, who was explaining in Chinese about her visit to her family's old house in Shanghai. Serena was cool. She looked at me for only a second and wrinkled her nose. She led the ambassador's wife away from the table. But I knew she knew.

Serena canned me the following Monday. Fired. She was very businesslike about it, and didn't mention the reason outside of budget considerations – it was very Chinese, avoiding the embarrassing reality. She said I could finish the week and I thanked her, but I said I would just work the rest of that day and that would be it.

Things happened fast after that. I got a letter from my dad that week out of the blue – and he told me he saw a Chinese guy touting a product called "Quick Rabbit" Word Processing on Lou Dobbs' *Moneyline*. He knew my interest in computers and thought it might be a good opportunity, so he called the station, and got an address in Beijing. Dad worried about me being thirty-six years old and still not sure what I wanted to do when I grew up.

Address in hand, I took the "323" bus down to Gongzhufen, the main subway and bus station on the western edge of the city. At Gongzhufen(The Princesses' Burial Mound) I got on the subway and rode for two stops to the Military Museum on Fuxing Lu. The address my Dad sent me was across the street. I had to climb three flights of stairs, and then I rang the bell. A small middle-aged man in a Mao suit answered the door. He had a thin mustache and for some reason, I thought of the Wizard of Oz opening the city gate in his guard uniform.

In Chinese. "Hello, my name is Nathan Schuett. I am an American and I would like to talk to your company about KuaiTu (快兔, Quick Rabbit)."

"KuaiTu. Ah! Come in, come in, you are here to see Tai Xiansheng." I didn't say no, and he ushered me into the building. After passing a dark, unpainted vestibule that looked like a toxic waste dump with old unlabeled canisters of paint or tar and a torn tarp lying on the floor, we entered a well-lit office with about ten occupied desks. On the desks were white monitors of Apollo workstations, all manned by intent Chinese men in their late twenties. On the left side, the glass-walled offices were occupied on one side by a young woman filing her nails and on the other by a middle-aged Asian man in a perfectly tailored blue suit and red tie. To the back was a large window, which opened to a porch overlooking Fuxing Lu and the Military Museum across the street.

The doorkeeper of Oz said, "My name is Ling Ye. As you can see our joint venture is working very hard on the products. Please come this way." I was confused by his attitude, which seemed to expect me.

"Oh Oz – *The Wizard of Oz* is an old American movie – not important. It had a character who wore what looked like a Mao suit."

I followed Ling across the room to the far office where the guy in the blue suit with red tie (and matching handkerchief!) was reading some documents.

In English. "Tai Xiansheng, here is the man you are expecting. Mr. Nathan?" The well-dressed Tai and I looked at one another.

"Hello." His English was accented but very clear. "I'm sorry…"

I smiled and stuck out my hand. "I didn't have an appointment so I don't think you were expecting me."

"No." He shook my hand. He switched to Shanghai-accented Chinese. "Ling, why do you say I was expecting him?"

"You said that a foreigner would sell our software!"

"No, I said that foreigners would buy our software!" At this point they got into a heated argument about the meaning of the Chinese verb "mai." In standard Mandarin, in one tone "mai"(买) means "to buy"; another tone "mai" means "to sell" (卖). People from south China have trouble with those tones.

Ling, who from his accent was obviously a native Beijinger, felt he was on solid ground since the standard National Language was based on Beijing's pronunciation. Their voices rose several decibels and soon Tai seemed to concede by politely changing the subject with a smile and then asking Ling to allow him to speak with me in private. Ling left us in the room, laughing as he closed the door behind him.

Qi stopped the tape and explained to Lang. They both started laughing – doing a popular Xiangsheng （相声） routine that I had seen on TV and recognized. Lang played the taciturn northerner (imagine Bob Newhart) who was trying to figure out what Qi, the moonshine-fueled southerner (Robin Williams), was saying. The three of us laughed for quite a while. Lang stopped me and shushed both of us. He got up, went out and came back with three cups filled with some kind of White Lightning, which was just what I needed. He said the brand, but I didn't recognize it. I gulped mine and held out the glass. Lang went to refill it and Qi restarted the recorder.

Tai sat for a minute, then in English said. "Stupid fuck. He doesn't listen and he jumps to conclusions." He looked at me with a helpless, "What am I supposed to do with these people?" kind of look.

"My father saw a show about your company on TV in America. I know about Chinese software on PCs and I was wondering if I could help you market it."

"Was it *Moneyline* with Lou Dobbs? That was me!" Tai's eyes opened up like Peter Lorre's. "I was on that show! What did your father think?"

"Well, I think he bought some of the stock," I lied.

"Really?" Tai looked out at the office, thinking. Ling was standing among the newly returned from lunch technicians, whispering and occasionally glancing over at us. The technicians were smiling, maybe even laughing.

"So how would you market our software?" Tai walked over and closed the door to his office.

"What's the price point?"

"We're thinking $700. We need to recoup $500. But that is too high – Chinese just copy software. But they can't copy KuaiTu – it requires hardware, a PC board."

"Let me market it to foreigners here in Beijing at first. Get it popular. It will get us a position from which to move into the Chinese market."

I just made up a marketing strategy on the spot and we ended up liking each other. That's how I got my job. I don't think Tai expected me to make much money, but he hinted that he wanted me there to be his spy. I mean a business spy – not Taiwan against China spy. He didn't have to pay me; the deal was straight commission, which was fine with me.

Chapter Seven

Qi translated and Lang laughed. "Spy for Taiwan now too?" Lang produced his little bottle of baijiu (白酒, white lightning) again and refreshed our glasses.

"So you just started selling software? How did you do it," asked Qi. He did not believe I could walk into a business and on the basis of just one conversation get a position making the money I did. We took a lunch break. The station was in Haidian, which is almost like a little suburban mall, with a few shops and other businesses that seemed to congregate around a busy bus stop. Qi and I both like cold shaanxi noodles (陕西凉皮), and we found a stand that was making them. I had tea rather than beer because I would surely fall asleep otherwise. The baijiu I had earlier was still driving my brain.

"I told you information that might get me in trouble," I said. He looked puzzled, so I foolishly reminded him. "What I said about the intelligence officer at the embassy."

"No – nothing will happen to you. You've broken no American laws." I wasn't sure that was true.

"Still – even if you are right – it wouldn't be a good if my country's officials found out..."

"This is a murder investigation. You're not a spy. You aren't even really a suspect. But you know something. You might not even know that you do. That is our problem I think."

Qi and I stared at each other for about five seconds. "There is one thing I need to get straight though," I said. "If I tell you things I know about the Chinese people I know and you learn things about them that you don't like, that they violated the special rules Chinese people are supposed to follow when dealing with foreigners. If what you learn has nothing to do with this case, will you punish them? Tell their bosses? Tell the Party? So that it ruins them?"

"No," said Qi. He seemed to understand what I was driving at and appeared sympathetic. "We will keep it all secret – and pass nothing on. It will be easy for us to keep it secret."

"Why should I believe you?"

He pulled a picture out of his wallet. It was a picture of himself and a blonde – she looked to be about ten to fifteen years older than he and they were standing in front of Beihai Park. She was smiling and he didn't look unhappy for a change.

"She is coming to Beijing again maybe next month. Maybe sooner. After this case perhaps I am going to resign from the force and leave China with her."

I looked at him trying to understand why he had just told me that. "So I can just talk to you?" I asked.

"You have to trust both Lang and me. If your Chinese friends are not involved with the murder of the Hungarian and West German, we will leave them alone. I don't care about other crimes – unless they can help me catch the killer. You know Kojak? – who loves you baby? That's me. I love you baby."

Kojak was very big in Hong Kong, but I had never seen it on mainland TV. I suddenly had a picture of Qi sitting around with his middle-aged American girlfriend watching HK porn to get in the mood. Maybe that was his plan, to say tell me the dirty stuff because I'm dirty too. Qi smiled as I just stared at him.

"That's the way homicide cops are in America, right?" I kept staring. "I am trusting you. You have to trust me. Are you finished eating?" I nodded and we returned to the station's upstairs room. Lang was waiting impatiently and he and Qi seemed a little testy with each other. Qi wanted to know more about my software sales job.

After Tai hired me and gave me the portable Compaq computer, Tai returned to Vancouver, Canada. I was on my own.

I built a database for the customers from information I got from western embassies. I would introduce myself and my product, the Chinese computer word processor KuaiTu. Then I would ask for a list of the businesses from their country. I gathered over 700 leads.

I wrote different letters that profiled people, based on prejudices and stereotypes that I found generally to be true. I would include glossy brochures that Tai sent me.

> *Dear (White Woman's name),*
>
> *Working in China requires special skills. Fluency in Chinese combined with your specialized business knowledge is often not enough. You need a tool that will allow you to quickly and professionally produce documents that look sharp and yet allow you to "personalize" your message.*
>
> *I would like to introduce you to KuaiTu, the next generation in artificially intelligent computer software. KuaiTu allows you to write, manage and print Chinese documents on your PC. The system learns your vocabulary as you write. KuaiTu allows you to compose impromptu as easily as writing in (Language). This product combines the scholarly requirements of the foreign expert with the hard tools you need to drive your business...*

The white guy lost in the sea of Asian Inscrutability needed a different approach.

> *Mr. (lastname),*
>
> *Communicating in the challenging business environment of Beijing can be frustrating. How can you quickly produce documents that look professional and convey your business message in Mandarin? Now you can with software developed by a Canadian-Chinese joint venture.*

*KuaiTu (Quick Rabbit) is a word processor that will allow
your staff to easily translate your company's documents into
a form that matches what is expected in the PRC. It is
inexpensive and can be installed on any standard PC...*

I had other custom letters for Chinese-Westerners,
talking up their native expertise and focusing on the speed
and technical advances that *KuaiTu* presented. A couple of
weeks after I mailed them, the inquiries started coming back.
I started to get more orders than I could handle. Install, collect,
install, collect – keep the inventory coming in – suddenly I was
making a lot of money.

"So you make money. How much?" asked Lang. I was finally
crashing from the baijiu （白酒） and I wanted to get up and take a
walk. "I made about $5,000 since I started selling last summer." Lang
and Qi conversed in Chinese, but I easily understood them since they
were calculating how much that was in Chinese Renminbi (people's
money). It was about ¥35,000 using current black market rates or about
¥15,000 if you took it to the bank. A lot more than their yearly salary.

"Don't you have a smaller tape player?" I asked, interrupting them.

"Yes, I have one," said Lang. He pulled out the small Sanyo (that
I think he borrowed from his wife) out of his jacket pocket.

"Can we get out of here and walk somewhere? Maybe walk over
to the Beida (Beijing University) campus and walk around. I need some
exercise or I am going to fall asleep."

Lang looked at Qi for agreement. I was coming up to something
that I didn't want anyone else hearing.

"Perhaps only you two will need to be the only Chinese cops who
listen to what I am going to tell you here?" They gave me the deniable
nods that didn't seem to disagree to my "terms." I plunged ahead,
feeling that I had to take a chance.

A year ago, I spent a week in Xian. It was late August;
Molly was in Hong Kong, and I was by myself with nothing

to do but roam around and look at the sights. I spent the last three days lurking about at a farmer's market called Xiao Zhai (小寨) on the south side of town.

I spent much of the time sitting in front of a blind erhu player. He knew I was there and I could tell he was annoyed with me. He would stop playing after a while and move somewhere else, and I was sure he sensed me in some way. Adding money to his empty instrument case only seemed to make his agitation worse. The second day he came late and played at a different place. He seemed to smell me and I felt like a creepy hippie worshiping some phony mystic from afar.

The erhu player and his melodies were the background music for the delicious and exotic food carts and the vendors whose booths surrounded the wildly active farmer's market. The "Weiwuer" Turks were running the most successful booths in the market. Their faces looked so Western that it seemed I had discovered the descendants of shipwrecked Europeans.

I met a Muslim named Kor'bin who ran a shish-kabob grill. Kor'bin looked like the American comedian Bill Murray and sold me shish-kabobs and a special tobacco-like product that he called "hash." He wouldn't take my money no matter how much I ate or smoked. We quickly became friends and spoke a kind of Chinese all our own. We made up our own idioms to match our common way of thinking, idioms that made sense to us because of our ancestors' common experience on the western end of the Silk Road I suppose.

We went back to the alley where he lived, which looked like the inside of a railroad freight car. One hundred kilogram bags of cumin were stacked six feet high in his room, literally tons of raw cumin, a brown spice that looks like caraway seeds before it is ground, and is the main ingredient for spicing lamb on shish-kabob. The fragrance was enough to get you high all by itself. Cumin was a spice, but has been used as a stimulant for thousands of years. I smoked the special plant-herb, the hash, with Kor'bin and his friends and relatives. They told me about plans to fight the Chinese like the Mujaheddin were doing in Afghanistan. Could I get "Stingers," one of them asked? I could have tons of hash for Stingers. The Americans gave Stingers to their brothers in Afghanistan, so why not help fight the Communist Chinese in Xinjiang? I smoked and smiled. Did they think I was crazy? I was pretty loaded that night and I passed out on the 100-kg bags of cumin and had lively dreams.

Chapter Eight

Qi turned off the tape player.

"Leave him alone," I said. "It wasn't him that asked me and besides, it was just drunken talk."

"I thought you said hash? You mentioned that before, but it was in the American Embassy, but now you plan to use that as currency to buy weapons? Isn't that a drug that the Weiwuers use?" said Lang. "We execute drug traffickers."

"It's not a drug," I said. "It is like strong tobacco. It is not opium."

"So you have ties to the CIA and you are talking about selling Stingers to Xinjiang traitors," said Qi. "What are Stingers?"

"It has nothing to do with the murder case," I said. "You said I could trust you."

"They are missiles, aren't they? If this ends up with American missiles being used against the Chinese in China then..."

"No missiles, it was just stupid talk," I said. Lang gave me a very hard look. Qi restarted the portable recorder.

The next morning when the blind erhu player arrived at Xiao Zhai, I broke away from my breakfast of tea and lamb, and barbecued pork on unleavened bread, and cold noodles with vinegar and cheap white liquor, and I found a spot to sit and listen. He dressed like a monk, except for his pork pie hat and fifty-cent-piece–sized dark round sunglasses. He alternated from very sad to madcap delight, matching the mood of the piece he played. I couldn't pull myself away.

Molding my body to the ground, sitting cross-legged and upright, I was put in a trance by the music, something so different from my past reveries that I was almost able to shed my so-called objective view of life. There really is a Dao (道), and it flowed through me and around me and was all mine, as long as I didn't try to own it or grab it or understand it. The erhu music rode on the currents of the Dao, pulling me into the way of old China, a China that was disappearing, right before my eyes. Unlike any hippie experience I ever had, this actually seemed real and genuine.

The next day he was gone and the next day as well. It was as if he was waiting for me to leave so he could play again, so I left and boarded a train back to Beijing.

"I am trying to explain to you something I am afraid you won't understand," I said to Lang. "You want me to explain myself - to tell you why - to tell you how I lived here in Beijing. If you understand me, then maybe you will see that I had nothing to do with killing Sandor and Erika. I was more involved with the affairs of Chinese people than I was involved with foreigners. But I am scared to tell you that because I don't know if you will hurt them or not."

Lang waved his hand and smiled, and I continued.

When I worked for Kone, I met a guy from the national health department who helped us land a pretty big contract. I think I told you that already. On the basis of huxiang bangzhu (互相帮助, mutual self-help) - quid pro quo - I met with his nephew, the cab-driving stomach surgeon who wanted to get advanced training on the medical equipment we were selling. Serena, my boss at Kone, told me to meet with him once, see if he was OK, find out if it would work out for him and for Kone, and she would arrange the visa and the trip, etc. A simple assignment it seemed. For a contract this big, expense money could be found.

Mr. Ding and I agreed to meet at the Quanjude (全聚德) Beijing Duck restaurant in the Qianmen (前门) district. I walked in and looked around for Ding, but didn't see him. About half the people in the place were Western foreigners, and there were a lot of them. I avoided their looks and was thinking about how I would have to reach for the check and "struggle" with Ding, who would pretend to fight for it. Fighting Chinese for checks at restaurants could be a nasty scene and I didn't want to end up on the floor, wrestling Mr. Ding, something I had seen play out many times.

I waited about ten minutes and still didn't see him and was about to go outside and when a young woman wearing clear, half-frame glasses like those worn by Jiang Qing,(Mao's wife) approached.

"Are you Mr. Na-tee Sihut?"

Close enough. "Yes," I said.

"I am very happy to meet you. I am Zhang Xi. My friend Quan Lileng is not here yet. Please come and sit down."

She had a deep throaty voice that did not match her body. She was about five feet tall, but was kind of chesty for a Chinese woman and was wearing loose-fitting clothes that made her look boxy. I didn't see her as beautiful until later.

"Quan is very excited to meet you."

I looked at my watch and made a serious face. "Really?" She looked concerned for just a second and then laughed, with a giggle that came from deep down. Her eyes lit up too, not squinting like some Chinese do when they laugh, but wide open, looking right at me. I looked back.

"Maybe I'm more excited to meet you than he is?" she said and laughed again.

"Maybe I'm excited to meet you too." We both laughed, and retreated to slightly embarrassed silence.

135

"Oh look, here he comes." Quan was stocky and bushy haired and looked more "Chinese" than Zhang did. He had a round face, but his eyes were not as round as hers. Zhang and Quan immediately started bickering about why he was late.

"Wawa hun"(娃娃婚) means baby marriage. Zhang and Quan's families had known each other for a long time, maybe hundreds of years, but they had known each other since they could crawl around together on their family's living room floors.

Quan liked driving a cab, but made it very clear that it was only temporary. He spoke very good English, better than Zhang's. He wanted to go the US and study X-ray and ultra-sound diagnostics. He had plans to be a "rich doctor". He knew that demand for modern medical care in China would eventually explode and expressed an obvious contempt for socialism, (and a subtle disdain for Party officials who worked for his father). And as I later explained to Serena, it sounded like a great opportunity for Kone to get a smart, well-connected young man trained on their equipment and not just a throw-away to get a lucrative contract.

But looking at Zhang as Quan talked about getting rich made me realize that his dream didn't really excite her.

Still, the three of us were enjoying ourselves and were into the first course when Quan's uncle, Mr. Ding, showed up with two Party hacks.

Mr. Ding introduced his two friends as officials from the Hunan Health Ministry, the ministry that was about to sign a contract with Kone. We ordered more food and drinks, with Maotai jiu (茅台酒) all around. I was actually beginning to like the stuff.

"When are you two getting married?" asked one of Ding's flunkies.

"Not until Quan gets back from the States," she said quickly.

"So what do you do, Zhang?" I asked.

"I'm a musician."

"Oh really..."

"She plays the old feudal stuff," said Ding, apologizing for her. "But it is important for China to maintain its traditions."

"We have too many erhu players already," said one of the other hacks. "Zhang should have become a doctor like Quan."

Zhang's face seemed to remain placid, but I saw the stirrings.

"I love the erhu," I said. "I heard an old man play it in the street in Xian last spring..."

"Oh...was he blind?"

"Yes."

"Maybe I know who he is!" Her eyes brightened. "There is a very famous street player from Xian. His name is Gang Xunzhu." Zhang looked at Quan for a second. "Ah Bing was his teacher. He was the most famous erhu player in China."

"Before Liberation, you mean." said Quan. The table became quiet for a moment.

"His music was very beautiful to me. But I know nothing about Chinese music," I said trying to break the silence. "Have you ever heard him play?" I asked.

"No," she said almost reluctantly. "I have never heard him myself."

"I know him!" said one of Ding's party hacks. "He drank something bad. Poisoned liquor, that made him blind."

"Like Ah Bing, his teacher," said the other Hack. He looked at me with a degree of suspicion and contempt. He was about my age, which meant he had probably been a Red Guard.

Ding looked very annoyed with the conversation.

"Tell me what he played," she asked me, ignoring Ding.

"I don't know." I decided to play it up a bit. "When he played, it sounded like a proud man whose soul was laughing and crying at the same time."

"Yes," she said, looking at me in way I had never been looked at in my life, a look that hit me pretty hard. The world seemed to stop. "I have to listen to him before he dies." Neither of us could look away from each other.

"I would like to hear you sometime," I said. Quan looked at me blankly and she looked away.

"No," she said, not looking at me. "You will be disappointed, especially if you have heard Gang play." Zhang looked at me again quickly, then not again for a long time.

As we were leaving (I paid in foreign currency, because I didn't want them to know that I was as corrupt as they were), I told Ding that the trip was all arranged and that Quan should leave in a month. I said to Quan that he should practice his English.

At that Ding said, maybe I could give Quan some lessons before he goes. I wasn't too happy about that, although I liked Quan well enough. I cursed myself for opening my mouth. I said maybe and left it at that. I tried to put Zhang out of my mind, and nearly succeeded until about a week later when I got a call at the Kone office from Ding saying that it would be good if I met Quan at the Beijing Hotel for a little lesson later that week. The contract wasn't completed yet, so I said yes. Serena said she would pay me for the time anyway.

I arrived at the Beijing Hotel lobby and sat on one of the large black heavy vinyl couches. It was not a crowded lobby, and everyone there seemed to be staring at me until I turned and looked at them. Twenty minutes after the appointed time, I was just about to leave, when Zhang walked over looking lonely and radiant, even as she fought some internal struggle not to draw attention to herself. The Beijing Hotel is just down the street of Heavenly Peace – Chang'An Jie(长安街) from Tiananmen. I was sure every person in the lobby was working for Chinese internal security.

We shook hands and Zhang sat down beside me, a chaste distance apart. She told me that Quan couldn't make it, that he had to drive somebody to Tianjin that day and would not be back until late. So Zhang and I sat in the lobby and talked and talked and the world stopped. Her English was not as good as my Chinese, but, oddly and out of character for me, I enjoyed giving her an English lesson.

Quan left the next month and I didn't see him again. But I kept meeting Zhang, about once or twice a month at various places from then (it was November) until last June, even after I left Kone because of that disastrous Christmas party at the American Embassy. Nothing more than mutual language lessons, I think we told ourselves. I didn't tell Molly about it, although nothing was really going on. Then in June, after months of begging by me, she finally agreed to play the erhu for me. We met in Tiantan (天坛), the Temple of Heaven, the most important of Beijing's Imperial Parks. It has some old pine trees away from the Temple center and we sat under them on a low wooden bench. She brought out her erhu and in the fading daylight she played "Autumn Moon of the Han Palace." Some people stopped to listen, but at a distance, and they left us alone.

When she finished she said, "You must go home now." She was fighting back tears.

"You played beautifully," I said, staring into her eyes.

"No. You don't understand...I play so badly. The more I practice the worse it sounds." When she saw her distress concerned me, she quickly composed herself.

We walked up Qianmen Street toward the subway station so I could get back to the Language Institute. "I received a letter from Quan. He is staying in Los Angeles for the rest of the summer." I hadn't asked about him and when she told me that, I was happy, and slightly ashamed for feeling that way. As we walked, she said she knew a place where we could stop. The sign said it was a publishing work unit. I stayed outside while she went in. After a minute a young woman came out and motioned me in. She said something in English, but I didn't listen to what she said. She took me up the backstairs and told me "Number seven" and left. I opened number seven, and Zhang stood just inside the door, looking up at me with her glasses off. She fell into my arms and we kissed. There was a cot toward the back. I put my hands under her bottom and picked her up. She wrapped her legs around me and I carried her to the cot.

That was in June and I didn't see her anymore that month or during July.

Then in August, after Molly left for the US, I met Zhang at her recital. After the recital and after we had made love on the sofa, in her fiancé's house, we walked together back to Tiananmen, in front of the People's Museum of Revolutionary History. I touched her hand and she smiled. We both understood that was about the limit to the public affection we could display, but it was OK, because we were still in an afterglow from earlier. A little breeze blew the late afternoon away, making way for dusk. We walked past the Monument of the People's Heroes in the middle of Tiananmen and then past Mao's Tomb. A couple of people were flying kites, and a squad of Young Pioneers in their red Boy Scout–like scarves was testing the limits of their chaperon's patience, running out of the formation that marched toward us.

As a young girl, Zhang Xi had scrubbed the marble floor of the mausoleum before they moved in Mao's body. She told me how she and the other young girls had been told it was a sacred honor to be on their hands and knees with tiny brushes cleaning the stones. I joked that in ancient times they might have buried her and the other young virgins with the Emperor. She laughed with a trace of dark irony. Her eyes narrowed and her lips pursed, as she stared at Mao's mausoleum, but she quickly smiled when she sensed me looking at her.

We turned back along the west side of the square and walked next to the steps of the Great Hall of the People. I kept my eyes on the lion on the left side of the main Tiananmen Gate, just under Mao's picture. Someone had told me that Li Zicheng (李自成), the rebel leader who overthrew the Ming and ruled as Emperor for six weeks, broke his spear against that lion in 1644 when he heard that the Manchus had broken through the Great Wall.

I get awed standing on historic masonry where great things happened. Tiananmen is such a place, and I was in love, walking with my Beijing girl, trying to suck it all in and make sense of it. At the height of the Cultural Revolution, some rallies would have a million people jammed in here at the same time, chanting in unison, "Mao zhuxi wansui! (毛主席万岁!, Long live Chairman Mao!)" After World War I, 3,000 students came here to protest the terms of the Versailles Treaty, which gave Germany's territory in Shandong Province to Japan. That protest, in a single day, created the generation that fought for Mao, and finally threw out the foreigners.

And now I was back, longing to crawl into bed with one of China's princesses.

When the shadow of Communism fades like some long-forgotten dispute among Confucian scholars, everyone will still remember that China had finally stood up after 200 years of decline. They will remember that Mao and those leftist students who stood on Tiananmen in 1918 had led that effort.

Each Tiananmen stone, about a meter long and half a meter wide, seems to have its own story, shabby, earthy, different yet the same; the slight imperfections in the individual stones make it seem real, and each stone makes a statement amidst the acres of stones that are almost just like itself if you don't look too closely. Each stone is different yet fits in invisibly, like Chinese themselves. When the Chinese overthrow Communism, the movement will probably start here, in Tiananmen. Like I said, I get weak in the knees standing on historic bricks.

I looked around and noticed an old Chinese man watching Zhang and me. He didn't look happy. I looked around for others who might be watching us, and well, I knew, without being paranoid, that they were everywhere but then again, maybe nowhere.

Zhang Xi didn't want to walk back to Quan's house via Nan Chang Jie, which runs like a walled-in alley between Zhongnanhai and the Forbidden City. "It's too close," she said. But I insisted ("It's the shortest way…"), and she shrugged.

As we walked, we talked about her concert. She told me she missed several notes. I told her I didn't hear any missed notes. "Just before I went on stage I heard someone say, 'There is a foreigner in the audience!' I had hoped you would come, but just before I went out, I forgot that I invited you. I was wondering 'Who is the foreigner?'" She looked up at me and I touched her hand again and it sent shivers through me. "I am so happy right now," she said.

"I am happy too."

A couple of hours ago we laid exhausted and naked, staring at each other, lying too close to see each other, but we just kept staring, afraid to break the spell, until she did, by saying, "I have to feed the pigeons." We went up on the roof. Her fiancé's parents' house was taller than any of the other houses in the neighborhood, other than the Drum Tower, which practically adjoined the courtyard. We looked down on all the roofs in the neighborhood. To the west, the houses around us were silhouetted against the blue sky and the afternoon sun. We sat on the roof, in silence watching the birds eat. The smell of Beijing was sweet perfume and I still couldn't take my eyes off of her.

Now, we walked up the narrow street that runs north-south along the western edge of the Forbidden City.

*The street is called Nan Chang Jie and Bei Chang **Jie** (南长街 和北 长街) – two ends of the same street, (Long South Street, Long North Street). It divides the Forbidden City and Zhongnanhai and, in a way, is the "no man's land" between old China and new China. Like all no man's lands, it is shunned and avoided. "Too close," like she said.*

Zhongnanhai was a huge private park for the Emperor, a playground, a place to keep the favorite concubines. Now it is China's Kremlin, as well as the Presidential Residence – Mao lived here, and now Zhao Ziyang lives there.

Zhang told me that Deng Xiaoping doesn't live in Zhongnanhai anymore. Too many bad memories for him, she said. I looked at Zhang and I could see that she had some bad memories too. She took a deep breath as we started walking down the street. Her slight fear excited me, and I was exultant under the illusion that I could protect her in her own city.

Several hours before, I watched her take the same deep breath as she walked on the stage for her erhu solo. The recital at the Beijing Music Conservatory was an informal afternoon affair that didn't draw many people from outside the students and faculty, certainly no other foreigners. I didn't recognize her at first, because her hair was up in a bun, she had on a long-sleeved, collarless white blouse and dark pants and was not wearing glasses. She stood alone on the stage, seeming tall next to her erhu. She was so beautiful, the rhythm of my breathing changed as I looked at her. She sat down and didn't start right away, but rubbed her eye, like she was getting sleep dust out of the corner, as if she were all alone and just waking up. She took a deep breath. The small hall was almost full and completely silent. Then she started to play.

The music evoked soulful melancholy, pushing me outside my normal consciousness, away from self-awareness, into a reverie of emotion and longing. It was like the trance I entered when I heard the old man in Xian play. I began to think it was the erhu.

I first heard echoes of the Gypsy violin, but it was much more than that, because Gypsy violin music is a bit corrupted by the Western instrument, while this was as pure as new snow on a fallow field. I just floated out of the concert hall into a dream that beckoned me like a shrouded mist-filled fantasy.

I was in a Chinese kitchen, and she was cutting celery and I was playing with a baby girl swaddled up, with a stalk of black hair on her forehead, and big round eyes. I was tickling her, goo-gooing her, making her laugh. An old lady came in and shooed me out of the kitchen, and I went out to the front stoop where two ten-year-old boys were playing with crickets, arguing about which one jumped higher. An old man smoked a long pipe, quietly, very content. I sat next to him and we watched the boys taunt the crickets. It was dusk. We sat outside without saying a word, completely comfortable with each other, taking in the soul of the neighborhood, the hutong. The neighbors were walking by, waving; kids were shouting and happy. Zhang Xi brought the baby out and squatted down next to me. I was invisible except to Zhang and the baby; the hutong was alive with cooking smell and gossip. There was pent-up rage too, controlled, wiped from the face, even from the eyes, you couldn't see it in the eyes, rage that could only be let out at certain times, or situations.

It was New Year's celebration, suddenly cold out and fireworks sounded and bottle rockets traced across the roofs. The little girl cried at the explosions.

Serene hopelessness and tight quarters produce strict rules and nobody breaks the rules or even calls attention to them. Discontent is not allowed, especially discontent based in individualism; the appearance of unfairness must be smothered even if it is not "gong ping," not a level playing field, not equal opportunity for everyone. You cannot break out. It is the most important rule. You bear it. You mildly complain and listen to the other mild complaints, but it is repetitive and useless, just empty noise to no end.

Still, living has exquisite rewards. Merge with the community, join the renao (热闹), the "hot noise," the controlled chaos of group enthusiasm, the loud laughter, the excitement, which wells up in everyone who joins in. Listen to the old people tell the same story again and again, laugh at the same parts even more than before; it gets better each time. Then politely withdraw, try and find a little place, a corner to read, to write, or just sit…night comes quickly, and desire comes, taking possession of you and her, the curtain walls flap closely, only a wall of fabric around the bed protects you. The teenagers are still up, and even if the children are in bed, they aren't asleep either. Quiet, quietly – and quickly too. There is just no space. Oh, for selfish time together, alone time, even only one night alone, a party, people, music, loud noise, more *renao*, the door closes, together in a solitary fortress then sleep...but morning also comes too soon, the humiliation and pain of being the last to wake...the curtain is jostled as the rest of the house begins the day...turn toward her, but she's up already. Is that her chopping garlic in the kitchen...?

She was standing on the stage, acknowledging the applause, which was not thunderous, polite really. I almost forgot to clap myself, but then I jumped in too loud, and then I stopped so as not to call attention myself and her. She left the stage and I walked back into the hall away from the stage door. After perhaps ten minutes, although it seemed longer (even though it went fast), she came out. She was dressed in a black pullover now and her hair was down, her glasses on. She looked small again. She saw me and smiled.

"You came to see me."

"You didn't know I was here? Couldn't see me? I was the one who wasn't Chinese."

She laughed that laugh, which came deep from her chest. "I couldn't see." She pulled her glasses down and crossed her eyes. "Don't like to know people are watching me. I don't wear my glasses when I play."

Walking back to Quan's house from Tiananmen, up Nan Chang Jie, we were almost to the old gate that connected the Emperor's palace to his playground. The true center of power in China, the Emperor's entrance to Zhongnanhai, the villa on the middle-most southern lake, where his favorite concubines lived in splendid isolation. The gate was sealed now though.

Zhang looked straight ahead and the twilight had changed the sky from blue to golden. It was starting to get dark and the man riding toward us on the bicycle was not clearly visible until he was pretty close. He was not Chinese and I looked at Zhang and she was relieved. With two foreigners she was safe. As we got closer, I saw it was a very old Chinese bike and an older man wearing sneakers and one of those sporty hats that bookies wear to racetracks in old movies. He came to a stop in front of us and I looked at him in silence, not sure what I was seeing.

"I seem to be a bit lost..." he said with a slight smile. It was the actor, Peter O'Toole. "Seem to be a bit turned around. I'm supposed to meet someone at the Peace Hotel in fifteen minutes and I haven't the foggiest idea where it is."

"Well," I said, composing myself, smiling and thinking, "The easiest way is to keep going and take a left at the next street. That is the Chang'An Jie..."

"Yes of course, the Street of Eternal Peace."

"Yes. Then ride past Mao's picture, past the History Museum, and up past the Beijing Hotel, maybe three-quarters of a mile maybe less..."

"I see."

"Take a left after you pass the Beijing Hotel, on Wangfujing..."

"Yes. Yes of course, where all the shops are, what? Something about a well, isn't it?"

"Yes, they say it used to hold very sweet water, centuries ago. About a half a mile up, you'll see a hospital on the left and there is a little alley on the right..."

"Yes, yes, yes, actually now I know it well, I just got turned around here. Thank you so much. You're a Yank, aren't you? Just visiting?"

"No, I live here."

"Really?" He looked at Zhang closely for the first time and smiled. "Well I'm making a movie. I hope a good one, but you never can tell. An Italian is running the show so who knows? Well, thanks again. Cheers." He shook my hand.

"Mr. O'Toole this is Zhang Xi. Mr. O'Toole is a famous actor." I looked over at Peter and said, "Zhang is a musician." I felt ridiculous, introducing them.

"How do you do, Zhang is it?" He shook her hand. He acted as if we were old friends, so I didn't even bother introducing myself. Instead, I decided to make a complete fool of myself, in case there had been any doubt. "I'm told, when the light strikes my face in a certain way, I am really quite handsome," I said quoting his best line in the movie *What's New Pussycat?* "I've tried to use that line myself, but it never worked for me."

"Oh." He looked at me as if he had just been served a weak drink, but then his eyes lit up, maybe at the memory of youth, who knows? That shy confidence of his is so cool. He smiled and nodded. "Well, nice to meet you both. Thank you for the directions." He paused, looking at me, then Zhang, slightly smiling as if embarrassed. "I hope you find your pussycat," he said as he rode off.

"The fucking fucker's fucked," Zhang said as he rode away. She had a concentrated look as if she were drawing something up from deep in her memory. "Long time no see, easy come easy go, no tickee no shirtee. You teach me English is very simple. I don't think it is simple at all. Why does he think you are looking for a cat?" In Chinese she asked, "Is pussycat a little cat or does it mean something else?"

"Yes. It can mean something else. It can mean something soft and furry," I said. She smiled and nodded. "Your English is much better," I said.

"Why is it better?" She was asking like an earnest student, trying not to laugh.

"Because we are exchanging ideas and little by little we are both improving our understanding of one another so that our two countries can strive forward in solidarity and friendship."

She gave me a look of resolute determination and then stuck out her tongue. "In Chinese poetry the image of a man and a woman together, like we were, is to make the clouds and rain. So when you say 'It is raining cats and dogs' - is that what we like to do? If so are you a dog?"

I barked at her. There was no one around and I kissed her. "I want you again," I said in Chinese. She pushed me gently away. We walked in silence for a while, moving past the point where Nan Chang Jie becomes Bei Chang Jie, crossing an unseen latitude.

Then she got serious and told me that she was leaving soon. The unspoken question was "What am I going to do?" If I love her, then everything else should be secondary, right? In literature, movies and poems, love conquers all. Is that really true I wondered?

"Can you leave Quan? Can you marry me?"

She looked at me with disappointment. She didn't ask me, Can I leave Molly? Instead she said, "No." She took the weight all on herself. Or else was she testing me? She didn't avoid my eyes. I was the one who looked away.

"Will you marry me? Will you come to America with me?" I felt desperate and cornered. Zhang continued to look at me, as if she were trying to figure out what was wrong with me, why I couldn't understand.

"I will be your lover, Nate. Always," she said. I felt a bullet enter my heart. "If I marry Quan or someone else, I will always leave room for you. Always. But when a Chinese woman marries a foreigner, she has to turn her back on…". She took a deep, seemingly final breath, as if she were about to die. I was transfixed. "I am Chinese. I want to be Chinese. I will never be able to…" She stopped and grabbed my hand and held it. Even though we had left the deserted Bei Chang Jie and were now in the crowded section around Jingshan park (景山), she held my hand and swung it boldly, leaning against me, flouting the great taboo of the Middle Kingdom. Older Chinese men in Mao suits scrutinized us. She wasn't scared at all, but was completely, fearlessly, thumbing her nose at her own society. "Anyway, it was all your idea what I plan to do. Remember?"

She had been planning to go to Xian to work and teach at the music college. She said she was going to find Gang, the blind erhu player I had told her about, and help him. When she gets back, then we can decide. She gave me hope, maybe only so as not to spoil the evening. I wasn't sure.

I walked her back to Quan's home. She was house sitting while Quan's parents were at Beidaihe(北戴河), the Hamptons for Chinese political elite, where Deng Xiaoping spent his days playing bridge with his old comrades, while grandchildren built sandcastles against the breaking waves. So Zhang had the place to herself. We went into the kitchen. She gave me a Qingdao beer, rare because Chinese are supposed to pay with foreign currency for Qingdao. We sat on the couch.

"Come (来, lai)," she said in Chinese – we went into a sitting room, and soon, again, we were making love just like we were two hours ago, passionately and unrestrained. It was perfect except that it wouldn't last forever.

We lay together exhausted. "We can't do that anymore," she said after a bit. "At least not in his house, at least not...I would lose everything if they knew about us and you would be deported."

I wanted to argue with her, but I didn't. I had to decide what to do and then do it, and then I could argue with her. I didn't even know if Molly was coming back or not. And what was worse I didn't know what I wanted. I could phone her from a hotel and say, "Don't come back."

We went out for dinner – walking down East Drum Tower Road to a little café. They knew her, so we could not sit too close to each other or act as though we were having a love affair. We pretended to have an English lesson. Everyone in the café was listening to us, but they were old and very traditionally dressed and hopefully couldn't understand English.

"Please explain 'The fucking fucker's fucked,'" she asked. Our old joke again. "I understand the grammar – article, gerund, adjective noun and verb. But in this sentence, one word is performing every part of speech in a sentence."

"Yes," I said. "It's a good sentence too."

"Why is it good?" She was asking like an earnest student, trying not to laugh.

"Name something you don't like."

She smiled and looked around. "I don't like this pencil. It writes too dark."

"Not hard enough," I asked.

"Not hard enough."

"Too soft?"

"Too soft!" She giggled. We both loudly said in unison, "The fucking fucker's fucked!" The old people looked on nodding and smiling.

After taking her back to Quan's house, I decided to walk back to the Institute. I ambled along the Street of Earthly Peace (named for the North Gate to the Inner City) and then turned north toward "The Direct Road to the Western Gate" (Xizhimen), which ran in front of the Zoo (I always got lost around here) and then…I saw him.

He rode by me, I could have reached out and pushed him, my own ghost, my Doppelganger. It was Rennie, riding his bike out of a hutong, out of Zhou's hutong!

He didn't see me. I wondered if he wasn't really me living the life that I was afraid to lead. Maybe I was just his shadow or maybe he was mine.

Part 2

Chapter Nine

Iang let me off at the PLO Mission apartment. He said that they would do some "follow-up and other investigation," and they would probably not need me for a few days. Naturally, he said with some embarrassment, I wasn't to leave Beijing. I walked into the stale-smelling flat and found a letter that had been slipped under the door. I decided that as soon as I got settled a little, I would clean the place top to bottom, starting with the refrigerator.

I took off my shoes and stretched out on the couch and read the letter.

I was sleeping when I heard the soft tapping on the door. It was Ibrahim.

"What time is it?"

"About 10 PM. I won't stay long," he said, smiling, as I came awake. "I just wondered how the interrogation went. Look what I brought!" He held up a bottle of French brandy. "Let me get some ice." He opened the refrigerator, made a face and closed it. He pulled a couple of glasses from the cupboard, and shrugged. "You should fill your ice trays."

"I don't know. I think I talked too much." I was angry at Ibrahim, and it was about more than him waking me up.

"Did you stick with our plan?" He sat at the end of the couch, just slowly enough for me to get my feet out of the way. He asked me the ritual Chinese question had I eaten (你吃了吗?) and I nodded, even though I hadn't.

"I told them about my business with the joint venture and about meeting that American missionary who never paid me for the software."

"Oh."

"And about Zhang."

"Oh. The erhu player?" I nodded – Ibrahim struggled not to laugh. "You never introduced me to her. So you told the Public Safety about...here, I think you can use a drink."

I took it, finished it and held out the glass for a refill. "Yeah – the personal stuff. How much I loved her and how she left me to go take care of the old street musician in Xian."

"It's OK. She is well connected. They wouldn't..."

"You don't know they won't!" I was beginning to feel really mad. "This telling them everything was a mistake. If the wrong people find out they can make anyone's life miserable."

I was worried that I had given them a real fulcrum on me. Talk or we will destroy the girl. "I am sure they think I know more than I've told them."

Ibrahim, still smiling, looked at the ceiling and shook his head.

"Look at this." I handed Ibrahim the letter, written in very clear simplified Chinese characters.

> *Dear Nate,*
>
> *I have thought about you these last months. I wish we would have had more time in Xian. There is so much we haven't said. But maybe that is best.*
>
> *Gang and I gave several successful concerts in the west and the south. We have played in Lanzhou, Chongqing, Changsha and Fuzhou. We played for more than 2,000 people in a park in Chongqing with no propaganda in advance. Gang is becoming famous again. He talks about you and teases me. He says I treated you poorly. Is he right?*
>
> *Quan is returning home on October 18 Sunday. He wrote me and said that he wants to see you very much. He believes that he owes all of his good fortune to you. He remembers that it was you who told me that Gang was in*

Xian, playing on the street. So we both owe our current situations and good fortunes to you.

Gang and I have been working on a new piece. It is a duet. I have been afraid to play with him, but slowly we have been making it sound well. He says that we will perform it first only for you.

If you will see me when I get back, I will meet you at Beihai Park. Let's set a date – Friday Oct 23 at 1 pm. It will be very crowded; people often eat lunch there. No one will suspect our situation. I will look for a tall American with red hair. I will be the short Chinese woman. (You are laughing now I hope!)

I'll contact you then.

Zhang

"That is five days from today. I have to see her," I said.

"That might not be wise," said Ibrahim.

"Why are we protecting him?" I asked. "Why am I lying and saying I didn't see him? Where is he?"

"He is innocent, I think, of this particular crime anyway." Ibrahim stopped smiling, and took a long drink and refilled his glass. He offered me a refill as well. "Besides, you have not told me all that you know."

"What?" I looked at Ibrahim. "Do you think that I know what these murders are all about?"

"Of course you do. You just aren't saying the truth to me."

I said nothing. Ibrahim laughed and slid over next to me and got right in my face.

"Look," he said. "You are in hell, right?" He started poking me on the shoulder alternating with his two index fingers. "You have to help them figure out who killed the German and the Hungarian if you want to get out of hell. At least you have to satisfy them that they know all there is to know. You have to confess. Chinese justice is based on confession. It always has been."

"I know," I said.

"It wasn't him. It wasn't me or you or your girlfriends..."

I gave him a cold look.

"You had to say something, you had to confess something. If you lied or didn't talk, it could have gotten very bad. You have no idea how persuasive the Chinese police can be. So far, you haven't said anything, except that you have a highly connected Chinese girlfriend. It is good you tell them this – they will not be so persuasive if they know you have important Chinese friends. And you are innocent! But the most important fact is that it is not to their advantage for you to be guilty. A guilty foreigner would be most inconvenient, especially if that foreigner is an American, even one who lives in the PLO Embassy."

Mission, I thought, it's not an embassy it's just a mission. Palestine is not even a real country, how could it have an embassy? "What am I supposed to...?"

"You know!"

"The stele!" I spit it out. I finished my brandy and held out my glass. It annoyed me that Ibrahim was guarding the bottle, instead of just putting it on the table in front of us.

"The stele." Ibrahim smiled. "Tell me when you first heard of the stele. Then we can decide what to tell the police."

Thurs Aug 20

My throat was sore that morning. I had been smoking too much, bumming cigarettes, and even opening the packs I saved to bribe the "receptionists" who guard the office doors at foreign businesses. I went in early to work, still half in the bag from the night before, but I wanted to get my messages and hopefully get a lead that I could work on. I hadn't made a sale in a week.

About 10 AM, Pan yelled to me that I had a call. The phone system looked as if it could transfer calls, but of course it didn't work, so I went into Pan's office and sat on the edge of her desk while I talked.

"Hello, Nathan." It was Preston. "Can you come by this afternoon?"

"Well, yes, if you think it will help us get closer to getting this deal done." I tried not to sound irritated.

"Absolutely. We can conclude our business. I have something that I think you will definitely be interested in."

***

A picture of blue-eyed Jesus hung on the wall. A well-dressed, smiling, late-thirtyish Caucasian woman was talking to Preston. The papers and documents that had covered the chairs and tables were gone and a plastic dustcover hid the Packard Bell computer. Two older white men, along with Paul and Hanna, and three older Chinese men, all of whom looked a bit frightened, were sitting or standing uncomfortably watching me with a paranoia I could feel radiating from their suspicious expressions and nervous gestures.

Preston brought me into the center of the group and introduced me around. I quickly forgot the names of everyone but Nancy Drinkwell. She smiled like a former beauty queen, very vivaciously, yet innocent-seeming and wholesome. I nodded to Paul and Hanna, who barely looked at me. Preston's wife pointedly looked away when I said hello.

A Midwestern American man (by his accent) with bad teeth, who had worn his cheap suit too long, stole creepy glances at me. He was talking to another white guy in a bad suit who looked like an autistic accountant.

Apparently they had been waiting for me.

I felt the eyes on me, and knew I would have to answer questions and socialize for a little while, if I wanted to get my money.

"Welcome, everyone," said the Midwesterner with the bad teeth. He was a pasty, bug-faced man who filled out his suit coat like a wire hanger and smiled nervously. "I don't know

how much Preston has told you about our program but..."
Paul and Hanna and two other young Chinese men stood
in the middle of the room talking to one another, which was
disturbing the speaker.

"...without further ado, I'd like to introduce Mrs. Drinkwell
as I think she has something astounding to tell us."

I noticed the woman flinch a little and give the most subtle
and slight single shake of the head. She looked at Preston and
his chin barely went up and down in assent. Then they both
caught me looking at them. It all seemed subliminal because
Preston then invited me over very warmly, and herded me
to his people. The bug-faced midwesterner looked at the four
Chinese people who were ignoring him with fear and anger.

"It is so nice to be here," Mrs. Drinkwell said. "It has
been a whirlwind believe me. Last week Hong Kong, Hanso
(Hangzhou), Chin Do (Chengdu), this week Sigh Ann (Xian)
and Low Ann (Louyang) and today – is it Tuesday? Thursday!
Then this must be Peking! Either that or I've been Shanghaied!"
This got a knowing chuckle out of the Westerners and complete
bafflement from the Chinese. She turned to the man who
introduced her and shook her finger at him with a mock scowl,
getting right up next to him. "And it is <u>Miss</u> Drinkwell!" He
seemed to shrivel up like a cockroach on a grill.

She then gave a bland, innocuous talk about faith,
teamwork, discipline and doing the little jobs well to make
the big jobs work. Was this a corporate pep talk for Preston's
conglomerate team? I still didn't quite get what was going on.

"The ancient Chinese always worshiped one God, Shantee
(Shangdi 上帝)." I felt the room begin to shift as she talked
not just to me anymore but to everybody else. She gave me a
slightly hard look. "We are in a battle for the soul of China,
don't ever forget that. The Devil is fighting for his life here in
China."

"Amen!" said Preston.

"China's psyche is rooted in the belief in one God," she continued. "The worship of the one true God! The characters – the alphabet that the Chinese use – they are from Genesis. Did you know that? Am I right, Paul?"

Everyone turned to look at Paul, who was trying to finish eating a cheese-whipped Ritz and talk at the same time. "The character for boat is 'chuan.'" He finished chewing his cracker then drew the character in the air with his finger, something Chinese people with different regional accents do to make themselves understood. But Miss Drinkwell winced as if she thought it a Popish gesture. "The character 'chuan' (船) is made up of three components," Paul continued. "a vessel(舟), the number 8 (八) and mouth (口). It means there were eight mouths to feed on a boat. There were eight people on Noah's Ark. And 'gui' (鬼) means the devil. The character for 'gui' is a picture of a man (人) in a garden (田) with a secret (厶)."

There are hundreds of books that analyze the characters for hidden meaning and many have religious messages. The Taiping controlled most of Southern China for ten years in the 1850s and spent most of their intellectual energy trying to explain how their leader was the flesh and blood straight-from-Mary's-loins brother of Jesus.

"Yes!" Nancy exclaimed. She looked at me and I gave her my "astounded and amazed" look back. "The great dictator was called Chin She Wang (Qin Shihuang 秦始皇)– he was the first Emperor. You know that God is called Shanti (Shang di - 上帝), in other words God is emperor who is above. Chin was the greatest Chinese leader, and people say he was like Hitler. There was full employment on the Great Wall, enforced unified culture, unlimited cruelty and head-in-the-sand religions like Buddhism and Taoism that allowed people to hide from the greater glory of God!"

She gave "God" a Baptist crescendo and everyone but me started clapping.

I didn't mention that Buddhism did not arrive in China until about three hundred years after Qin's reign.

"…but of course Moe (Mao?,毛) was the worst of them. Nestor's church was in Sign Ann way back in the Middle Ages, and the Catholic Jesuits were in Peking when the Mongols controlled China. Sun Yatsen, who overthrew the Emperors, was of course, a Christian – he had lived in Hawaii and was taught by Missionaries…they all brought a particular idea of Christ to China. It was never the correct idea because it always tried to mix Chinese idolatry and superstition with Christianity and that is nothing but blasphemy! Of course Mrs. Chiang Kai-Shek (蔣介石的太太) is a true Protestant Christian but unfortunately the Communists never gave her a chance to truly change China."

I was still thinking about my commission on the software Preston had purchased, but not paid for yet.

"Moe and his Satan-inspired Communists fought Christ in China." She looked at Hanna. "But we think that the time has come to witness to China again using all of the financial and technological power available. Don't we, Preston?"

Preston smiled knowingly at Miss Drinkwell and waited half a beat. "Yes we do, Miss Drinkwell." He put his hands up in the air and closed his eyes.

"Dear Father in Heaven!" He paused and looked around until Hanna and Paul had raised their hands like he and Nancy did. "Lord give us the strength to stand unscathed among your enemies! Give us the courage and the wisdom to go forward and seek out those that will hear your word – here in the land of Devil-inspired Buddha and godless Confucius are the new Catacombs from which we must emerge into the light of your righteousness! We must tread carefully but be fearless. We must follow your word in all things…"

I stood with my head tilted down, wondering what the fuck was I doing? Still, I wanted to think for a change before I started pissing people off.

The prayer over with, I talked a bit to Miss Drinkwell; in fact I think she was flirting with me. As we chatted, I was trying to not pee on their parade, because I was there to collect what Preston owed me – at least $700. He had also promised to purchase five times that amount and I was prepared to deliver it! But here, among these people, I felt like there was no graceful way to demand it. I was beginning to feel like the whole deal depended on me joining their ridiculous Crusade to convert China. All I wanted was my money.

It was about 5 PM. I excused myself, saying that I had an important client to meet for dinner. Miss Drinkwell flirtatiously insisted that I come back after dinner. Preston didn't look happy as he escorted me out of the apartment.

Chapter Ten

I don't know what that has to do with the stele," said Ibrahim. "I don't see how any of this can help you with the police."

"No, I don't see any reason to tell them about this, but you asked me about when I heard about it..."

"And you tell me about a bunch of..."

"OK, OK, I am getting to it," I said. I reached over him and grabbed the bottle and poured my own drink. After I set it on the table, he picked up the bottle and put it back on the floor next to him.

It was about 8 PM. I had been sitting at the Youyi bar for the last three hours, so I was a little loopy, figuring I would wait until his guests left and then return to Preston's place and collect. I knocked on the door and his ghostly wife, without a word, let me in.

Preston's guests, except for Nancy, Hanna and Paul, were gone. The room had been put back to the way it was, and even the grandmother smell seemed to be back in its original condition except that blue-eyed Jesus was still staring down from the wall.

"...and Lord, give us guidance as you gave guidance to those who had carried your word forth from the Catacombs to those who would persecute them. Give us strength and courage in the face of our enemies."

"Amen."

Catacombs again – made me think of Satyricon. Or was that catamites? Like I said, I was a little loopy. All I really wanted was my money. Preston had ordered five copies of the KuaiTu software. I wanted my MONEY!

Miss Drinkwell invited me to sit down. Preston avoided my eyes. "Nathan – Preston tells me you are a very capable young man."

"That's nice. I am just trying to make a living."

She put her hand on my wrist and smiled as brightly as she possibly could. "Don't you think that China would be better if it accepted Christ?"

I looked at her unable to answer.

"I can tell just by looking at your eyes," she said.

My eyes moved involuntarily to her breasts.

"You do believe in Jesus, don't you?"

"Yes," I said. "But not in the way that I think you do."

She smiled again, giving me the treatment. I wondered what kind of fuck she would be. I had a feeling it wouldn't be that hard to find out.

"Nathan, we have something to tell you, but we are not sure that you are ready to hear it."

"I think you are right. Perhaps I am not ready…"

"Nathan," Miss Drinkwell stopped me just in time. "You are ready." To fuck you I thought. I saw Preston's wife look out from the kitchen. That old crone knew what I was thinking even if Miss Goody Juice didn't. "We have something to show you that is so fantastic that I am not sure how to tell you. But you might be the bridge we are looking for, Nathan. You are the one who can play a role in China so great that…"

"I am the person that…" I said. I stood up. All I wanted was my $3500. Or at least the $700 FOR WHAT WAS ALREADY DELIVERED! I really didn't want to be impolite, but…

"Are you a Christian?" she asked.

"I don't think that Jesus…the Gospels represent different points of view of the same story." Uh-oh, I thought, I was half drunk and trying to get theological. "I think the story might be true as far as it goes. As for the empty tomb…something happened…I believe that something really amazing might have happened. Christianity is a strange religion. It makes the enormity of the infinite as a source of belief in a higher power more approachable than Eastern religions, without being completely anthropomorphic, if you catch my drift. The gods of Olympus are a cartoon for a reasonable person. But the worship of a malcontent who turned the tables upside down in the Temple and who was executed by the state in a hideously degrading manner, in some ways it is a pretty absurd concept for a religion. But I think that is the reason it is appealing, because in a weird way, that part rings true." But when it got into missionaries and crusades and Creeds and heaven and hell, forget it. I didn't say that though.

She frowned. "You are familiar with the Old Testament as well?"

I shrugged.

Nancy looked at Preston. He got up and went into his bedroom. Nancy continued to give me the "God's love" smile. Preston brought out a large piece of thin yellow paper, about the size of a newspaper front page. It was a stele rubbing. It was only a fragment actually, about six inches high and twelve inches wide. It wasn't completely legible.

"It is fascinating the way the Chinese use the slate stele," said Nancy. "It is like a perpetual printing press. You put the paper over a stone carving and rub the front with a pencil or ink and the carving appears on the front reversed. This was from a stele that was found. Where was it from, Hanna?"

Hanna looked slightly uncomfortable and said very softly, "It is from Shaanxi province."

"Where," I asked.

"The place is near Xianyang on the Wei River."

"Just west of Xian," I said as I looked at the rubbing. "The old Qin capital."

"Yes."

"I've been told," Nancy said, "that traditionally the people from that place are descended from one of the twelve tribes, the Menashe. Isn't that right, Paul?"

"Yes – I have heard that," he said. That sounded like bullshit to me, but I let it pass.

Hanna said, "It is dated between 200 and 300 BC. It is very old for a stele, older than any ever found before. But even at that it is likely a copy of something that is much older. I have training in Chinese archeology, and there are several technical reasons for this."

Classical Chinese is very difficult to understand. You can know the modern meaning of every single character in a sentence and have absolutely no idea what the sentence means.

"Here is the translation." Nancy handed me a typed page centered in the very middle.

OUT OF THE LAND OF THE SNAKES AND WATER HE SENT HIS BROTHER TO FIND HIS FATHER AND BRING HIM AND ALL OF HIS FAMILY INTO THE LAND OF PLENTY. FOR THE KING FOUND FAVOR WITH HIM.

WHEN THE BROTHER RETURNED HE AND HIS FAMILY DWELLED IN THE LAND BY THE RIVER AND TENDED FLOCKS, AND PROSPERED AND MULTIPLIED.

Two lines? That's it? Nancy took the translation back from me and handed it to Preston, who handled it like a sacred scroll. He put it between two pieces of heavy parchment and slipped it into her briefcase.

"I don't know if there are any other copies. A communist academic, who was later infused with the Holy Spirit, made this rubbing. According to our information..." here Nancy quickly glanced at Preston's wife and when I looked over as well, Preston's ghost wife suddenly went as stone-still as a Terra Cotta Soldier standing guard at Qin's tomb, "...this professor disappeared many years ago. This is only a small part of the writing on the stele. I think this stele was one of a series of steles that contained the complete book of Genesis. I am taking this rubbing back to be studied. This is why I came to China on this tour." She looked at me with serious eyes.

"So you see, Nathan," said Preston, "we're here for more than business."

"You believe that this is part of the story of Joseph bringing his family to Egypt?" I asked.

"Of course it is," said Preston. "What else could it be?"

Nancy continued. "The Great Emperor Chin burned all of the books. A few survived – some poetry and some of the works of Confucius and his followers. But something very fundamental was destroyed. The Chin, the ancestors of the modern Chinese people, are one of the lost Tribes of Israel. That was something that Chin She Wang wanted forgotten."

"Don't you see, Nathan?" said Preston, almost grabbing me. "That means that they will be saved from the horrors of the Final Days. The Chinese need not die and be condemned to hell. Because God has a special plan for the Jews!"

I stared at them both, and they were watching me very closely. I tried to remain impassive and not laugh. "So," I asked, "are you still going to build the computer chip factory?"

Preston gave me a disappointed look that said I had missed the whole point. After half a beat he said, "Of course, that and the other projects are the cornerstone of all this. It all works together."

"But most importantly, we need to find that original stele, Nathan. It could be the proof that the Chinese are descended from one of the missing twelve tribes. And if so then Jews will suddenly become the largest nation on earth."

Chapter Eleven

"Iwouldn't mind that," said Ibrahim. "Just so as long as they don't all want to move to the West Bank."

I smiled weakly.

Ibrahim looked at me smiling, shaking his head.

"I need to think about things a bit," I said. "I can't tell the cops this."

"OK," he said with a relaxed, easy-come, easy-go lilt, "we can talk about it tomorrow."

"Is he still alive?"

"Oh yes. Very much alive." Ibrahim picked up the bottle and poured a sip into his glass and drank it.

"Did he...he was carrying something when..."

Ibrahim lit up with a very bright and deliberately enigmatic smile. "We'll talk about it tomorrow." Ibrahim got up, laughing to himself.

"Why are you laughing?"

"You didn't even ask him for the money he owed you, did you?"

I gave Ibrahim the finger.

"I'm going to bed. You have another long day ahead of you. You better get some sleep." Suddenly I wanted to talk, but he didn't give me the chance, he just got up and started to walk out. Then he stopped.

"Here," he offered me the bottle. There was still about a quarter of it left. I was pissed off at Ibrahim, but what could I do? I grabbed the Courvoisier and he walked out.

I fell asleep watching a Chinese TV show. It was about life in Japanese-occupied Beijing. The collaborator, a stock character on mainland TV soap operas, wore a long Chinese scholar's gown and he carried a broom-handled Mauser that he used to pound on the door of the patriotic Chinese hero. The collaborator was constantly, but so far unsuccessfully, trying to seduce the hero's sister. The collaborator used the butt end of the big pistol to pound on the door.

I don't know how long the pounding had been going on when I realized it was at my door and that I wasn't in Beijing in the 1940s. It was 1987 and I was staying at the one of the apartments meant for guests of the Palestine Liberation Organization. I was still fuzzy minded as I pulled on my pants and answered the door.

It was Lang, although I could barely make him out. It was still pretty early.

"Quickly. Get dressed." There was no friendliness in his eyes this morning.

We didn't speak at all on the trip around the north ring road toward Haidian. I was still half asleep and a little hung over from the rest of Ibrahim's cognac.

He drove us to the Foreign Language Institute instead of the police station. We drove in silence and after passing through the Institute's gate we slowly made our way to the back. As we puttered past my old apartment, I saw Mr. Liu walk out of the entrance we used to share, on his way to teach his 8 AM class. I waved and he looked at me, but there was no recognition of me in his eyes. I was suddenly afraid. We pulled up to Erika's apartment building and Lang reached back into the backseat and grabbed an eight-inch thick pile of newspapers bound up with cord.

We walked into the apartment building and down the dark stinky hallway. The door was half open and a young man in a *Gong An* uniform was watching TV and sitting on the couch where I had found Sandor and Erika. He jumped up and Lang berated him for sitting on the sofa. I could still smell the faint odor of human shit in the air and wondered if the guard had turned the cushions over. Lang put the newspapers down on the couch and picked up a walkie-talkie.

"Use this when I tell you," said Lang, pointing at the pile of newspapers. Then he turned to leave as quickly as he entered, motioning me with him.

We went up the stairs one floor and Lang knocked on an apartment two doors down from the one above Erika's. An old Chinese man answered and Lang introduced himself and ignored me. The old man looked at me and suddenly straightened up and kept shifting his eyes from me to Lang.

"The afternoon that the foreigners were killed, were you at home?"

"Yes." The old man straightened up visibly as he answered.

"All day?"

"Yes. I heard them around noon laughing and they were out on the porch talking and cooking. It smelled very bad." He realized I understood him and suddenly was embarrassed that he referred to Western cooking as foul smelling. Standing in the hallway outside his apartment was nearly gagging me.

"You were home all day? Did you go out at all?"

"My daughter and her husband were gone, but I was at home. I was working on my cage. See?" A black, multi-tiered, recently lacquered, bird cage perched precariously on a newspaper-covered table. The bars on the cage had the diameters of tooth picks, yet were perfectly tooled and seamlessly fitted into the whole structure. He smiled at me, as I comprehended the magnificence of his construction, but then stopped smiling as he looked at Lang.

Lang held the walkie-talkie up and said, "Su Ma! Ready? Hurry up! Ready? Fire!" He paused. "Shoot into the newspapers, you fool!"

We heard a loud retort that sounded like a gunshot.

"Did you hear anything like that the day the foreigners were killed?"

"No!" The old man snapped to attention as he answered.

Lang looked at the old man for fifteen seconds or so as if he was trying to decide whether to believe him or not. Neither one of them moved. "Thank you. Sorry to bother you."

We walked back to the car. "Do you understand what that means? Someone used a silencer. Did you see a silencer?"

"It was a strange-looking gun." I said. "Was it the same gun..."

"It was 7.65 semi-automatic, standard issue, People's Liberation Army. That is what Su Ma fired just now – a 7.65 semi-automatic. The actual gun is evidence."

"Do you have a time of death yet?" I asked.

He didn't answer. I tried to remember the gun, it wasn't exactly like a Luger...or like Su Ma's gun...

We got back into the car, and Lang sped out of the Foreign Language Institute's campus, barely slowing down as we went through the gate. I went over in my mind what I remembered from when I found the bodies, trying to figure out what I was missing.

"Was the gun I found the one used to kill both of them? Did you find the bullets that killed them? Do those bullets match that gun?"

He kept his eyes on the road. "There was another gun. The one you found must have been planted."

"Did Sandor fire the gun? Did you find any other bullets in the room?"

Lang stared at me for a second then turned away. "Today what you learned – that is police business. Do you understand? You are not to tell anybody, regardless of anything else. If you tell anyone, we will lock you up for five years for revealing state secrets, even if you are not found to have committed the murders themselves! Do you understand?"

I nodded.

We drove into the front gate of the Friendship Hotel and like cops everywhere, Lang double-parked and told the valet to go fuck himself as he flashed his badge. He ran up the steps and I followed, not too fast but not too slow either.

We climbed to the roof. A cop was guarding the door. Lang and I walked in. Qi had everyone there. They had put three long tables together in a horseshoe shape that everyone was seated around like a séance. It was cold, and everyone had on jackets and sweaters, except me. Qi was sitting backwards, straddling a chair in the middle of the horseshoe, holding a pen and a thick notebook covered with a scrawl of Chinese characters.

The first thing I thought was of Hercule Poirot gathering the suspects in the drawing room. I wished I had worn a heavier coat. Gregor – how did Qi wake Gregor up this early? Yevgeny, pretending to sleep, Boris was reading the paper, the East German Party Hag, Rennie, Zhou, (but no Chen), Monique the French girl who never speaks to me, and MOLLY! She was sitting next to Dexter, wearing a white fur hat like Doctor Zhivago's wife. Which was new, because she hadn't had a hat like that when she lived with me. Harold and Mikku were sitting off to the side. No one seemed surprised to see me.

Qi started out explaining that it was important that they explore the facts of the case. "This is a Chinese affair but it has complications. It is important that the foreign community understand we are doing our best to find out what happened and why."

"And quickly," said Lang in Chinese.

"Yes," agreed Qi. "There is pressure to close this case. As some of you know, the foreign press has reported on this affair and the case has the attention of the highest levels of the Chinese government."

I squeezed in next to Harold and then Lang pulled a chair next to Qi's and set it facing me, a couple of feet away.

I leaned over and whispered to Harold, "How'd you get here?" He pointed at the six or seven cops in the back, sitting around the bar, eating baozis (包子, steamed buns with meat inside), ignoring our mass interrogation.

"Personal escort."

I was still thinking about what had just happened over at Erika's apartment building, and was barely following what Qi said. Molly quickly glanced at me and then grabbed Dexter's hand and moved it to her lap. He was wearing round glasses, and an ugly Christmas muffler around his neck, like some stupid British schoolboy, and had let his sideburns grow to muttonchops. Good, I thought, she is stuck with a douche bag. Maybe there is a God. I'll have to tell Preston the good news next time I see him.

Harold asked if they were sure it wasn't murder – were they absolutely sure it was double suicide? I thought at first I heard him wrong, and almost started to correct his misunderstanding. Are they sure it WAS murder he must have meant.

Then Qi said that at this time they had no reason to suspect any involvement by a third party, that it was either a weird double suicide or murder suicide. I looked at Lang and he shifted his eyes ominously toward me, and with just a simmering look, he warned me not to speak, then looked away.

Molly asked, "Wouldn't somebody have heard the shots?" Dexter leaned toward her, squeezing her hand.

"We have witnesses who heard the shots," said Qi. "Unfortunately they did not report it immediately. We are investigating why they failed to notify anyone."

Lang stood behind Qi and didn't move a hair. Somehow, for obvious reasons, I didn't scream bullshit. Why were they doing this? I was being used for something, but I wasn't sure what yet.

"So," said Qi, "this is just a chance to review what we know – so we can explain why the Hungarian killed the German and then killed himself. Since you were all at her apartment that afternoon I wanted to bring you all together to see if we can work it out together."

"What are you talking about?" I said. "What do you mean 'all at her apartment'?"

I looked at Mikku. She looked ashamed and seemed about to commit harakiri (腹切り).

"She had a 'going away lunch' that day," said Harold.

"I didn't tell you because – Molly was there and I didn't want..." Mikku looked almost tearful.

"What?" I looked around. No one would look me in the eye.

174

"So what happened?"

Molly shook her head in sad disgust. "Nothing happened! Dexter and I were planning to take that evening's flight to Hong Kong. And you stopped us at the airport! Why?" she said to Qi with disdain. "Can we still make that flight tonight?" she said in a slightly lower voice to Dexter.

"What time did you get to the German woman's apartment?" asked Qi, ignoring her question.

"About noon."

"We walked in together," said Monique.

"Yes," said Molly. "Most everyone had already arrived. Erika was distressed, but I don't know why. Dressed nicely, but then she always was."

"I gave her my mother's address," said Rennie, as if it were an important clue. "My mother often stays in Zürich and I thought when she got back to Germany, it would be nice if we got together. Zhou and I are going back to the US in December and are going to be married. So I wanted..."

Qi nodded and tried unsuccessfully to avoid a disdainful look.

"We had planned to leave tonight or..." Molly shook her head in disgust. "It looks like now, not until tomorrow." Molly shook her head and looked at Dexter in distress.

"I see. Yes, so perhaps you can help us out..."

"We fixed chicken and rice," said Monique.

"Yes," said Molly. "No drinking for a change and that was nice. People talked quietly, exchanging addresses, like Rennie said."

"What did you talk about with her?"

"Wedding plans and where we were going to live. Things like that. Then Sandor arrived with the Chinese guy who lived above – in Xilou. Nate's friend." She looked at me for the first time. "Erika greeted them but didn't seem happy to see either of them. It seemed to make her nervous."

"Why? Why did Sandor and Bing make her nervous?" asked Lang in Chinese, after consulting with Qi about the meaning of nervous.

Silence. I looked around. Monique was quietly talking to the Party Hag, Gregor was eating and Yevgeny was still pretending to sleep. Boris was reading *China Daily*. It was like a Communist Party meeting at the work unit; nobody was paying attention.

Lang looked at Qi and shook his head. "Perhaps you can describe when you first discovered that she was romantically involved with the Hungarian," said Lang.

"She wasn't involved with him. Are you saying that Erika and Sandor...?" Molly gave them a look of condescending incredulousness. "No." She started laughing and looked at me. "Did you tell them that?" Both Qi and Lang lost their blank officious stare, looked at each other, then at me, then quickly away.

"I never said that," I said.

"But I thought..." Lang looked at me very hard. I almost smirked back, but kept my expression blank.

"She was involved with Zev," said Molly. "Now what happened later – what happened later that day when they – when they died – I don't know – maybe then – but –"

"Please explain. What happened when you came back?" said Qi.

"Back in September," I said helpfully, feeling pleasure of ever so slightly twisting the blade. "You had just gotten back – remember?" I smiled because I know she did remember, even if her expression stayed frozen as I talked. "The night you met Dexter. I didn't want to go that night; I wanted to stay home." Molly looked at me and would have continued to, if Dexter hadn't leaned over and bussed her cheek, like a pussy-whipped dickhead.

Qi said, very gently "Miss Barton, perhaps explain this for us? When was this..."

"It was the day before school started – it was a Sunday I think... Yeah – I'll explain it." She glared at me.

"That would be September 7," said Qi.

The night we went over to Erika's, to meet Zev, you did say, "I don't want to go." I do remember that. You wore a tee-shirt and shorts and I put on a blue dress and tried to look nice.

It didn't bother me that you looked like a – like you were trying to insult me by dressing like a bum so I could be your whore.

Erika answered the door, giddy. We hugged and the first person I saw was Sandor. I thought it was strange that he was there too. I was sure that he wasn't her new boyfriend – that she had been coy about it, to surprise us. It made a little sense from what she told us before, about her new boyfriend being of the Jewish persuasion, but Sandor? He acted sheepish and I tried to smile and make him feel – Oh I don't know what I thought. But it didn't make sense to me.

But then I heard another voice coming from the patio. "Snags on the Barbie!" In from the balcony came a big, hairy guy with an Australian voice, in a Polynesian shirt, holding a large greasy sausage on a skewer. The first thing I noticed was that Nate and the Australian recognized each other, and then they both tried to pretend that they didn't.

The Aussie guy pushed the sausage toward Erika and she ate it right off the skewer, while standing in the kitchen, devouring it while dripping grease down her chin, barely avoiding dripping it on her pretty green smock. I'll never forget that as long as I live. Erika was so particular. She complained if the waiters put the knife and fork on the wrong side of the plate when we ate in a restaurant. Then Zev looked up and down at me and said – "Let me get you one, love."

"Oh, I think I will wait," I didn't let him fluster me like he was trying to do. "It looks good though." Erika took another bite while her mouth was still full. I was flabbergasted!

"So," Erika trying to talk and chew at the same time, "You know Sandor of course…"

"Yeah – Sandor…hey…" I said. Another round of over-friendly shaking of the hands…he looked at me with an expression between bewilderment and pitifulness.

"And this…" here Erika snaked up next to him, chewing and swallowing the grisly sausage, putting her head in the crux of his arm and chest, "…is Zev."

"Zev. Well Bob's your uncle, Zev!" Nate said. What did you mean by that? Zev broke up laughing. "Son of a bitch! Have we met before? I could swear…"

I was sure that Nate and Zev had met before and I asked Zev about it.

"Bob's your uncle! It's just an expression, love," said Zev, "English expression actually not Australian – although I am not sure that – Nathan! Right? Not sure that Nathan can tell the difference. And what do you mean 'haven't we met before' – Blow it out your bum, Bluey – over at the Jianguo Hotel bar of course…" I am not kidding that's how he talked!

"Yeah, you were talking to that guy from New Zealand…" Nate said.

"New Zealand? Poor bloke…" said Zev.

It seemed like they were hiding something, but I never figured it out – that is typical of you, Nate.

Chapter Twelve

"So then what happened," asked Qi, pretending to pretend he did not completely understand what was just said.

"We came over here to the Youyi – up here on the roof – the four of us walked over here and came up here. It was a beautiful September night and my first night back since I got back from the States and everybody – all of you were there. Remember? You were, Dexter." Molly looked around.

"Everybody was drunk," said Gregor. "But, something was different about that night."

I looked at Gregor, who was just trying to instigate something, anything for his own cruel amusement. But, of course he was right. That was the night my house of cards started to fall.

"Dr. Nate – Is she correct? Had you met this," here Qi consulted his notes, "Zev before?"

"It's true – we did meet before." I said. "At the Peach Orchard."

Lang glared at me, but I was unfazed. He looked at Qi, who almost shrugged. "Peace Orchard?"

"Peach Orchard," I corrected using Chinese. "Tao Yuan. The place where the Monkey King threw the peaches at the gods, peaches that gave eternal life to whoever eats them. The gods were meeting in the sacred, heavenly Peach Orchard. The Monkey King was saying take your immortal fruit and put them in your ass, I believe. But this Peach Orchard, where I met Zev was a little different." I allowed a slight smile to pass over my face and Lang looked at me with daggers shooting from his eyes.

I looked at Molly, back in English I said, "I have wondered ever since then if Zev followed me to the Peach Orchard that night. I don't think it was an accident that we met." I said.

Two waiters came up and asked us if we wanted steamed buns and tea, which I did, (and so did everyone else, except the East German Hag) I was suddenly very hungry.

It was getting a little warmer as the sun rose, it was still very early, and chilly, about 9 AM. It was a great day for late October but not meant for sitting outside.

"I am going to give you your confession, Molly. The confession I should have made a long time ago."

"You are just an asshole, Nate," she said.

"When did you go to this Peach Orchard?" asked Qi.

"About a week before Molly got back from the States, last week of August I think." Qi scribbled intently in his notes ignoring his partners obvious displease at allowing me to speak uncontrolled, in public.

I looked at Molly and Dexter and suddenly felt happy she she wasn't my problem anymore.

The Peach Orchard. I wasn't sure if Molly was coming back or not. Not that that mattered because, you know, I needed a job, and I wasn't going to do or rather in this case, I was going to do what it took to make sure I got the job. Or what I thought it would take, anyway.

Pan, the executive secretary where I worked at ITMS knocked on my door about 9 AM. I was actually just about ready to catch the bus down to work, so I asked to catch a ride with her.

"Don't you have any nicer clothes," asked Pan as I got into the backseat of the Hongqi. She looked very hard edged in a perfect sort of way. She was dressed that morning like a Japanese schoolgirl, with a white blouse and black skirt that was tight and short. Her legs were covered by blinding white stockings, the tops of which were tangent to her hemline. I sank into the soft, musty, velvet-like upholstery of the Hongqi's backseat, sneaking a peek at what might be holding up her hose.

"The boss is in town. Tai came in last night and wants to see you!"

Pan flirted with me all the way down to the office, dropping hints that I could meet her after work. I stayed vague and mysterious with her. We walked into the busy office together, and that seemed to shoot even more air up her skirt.

Then she sorted through the mail on her desk, and with a sad pout, gave me a post card from Dagmar.

Lang was gripping his chair and seemed like he was about throw it at me.

"What did this postcard say? Why did you get it?"

"I told Dagmar to write me at the office where I worked."

"So I wouldn't see it," said Molly.

"Yeah. So you wouldn't see it."

Ah, fuck, Molly was welling up again.

What did the postcard say," asked Qi.

"Here it is." I took it out of my wallet, unfolded it and handed it to Harold and he read it with his upper class British accent.

> Aug 26
> *Ulan-Bataar*
> *Dearest Nate,*
> *I know you are OK. I will never forgive my country for that. I told you not to come to the train station! Please be OK!*
> *I have not even been gone two days and already I am stuck in Mongolia. Apparently some big shot is traveling to Moscow and he needs his own car.*
> *The first time I met you, you said "She's not my wife."*
> *Then what is she?*

I am sorry. I will probably marry Markus when get back to Berlin. So I cannot speak to you about your personal affairs. I wanted you to know me the way I am. I want to know you too – How can I learn?

Dagmar

Molly got up and ran out of the room, followed by Dexter. Too much? Ah, fuck it, I thought.

"Please continue Professor Nate," said Qi.

Tai was in his office with Ling, had the ledger books opened and was comparing them to a computer printout. Ling, dressed in his gray Mao suit, hovered nervously over him, pointing occasionally at a figure on the page. I waited outside with the geology engineers, gossiping and joking.

Tai was obviously interrogating Ling Ye, but from his gestures, Ling was not accepting any blame for what I assumed was declining profits. Tai used the intercom several times to order Pan to bring a copy of this or that record. She put down an emery board and made a face, which was for her, jumping right to it. But she seemed worried and eventually brought the documents in to Tai. Then suddenly it was over.

Ling walked out staring straight followed by Tai, who came out of his office clapping. Pan walked out of the storage room on cue, smiling broadly and guiding one of the technicians who carried a large travel bag of gifts. Toiletries, pens, little flashlights, calendars, Seiko watches with Jackie Chan on the face, his arms as minute and hour hands, ready to chop, his eyes ablaze, made in Taiwan, all handed out by Pan. Everyone became happy and talkative as if on cue.

Ling Ye started things off. "Welcome Tai Xiansheng!"

"Thank you for all of your hard work. We have made great progress in the last six months. Negotiations are proceeding with the National Land and Resource department. Each step we take leads to the next one. Your hard work is essential for the success of the organization."

Big cheer. He introduced me, and I stood and accepted the applause then sat down to listen to Pan's father, an odious little man, who droned on and on, pointing out the debt was really owed to the Party for recognizing the importance of technological development, etc., etc. Tai signaled to me from across the room and I got up and walked over to him.

"Nathan, come with me."

We grabbed Lin, jumped in the Hongqi and drove off to the Great Wall Sheraton Hotel over on the Ring Road on the east side of the City. The waiters at the French Bistro smiled at him with familiarity. Tai spoke French and spent a long time ordering the wine.

With me he stuck to English. "What do you want to do? Do you like teaching?"

I knew that the next five minutes would decide my future.

"In America, until recently, Chinese was taught as a classical language," I said thinking of the power struggles between the younger and older Chinese faculty at the University of Oregon, where I studied before coming to China. "But now when Westerners learn the modern language, from simplified characters, using the unadorned Communist rhetoric, it is a political statement by itself. It gives the mainland legitimacy. It is choosing sides – choosing Beijing over Taipei."

"Yes." He chewed slowly and spoke even slower. "That is true. The Taiwan government for many years did not encourage Westerners to contact Beijing." He continued eating as if the conversation only half interested him.

I discussed the technical features of the product that I liked as if I was trying to sell him the product. He looked at his watch.

"You've done pretty well, but we have to do much better and soon." Tai put his fork down and took a sip of wine.

"We have decided to invest, to seriously invest, in China. We want to get big contracts for the Tectonic Measurement software of course. But with the personal computer about to explode, KuaiTu is really our best hope to quickly crack the China market." He took a bite and chewed thoughtfully.

"I see." I drained my wineglass and helped myself to another.

"Here it is. You will market KauiTu full time. Crack the Chinese market – make contacts – go out and meet everyone you can, all the time, pushing, pushing, pushing. Use your contacts to sell. We'll give you a salary and housing and get you a visa. You start October 15. We'll have everything arranged by then."

"So I have to quit my job at the University...?"

"Of course, I would wait though." Now he paused to take a sip of wine. "I would not resign now. Wait until two weeks before October 15. Give them two weeks' notice. That will guarantee you have housing until you move in with us."

So that was it. We briefly talked money, to my great satisfaction, and then shook hands. Of course that meant waiting until the school year started and then quitting after a month. It would be hard for the school to find a replacement by then, but there are always foreigners hanging about, at least that is what I told myself.

"You will get a lot of offers once you decide this," said Tai as if reading my drifting mind, "to moonlight or just to switch jobs. It is a very expensive process to get your visa changed to a business visa. And the apartment is even more expensive. We expect you to stay on and make this successful." He gave me that look that said he knows guys...

I blew my main chance in the States a long time ago. Too many hangovers, too many middle fingers extended toward the wrong people. But Asia, and China in particular, has always been a place where low class, lazy Westerners could get a second chance to make their mark. And that was me. I really thought this was going to be my shot at success in life.

"Well we should celebrate now – I'll show you a Beijing that maybe you don't know." He smiled.

Tai released Lin and his plush Hongqi Limo for the evening, and we hailed a cab. We drove south on the ring road past Jianguo Road about five kilometers and then turned west until we came to a driveway in front of an unusually high wall. The guard waved us through, and we got out just inside. It was dusk and though the haze of the late afternoon we looked up at a three-story, dirty yellow building. The small parking lot was a patch of dirt with ruts and weeds and scattered paper wrappings and containers from Chinese fast-food. The characters on the gate said "Tao Yuan" (桃园, Peach Orchard). The garbage looked to be of a fairly recent vintage. Three guys hung out at the entrance; two of them were chunky and the other looked like an over-sized rat, down to the three or four hairs that passed for his mustache. They wore white shirts and black slacks, the usual low-level Commie attire. They approached us.

Tai pulled out his crispy new roll of twenty yuan (元) RMB (¥) bills. The little Rat talked like the leader, but Tai ignored him and passed a twenty to each of them and it was all smiles after that. Tai similarly tipped the guy at the front desk. Then a tall, long-haired, elegant charmer with mischievous eyes and a long slit skirt directed us to the elevator, pushed the third-floor button and blithely stepped out with sly smile. The door closed too fast for me.

We entered into a large common area with three doors on one end and two on the other, with the windows completely covered over with white particle board. It was dark, lit by candles and imitation oil lamps in three of the corners. On the far end of the room, a large-screen Sony TV was tuned to a Chinese variety show that was panning across the audience, middle-aged military in full regalia, grim-faced second-tier politicos with plump, resolute wives and bored Young Pioneers, their red scarves tied like Cub Scouts'.

I looked for the beautiful Chinese women gliding gracefully in long flowing gowns, with their perfect hair held up exotically by jade clasps, their pouting lips framed by languid eyes of sensuous mystery, but it was soon clear that this was a different fantasy. Four girls, none over five feet tall, bounced around like an X-rated circus variety act. They wore only tight nylon light blue sweatpants, and jumped from one giant Persian puff couch to another, pulling at their colleagues' pants playfully and acrobatically, revealing perfect round little fannies. They tossed flesh-colored, inflated vinyl balls that were impressionistically encircled with cartoons of tits and asses. They ran to us as one, still pulling each other's pants a quarter down, giggling, escorting us to our respective positions, enthroning us on the puffed-up Persian couches. Tai had it down, laughing and clapping at their antics, very much enjoying the show. I was still interested in the one who pushed the button in the elevator.

I had never done it with a whore before (at least not while she was working) but Tai was handing out the cash, for the first round anyway, so who was I to be ungracious?

I landed with a girl from Guilin (桂林) whose Mandarin was actually worse than mine. I gave her pronunciation lessons which annoyed her so she started giving me a blow job while I drank sake that was efficiently served by another bouncing courtesan, so as not to interrupt the work in progress. Most of the customers seemed to be Japanese or Taiwanese, at least if the porn magazines that were lying around the tables were any guide.

My little Guilin girl was pretty good, because I was just coming into the back stretch of the bell lap, when in walked a big, well-muscled olive-skinned man in khaki shorts, a Polynesian shirt and an Aussie cavalry hat with one side tacked up and the other down. Seeing him, my Guilin girl stopped in mid-stroke and jumped down to revive her tumbling routine with the other girls, "pants-ing" each other and running to welcome the new customer. It was cute the first time, but now it was beginning to get old.

The new customer looked at me, then my crotch, and pulled himself up into full salute and attention. Funny.

"I think I'm in the right place, mates."

Our new friend, an Aussie soldier, about forty or so, made himself at home very easily. We learned about him very fast, which is typical for Aussies I suppose. He pulled out his wallet and laid at least 500 kuai on the bar. - "Bring more!" It promised a full evening of fucking and drinking.

"Bob's the name," he said. I guess I gave him that "Oh we're not using real names here?" look.

"Bob, I bet we would have known you were Aussie even without that fucking hat," I say.

He looked at me hard for a second and started to say something, but stopped and hoisted a drink in my direction. The guy was about 6'2" 200 lbs, dark hair and clear brown eyes. He didn't look like the typical crab-faced descendant of gin-soaked English criminals and syphilitic Irish barmaids that usually passed as Australians.

"I need a raincoat!" he said, pointing at his flaccid dick which a team of girls had just pulled out for inspection after pulling his pants off. None of the whores had a clue what he was saying. Christ, I could barely understand him and I speak English. I was developing a bit of a passion for my little Guilin acrobat so I really didn't want to have to pretend to listen to Bob anymore. I translated condom ("taozi" 套子)into Chinese for him (and me) and rubbers appeared, instantly solving the problem.

"Listen, Bob, why don't we get phase one of the campaign rolling and reconvene out here at say twenty two hundred hours?"

He saluted me with a faux-grim face, and we each retreated off to the little rooms that surrounded the main lounge.

Youth and enthusiasm go a long way against age and experience. Case in point – my little ball of Guilin energy didn't seem familiar with doggie style (狗肏式). I know I surprised her with that move. Her little Thumbelina butt went up, and then moved wherever I steered it. When I finished, she looked happy, but a little shell shocked.

"Too big! Very good" was all she said. And that was in clear Mandarin, showing that she could speak the language if she wanted to!

"How long have you worked here?" She lit a cigarette and offered me one. I had been smoking too much lately, but I lit up anyway. I actually quit when I left Louyang, but recently it had become a habit again.

"This is my first day," she said. Of course every whore would love it if her customers thought she was a virgin. But you know…ah fuck it. This has got to be better than wading through a rice paddy. That's what I told myself at the time anyway.

I lay there watching Hong Kong pornography with her for a while. Another girl brought in food and more sake. I was wishing for some hash, but the Chinese really don't go for highly refined hemp. Hash is one of those universal words, but she didn't know it.

"Yapian (鸦片)?"

"Yapian!" My little gymnast's eyes lit up. Opium! Jackpot! She bounced out of bed like a flying monkey.

She returned with a traditional pipe the size of a flute and what looked to be a genuine antique smoking tray. She set it up for me with slow elegant precision, rolling the gooey, dark green ball around and heating it up, and got the pipe going good before she passed it to me. I was developing a profound respect for my little Guilin sex fairy. Oh wow. She put on some erhu music, but I didn't really want to listen to that. I did, but this wasn't the time or place to get emotional. So I asked her to change it to some Suzhou Opera instead.

After about – well, I don't know how long, quite a while – I excused myself, had to pee. She stood up in one smooth move, from sitting flat on the floor to the balls of her feet. Her hands never touched the ground. She pulled a Ming scholar's robe out of the closet and put it on me. I put my wallet in the robe pocket (habits sometimes overcome forgetfulness) and let her lead me out. I dismissed her. I wanted to experience it all myself. Everything was pleasurable. The bathroom was in the center of the hall. I could have peed all night! I could have peed all night! It actually got scary, maybe because I started singing and maybe because I was afraid I was going to drain myself completely into the toilet, turn myself inside out into urine and that it would never stop.

Finished, I came out and noticed the stairs. What else is in this place? I glided up, almost not touching the steps, yet I counted every one of them. Six up to the landing, turn, then nine steps up to the next floor. No fuck rooms here, looks like the business office.

Everything was brown unlike the red-pink downstairs. I came to a door with a small gold-colored tag on the front with three characters - "Fa er ben" (发迩本). Farben? IG Farben? Maybe Yoyodyne has an office here too? A light was showing under the door. I turned the knob and it opened.

I walked in quietly and listened. It was small – on the other side of the wall was a little office, and from inside it sounded like a washing machine on rinse cycle. I pushed the door open.

I heard a scream and shouting, then laughter.

"Ni – shei? (你 – 谁, You – Who?) – Ah – duibuqi! – duibuqi (对不起, Sorry! Sorry…)" The tiny rat-whiskered guy from down in front had his pants down at his ankles, and was fucking a tall girl who was much prettier than – it was her! The elevator button pusher! This was the one I was dreaming about. She pushed down her long silk skirt and laughed. "You duo you wan'r! (有多有玩儿), The more the merrier!" she said. She came over and pulled me toward the desk.

"Sorry – sorry…" the rat continued. "She is…she does not work here," as if reading my mind.

"I do too work here!" She came over to me. "He did not finish," she whispered to me. All oiled up, but not really sloppy seconds, eh? Mickey Mouse pulled his pants on and put on his oversized coat and left even as I was really trying to give him some money and half trying to get the hell out myself.

Interception! She took the two twenty-yuan notes that I was holding out for the guard. "Sit down!" she ordered me with a leer, pushing me onto the desk, then pulled my robe open and straddled my waist. Her feet on the floor, she began the work. I couldn't believe it – oh!! - so pleasurable I could barely stand it. Time lost all meaning at that point. I turned her over on the desk and fell into her, licking every inch of her body that I could reach and still maintain my mount. At some point I came. I felt as if everything suddenly left me. I was gone. There was nothing left of me. I was barely still there, in fact for a while I was inside her pussy! I mean me – all of me, not just my dick! I drained out of myself and my consciousness took up residence in some of my sperm (assuming I had any left) and there I was trying to whip my tail as hard as I could heading up toward – nothing – totally dark! Where is the light? There is supposed to be a light!

There it was. Shit it was bright. I was on my back and both my legs and head were hanging off the edge of the desk.

"Where do you live in Germany?" she asked me, as she counted out the fifty or sixty kuai she had relieved from my wallet in addition to the forty I gave her.

"Hamburg," I said. It is easy to say in Chinese.

"I would like to go to Germany someday. Not the East. It is Communist like China. Is that true? Is it like China?"

"Nothing is like China," I said. I was pretty sure that was true.

After who knows how long, I sat down in the chair behind the desk and she took the seat across from me, as if she were interviewing for a job. I opened the desk drawer. And there was Dagmar. I pulled the picture out. I stared at it in shock.

"She is pretty," she said, grabbing it out of boredom. "Is she your wife?" I thought about that question. Does she think I work in this office? Do I? I was reeling from cognitive vertigo. I was getting nauseous; opium doesn't complement sudden exertion.

I looked up at the girl. "No. But I love her just the same."

"Ah..." She gave me a look of understanding.

***

Tai and I didn't talk much in the cab ride home.

"You have fun?" I looked down at the black and white photo of Dagmar. It was her at the Beijing train station, taken less than a week ago. She was smiling, but her eyes were sad.

"Yes," I said. "Thanks."

"It will be good to have this memory in a couple of weeks, when we are into the work. If we can get the business off the ground then, we can do this again. Only in Hong Kong or Las Vegas. They still are behind the times in Beijing."

"Well, some products really can't be improved on that much."

"Yes," Tai laughed, "the demand for sex is somewhat marginally inelastic."

In some odd manner, I knew what he meant. "Did you see that Australian again?"

"Yes we met for that drink afterward – where were you? In the penalty box?" Tai had a Canadian passport.

"Yes, and then went into overtime," I said. We both laughed.

"The Australian asked a lot of questions about you – at first I enjoyed his company, but...he's Israeli originally you know. Army guy. Interesting. You'd never know he was a Jew if he didn't tell you."

"But then, I'd never know you were Chinese if you didn't mention it."

Tai grunted a laugh but I don't think he thought it was that funny. "Fuck off, Hose-head," he said.

I laughed, but I don't think he meant it to be funny. He didn't say anymore, and soon he let me out at the campus gate, where I had to ring for the guard.

Chapter Thirteen

"**D**r. Schuett. Please...the train station," said Lang. He looked at me with friendly, almost pleading eyes as though our visit to Erika's neighbor who heard no gunshot that morning had never happened. "We've waited to hear about what happened for quite a while."

"Now?" We looked at each other and he shrugged.

"Please..." he said again.

Dexter, who had returned back to the table with Molly somewhere near the end of my story about the Peach Orchard, suddenly looked very concerned.

"Yes," said Qi. "Tell us about the train station."

"Why was Dagmar's picture at that office," asked Harold, cutting off Qi. "You said it was at...Do you still have the picture?"

"No," I said. "It had gone missing sometime before I moved out of Xilou. I thought at the time I had thrown it away, but..." I noticed Dexter was almost smiling.

"I'll tell you about the train station," I said. I looked at Zhou and Rennie. Zhou looked inscrutably pissed off. I don't think she expected me to be the whorehouse type. I don't know why. I thought about what happened after the train station, after Dagmar left and after I was nearly strangled by the East Germans.

Zhou leaned against Rennie and looked at me with sad eyes. I smiled at her, so she wouldn't worry. We looked at each other and I knew what she was thinking, because I was thinking the same thing.

It was about 3 PM. I felt sick and could barely get my breath. My Adam's apple felt like it was broken. I left the train station, walked out to Chang'An Jie *(長安街)* and jumped on a bus to the Drum Tower (Gulou, 鼓楼). I had to find Zhang Xi.

From the Drum Tower I crossed the footbridge over Qian Hai *(前海)* and ran to the office at the music school just before 4 PM and by some luck I found a woman friend of Zhang's that I remembered from her concert. I assumed she remembered me, even though we hadn't been introduced and she was nice enough not to stand on ceremony. She told me that Zhang had left for Xian that morning. I was shaken by that news because I didn't think she would be leaving for another two or three weeks. We had left everything so vague. Maybe I'll go to Xian to see her. Maybe I should just leave her alone. I didn't know what to do. My Adam's apple still hurt, and I felt dizzy.

I didn't know if she was leaving Beijing to get away from me or to do penance by helping the old erhu player. Or maybe both. So maybe I've ruined the lives of two women on the same day. And if Molly didn't come back from the States – if only I'd have just stayed out of everyone's life...

I didn't go home to the Foreign Language Institute, but took a bus straight to the Youyi. The clouds had moved in and the temperature was dropping. No one that I knew was at the pool. I went over to the bar and there was Chen and Zhou and...the fat Croat was back from Tibet! I guess it was time to talk to Gregor.

He treated me like a long-lost friend. "You would not believe what animals they are in Tibet," he said. "No wonder the Chinese shoot them." He ignored Chen as she picked some crumbs out of his beard.

"We don't shoot them," she said in Chinese. I didn't understand Chen's selective knowledge of English. Gregor shrugged, like she was an idiot speaking gibberish, because he could barely speak Chinese himself and I doubt he understood what she said.

Zhou gave me her shy little wave with just the top of her fingers. She smiled warmly and made me almost drunk with desire. She was wearing a blue and white knee-length dress belted at the waist that was as light and flowing as silk but probably rayon or some synthetic. She wore her hair long and wavy and smiled at me with sparkling eyes that lit up the dark place I had just been in. I sat next to her and suddenly felt happy. She studied me as if looking for signs of stress or injury.

"Your eyes they are red." She barely touched me with her finger on the corner of my eye. There was a slight formality to her actions, and she evoked a vision of the beauties of The Dream of the Red Chamber (红楼梦). The Ming Epic unfolded the tragic lives of beautiful young women who seemed to know it won't end well, but who continued on their appointed course. Beautiful, posed, available, withdrawn, interesting while maintaining dignity even when completely at the mercy of family and husbands. As I fell into her perfectly balanced, but wildly elliptical orbit she elegantly pushed back. She was the perfect Chinese woman, a piece of translucent jade.

The General's daughter, Chen, asked me, how have I been? What was I doing? Where were the American women I had given to the Arabs? Zhou, laughing behind her "stern" manner, translated for Gregor.

"What American women? You give them to the Arabs but not to me?"

"You don't need American women!" Back and forth they went, all for me, Zhou translating and looking to me to help her, but I just smiled and let her struggle. She told Gregor about Margie and Judy and Ibrahim's PLO boys, but it came out like some kind of sexual prisoner exchange. The mistranslations and the answers based on misunderstandings compounded the hilarious confusion. My mind was only half there.

Zhang was on the train to Xian. She must have been at the Beijing station a couple of hours before I got there, otherwise how could I have missed her? Or rather how could she have missed me! In a couple of days she would be sitting on the steps of an abandoned shop, at the market, in the shadow of the Big Wild Goose Pagoda (da yanta, 大雁塔) sitting with blind old Gang, the erhu master. I could see her dressed in old clothes that would match his in age and poverty as if she were his daughter, preparing a small lunch of cold noodles while he played his erhu for the shoppers who mostly ignored him. Chinese stories recurred like the Dharma. She would not be ignored. Not for long. Maybe after a while he would let her play with him. By October they will be famous, probably have their own TV show by then, set outside the walls of a rich family filled with perfect Ming Beauties. Maybe Zhou will be inside those walls and me too, a seedy Western silk merchant whose ship left without him.

Gang, the Xian erhu player, would be an itinerant Daoist monk and Zhang his beautiful but wily daughter. Or maybe only posing as his daughter...she could be hiding from the Imperial police...perhaps she is the daughter of the deposed Emperor in disguise.

Had I already forgotten about my forlorn Fraulein, Dagmar? It had been at least four hours since I'd seen her at the train station. I felt like I was losing my grip.

I came back to the Friendship Hotel with the fat Croat, the General's daughter, and Zhou. Gregor could speak almost no Chinese and acted proud of his ignorance. His relationship with Chen was funny because she spoke very little English. "I missed you." "Huh?" Quizzical look at Zhou – "Ta xiang ni. 她想你" Chen – "Wo ye xiang ta. 我也想他" Zhou - "She also miss Gregor." Gregor – (whispering to me) "I missed her big fat Chinese ass!" Zhou – "What?" Gregor – "I have keys to an apartment." Some Italian he had met in Tibet had lent him a small place on the Youyi grounds for the next week.

The four of us walked out the back of the Youyi toward the guest houses. It was just beginning to rain. We stopped at the Friendship Hotel Shop, an overpriced tourist trap. I bought a couple of pre-cooked chickens, a bag full of baozi buns and about six liters of cold beer. Gregor whispered, "Get some rubbers." The girls were looking at jewelry, so I got a box of prophylactics too.

We ran through the late August rain to the apartment, sliding on the grass, laughing and splashing and pushing each other. There was a crack of thunder and the late summer air carried a clean, purifying, electric tingle. Soaked through to the skin, for just a moment children, jumping at each flash of lightning, we ran into the apartment's vestibule and the rain turned to torrential downpour as we reached shelter.

The apartment was on the south side of the Youyi grounds, a campus setting like that of an upscale New England college. The older brick building looked stately from the outside, but there was no air conditioning and the humidity was stifling. We opened the windows in the apartment and the breeze instantly refreshed us with the smell of the late summer rain.

The bathroom had a small shower in a bathtub, something that my own place lacked. I stripped off my wet clothes and turned on the hot water. Zhou came in, without looking at me, but without embarrassment, peeled off and *stepped out of her flimsy blue and white dress, hung it over the towel rack, then took off her bra and panties and delicately stepped into the bathtub. I drew the curtain and the water was hot and my eyes were soapy as Zhou slowly enveloped me with her long smooth legs.*

"Birth control (节育, jie yu)," I asked in Chinese.

"Don't worry – it's safe."

I pushed into her and arched my back, picking her up, driving us deeper, closer together. She put her feet on the back wall and did wonders by merely flexing her ankles. We found a good rhythm and the hot water was unending. Her body was much stronger than what it seemed with her flimsy clothes on. The one-piece bathing suit that she had worn at the pool had concealed her strength. She helped me keep my balance without touching the floor, undulating endlessly until the bestial rioters stormed unbidden out of my burning Pleasure Dome and we slowly, gracefully, slid into the tub without losing our place. We filled the tub with the inexhaustible hot water and somehow started up again. Her flexibility was astounding. After a while, there was nothing left but a vague timeless awareness.

It was more than an hour later when we finally got out of the tub. Not much talk, she softly sang a popular song about love and sorrow. When she finished, she brushed my hair and I sang a song I had made up with some foreigners in a bar in Guangzhou the previous spring.

***

The Shanghai girls are hip, I really dig those styles they wear,
And the Guangdong girls, You know the way they talk,
They knock me out when I'm down there,
Ooooh,
The Sichuan farmer's daughters, Really make you feel all right,
And the Xinzhang chicks, You know the way they kiss,
The keep the Weiwuers warm at night,
Baboom, baboom,
I wish they all could beat Beijing girls,

197

I wish they all could beat Beijing girls,
I wish they all could beat BeeeeiiiJingggg girrrrrrls......

***

We toweled each other off and came out to the living room. Chen and Gregor had found robes in the bedroom and between them had already devoured both chickens. That was fair (公平) since we had used up the only two towels and all of the hot water. Gregor wiped grease off his chin with one of the baozi rolls. A European soccer game was on the TV so we all sat down to drink the beer.

"So," asked Gregor, "when does your wife come back?" I suddenly thought of how hard it had been to kill Rasputin, with the poisoning and the shooting and finally, the drowning.

I looked at Zhou.

"Bu zidao (不知道, I don't know)." "Ye xu (也许, Perhaps)." I squeezed her hand.

"Don't worry. She'll be back." Gregor and Chen laughed like hyenas.

Chapter Fourteen

I looked at Zhou and she smiled at me and waved with a tiny motion of her finger's upper joints. I wondered if we were both thinking about the bathtub last summer. Yeah, we were; her innocent smile brimmed with erotic complicity.

I was dreading what was coming. The stele, I thought, was going to change everything. I knew, at least I was pretty certain, that Erika and Sandor died because of it, but I didn't know why or by whom, or even how. But Zev knew, and Ibrahim probably knew and maybe even Dexter, Mr. CIA, he might have known something, although thinking about it, I seriously doubted that. I was sure he hadn't told Molly, because she couldn't play it that closely. But in the end, I don't think he could keep it from her, because he was head over heels for her pussy. So Dexter almost certainly didn't know. Except, why did he seem to smile as if he knew what happened to Dagmar's picture? OK, I thought, let's put it on the table and find out.

"Professor Nate, you keep avoiding discussing what went on at the train station. Why?"

I looked at Lang who no longer seemed interested in what I might say. He was diving into a second baozi and had ordered one of the Gong An uniforms to leave a bottle of baijiu with him. He didn't offer any to anyone else, including Qi.

"It is simple, I only wanted to say good bye to a friend and I think there was a mix-up as to my intentions. Its not really a big deal." I tried to act nonchalant.

"This friend, she was the young woman from the German Democratic republic who returned to her country," here Qi again flipped through his notes, "When did she leave, what day?"

"Sunday. It was a Sunday I remember."

Qi found the page he was looking for and nodded self-satisfied to himself. "August 23. A Sunday again. I thought you westerners rested on Sunday?" He looked up smiling evidently expecting some laughter. Nothing. He was working a dead room and had no backup quip to hide the silence.

"She told me she had to leave at lunch. We had been eating every day this week over at the campus cafeteria. That was when she told me that her leaders had decided to give her an important assignment, managing the transport of important artifacts back to Berlin."

The fucking commies! The fucking commies! The fucking commies! Commies. Nothing comes close to the hatred I feel for the pompous apparatchiks that end up on top of the socialist dung heap, and even worse, the arrogant, self-righteous intellectual, bourgeois, leftist bastards that support them. They are the real enemy. Look in the mirror, dumbfuck! You fucking useful idiot! How could I have ever supported any cause even remotely to the left of Francisco Franco! I want to join a fascist death squad so that God can forgive me! Machine gun all of those fuckers! Small-minded, pecking order–bound, conscienceless, spawn of filth, why should they walk the earth? How do we let them walk the earth? Torture and shoot anyone who even pretends to have sympathy with these left-wing monsters! "All men are brothers!" They are failures, wanna-be-artists and second-rate minds that misunderstand the one or two books they tried to read – saps and losers, promised some token of group orgasmic oneness with humanity, wasting away in the upper rooms of the hell on earth they have created for the rest of us!

Killing them won't help though. Cockroaches don't care if other cockroaches die. It won't make any difference!

They are sending Dagmar back to East Germany tomorrow!

We ate that day at the campus jiaozi house, behind Xilou.

...A dirty little place behind Xilou that made two decent Sichuan dishes, good jiaozi, and served cold beer...

"We had a similar sense of humor I guess because we laughed at the same things, and had similar interests. We laughed together, and learned about each other and about our cultures, trying to forge bonds of friendship...It was innocent of course, just the pure curiosity of two people who's nations had been separated by politics for many years. We talked about helping overcome the walls that divided our two nations."

The Hag, who might have been attractive when she was young, but is now a middle-aged Babitchka, wearing a black leather jacket, even in this August sun, and is a sunken cheeked razor-face who cultivates her power by giving long deep looks to any one of her charges who seems to show the least degree of personality...she has been daring us to continue, which we have.

I laughed openly at her while Dagmar sat next to me in the cafeteria. Perhaps that wasn't too smart. I bought Dagmar a silk blouse and some very small jade earrings and she's been pretty mouthy to her comrades. She was constantly tantalizing them with her sharp yet somehow languid eyes, wearing open-necked blouses instead of tee-shirts and pull-overs, putting her hair up disheveled like we just had come straight from an afternoon of fucking, which generally we had. The Russians, Boris and Yevgeny, stopped acknowledging my existence.

I looked up. Boris was looking at me as if I was transparent and Yevgeny had his eyes closed.

"I have to go back," she said. No one was looking at us today as we sat eating lunch alone and happy...

"Why," I asked. I was not getting it, hoping that she would fail to understand as well.

"I just do," she said.

Dagmar wouldn't go to the Youyi anymore. She didn't even like to spend time in her dorm room, or talk to anyone else, not even Erika. People had been very cruel to her, spreading false rumors about her and now that she was returning to her home, I think she was relieved, in some ways. She told me she was excited for the opportunity to serve her country on an important mission.

For the last three days we had been in my apartment making love repeatedly, vengefully. We were both exhausted.

We had very frank discussions about the issues that separated our two countries as well. These discussions were not always comfortable, to say the least.

"What discussions?" I looked over and saw it was the Stasi bitch herself asking. I could have ignored her question of course, she had no standing to ask me anything, but, yeah, I answered her. Fuck her.

We sat in my kitchen sharing an orange. "You must know something about Communism?" She said it not to mock me, but truly wondering just how naive I was.

"But, what did you do?" She looked out the window. "Why do you have to go back? Is it me?"

She turned to me and started to laugh, but stopped when she saw my face. "No. no, no. In fact, normally I would be encouraged to…"

"To spy on me?"

"No. You? Please, Nathan, you are sweet but…"

"Then what?"

"Bad luck mostly. You know how I am. I was a good girl in Berlin, cheering at the right time, asking questions in the right way, not really challenging anything. But I hated it and now that I am here, seeing you and everyone else, I started to cheer incorrectly." She mis-clapped her hands together and smiled. "You cannot believe how wonderful I feel," she said. "The world doesn't end if you are not afraid of them. Anyway, the

Attaché for the Party at the GDR Embassy had some art work he needed escorted back. I am just convenient now."

"Why?"

She laughed again. She looked at me and seemed to say – Don't you understand? Don't you get it, her eyes seemed to ask me.

"What do you mean art work?"

"Vases, paintings, silk costumes, and a huge wooden screen carved in a most hideous manner. And jade, and statues and even a small stele, with ancient Chinese writing that they recently dug up. The attaché told me it is from the fourth century BC, which seems very old, doesn't it? I don't know Chinese artifacts very well. Also, I think there are some old coins, actually a lot of them, and some old documents too."

"I didn't think you could take antiquities out of China?"

"I am sure it is very complicated," she said. "The attaché is probably doing it to enrich some high party officials, in China and Germany. It will be sold in Geneva I am sure."

I fumed with anger and self-loathing.

"It's about money of course," she said. "You should understand that, Mr. Capitalist American! It doesn't matter. There is nothing anyone can do."

"So why do you...?" I didn't understand.

"Seven days on the Trans-Siberian. Then at Moscow, get the car moved to another train. Papers, reports to fill out, some bribery as well. I have to bribe Communists! It is in the budget!" She stopped and laughed. "Then to Berlin. They said I was chosen because I am the most capable, the one who could handle the Russians best." She smiled as she told me this.

"What was in the box car," Lang asked. "A fourth-century stele? Zhou dynasty? I've never heard of a stele that old. Are you sure it was that old?"

"How would I know?" I said. "She mentioned something about Chinese antiques. I might have misheard her."

"I could..." I stuttered, *"...I could tell the Chinese students that they are being robbed, that their fellow socialists were ripping off their heritage. The Chinese are starting to get pissed off about a lot of things their government does."* I think my eyes started to tear up. I knew this was my fault somehow.

"Oh, you are so sweet." She kissed me. *"Are you too tired..."* her head nodded back to the bedroom.

"No, I'm not tired." I poured a big glass of water. I was very thirsty.

"But it would be a very bad thing for you to do that. I know that you would do it for me. But excuse me, Nathan, how would telling the Chinese that German Socialists are stealing their treasures help me? How would it help us?"

Help us? How can I help us?

"When...?"

"Tomorrow," she answered.

"Did you know, Nathan, I have a fiancé in Germany?"

I led her back to the bedroom. We both reeked of the smell of recent sex, but I was getting recharged in a hurry.

"I thought everyone knew. I guess I never talked much to you about myself until recently. Anyway," she continued, "your fiancée will be back soon and you will forget me," she said. "Not forget, but you know, forget a little. As I will you."

"I won't forget you," I said,

as I ran my head down her body on the rails of my tongue.

"I have seen your Molly and listened to her. She is wonderful, I know this, even though she has never talked to me. I always admired her from a distance, wondering what it must be like to be so confident and so free. Everyone envies her. She is beautiful, and she is your lover. She will be back. And you will be happy when she is back."

We fucked again and spent the night together, but didn't sleep. I told her as much of my life story as I could remember, such as it was. So little time, the clock was a ticking bomb. She asked me so many questions, but the normality of my life seemed to disappoint her, as though she expected an unending series of triumphs over the oppressors. I told her my fears too, like I was confessing to a priest. She told me about her young man who was waiting for her. She wrote him faithfully every week. He was her best friend. They talked about everything. "...Everything?" – "No not quite everything..."

Dagmar had been a good communist since early childhood. She had never been to the West but spent her summer vacations in the Crimean, or in Sarajevo. Her father was an engineer and her mother, an English teacher.

Boris had been her first Russian, and then of course there was Yevgeny whom she now hated (but it was the hatred of disappointed love, I could tell). She was very happy that she had had a chance to leave and disgrace him with an American. Everyone knew about us, even though we had not been out together, except to the diner on campus.

"Boris was nice, but Yevgeny pretended that it didn't bother him and told me that he only used me as a whore. I hate him now."

I won't say where we'll meet!

"Where will we meet again after this?" I asked.
"We must go to the end of the world," she said.
I said nothing. I thought that is where we were now.

"It must be near Kashgar, or Tashkent, or Almaty. I want to live as a bandit in the Tianshan mountains. I want to be a white-haired legend, like a Valkyrie – yes a Valkyrie but not in Germany! – I want to be Queen of Kyrgyzstan! Perhaps you can come and be my bandit lover?"

"I guess you are not a Communist anymore," I said.
"We can become Muslims when it suits us," she said.

Bending toward Mecca ohh! Bending over toward Mecca every day is very good for the back.

"Afterward we can...again. And again! See...now you bend over too..."

"Allah Aqbar!" I said, half in jest.
She left early that morning.

She told me to be careful of the Russians. She said, "If I get the courage and you get the courage, then meet me in Tashkent."

Chapter Fifteen

"She was lying." Babitchka in her leather coat looked at me with cold hatred.

"Dummkopf," I said.

She stood up and walked toward me. "She is a traitor." I just stared at her. "And will pay for her crimes, in due time."

"We are not here to discuss stolen Chinese art treasures, which may or may not have been smuggled out of China. This is about a murder," said Lang. Then he corrected himself. "A murder and a suicide. Or two suicides."

"Well, perhaps not murder but...the strange and unusual deaths of two foreigners." Qi smiled proudly at his English pronouncement on the whole thing. "There is no proof that anything has been stolen. It is not connected to anything we are talking about!" I looked at Lang. He and I stared at each other. I was still confused why he insisted (but only to me!) that the gun I found was NOT the murder weapon.

"But what if those treasures never left China," asked Dexter.

"There were no treasures," said Qi. "Who said anything about treasures?"

"But Nathan said..."

"Little pieces of 19th-century Qing trinkets – perhaps. Maybe not even that. I may have heard of some investigation but – it is unrelated," said Qi.

"What if one of those treasures never made it on the train," said Harold. I looked at Gregor, who smiled back at me. He was being strangely quiet. I didn't know what to say, so I said nothing.

"Perhaps, perhaps, but we've no evidence of that!" Qi was strangely emotional.

"But what happened at the train station?" asked Lang. "The train station! It is very interesting to hear about your sentimental time with the young East German woman, Professor Schuett, but we must know about the train station!"

"This is on the 23rd still, correct?" Qi was scratching his head, still flipping through his notebook.

"Professor!" Molly broke up into cackling laughter. "What a joke! You barely got your BA degree!"

I forget how I felt. She told me I would forget her and that she would forget me. I am scared that she is right.

She left early. Several hours later, I went over to the little shop across from the foreign students' dorm. The black GDR Mercedes was parked right up next to the entrance, as if to block any last-minute change of heart. I had a good vantage point for her departure from inside the campus store. I studied the inventory of the shop to avoid thinking, to avoid hating them, to avoid hating myself. Peanut oil, canned water chestnuts, vinegar, rice, tea, lychee nuts, notebooks, little toys, paddle balls and plastic monkeys that spun around uneven bars. Pineapple that could have been canned during the Boxer Rebellion.

I wandered through the store, occasionally looking out at the two blond hulks in black turtlenecks leaning on the black Mercedes. Most of the Russians, all of the North Koreans and a few people from the other east bloc countries were also standing around, as well as people whom I didn't recognize but were probably from the GDR embassy. Then the East German Party leader came out wearing her customary black leather coat in the August sun followed by Erika, who carried a bouquet of red roses the size of a beach ball. And there was Sandor, the Hungarian.

Sandor and Erika have been sitting with each other all the time lately, chatting it up like an old married couple. But Sandor had always shown a vague dislike for Dagmar. She was German of course, and she had slept with most of the men in the dorm except him and the Koreans (and Gregor – I hope!). It was strange to see Erika there because she always talked about how much she hated the East. But she had become Dagmar's friend lately, and seemed almost as close to Dagmar as she was with Molly before she went back to the States.

Boris and another Russian came out carrying her luggage. I didn't see Yevgeny. Dagmar walked out, her head up, forcing a smile.

Wearing her leather jacket in the August heat, Frau Party Leader went on for a couple of minutes in German. It must have been a party boilerplate farewell because no one was even pretending to listen. Dagmar and Erika talked through the whole speech. Dagmar hugged her friends goodbye, forced a smile and waved and got in the car. I bought a little notebook and walked out to the bus stop. The car drove by me, but because of its tinted windows I could not see in.

***

I got off the bus at the corner of Chang'An and the street south to the railroad station (站街), and tried to be inconspicuous as I walked down to the station. It was very hot and muggy, with dark clouds to the east. It felt like a heavy rain was coming. The crowd waiting outside the train station was thick and jostling as usual, and it took me almost ten minutes to push through the last hundred meters.

I walked into the nearly empty, cavernous main hall. The "old hundred names," (老百姓), the common people, the poor and peasants, were not allowed to wait inside, but had to stand in the sun until just before their train leaves. Foreigners of course have their own waiting room, where you could feel the eyes of state security police staring at you from every direction.

I was hoping for a chance to say goodbye, but I realized as I walked in I could not go near her. What would be the point? I went out to the platform where she was hugging people again, just as she had in front of the dorm two hours before, waving, and crying. I stood off to the side so she could not see me. There really was no point.

Then I glanced across the station, to the far entrance to the platform. Standing in front of the big doors on the left side of the station I saw Dexter, looking detached and collegiate, the CIA boy from the US embassy, eating an apple, holding a LL Bean overnight bag. He didn't look at me, and I couldn't tell if he was really there to travel or to spy. I hadn't seen him since the Embassy Christmas party that got me fired from Kone Instruments.

I was dizzy and the noise level of the crowd on the platform rose steadily. I hadn't eaten all day and it was mid-afternoon and hot. Large and small crates sat on the concrete loading area in front of an open, white boxcar. Two Chinese men were pointing at, and waving away two Germans in bulky suits, and it was clear that language was a problem. The two Germans saw me, pointed at me and started walking toward me fast, leaving the open white freight car. There was cold vapor wafting out of the open car door with a sign above that said **Kontroll Klima.** As I wondered what they wanted, I heard a scream in the other direction and the Chinese guys they were arguing with ran in the opposite direction. I walked faster up the platform, and as the Germans started to catch me, I started running and pushed my way through the crowd and reached Dagmar as she stood on the steps of the train. I reached for her and her eyes got wide. She moved toward me and looked fearful and then someone grabbed me around the neck. I was pulled down and I lost sight of Dagmar and then blacked out. The next thing I knew I was being held up and fanned.

Frau Party Leader, still wearing her black leather jacket, opened a can of 7-UP and offered it to me. The train was pulling away. She looked at me blankly but with a hint of a smile. No one said anything. I got up and slowly walked away.

Dexter wasn't standing there anymore. I walked out the front of the station, dizzy and nauseous, oblivious to who was watching me (and oblivious to anything else for that matter) and I saw Sandor – holding a satchel, standing in line for a cab. When he looked up at the same time and saw me, an Asian in an expensive Western suit jumped in front of him and stole his cab.

He waved for another one and looked around, seeming to pretend he had not seen me. I yelled and he looked at me as he was getting into the next cab, but just for a second. The black Mercedes pulled up behind it and the driver got out and ran into the station. I knew I didn't want to ride back with them, so watched his cab pull away and then I walked away from the station toward the music conservatory hoping to find Zhang.

***

"We were taking 100-year-old eggs back to Our Leader, GDR Staatsratsvorsitzender Erich Honecker," said the Hag. "Ten or twelve cases. They were a gift from Premier Deng Xiaoping. It was a little joke they had with each other about their age. That is why we had a refrigeration car. Those were the 'antiques' that Mr. Schuett was talking about."

Even Qi didn't try to hide his disbelief. I said nothing. I wanted the focus off of me.

"Oh, by the way," she said looking around with a mock serious look on her sunken face, "all the eggs arrived safely." The Russians laughed.

I looked at Dexter. There was blankness between us. He stole my girl. I could have been killed on the train platform and he would not have lifted a finger. I didn't care about any of that. But I suddenly

I felt terribly responsible for Molly. It was not about jealousy, I didn't love her anymore, but I didn't want to see her hurt and I realized that I could never, ever hate her. I wondered if he was just using her to get to me, and that made me hate him.

Qi and Lang were whispering together again, so I just walked up to Dexter and signaled him to walk over to the parapet with me, away from Molly and everyone else.

"Why were you there?"

He looked at me quizzically, but quickly saw I wasn't fucking around.

"I am not required to discuss Embassy business with you. I am here as a courtesy only. You are an American. What happens to you here in China is my business as an embassy official. Up to a point..."

Qi walked over. "So, Dr. Schuett. Is that it? For some reason, I thought that there was a great secret to be revealed when you told us what happened at the train station," said Qi, coming into the tail of our conversation. "We knew that the Democratic German security detail might have over-reacted to your impetuous breach of their cordon, but...there is nothing here that relates to our case. Is there?" Qi spoke Chinese, I think to piss off Dexter who was obviously lost. I answered, speaking quickly, with a bit of a Beijing brogue thrown in for spite.

"Everyone knew the story about me at the train station. I lost my cool and tried to grab Dagmar and the Stasi goons choked me. I honestly don't know what I was doing myself. I couldn't help wondering if they were punishing her because of me. I know nothing about any Chinese treasures."

This seemed to satisfy Qi and I promptly shut up. Dexter looked at me, hoping I would translate what Qi and I had just said. I smiled at him and we returned to the table.

"Is everybody full?" Qi said. "Let's go back to the night when when the deceased West German woman met the missing Australian. Ms. Barton, you said you were there. Could you tell us what happened that night?"

Molly said –

We all walked over here, Zev, Sandor, Erika, Nate and me. Erika and I talked about my trip back home last summer, and she caught me up on some of the gossip. She told me that the East German slut, Dogmouth or Dartmar, whatever, had left in August. I remember she said something about the East Germans forcing her to leave, probably because she had been sleeping with too many Western European men. I remember that she told me one night the slut walked back to the boys' dorm, about once an hour, and grabbed guys by the wrist and took them to her room. But I didn't suspect she was sleeping with Nate too! Oh, it disgusts me!

Molly needed a moment to compose herself and Dexter gave her a slight hug and whispered to her. She continued.

I remember how quiet you got Nate when she was telling me that, and how Zev was smirking.

Anyway, it was so funny to listen to Zev talk. It was like, you know – g'day mate. Crocodile Dundee, that who he reminded me of!

Yeah, I remembered how he talked.

"We used to hide out up north in Laos on the Ho Chi Minh Trail – just dillydallying in the bushes waiting for Charlie with the Lops – bloody business – Charlie got scared when he didn't know it was coming and believe me – you didn't put the wind in him very easy."

The weather was warm that night as we walked and Zev's Star of David was visibly nestled in his curly black chest hair where his shirt was unbuttoned. I asked him when his family came to Australia.

"Ha huh. Don't have a family, luv. They all disappeared – the French, bloody Vichys, dobbed'em to the Germans. Originally from Spain. Marranos for a while, then a couple of hundred years ago we became Jews again. I grew up speaking Ladino. Sephardic, you know. It's funny because if my family could have made it back to Spain where we started from, it probably would have been all right. Franco wasn't so keen on killing us.

"You've seen the movie Exodus? I was a bit bigger than an ankle-biter on that boat, the Exodus 1947. Grew up on a Kibbutz for war orphans. Parachuted into the Sinai in '56 – I was sixteen – that was all a long time ago."

He said he was an orphan and came to Australia after some war with the Arabs. He didn't look that old. He looks a year or two older than Nate.

"In '67 I was a Lieutenant Colonel in the IDF, not even thirty yet. Would have made General if Sharon hadn't hated me for some reason. My boys were the first ones to the Wailing Wall. Those were good days let me tell you. General Dayan – Moishe – and I went on quite a party after that one. A three-legged toad wearing an IDF beret could have gotten laid that week."

"You'd be a big shot if you would have stayed home," I said.

"Home. Let me tell you, it all went to shit after that war. I wasn't about to stay on and be an occupier. Garrison duty is not my thing. We finally get our home, and then we end up just like any of a hundred armies who have occupied Judea in the last 3,000 years.

"I quit the Army, supported Peace Now, got arrested a few times, was probably drinking too much and finally decided, bag it. I moved to Australia. Problem is, I had no money and the only thing I knew was soldiering. So I ended up in Vietnam. Anyway, that shit's over for me."

It was completely dark by the time we got to the Youyi and the place was packed as we walked up to the rooftop bar. The four big tables in front of the bar were occupied, but people started making room for us almost right away. Erika was so happy that night. Zev seemed like a good match for her, even though he was older and a…you know, different.

Chapter Sixteen

Dexter was looking at Molly and whispered something to her. We were all getting tired of this little group therapy session, none more so than Qi and Lang, if their expressions told anything.

"Does anyone know anything about the Australian," asked Qi. "We don't believe he is in China any longer, even though there is no record of him leaving. This is troubling, needless to say." Lang looked at me, and I just shrugged.

Molly started giggling. Maybe she is happy, I thought. Maybe it's OK. All the huggy-dubby she was doing with Dexter seemed a little too forced to me. I didn't trust the fucker, but it wasn't my problem. She was intent about telling the story of how she and Dexter met, even though none of us, including the cops really cared, but I supposed they hoped she would drop clues inadvertently.

Anyway Molly, continued on and on about the magic of the evening and how heartbroken she was when she finally realized she lived with me, but was in love with Dexter. The strange thing was I didn't even feel that insulted.

"Let me explain how I remember it," I said. "I think you were too busy falling in love to remember everything clearly," I said, with no rancor in my voice.

"Go ahead," said Molly. "Say whatever you want. I am so passed all that."

Mikku and Rashid were sitting right near the door with the East German woman, I am sorry, I don't know your name, but I love your leather coat, it is like ultra...1930s Gestapo-chic, anyway, some new people, mostly Euros, at the other table near the door, and in the back were Yevgeny and Boris and the other Soviet guys. They didn't look up. Still pissed off about the Chernobyl joke I guess. Across from them were Gregor, Chen, Rennie and Zhou.

At a table next to the bar a couple of Americans, a black guy in St. John's red and the white guy in Stanford gray, were setting up a boombox. It was a first for the Friendship Hotel as far as I know – they were playing Motown.

A bunch of well-dressed Euros and Americans with $50 haircuts crowded into the back. Embassy Row was slumming that night.

Molly and Erika walked in with their cobweb thin short chemises and everyone seemed to pick up the scent. Molly, blithe and breezy, greeted old friends whom she hadn't seen all summer. We walked in holding hands and then split up just to mix. Zev and Erika sat with Mikku and Rashid and the Hag. Yeah, I mean Marlene Dietrich's ugly sister over there. All she needs is a saber scar carved on her face.

"Dr. Schuett, please..." said Qi, gently interrupting me.

Anyway, we walked into the Youyi rooftop and Erika was talking German to her. I stared at her and started to speak, because I was ready to strangle her over what she had done to Dagmar, but, being with Molly, I said nothing. Then Gregor put his finger in the small of my back and said, "Don't move American pig – Stasi bitch has questions for you!" He nodded me over to his table. Zhou, Rennie and Chen moved over to make room for me. Molly headed over to Stanford and St. John.

"So, Sandor," Gregor asked, "you come to the bar finally? Who is the big one with Brunhilde?"

Sandor seemed to go shy on the subject and lowered his head and shook it like a horse trying to shoo a fly away. Sandor looked away from everyone and seemed equal parts ecstatic and depressed.

Molly broke out into a high-pitched laugh. Zev was conspicuously buying his table drinks so I shouted over to Molly, "You want something?" She looked at me and ordered something directly from the bar while asking Stanford and St. John what they wanted and then pointed to me.

At that moment the waiter was standing over me, "Gregor, do you want a drink? Rennie, Sandor..."

"He is a Samson," Sandor answered out of the seeming blue as he smiled.

Gregor didn't miss a beat. "So Brunhilde is now Delilah?" Gregor was laughing in his beer, very entertained by his own wit. "When does he go to the barber?"

"You have learned our stories well, you fat, Ustasi Croat!" Sandor grabbed the little glass in front of Gregor's beer and pounded down the shot of vodka like a Cossack.

"...and now she is getting her Kosher salami from another butcher!" Gregor pulled his secret bottle from under the table and filled Sandor's glass. You could tell Gregor liked Sandor, admittedly in a funny way.

Molly laughed again, from way on the other side of the bar, and her laugh echoed across the roof and everyone was looking at me, smiling at what I sensed they took as my "comeuppance."

Earth Wind and Fire, which I hadn't heard in three years, was wailing out of the boom box.

Gregor, never one to miss a chance at tormenting a weakened comrade, assumed a conspiratorial tone. "You should try to fuck her when Samson is out smiting the Philistines."

"You are a miserable Nazi man servant! You are an ogre from the basement of Nuremberg!" Sandor said as he pounded another vodka.

After all the reasons why...

Oddly, Gregor looked a little hurt by Sandor's outburst. "My uncle didn't kill anyone and the Communists, your liberators, they killed him."

"How do you know?"

"Because he wrote my grandmother letters from prison camp. You don't believe this, but not all Croats were in the Ustashe. But he was a Croat from Zagreb so what could he do? The fucking British – Harold MacMillan was in charge, remember him? In May 1945 he just turned over thousands of innocent men, women and children to be killed by Tito, including my uncle."

"Tito was a Croat though, wasn't he?" Sandor smiled. "You people eat your young. Anyway, please don't tell me your sad story. I am Hungarian Jew. I think that is all I need to say."

The fucking Balkans again – I didn't want to go down that road tonight.

"Do you think Zhou is smart enough for me to marry?" Rennie asked me.

"Are you serious? Her English is better than your Chinese and she's never been out of China!"

"That is different. Everybody in China is learning English. It's just – she seems so naïve."

"Yeah," I said, looking away. Zhou was talking earnestly to Chen, sneaking a peek at me and Rennie, while Gregor and Sandor were back somewhere arguing about where the Hapsburg Empire went wrong.

"Why doesn't she try to learn something besides English? I don't think she has a clue about life."

"So why do you want to marry her?" I asked.

"Because she is so elegant and mysterious, I can't think about anything else. I am tied up in knots."

"Can I ask you a personal question?"

After a moment of puzzlement, Rennie gave me a look of understanding, and for a second I thought he knew..."No, I have not. Not yet. I am sure no one has. She is so pure in everything, her movement, the way she looks at me. Now – I can't spoil her perfection yet. It has to be the right moment."

"Well," I said, trying to think, and Rennie looked at me earnestly, and of course that made me uncomfortable...shit. "Sometimes that makes it easier for a woman to make up her mind, one way or the other."

"That's another reason...I am afraid she will make up her mind the wrong way."

"You've slept with Chinese women before?"

"Of course. You know – my previous fiancée," and here Rennie gave me a long look, one I had never seen before. I looked back with a blank stare. "You remember Jin Pingli," another pause, and we stared at each other, but I gave him nothing. "The one whose cousin got you the job?"

"Sure, I still say hi to her when I see her. She is working in the party mimeograph room next to the dorm."

"Yeah...her – and in Hong Kong once, but I paid for that."

"So..."

Rennie thought for a minute. "Maybe you're right. Maybe tonight..."

Harold tried to distract Sandor and Gregor, "Did you hear? Rudolf Hess died last week. Now World War II is really over. He was the last prisoner of Spandau and without Spandau there is nothing left of World War II except history."

"Hess was killed. He didn't hang himself," said Gregor, who already was tuned into the still being imagined conspiracies.

Gregor had been slyly eavesdropping on my discussion with Rennie about Zhou with barely disguised amusement.

"I wish I could have kicked out the chair," said Sandor.

"Don't you see?" Harold was excited. "There's no reason to keep Spandau opened anymore, and that is the only reason for the Russians to be in Germany – officially anyway...that means World War II is finally over! Maybe the Cold War is over too. With Hess dead there is no reason for any of this."

"So you think that the last forty years of nuclear terror have been about Rudolf Hess?" I asked.

"Who is Rudolf Hess?" asked Rennie.

"Him dying is like the beer running out at a game of cards," said Gregor. "It might be an easy excuse for everyone to call it quits and go home." I nodded and looked at Zhou and we smiled at each other. I didn't have the energy to ask Boris and Yevgeny what they thought.

Gregor and Sandor were yelling at each other again. Harold had this theory that, regardless of Hess, the Cold War had been over for a while but no one realized it yet. Gregor said not so fast – there was still going to be a reckoning in Yugoslavia – among Croats, Serbs, Bosnians, Hungarians, Romanians, Albanians, Macedonians, Slovenians, Bulgarians.

Sandor said the Balkans are like a little pool of water filled with tadpoles, crawdads and water bugs in endless variety, lively and entertaining, but ultimately you look up and realize you are staring at a stagnant, polluted little pond. History is a swamp in the Balkans. Everyone else drank faster, hoping someone would change the conversation.

Zev joined us. "You know, that Circassian speaks pretty good French."

"He's PLO, you know," I said, looking for a reaction.

"I gathered that. Said you pimped him a Yid-American tart."

"She was a tourist looking for adventure. I'm sure she is back at her comfortable American college by now, with a story to shock her classmates."

"Good for her! Aren't we all just looking for little adventure? Isn't that why we are all here?" asked Zev, smiling.

I walked over toward the bar again so I could refill my drink without paying for everyone else's. I looked over at Molly shaking her bra-less tits through her flimsy blue smock. Five guys with monochrome ties and sweat stains on their off-white button-down shirts were taking turns grinding her. As Molly danced, I had a very nervous feeling in my stomach, vertigo – like an opium flashback – I begin to think somebody slipped me a "mickey." Everyone was talking and none of it made sense. The Stasi bitch, what was she doing here? I walked over to her table and leaned in between her and Erika. "Fuck you." I looked at Erika. "Why are you talking to this horse-faced bag of shit?" I didn't shout, I just said it and walked away. Pretty much killed the conversation at that table. I came back and sat down next to Sandor.

"Was it really you at train station?" asked Gregor. "Did they choke you right in public?"

I looked at Sandor.

"Why did you try to stop her from leaving?"
"What?" I said laughing.

Sandor looked at me very closely, as if he were worried about something.

"I didn't try to stop her. I didn't know what I was doing. I just wanted…" I looked over at Molly who was slow dancing with St. John. "I just wanted to say goodbye. You know. But those fucking goons did not need to choke me."

Sandor shook his head quickly and looked away.

"According to what I heard it was a big deal. Was it a botched snatch job by…whoever…to kidnap – or steal…?

"Who told you about the train station?"
"I did," said Sandor. "I saw you there. And you saw me, right?"

"I thought it was wrong that I couldn't say goodbye," I said finally. "That is all I wanted to do. Snatch job? What?

Nothing brave happened. What are you saying, Gregor? I don't know anyone in the CIA." I forced myself not to look at Dexter.

Sandor was looking at Molly. She was dancing with…

All our illusions were just a parade

…she had traded St. John for – Dexter. Dexter was dancing with Molly. It hit me right away, the embassy, my summer of love in Beijing – the piper with his hand out…

He stood right there – that fucking scumbag let me get mugged by the East German goons.

"This makes no sense at all," said Qi. "You were all up here – it was the last night of your summer vacation. You are spreading rumors, its all fart talk! As far as I can see this gets us no closer to understanding why the German woman and the Hungarian man are dead! As of now, we are very certain that the Hungarian killed the West German woman because of a lover's quarrel. It was jealousy. He then turned the gun on himself. It had no connection to any events outside of that. It is consistent with the facts, correct?"

"So why are we here?" Rennie asked. A good question. Rennie, maybe he knows more than…

"Because if that is not the truth, if it wasn't murder-suicide, then we want to discover the truth. You must believe that China is not hiding anything! We are not! If you think something is hidden or secret or that there was some plot, speak now! But don't spread rumors that China's justice toward foreigners is not correct!" Lang said it in Chinese. Not everyone understood, but no one had the courage to ask Qi to translate it.

"Let's finish with that night. Who else was there? What else happened? Please, Professor Schuett - continue."

I felt eyes shift. I turned and saw Ibrahim at the door. I walked over to greet him and he hugged me like a brother. He pretended not to see Mikku, but walked toward her table just the same. We sat down with Mikku, Zev and the Russians.

Without a word, Mikku got up and walked over to Molly's table. Ibrahim looked at me, as we continued to shake hands. "I pray to Allah every night. I say, 'I want my fucking rib back!'" Everyone laughed and Ibrahim had a deadpan look as though he didn't get his own joke.

"Have you met Zev?" asked Yevgeny. "Zev used to be Israeli, but now he is Australian. He changed nations like I change my socks."

They ignored Yevgeny and nodded to each other. "Where did you live in your former country?" asked Ibrahim. He was smiling slightly as was Zev.

Zev named an unpronounceable place and was smiling as well, as if they were playing out some formal ritualistic ceremony.

"Oh yes, the Kibbutz. I know it. My uncle's orange orchard used to be very close. It is near ***." The village name sounded like Ibrahim was clearing his throat.

"Yes," said Zev. He was quiet for what seemed like a long time, nursing his drink. "You used to shell us from there. 1965. Boom. Boom. Boom. Nine dead."

"But we always lose more, don't we?" Ibrahim laughed while Zev remained impassive. "So you leave for Australia in 1972?"

"Yes…the lucky country. It suits me better."

"I know how you feel. China suits me better too." The table was quiet for a moment. "There is no happiness back there anymore for me."

Ibrahim was not at Qi and Lang's little get-together of the foreigners at the Youyi. Diplomatic privilege I suppose.

"Was there any animosity because of the Middle East? Could that be related to the strange deaths of the Hungarian and the woman from the West German Federal Republic?" A few of us shook our heads and a few of us shrugged our shoulders. It was clear now what Qi and Lang were doing. They were shifting the burden of proof to us. Accept our version of what happened or tell us otherwise, and tell us now in front of everyone. I continued.

"You know," said Boris, "So many Russian Jews go to Israel yet we help the people of Palestine. It is a strange situation."

No one said anything. Boris answered his own statement. "Yes." He both had Zev's attention and completely lost Ibrahim's. I was watching Molly being dipped by Dexter. "It's a problem, no?" No takers.

"Palestine is becoming more Muslim," said Yevgeny. "And Israel is becoming more Russian."

Ibrahim got up to talk to Harold, the fat Englishman. Zev said nothing, but turned to Erika and began tickling her neck and too whisper.

Boris looked at me with contempt. "Dagmar – the German whore! We all fuck her you know."

"Yes," said Yevgeny. "I wait next to bed reading newspaper while Boris fuck. Then I climb on, from behind. I fuck her like dog! Was she that way for you?"

I said nothing.

"I am sorry, Nate. So sorry." Boris smiled and stood up unsteadily, "To Nate!" he proclaimed so everyone, including the Americans on the other side of the bar, can hear. "The best American!" He and Yevgeny laughed. Everyone on this side of the bar stood. Gregor, Sandor, Harold, Mikku, even Erika, they all stood to drink to me. They pretended for me, as if it were all said sincerely.

Then there was a scream. Molly saw Ibrahim and ran over and hugged him with her leg up on his hip – her blue dress was short and everyone on the front side of the bar could see she was wearing tiny powder blue panties.

"Nate, get me another drink. How are you, Abe?"

"Good, Molly. Welcome back. We all missed you this summer. Nate told everyone that it was killing him every minute you were away!" Molly and I looked at each other.

"I never told anyone that," I said. We all laughed.

"Do you even tell people I am your fiancée, Nate?"

"Of course I do."

"Oh. And did you really miss me this summer?"

"Of course he did," said Ibrahim. She smiled at me. And I smile back as I went to get her a drink.

Chapter Seventeen

"OK," I said. Suddenly it was gone. I looked at her straight on, no avoidance, no shame or anger. I felt a huge happy void; it was like I had just taken a humongous dump. I expected to well up with emotion but it just wasn't there. Nothing. It wasn't going to kill me after all. It wasn't exactly relief, but it felt a little better.

Molly continued -

He came over as Nate was bringing the drinks back to me and Ibrahim. It was so good to be back, the weather was so beautiful that night. I was drinking and dancing and wondering why Nate was acting so strange. Like he was guilty or something. Nate said he met Dexter at the embassy. I said I start work there tomorrow at the International School.

Then Nate introduced you to Ibrahim, and after I pulled on his sleeve to remind him, and he introduced you to me.

"Well I guess we've sort of met," I said, a little confused. "I've seen you around I mean." Anyway you said, "You and I both work at the embassy and…" Remember, Dexter?

"And you were a great dancer!"

Dexter, then you said, "I'll get the next round." This got me smiling again and I gulped the one in my hand. I remember, Dex, you looked a little taken aback like you thought I was drinking too much. I didn't want you to think that I was a lush, but my head was spinning so much from meeting you and dancing and being back in China. That was my first day back from the US! So, I didn't know what else to do! Meanwhile Ibrahim had been standing there all this time. I remember he asked you, "Have we met?" Ibrahim said, "We've seen each other at briefings. I am Ibrahim Abu or something like that, an engineering student." But he's not here. Where is Ibrahim? Isn't that what happened, Dexter?

Molly still had her arm around Ibrahim and it seemed to make Dexter nervous. He looked at me, still trying figure out who was what. "I finally made it over here to your side of town." Dexter said to me, but was looking at Molly and she looked a little embarrassed.

"PLO, huh?" said Dexter, looking quickly at Ibrahim, then back at Molly.

"Yes." Ibrahim was not enjoying making Dexter so fidgety. He knew he could not make an enemy like that in public. Molly leaned drunkenly against Ibrahim while she stared at Dexter.

So Dexter and Ibrahim finished talking about some boring diplomatic stuff when, turning to me, Dexter shook the ice in his drink. It was like the beginning of a scene in a movie where we had to talk about something real for a change. A waiter walked by and he ordered another drink for me and him. I gulped mine just as he ordered and put it on the waiter's tray. I pointed at Nate to pick up the tab. Nate had been giving me looks all night about me ordering drinks, not that he cared if I got drunk and sick but that I was spending too much money.

Then, Dex, you asked me, "Molly, you sound like a country girl?"

"Yup," I said.

"It was like you were daring me to make something of it," said Dexter. Molly's cheeks got so red when she drank. They almost matched her lips. I didn't care that much about the bar tab; I really didn't want her to get sick.

"A real ranch."

"Horses and everything?"

"Horses and…" Dexter got excited then as he talked and we were galloping off, Appaloosas, Mustangs, Quarter Horses, Andalusians, Morgans, Palominos – between the two of us we had ridden them all. Dexter is from Virginia, but had worked on a dude ranch in Oklahoma. That's when it started.

Molly and Dexter stared at each other nuzzling, even as she continued to sob.

Qi looked at me. He was tired and hearing nothing that could help him and Lang. Everyone else wanted to get out of there. I got a look from Harold that said, "You got off easy!"

We were all quiet. Molly wouldn't look at me. She looked in shock, deadened, wishing she were someplace else. I realized that I had succeeded in turning the attention away from me, and Zev, the stele and Ibrahim and Rashid by airing my emotional laundry. I tricked her into blathering about how she left me, that night, but punishing her was giving me some sadistic pleasure, and I was ashamed of myself for that. She put her head in Dexter's lap.

"Alright well," said Qi. "One more thing before we go. Does anybody remember anything else about the lunch the day the Hungarian and the German woman died. Anything?"

"Everyone here, except Nate, was there," said Harold. "It was really like we all ate and ran. Erika was distracted. She wasn't comfortable and I guess we thought she wanted to be alone, so we all left together. Only Sandor and Bing stayed, to help clean up they said."

There was a silence.

"Where is Bing?" asked Harold. "Have you arrested him?"

"That is police business," said Lang in Chinese.

Anything else?" asked Qi. Nobody said anything. "You are all free to go. Please be very careful what you say about this affair."

We walked down the dark brown wood-paneled stairs and into the lobby. I got to the bottom and Molly grabbed me by the arm. "I need to talk to you. Please," she pleaded. She squeezed my arm and I nodded.

We walked down by the pool. It was cold out now, and she was shivering.

"Listen," she said, "we can't keep killing ourselves. Please just tell me. Why were you at the train station when I got back from Montana?"

"I went to Xian like I said. You know."

"You mean to see the Chinese cello player."

"Yeah..." I knew she was just guessing, but I decided then that she deserved the truth, "...but it's not a cello, it's an erhu." I realized I was doing it again, playing Professor Higgins to her Eliza. I had to go Bogart on her. "It was over with her when I met you at the train station. It was all over." She looked at me, and for just a flash, she seemed to relent, to be holding out...but I had finally and truly had enough. "Look, this has been hard on both of us. I wish you luck with Dexter. Let's just let it go at that."

She looked away and swallowed.

"What were you really doing at the train station when Dexter saw you? Tell me the truth!"

"What are you a spy now too? I went to say goodbye to Dagmar. Just like I said. That's the truth."

"You really went to say goodbye to that slut? That whore? You had me! I can understand the Chinese woman. But I don't understand her. Christ."

"She's not a slut."

"Oh I'm sorry. I guess you are the only white guy in Asia who had a 'platonic relationship' with her."

I let it go.

"Are you sometimes sorry that we lost each other?"

I nodded, but felt like I was lying, but then, maybe I was sorry. "But it just wasn't our time." I felt stupid saying that, but she nodded and accepted it. Maybe it wasn't stupid. She might have spit at me.

"So when I met you at the train station when we both got back to Beijing – that was just coincidence then, right?"

"Yes." I smiled. "That was something, meeting like that wasn't it?" I said. She smiled.

"Yes, it was something." We looked at each other for a whole second; it seemed much, much longer, almost too long, too inviting of more pain, so we both moved away at the same time, like two repelling magnets.

Chapter Eighteen

It was lunch time. I needed to get away. I saw Mikku coming down the stairs. "Mikku, would you have lunch with me?" We grabbed a cab and I picked up an *International Herald Tribune* someone had left on a table and we got away from the Friendship Hotel as fast as we could.

It finally made the papers – on page five.

> Erika Neibender, 28 of Stuttgart and Sandor Munkácsi, age unknown, of Budapest Hungary were found shot to death in Ms. Neibender's apartment Saturday, on the campus of the Beijing Foreign Language Institute.
>
> A spokesman for the Beijing Public Safety Department said it was "an apparent murder-suicide." The man and woman were found next to each other, both shot to death in the head. The murder weapon, discovered in Mr. Munkácsi's hand, was confirmed to be the gun used to kill both of them.
>
> The apparent murder-suicide of two Europeans in an apartment at one of Beijing's most prestigious universities has sent a chill through the expatriate community. Several of the expatriates who knew the pair question the findings.
>
> In what Chinese government sources call "an unrelated event," three North Korean language

students were quickly dispatched back to Pyongyang. A student who wished to remain unidentified said that Neibender had been "close" to the three men in question.

The West German embassy issued a statement saying they are satisfied with the progress of the investigation. The Hungarian Embassy did not comment.

Mikku and I raced out, to avoid talking to anyone. We held hands, instinctively, like Hansel and Gretel trying to get out of the Gingerbread house. We had almost made it when I heard Gregor.

"Nathan – wait." We didn't stop or turn around, but by the time we got to the bottom of the steps he had caught us, breathing so heavily that the vodka fumes would have singed all of us at the slightest spark. "I need to talk to you."

I looked at Mikku and she lowered her eyes.

"Oh," he said, as though he had found us *in flagrante delicto*. "It's important though. I know about Bing!"

"Get in," I said. The three of us squeezed into the backseat. I sat in the middle so Mikku wouldn't have to suffer as much from his foul body odor. Who said chivalry is dead? "We are going to get some lunch." Mikku knew a little luncheonette in the northeast side of town, in the Dongcheng district (东城区). We sat in silence as we drove because the three of us knew that cab drivers who pick up at the Youyi are wired into the *Gong An*.

The China Japan Friendship Hospital (中日友好医院) was a block away from where we stopped. We went into what looked to be a fancy noodle shop but they also served mini lamb kabobs, exotic salads, Xian jiaozi, Vietnamese soup, dim sum and sushi. The shop was full of Japanese medical people. The menu was bizarre, Chinese, Turkish, Vietnamese, Thai, and Japanese. A couple of flamboyant men (one Chinese and the other Japanese) in their thirties ran the place, and Mikku stayed at the counter to talk to them while Gregor and I repaired to the table. We ordered a big bottle of hot sake to start.

"They don't know where he is," he said. I poured and we both toasted and drank with one move, like veteran infielders instinctively working a double play. I didn't have to ask him how he knew. He was dating the General's daughter after all. "Right now their theory is that he has left the country. They assume he has stolen whatever it was that Sandor and Erika stole."

"So you are saying he killed them?"

"I don't know." Two cups, one pour, no spill. I waited. Gregor made a great show of thinking, rubbing, furrowing and scratching. I was afraid his brain would overheat and explode. "I think that is what the Chinese think. Bing worshiped Sandor. At least I thought he did. In spite of all our arguing and fighting about politics, Sandor and I were friends." Gregor was suddenly almost crying. "We understood and forgave each other. I loved him – you cannot possibly understand that!" The fucking Balkans again.

"I liked him too, you know that. And Sandor never said anything bad about Zev, even though he was fucking Erika." We toasted, more formally this time, looking right at each other. Gregor's eyes welled up like a lost child.

"Sandor went over to your building almost every day. You know that, don't you, Nathan?" He sobbed for a minute and then suddenly snarled. "That bitch got him killed!"

"I didn't know Sandor came over that often. I did see him come or go a couple of times," I said. "I thought he and Bing were a good match as friends." I was trying to be sensitive, but yet, at any moment, I was half afraid Gregor would laugh at me for falling for his drama.

"I thought he might be visiting you at first," Gregor said. "It happened right after we introduced them, that night we drank lychee martinis. I think Bing is out of the country now. Somewhere. He has that stele, doesn't he?" Gregor, behind his reddened eyes, looked at me sideways.

"Do you know what it is? What the stele is actually?" Gregor did a double take and slowly shook his head.

"I think you know better than me." He looked up at me with hurt eyes as if I didn't trust him. He was right about that.

"It is some old stone, isn't it? Like the Ten Commandments or something – only it is real old and in Chinese," he said. I nodded. Close.

"So Israel would be interested in it for sure, right?" I asked.

He poured himself another cup of sake - I wasn't even close to finished with mine. "It's got something to do with Zev. You know something," he smiled through his tears, but I didn't bite. I shrugged my shoulders. Mikku rejoined us.

"OK, forget that. But Bing? Why is he hated so much? He walked around the campus like a ghost. I watched him walk across the courtyard late one afternoon. All the Chinese people at the school stopped and talked to all the other Chinese. It must take two hours for them to walk a hundred meters at that time of day. Everyone has to say hello to everyone else, and chat, but not him. It is like he is dead, and only we foreigners can see his ghost. Even Chen won't tell me anything about that. It apparently is too close to home even for her. What is it? It's something from the Cultural Revolution, isn't it?" Gregor asked.

"I just went ahead and ordered for us," Mikku said. "Perhaps you will like it."

"Gregor wants to know about Bing, the Chinese guy who lived in my building. You know the guy, about my age, no job, the guy nobody ever talked to?"

"I talked to him once. He spoke very good Japanese," she said.

"I'm not surprised. OK, I'll tell you what I know about Bing," I said. "This happened back in the middle of August."

I was in the kitchen watching water boil when I heard a rustle of bushes just outside the window. Something had fallen from above. I was puzzled, but didn't think too much about it.

It was early, and I stood, squeezed into a shaft of sunlight away from the kitchen table, reading an old *China Daily*. I was rubbing my bare back against the corner of the wall, in the little kitchen, trying to scratch an itch, occasionally watching the pot so I could make a couple of cups of instant coffee. Then I heard another noise just outside my window. After the first rustle of bushes, it was followed by a thump.

My window was painted stuck, so I couldn't open it to see what fell. Then I heard her moaning, followed by a scream from up above. Across the courtyard, people were gathering in windows, looking toward whatever or whoever it was outside my window. I saw someone from the other side of the courtyard come running out.

In my underwear, I waited for the coffee to finish. I turned off the boiling water and poured two cups of freeze-dried instant and went back to the bedroom.

"What's going on?" Dagmar asked, sitting up, stretching and displaying her small but perky tits. She sipped the coffee and made a face like it was the most pleasant experience of her life.

"Something or somebody fell..." I sat on the edge of the bed and put on my pants and shoes. "I'm going to go see what happened."

"I am going back to the dorm when I finish my coffee. I don't want your neighbors to see me here." She held the cup with both hands and closed her eyes like she was dreaming of something very pleasant. "I'll see you later?"

"Yes. We'll have lunch together." I kissed her.

I walked out and as I walked around the bottom of the stairs, I was almost bowled over by Mrs. Gao and her daughter-in-law. They were running and very upset. When I got outside people were running out all four exits of Xilou and sprinting to the courtyard. The people on the far end were running around the north end of the building and from my exit they were running around the south.

There must have been forty or fifty people in the courtyard by the time I got there. As I walked up toward my back window, I heard a baby crying. The baby was in a blanket and Mrs. Gao's daughter-in-law was holding the child, crying and laughing at the same time. Dr. Wang ran up to her, gently took the baby, carefully laid it on the ground and began to examine the infant.

A young woman was lying on the ground with broken legs; in fact the bone on one of her shins was visible, and she was moaning deliriously. Two people were standing over her, looking at her, but not really attending to her. Old Mrs. Gao left the baby to the doctor and her daughter-in-law and started screaming curses at the poor woman sitting splay legged on the ground. She continued to moan.

"It is horrible," said Bing, as he sidled up next to me.

It was the second time in as many days I had talked to Bing. He had shyly accosted me the day before as I was walking into Xilou, as if he knew a secret. I was a little wary of him, because Mr. Liu had told me about him, calling him a "black egg."

I had met Mr. Liu, the husband of the early morning garlic chopper, my upstairs neighbor, in the hallway when I first arrived last year. He invited me up for tea, and our afternoon talks in his apartment have been a monthly routine ever since. We never saw each other outside of our teas; in fact he tended to ignore me when we passed each other outside the building. We usually talked for about an hour or so and it was always enlightening. Liu told me about his life as a translator for the Americans with General Stillwell in Chongqing, when he worked for the Guomingdang. Working for the nationalist Chinese during the war was still a politically charged subject, but Liu was almost eager to tell me about his past with the Taiwan-based Party.

Mr. Liu, who was almost retired, but still continued to teach an English Lit class, told me the American General Stillwell had been a true friend of China's. Stillwell made it clear he understood that Jiang (蒋介石), or Chiang Kai-Shek as he is known to Americans, was a gangster. All of the Chinese translators knew that Stillwell called Jiang "Peanut Head," pronounced Huasheng Tou(花生头), which sounds almost like "Washington," to make the absurd point of comparison...well not so absurd since Jiang was completely bald and his head did look like a shelled peanut. Liu told me, "If Stillwell lived, we would not have had the Korean War, or at least China and America would not have fought. I don't know what would have happened. I am sure Truman would have listened to him. Eisenhower knew Stillwell was the smartest general of his generation. But of course Mao still would have been Mao."

Mr. Liu invited Molly and me to dinner last spring with two older Chinese couples. I had brought Bing's name up and one of the other guests said that she would "never talk to that bastard." She was an English professor and said it in English, but was hushed up by a look from the other woman guest, Mrs. Lü, my benefactor and the party chief for the University (and Liu's secret paramour I think). Talk of Bing was dropped.

When I had tea with Mr. Liu it was very informal and yet correct in the way that conversation between a younger foreigner and older Chinese man required. Mr. Liu was tall, thin with a full head of dark hair, just a little gray, and wore Ivy League–looking wool sweaters, with patched elbows, and horn-rimmed glasses. I know he used me to practice English, but I think he enjoyed talking to me as much as I did talking to him.

"Chinese will always love Americans," he said. "We always did. Even during the Korean War or at the height of Mao's insanity, people remembered it was the Americans who freed us. We will always remember that it was you who dropped the Atomic Bombs on the Japanese devils and burned them like ants. That was a great gift to us."

I asked him again about Bing. "He always walks and eats alone. People want to talk to you, Dr. Liu, but people go silent and walk away when they see Bing."

"We say 'Ta chi bu kai' (他吃不开). He eats alone, which is a big social 'sin' for us Chinese. He is a pariah," said Liu, smiling at his 50-cent word. "We pretend that we don't see him.

He was once so powerful and so cruel and so young and so…" he stopped and took a breath.

"I remember when we moved into Xilou, he was a very bright seven-year-old boy." Liu smiled as if for just in that moment he liked Bing again. "He was bullied by the older children, but was a very good student. His mother died right after we moved into Xilou. That was hard because finally his family had a comfortable place to live and then – she died. She was a very lovely woman. She sacrificed for her family and her neighbors. After that his older sister moved in and cooked for him and his father. I think she was from a different mother. I don't know his father well even to this day. Most people think he is stupid. I am not sure. He seldom leaves the apartment anymore. He marched in step with whatever the Party was saying at the time, regardless if it contradicted what they said the day before. But even he was exiled, and treated harshly by his teenaged son."

Then for several minutes, it seemed, silence. It was very difficult for Mr. Liu to talk about the Cultural Revolution.

"I don't know if it would have been so hard if he had not denounced each of us. He came to each door in the building." Liu showed me a scrapbook. Toward the front the pictures were stained and smudged as if they had been scattered on the floor and walked on by many people. Mostly formal family pictures, they were taken in the old Chinese style.

"That's me," he said. Liu looked about seventeen. He was in a traditional scholar's robe, wire-framed glasses, standing behind a sitting old man and several women, also dressed traditionally. It was titled "Shanghai, 1935."

"I was downtown when the Japanese bombed us in August of 1937. Fifty years ago! Almost to this day!" He paused, thinking with a bit of self-amazement about the dreadful anniversary. "I was about 200 meters from the Sincere Department store on Nanjing Road when a 500-pound bomb fell. I felt the force and could not hear correctly for several days. I never saw so many dead people. "Peanut Head" should have fought a guerrilla war in the streets. At least it might have involved the English and Americans sooner. He would have united the country. Maybe not though. China is hard for even us to understand." Liu shook his head and turned the page. More pictures, one a group shot of men in army uniforms, then academic photos in the Chinese style, black and white renditions of young scholars resolutely pushing the boundaries of knowledge for Chairman Mao, with party leaders sitting front and center. Liu silently pointed himself out in the back. "I can't remember his name," he said softly to himself in Chinese. Pages turned, and suddenly the photos were in color, and Liu is an old man holding his youngest grandson.

"Bing knew us," Liu said. "He played in this room constantly when he was little. He was in everyone's home as a little boy. He was so smart. We all said that. That is what still astounds us. He knew what we had, he had seen us all in every way that families can be. I know I had shown him our family pictures several times. Most of us were well educated. Every educated person from my generation in China was connected with the capitalist class. How could we not be? Of course they were the only ones who could afford to educate their children. Now that I think about it, even though Bing made it easy for the Red Guard to take us away, he probably saved us a lot of bother as well. He made us show our family pictures to prove who we were. No long interrogations necessary. The pictures talked much more eloquently." He paused to sip tea. He looked at me very seriously.

"It was so different back then. Chinese people were civilized, we had a sense about life, a sense of...I think you English speakers must have French words to describe what I am trying to say."

I smiled and Liu looked very annoyed at me for a second. "I told young Bing all about my life in the Guomingdang (国民党) working for Peanut Head. Almost everyone in the building had lived in Beijing through the occupation. That experience dirtied everyone in some way, and everyone knew everything about everyone, but we believed that the Revolution had cleansed us of all that. There was nothing to hide, but we were dependent on some basic common sense. It seemed so obvious. Little by little, starting with things that happened in Yanan, and continuing through the '50s, we Chinese gave Mao more and more power, until finally in 1962 we said enough. Liu Shaoqi and Deng, we knew them, they were smart, we were sure they would lead us out of the hell we had created. If things had taken a 'normal' course we would have been a 'normal' nation by 1970, but the 1960s were not normal. We didn't think that Mao would pull a page out of European Medieval history and start a Children's Crusade. But he did. You see, there were a lot of – contradictions…" he looked at me to see if I got his joke, "… in our society, but people like Liu and Deng understood those contradictions. It took an angry seventeen-year-old boy to say it so openly, so cruelly, "You don't believe in the Revolution!" Of course there were millions of young boys – and girls – just like Bing. The girls were often the worst! Of course we believed! I didn't have to stay on the mainland. My brother went to Taiwan and made a fortune. I stayed because I believed the Communists were the best hope for China. I believed that capitalism had created an unbreakable class system and that Communism would make all Chinese finally equal. I was a fool." Liu took a sip of tea and offered to warm up mine from the pot, but I declined.

"Bing was only a boy, but still, I'll never forgive him. If it hadn't been him it would have been someone else. But it was him. In 1967 we were packed up and moved into pigsties about 500 km from here. Eight people who lived right here in Xilou never came back. There are various stories of their last days, all too horrible to think about. Beaten, starved, isolated. Lü's husband was my best friend. He was badly beaten and left dead in the cold for two days because he wouldn't 'confess' to Bing. I'll never forgive him."

That was what I knew about Bing. So when he sidled up to me yesterday as I was walking back to my apartment, he approached the road in front of our apartment house from a lane perpendicular and I came straight on. He couldn't have seen me coming until it was too late.

I smiled at him first, even as I realized that he was a criminal, suffering a very peculiar punishment for his crimes, which was that he had to remain neighbors with his surviving victims. Bing was the only male my age living in Xilou except for a guy with Down syndrome who lived with his parents. Bing approached me and without preamble recited the first stanza of a Rolling Stones song.

...Supposed to fire my imagination
And I can't get no satisfaction

"What does that mean?" he asked.

"Well..." I felt like a fish suddenly ripped out of the water.

"Is it existential protest against a meaningless existence in a materialist society or is it something else?" he asked before I could form a thought.

"That is pretty much it...except..."

"Of course, yes, sex." He had me on the ropes. "No sexual satisfaction right? But I know nothing of that of course." He smiled a bit too brightly.

"Well, I think the feeling is pretty universal," I said. "I mean, I see bored, anxious people here too."

"Yes - 'The mass of men lead lives of quiet desperation. What is called resignation is confirmed desperation; ... unconscious despair is concealed even under the games and amusements of mankind.'"

"You like Thoreau?" Freshman year bubbled up into my consciousness. My Philosophy 101 Prof called Transcendentalism "American Daoism."

"Yes. Thoreau and the Rolling Stones. I love to read Thoreau. I wish..." he smiled again. "If you have some time, would you like some tea? Or perhaps something stronger?" He smiled. I felt a little queasy and sensed more than one set of eyes on me as we stood in front of the door to my apartment so I took a rain check.

Anyway, here we were again in the courtyard, looking at a young woman horribly injured, surrounded by many of the members of the senior faculty. They had come out like I did, to see what the commotion was about. The Gao family was joyfully happy that their little baby grandson was OK, and angry at the poor girl who had apparently let it happen and who tried to kill herself out of shame. And Bing was explaining the scene to me. The girl was moaning in agony and the Gao's baby was crying and then cooing, miraculously alive, apparently having survived a fall from two stories above.

Everyone was talking at once.

"It looks like the baby is fine," I said. "Do you know what happened?"

Bing nodded almost gleefully. "The young girl blamed herself for the baby falling out of that window," he pointed up at the second story, "so she jumped. But the baby is alive. It is both very wonderful and very sad."

Bing pointed across the courtyard to an ambulance being directed by three men with three different ideas of where it should back up. "Everyone tries their best to help when bad things happen in China. Sometimes it is better to stand back," he said.

Dr. Wang left the Gao baby and turned his attention to the young woman on the ground. Mrs. Gao's daughter-in-law was semi-deliriously showing her crying child to her neighbors, who were laughing and poking the baby. The young girl on the ground continued to moan.

"Maybe now would be a good time to come up and have tea?" I think he meant that with all the commotion and the neighbors outside I wouldn't be observed going to his apartment, but once again, I wasn't sure. I wanted to allow Dagmar time to get away before I went back to my place anyway. So we went back around Xilou, and walked up, passing my landing on the first floor to his family's apartment.

It annoyed me when I would speak in Chinese and Bing answered in English. It was just as well, because I didn't want to be friends with him, at least not here around Xilou, especially considering Thoreau, who must have been a real prick to know, and course, there was all that Mr. Liu told me about him. But I was curious.

His family's apartment was almost primitive compared to the Liu apartment. Bare, sparse, no TV; the radio was a boxy 1950s style noise-box, tuned to a droning Communist monologue that sounded like a janitor lecturing the summer help on the importance of emptying the garbage. In the shadows, Bing's father sat by the window looking out at the barren construction site in front of Xilou. I gradually grew accustomed to the semi-dark apartment and noticed that it was as clean as it was devoid of anything ornamental, no pictures on the walls, no cushions on the chairs, plain, hard and drab from top to bottom. It looked like the interior for a Clifford Odets play. His father did not seem to notice me.

"What happened out there?" I asked.

Bing brought out two shot-glasses and a bottle of syrupy wine liquor. He poured it. "Have you noticed all of the young farm girls who live on this campus? I don't see how you can miss them, their clothes, the way they eat sugar cane while they are walking and talking. They are usually taking care of children."

I nodded. I had noticed them. "Aren't they part of the family? That's what someone told me?"

"You cannot possibly believe that, can you? It is not family, it's slavery! Many families on this campus have an Ayi, an Auntie. An Auntie is a young girl, twelve to fifteen years old, whose family is from some village in the countryside, a family so poor that they actually sell their daughters to be house servants. The Gaos' Ayi is from Anwei, so she is very far from home. She is the girl with the broken legs."

"Does the Party allow that?"

"That is the funny part." He seemed to mean ha-ha funny because he chuckled a bit. "It is permitted if it is a relative that is coming to live with you - 'Ba bai nian yiqian, women shi dou yi jia de!'(八百年以前,我们是都一家的!"

Eight hundred years ago we were in the same household! You say that if you meet someone with the same family name as yourself. The common people are called 'Old hundred names,' which is about the number of family names in a nation of one billion people, so many people share the same name.

"If your name is Gao, you find a Gao Ayi in the countryside. It is all very well understood by everyone. The local party leader is going to take your word she is a cousin if you buy something nice for them." He picked up his glass and waited for me to pick up mine. Clink and drink. Yuck! Sugared turpentine would taste better.

"So, what happened?"

"The Ayi put the baby in the open window so she could watch it and do dishes. The baby tumbled out the window. The Ayi tried to kill herself because she thought she killed the baby. The shame would have killed her if the fall didn't. But the baby landed on that thick bush and seems fine. The Ayi is seriously injured."

"What's going to happen?"

"Well I think the Gao family will have trouble. It could be trouble for four or five other families." Bing smiled a little.

"The Gaos will pay a big fine. This can't be ignored now. They will have to take care of the Ayi, pay her hospital expenses and see that she gets home and can support herself. It will be very expensive. It won't change anything but it will make some people uncomfortable." Bing's eyes brightened and he seemed to savor the situation. "The poor girl..."

"It is amazing the baby survived the fall," I said.

"Babies are very flexible."

Bing motioned me into his bedroom. I would say less than one percent of the country sleeps in a room alone, particularly in the cities, but Bing did. His room had a chair, a desk and a bed and was surrounded by brick and board bookshelves, from ceiling to floor, stocked with paperbacks mostly, Chinese, German, Russian, Japanese, English novels, all original language editions, biographies, philosophy tomes and histories. He had it better than Raskolnikov in St. Petersburg, with heat in the winter, food and a housekeeper. Bing seemed to have made the best of his invisible prison cell, his life sentence, with all of the living victims of his crime serving as the jailers.

"Where's your sister?"

"I don't know. Perhaps she is at the market." Bing had the only bedroom. His sister and father must have shared the pull-down bed in the living room.

"So you never answered me, what is satisfaction?" he asked, taking up the topic he had had brought up several days previous.

"Satisfy? Of course there are many forms of satisfaction, but when you talk of that deeper feeling of emptiness, I don't know. We come into life knowing nothing, only being driven by the hunches and whims of people who came before us. And then just when it is beginning to make sense – it's over. We're dead. What kind of satisfaction is that?"

"Yes it is elusive." He laughed, and then became silent.

"So," I just came out and asked him about his time in the Red Guard. We had had three shots each of his sorghum-based cheap white liquor.

"Tell me about what you did in the sixties first," he said.

"In the spring of 1970, Nixon invaded Cambodia. The military shot down students in Ohio who protested it. We went on a rampage at my college. We destroyed the Army's building on campus. I was in the mob that broke every window, and smashed everything inside. They chased us. I was a very fast runner back then, so I was never caught."

"Yes. I have read about that. Was that before or after the 'Summer of Love'?"

I laughed. It was funny to me because if ever I had a Summer of Love, this was it.

"After. I missed the love – by 1970 – it was only sex..." I meant that as a joke but he nodded very seriously.

"I met Chairman Mao."

"Really?"

"It was 1968 – there were ten of us. We were taken to Zhongnanhai and he told us to continue our work, that the Counter-revolution must be stopped at all costs. He looked right at me. He was sitting back on a reclining chair in his robe, next to his swimming pool. He said that my work was especially important because the Foreign Language School would be one place where the running dog Imperialists would hide."

I looked at the titles on his bookshelf.

"How could I not believe I was doing good work? He was as close to me as you are. His picture was on Tiananmen. He looked at me and said my name! He knew where I was from! As we were leaving he shook my hand! He shook my hand!" Bing's voice trembled as he repeated himself. "I didn't sleep for days after that. 'Chairman Mao is watching me and likes what I am doing!'" Bing looked down at his hand.

At that moment his sister came in the door. She had some chores for him. He meekly complied with her and I left.

Chapter Nineteen

"That happened back in mid-August before he met Sandor. I think Sandor had a strange effect on him, because he never brought up the Rolling Stones after that," I said.

Mikku laughed.

"What is so funny?"

"Have you ever dated an Asian woman?" she asked. "I know about you, Gregor, but Nate. Now that you and Molly are not together?"

"Do you consider Ibrahim a Westerner?" Gregor asked.

"Of course he is. Even India is really Western to me."

"Where is the border?" I asked.

"There are no borders. Being Western or Eastern is a state of mind. Ibrahim is definitely a Westerner."

"Well, in China it is hard, relationships like that are not exactly encouraged, except apparently for Gregor."

"The General's daughter can date who she wants. Even Croat pig," said Gregor.

I laughed.

"Fuck you," said Gregor. Mikku laughed.

I looked at Mikku, not sure what she was asking. For just a second, then the spell was broken. "There was one Chinese woman..."

"Just one?" she asked, teasing me. Gregor looked away, discreet for once in his life.

"But it didn't work out," I said.

"Oh. The 'cello player.' What happened?" Mikku asked.

It was the Friday before Molly came back, and I decided on a whim to go to Xian for the weekend and try to look for Zhang Xi. I booked a soft sleeper and caught the 8 AM train from Beijing. I could only stay Saturday and maybe Sunday because I had stuff to do for the Joint Venture Monday morning that I suppose would wait until Tuesday and the school would start on Wednesday. Molly was due back soon. But I had to see Zhang Xi before all that for reasons that weren't perfectly clear to me.

I arrived Saturday afternoon and walked from the train station to the nearest bus stop. When I walked out of the station, I suddenly had a feeling that I had made a big mistake. The bus station in Xian was dusty and crowded. It was 9 AM Saturday, she didn't know I was coming and I didn't know where she would be. She was probably at the Music University, wherever that was and whatever it was called, something like the People's Institute for the Performing Arts.

I looked at the bus routes, and saw most of the colleges were by the Big Wild Goose pagoda. Of course that was where I had seen Gang Xunzhu, the erhu player that Zhang had told me was famous. So I got on the next bus going south on Zhuque Street (朱雀大街, Scarlet Bird Road), got off at the xiaozhai (小寨, the Small Stockade) stop and saw them both right away.

She was dressed in white, ominously, the color of death. I waited in the distance, wearing a cheap cap, watching from the same old hiding place that I had used the previous spring, from across the street. Gang still dressed like a '30s Shanghai gangster, but now he looked and acted like the boss, not the over-the-hill henchman of the earlier trip. The pork-pie hat was jaunty, the round sunglasses slid down his nose a bit, and the long scholar's robe was well mended and didn't look like a horse blanket anymore. He looked much happier than last time. I saw him laughing. They were playing a spirited duet, and there must have been three hundred people listening. Everyone within listening distance was watching. It didn't take her long, I thought; she had only arrived in Xian a couple of weeks ago and already she had him.

They finished playing and were surrounded by people, but they remained disconnected from the crowd. People were waiting in line to put money in his erhu case. Zhang's white French Foreign Legion–style cap had a sun flap in the back. She wore a baggy white tee-shirt and white nylon sweatpants and white sneakers that gave her "the look," to her audience, of a shroud-draped ghost. The old women gossiped intently as they pointed at her. She paid no attention to anyone but Gang, helping him, putting away the instruments; all the while he scolded her, like a grumpy grandfather. She gave him complete respect and ignored his tantrum. I followed from a distance without hiding, staying in the background until they were away from the market. Something made her turn around as I got closer.

"You?!" She didn't exactly look pleased to see me.

"Waiguo ren (外国人), Foreigner)!" said Gang, touching his nose then pointing at me. The train had been hot, and I hadn't showered in the last thirty hours, so you didn't have to be blind to smell me. Or he might have just meant my big nose.

She smiled and came up to me, close, very close for a Chinese woman approaching a man on the street, outrageously close for a Chinese woman to get to a stinky foreign man. I told her I was only here for two days and she suggested I stay at the Scarlet Bird Hotel, a Chinese-owned and -operated place. We went in, I got a room, and the three of us went up. They waited as I went into the shower. The room was red, almost too much red. I came out of the shower and Gang was gone.

"He is waiting for us downstairs. I think he wanted to leave us alone." She came up to me and I picked her up and carried her to the bed and pulled her clothes off. Then we were making love.

"We can't. We cannot make a baby today," she suddenly said, in English oddly considering the urgency of the request.

I had no condoms, dumb me. I had always carried them since Molly had left, but not today. I almost argued with her, why not make a baby?

She told me about how happy she was with Gang and how things had worked out exactly right. We kissed and played and both ended up breathing hard, without any possibility of a baby. I lit a cigarette, something I had recently started doing again for some reason. I was happy to be with her, and thought, why not?

We got a taxi for downtown and ate jiaozi (饺子) and moon cakes (月饼) on Jeifang (解放) (Liberation) Road and Gang and I got a little drunk, which annoyed Zhang. I drove with them back to the Institute and neither of us brought up the idea of staying together. She was giving me the silent treatment, which I assume was because I encouraged Gang to drink. Anyway, I was so tired I could barely keep my eyes from closing so I took a cab back to the Scarlet Bird and slept.

The next day, I was up early and came back to the institute and found my way to the recording studio, where Zhang was producing a record. She over-dubbed Gang and then over-dubbed him again, then slowed down one track and sped up the other so it had a very ragged and almost natural sound that was haunting to listen to, echoing itself in the distance as if the erhu was being recorded in a mountain valley. It was amazing to watch her figure out how to create the sounds she wanted. She told me that before coming to Xian she had never seen a Sony Synthesizer, with its confusing panel of switches and knobs and gauges. I watched from the corridor, listening through headphones.

Gang seemed completely unconcerned about technique or (Zhang explained this to me) even being faithful to the music. A Glenn Gould of the erhu, I thought. You can feel that each time he picks up the bow, it is a one-time experience. Zhang said that he hadn't recorded since 1962. I didn't imagine that this deadpan Daoist could look so earnest, while playing so wildly, so close to the edge of losing control but always finding his way back to the theme. He played one song and it reminded me of an Appalachian fiddle tune, yet still completely Chinese. I listened to him for over an hour with little breaks between songs for tea and once for his medicine, but he wanted to keep going. I looked over at Zhang and caught her looking at me. We stared at each other and it seemed like she was trying to tell me something that I didn't want to know.

They planned to leave the next day for a concert in Lanzhou. Zhang didn't waste time once she decided to do something. She dispatched students to get train tickets and arranged the trip with the Public Safety office, all time-consuming tasks that required standing in lines, yet the students vied for the opportunity to serve Gang and Zhang. Zhang carried her erhu case, but except for the duet in the street, she hadn't taken it out.

We walked to the other side of the building and it seemed deserted. She took me into a darkened office with a velvet-covered couch and we began to undress. I had condoms this time. We heard a noise outside. I pulled up my pants and hid behind a closet door. Zhang chewed out the students, a young man and woman who lost out in the bid to run her errands. She was trying to take a nap, she said, been up all night planning the recording, the concert; she broke out in tears and ordered them out! They left. She was crying and then stopped and we tried again. It was as if we were keeping the beat to one of Gang's sad erhu songs. We kissed and she was almost instantly asleep on the ratty couch. It was hot and I sat in an over-stuffed chair and watched her sleep.

Later, I don't know how long I sat there staring at her, sleeping, the student in charge of Gang came to the door. I was dressed and she didn't ask who I was, even though I only arrived yesterday. Gang had gone out and he left his medication and the woman was worried. She wanted to wake Zhang, but I said I would deal with it. Apparently he convinced one of his older fans to take him out. She thought he was at Yi Shanlou, drinking.

Yi Shanlou (乙陕楼) is one of the most famous restaurants in China. It is not large. It's a true workers' canteen, run by Chinese Muslims. Bare wooden tables and chairs, bowls, chopsticks and one entrée, always one entrée – Yangrou Paomou (羊肉泡馍) – mutton stew poured over hard crumbled biscuits, all washed down with cheap, nasty white liquor, a sorghum-based spirit with a vicious kick and the smell of fermented toe jam. Gang was playing for the workers, little thirty-second, one-minute riffs from famous pieces that the workers knew and asked him to play. In between, he was bragging about the crazy Beijing Princess who has been taking care of him. He was a little vague, but never suggestive. I was hungry and I ate as he told his story.

The drunken Monk lets himself be saved by the Princess in disguise whose motives he can't quite figure out. It is an old story and he took his time telling it, drawing out the descriptions with fragments of ancient poetry that I didn't understand. He told it with a classical rhythm. The Epoch doesn't matter, it means nothing, the story could have taken place in Ming times or Han times, but my guess it's a Tang story, because he told it as if Li Po and Tu Fu were in his audience competing to put his story into verse. Xian is first and foremost a Tang city, the Tang city, Chang'An, center of the world 1300 years ago, and the patrons of Yi Shanlou love him.

"And here is her foreign friend." He paused significantly on friend, pengyou (朋友). They gave me sullen looks. "So," he said, playing to his crowd, "the Beijing Princess tells me your taitai (太太) – (old-style word for wife) is returning soon. Are you preparing a warm welcome for her? Why do you need a wife here anyway?"

"To entertain me," I said. I knew the old term for entertain – kuandai (款待), the word that describes how a young concubine entertains the emperor. This got them all laughing and toasting me.

Beijing is a Qing City, home of Manchus, not really Chinese, like Chang'An. In Xian, the last true Emperor was Li Zicheng (李自成), the Shaanxi peasant who overthrew the Ming. Beijing Princesses are the daughters of Manchu usurpers. If you act the man's man with these Xian guys, that is all it takes, getting a little in Beijing and keeping your foreign she-devil happy, yes that was OK, even for a foreign devil like me here in Yi Shanlou.

Xian was the greatest city in the world when Beijing was a backward Jurchen village. I knew the drill, stylized modesty, that barely revealed who I really am. The workers, the truck drivers and the loafers, they loved it. I bought a bottle for each of the tables and one for myself and passed out cigarettes and lit one for myself. I surreptitiously showed Gang the little bottle of his medicine.

He played some more for the workers and I drank and smoked. The white lightning and the good company had me on a cloud. Gang was a bum who sat on the street and played for pennies not more than two months ago. Now he is lord of the most famous workers' den in China. During the war, Mao, Zhou Enlai and even Peanuthead himself, Chiang Kai-Shek, ate and drank here at Yi Shanlou as the City changed hands. Now, this afternoon, Gang was the Emperor of Yi Shanlou. After playing a couple more songs he suddenly wanted to leave. He took his medicine and I called a taxi.

Zhang had told me that Gang's blindness was glaucoma, not alcohol poisoning or the result of mistreatment in the Cultural Revolution. So sitting in the back of the taxi, I gave him a tiny piece of hash for his pipe. He mixed it with his tobacco and smoked it in the cab.

"Very good!" He was leaning back against the backseat cushion smiling like the Cheshire Cat.

Zhang was awake when we got back. "I love you, Nate," she said it again and looked at me. I am not sure what she saw.

"But..." Was this what I thought it was? "...we are too busy for love. You can see that. Gang is so important to China."

I was getting dumped.

"And anyway – your wife..."

Zhang knew she's not my wife. I didn't say, "she's not my wife."

"...When does she return?"

"I don't know."

"Quan returns from the US next month. He will want to see you and thank you for all you've done." There was no irony in her voice or eyes.

"We love each other. We should tell them and everyone else and try and live together." To her I said this.

"In China?" she asks me. Could I be a scholar for the rest of my life, quietly hidden in my room, coming out for holiday festivals but only if I smiled and made very small talk? Isolated, devoted to her and my work – could I do it? Teach my theories of history and literature, reading and writing and looking into Zhang's eyes every night?

"I don't want to go to America," she said. "I would be lost there, useless."

At that moment I felt my stomach turn upside down. There was a squat toilet down the hall and I thought I might need to use it. Squatting. I thought about shitting every day into a squat toilet. It just flew into my head.

Zhang looked at me as I thought about it and I felt a cord snap at that moment. We lay down and slept together the rest of the night not touching. Monday morning came quickly, and all three of us had to be at the train station at the same time, Gang and Zhang to Lanzhou, me back to Beijing. We claimed the last open bench in the station. The mood was alternately light and heavy between the three of us. We joked and Gang softly recited a ribald drinking song, making everyone around him laugh except Zhang. After that we alternated between whispers and silent sadness.

Police were everywhere. The station was filled to capacity. Gang and Zhang had a soft sleeper reserved. I hadn't yet bought my return ticket, forgetting that the students started traveling this weekend. Zhang stood in line with me and apologized for not getting mine yesterday; she assumed I had a round trip ticket and I of course didn't think it would be a big deal. So we didn't talk anymore and I was only able to get a hard seat ticket. Zhang started to argue with the ticket seller, but I asked her not to plead my case and we returned to the benches. Gang got up with his cane and walked and tapped around, leaving us be, but it changed nothing. She looked at me too kindly, too tenderly.

"I must go to Beijing in October," she said. "I hope we can finish the recording. We have at least another fifteen hours of music – we are doing every erhu standard ever written, along with many new folk tunes. And perhaps...", she looked at Gang, who was alert, walking and tapping his cane around the train station, turning his head this way and that, looking healthy actually, "perhaps we can perform in Beijing."

I knew we couldn't kiss goodbye, so we shook hands and looked at each other. I am a coward. The dream wasn't real after all. Everything I had dreamed about her tumbled in and out of my mind uncontrollably. I had lost her, irrevocably, and yet there she still stood in front of me. The numbness and shock of the disappointing self-discovery was like a bone-shattering injury. After the first shock I stopped feeling, but I knew it would hit me later. There was no crying.

Chapter Twenty

"So that was it? Are you never going to see her again?"

"I don't know." The memory was so bittersweet, I didn't want to let go of it. Mikku looked at me with sad disappointment along with something else. There is a part of Mikku that I don't understand at all. Japanese are more alien and exotic than Chinese. I am not sure why. I can't understand Mikku in the way that I do Zhang or Zhou. There is a shell around Mikku that I don't think I could ever pierce, in spite of her pitch-perfect fashion sense and style. I looked at Mikku trying to figure out what it was she was really thinking.

"How could you just walk away? Why didn't you fight?"

She grabbed my wrist and held it firmly, yet softly and squeezed it in a way that sent an electric current through me. Some kind of acupressure or maybe something else.

"When I got back, everything just fell into place; it was just too easy to let it go."

"What happened?" she asked again. I couldn't look at Mikku out of fear of her beauty and what that would mean, so I continued the story about my trip back to Beijing from Xian.

I had about two hours to kill after Zhang and Gang left for Lanzhou. I wasn't leaving until noon because my train had been delayed for two hours and the station was filling up very fast. The delay was pushing into the schedules of the trains leaving later, and of course everyone wanted to get out sooner.

Almost everyone in the Xian Station seemed to be a student or related to one. Groups of ten to twenty collected throughout the floor. I was amazed at the loud self-confidence that the young "freshmen" displayed. I had never seen that kind of assertiveness in Chinese students.

A Chinese college student is the one-in-a-thousand, maybe one-in-ten-thousand, high school student who gets to advance in school. These students were the best hope for the family to rise up and succeed. Having survived the College Entrance Exams, these were the kids who dreamed of going to a Beijing university and now were actually doing it.

They were not very healthy looking, kind of pasty faced and seemed to really need their thick glasses. It was as if they had recently been released from a long detention, happy, but not quite knowing how to express it. I watched family goodbyes with the group pictures, last minute instructions, and the "secret" passing of money. The fathers pulled mothers away, the little sisters looked up in awe, and the older brothers looked on in envy. In spite of their shyness and nebbishness, these kids weren't the dour, beaten-down factory managers and technicians whom I taught last year. They believed in the future.

Finally it was time to board the train. Pushing and shoving made me forget the happiness I had just witnessed and made me think about Zhang. It went bad. We were just too rushed, had too much to do and worry about, we couldn't be in the open, but it wasn't just that. How could I leave Molly? She probably would be coming back next week. Probably. Maybe she wouldn't. I should have told her not to come back and told her I love Zhang. Who's Zhang?

If only it could have been like it was...I never felt that good ever before, ever. And afterward sitting with her, just being with Zhang. Or was it Dagmar? I am too old for this Romeo and Juliet shit. Why didn't I tell Molly? I thought I should call her as when I got back to Beijing and tell her not to come back. Save the plane fare, save the hassle, and make sure I stay at least a thousand miles away from Montana for the rest of my life.

I found my car, tracked down my seat and the whole row was filled with peasants and their big red and white plastic bags full of all kinds of low grade things that made up the sum of their material life. My seat was taken by a couple, a young man who looked old already from smoking and working outside, and his very young wife. I wasn't ready to get into it about the seat.

So I stood. I found a post to lean on right next to the woman...on closer inspection of the number on my ticket – the husband was sitting in my seat. Fuck this, I thought, it is my seat.

"Da rao ni? (打扰你?)," I said. From his startled reaction, I knew he heard me, but both he and his wife recovered quickly and pretended they hadn't. I stood right in front of him and showed him my ticket. "You piao ma? (有票吗?)" That was the wrong thing to say. That is what a rude conductor on a bus says when he thinks you're stealing a ride. "Have a ticket?" I didn't mean to sound that way, it was just my simple Chinese.

"Shei shi ni? (谁是你?) Bie darao! (别打扰!)" - "Who are you? Don't bother me!"

Apologies and meekness flowed from me. It didn't matter, the whole family would lose their seats if I persisted, but I would still have to sit there for the next 24 hours. Nothing is worth that kind of unpleasantness. I smiled back and moved back to my pole. Everyone in the whole car seemed to take in our discussion.

A tall, heroic young man suddenly stepped up and said, "Shei shi ta? Shei shi ni! Ta shi laowai!" - "Who is he? Who are you! He is a laowai!" A laowai (老外) is a foreigner who helps China.

Another young man, shorter and with glasses, said to the peasant, "Let me see your ticket?" Then from the back, "Yeah let him see it!" More shouting, "let him see it!"

The young man in glasses reached over and took the ticket and compared it to his own.

"Jia de! (假的!)" he shouted as he held it up. "It's fake!"

A heated argument proceeded that obviously had deeper meaning than who sat in my seat. The children of the newly restored class that had fallen when the worker-farmer-soldier class had ruled during the Cultural Revolution were asserting their new power. The merits of the argument were quickly lost in a battle of class vengeance. Before I knew it, I was escorted to my seat between what appeared to be the wife and the sister of the peasant with the phony ticket.

The peasant man took my place at the pole and left his bags at my feet. At that point the students kicked and pushed his cheap disheveled luggage toward where he stood.

I felt bad and was still a bit nervous about the people next to me. But they were more nervous than I was. On closer inspection it looked like most of what they owned was in the red and white plastic bags that had just been roughly kicked away from them. Since they had a counterfeit ticket, word would get around and they would be checked for documents, that, from the look of them, they did not have.

The students who successfully drove the peasants out of the seats were perched around me, proud of themselves and of the victory they had won against those who prefer the Gang of Four. It was a victory for a legal system and for Democracy!

I wasn't comfortable, and I tried to start a conversation with the wife who now sat next to me. She smiled and told me that she and her family were looking for work. She was a cook and her husband a laborer who recently hurt his back.

I stood up and pushed through toward the peasant standing at my old spot at the pole.

"Mai piao ma? (买票吗?)" That's what a conductor says when selling a ticket. "How much?" "One penny." I said. He found a one-fen note, worth about 1/7 of a US penny, dirty and crumbled, but surely not counterfeit, and handed it to me. I gave him the good ticket. My new friends were puzzled and disapproving of my action but I didn't care. It was a "legal" transaction.

The family invited me over to share food. I took a baozi, a big roll and some tea. It tasted good because I hadn't eaten since Yi Shanlou yesterday afternoon. I couldn't understand them very well, because they spoke a heavily accented northern Shaanxi hua (陕西话), but at least I didn't have to give English lessons.

I didn't want any more drama. It was very hot and I tried to sleep on my feet.

"Da rao ni?" I opened my eyes to a very pretty, stylishly dressed girl, about twenty, short hair and glasses, addressing me in clear Chinese. She said she represented the "The Ad Hoc Xian to Beijing Democracy Committee." They needed a "Foreign Adviser." If I accepted the position, I could have a bed in the hard sleeper car. Would I accept the position? I said yes and she said in English this time, "Please come with me. My name is Xiao Hong."

We pushed our way through the tight crowd; people were even standing outside on the coupling platforms between cars, and I was marched into the hard sleeper, led by Xiao Hong, as if I were a captive barbarian chieftain. They were talking in twos and threes laughing behind their hands, amazed at the sight of a big red-haired Westerner. Freshmen on their way to college, the brightest of their generation, who had never had a foreigner as teacher. We came to the center of the car where Xiao Hong showed me a perfectly clean, hard sleeper, the middle bunk, with the blanket folded at the foot of the bed, and the hot water and cup within easy reach. Xiao Hong introduced me to my upper and lower neighbors, a boy who couldn't have been older than eighteen and a woman about thirty. The woman was very submissive and obliging, checking to see that I had hot water (I did), etc. Undoubtedly she was a Party chaperon. Then she lay down on her bunk and I didn't see or hear her for the rest of the journey.

A big banner in English: "Welcome to the Democracy Train Car!" hung across the aisle. "Strive to keep the Needs of the People in the Forefront!" - "Struggle against Corruption!" I would have to sing for my supper by giving a continuous English lesson, and follow the path that the banners laid down for me.

The big universities had the freshmen come in a few days early for political indoctrination. The Party's message was "We're the Communist Party (共产党) and we are going to teach you that you better not fuck with us!" But it was clear these kids had something else in mind. They weren't impressed with the Party. Since the demonstrations last December, the Party was pulling out the stops to get discipline back in front and center, although from what I could see, the people of Beijing were laughing behind their hands at the effort. Case in point, the chaperon pretending to sleep beneath my bunk. I would start teaching this week because my students at the English Training Center were older and already out in the working world. They didn't need political training.

The train started rolling and it was a continuous buzz of excitement and chatter. I planted myself in the middle of the car and asked questions and listened to the students tell their stories in English. I drank green tea and luxuriated in the fact that I didn't have to stand.

At 2 PM we pulled into Weinan (渭南), the southern-most point in the Wei river valley and the entrance to the big bend where the Yellow River turns from flowing south to east. Huang He (黄河, China's sorrow)! The Yellow River is the blood of the Yellow Dragon, which was punished by being crushed under a mountain for helping man. In a final act of self-sacrifice the Yellow Dragon turned itself into the Yellow River so that it could always help man. Very Promethean when you think about it.

It is also China's sorrow because its floods have killed hundreds of millions over the last five thousand years. Its shores are the cradle of China's culture. Chinese history is almost incomprehensible without understanding the ebb and flow of the Yellow River.

I had a hard sleeper because I was a foreigner. Maybe I was the Dragon. Maybe my coming to China was the real "Return of the Dragon," not a martial arts movie. Or maybe I was just "Chasing the Dragon," sucking a high out of the rich opiated feeling I get from living here. I couldn't imagine having to go back to dull predictable life in America. It's never going to be this good again, I thought.

After a day and a night, the charms of a crowded Chinese train began to diminish, even with a rack to sleep on. The sun came up as we were pulling out of Baoding – I was not sure if it was the sudden lurching of the train, the sharp sunlight shining in or the Chinese smokers hacking and retching that pulled me out of my dreams of chasing Zhang across a desert. We were both on horses, but I couldn't catch her. I wasn't sure if I had seen the same scene in a silly Chinese Gongfu movie or not but there was probably a dragon in my dream too, I don't remember.

She was just too high class for me. I was a foreign bandit. That is what it's all about. She doesn't need a foreigner to get what she wants. I'm a novelty act for a young woman having a last, or maybe first and last fling. I was her foreign adventure, her Roman holiday. Most of the time romance doesn't last forever for anybody, and maybe it is not supposed to. I have found that women generally understand that better than men. Men are expendable when you come down to it and at the core all women understand and accept that. That's why hunters only shoot bulls and bucks.

But I knew that was all bullshit, and that I was making it up to assuage my own guilt and cowardliness. She was as real and genuine as the good earth. It's either a cliché or an enigma, nothing in between. Two floating ships crossing by a mist-covered mountain-top. It's just China. I know I'll never feel that way again.

The morning was proceeding and I felt like an expendable beer-soaked butt in a dirty ashtray, but otherwise not bad. A cup of tea and a good shit fixed most of it.

It was crowded, yet things were fine in the car. Chinese play a game where manners are the gifts at a private low-key potlatch. Whoever is the politest, for the longest, while being most uncomfortable, wins. It makes semi-miserable situations like crowded train rides tolerable. Besides, the hard sleeper car was in a whole other world from hard seat. Life was pretty good all and all on a hard sleeper. I looked around and many of the democracy car pilgrims were in pissy moods. Sore necks and backs had people snapping and snarling at each other. The lack of stoicism among the young ones seemed more American than Chinese. Those who managed to find space on the floor seemed the best off. Only about half of the people in the "Democracy Train Car" actually had beds of their own. Somebody gave up their bed to me, the foreigner, and now they were probably curled up, perhaps with a potential sweetheart, only to wake in agony from being twisted on the hard deck of the train car. But they were young and I was an "Honored Laowai." We all rode in relative silence for the next three hours.

A young man going to Shifan Daxue (师范大学), the Beijing Teacher's College, wanted to talk about President Kennedy. It happens I saw Kennedy up close about a year before he was shot. He was behind the wheel, driving a big white convertible Cadillac down Worth Ave in Palm Beach. The Secret Service were not tense at all, almost jaunty. My dad took me and my sisters over the bridge from West Palm Beach where my grandmother lived to rubber-neck rich people and Kennedy just showed up, on his winter vacation, just like us. It must have been Christmas time, 1962. As he drove by, Kennedy looked at me and it was not a meaningless look by any means.

It was a look that haunted me through late November of 1963 and beyond – to this day really. I told the kid that Kennedy was very important, but that no one knew exactly why yet. "Kennedy bridged a gap, but he didn't live long enough to make a huge difference himself," I said. "However," - here I laughed at myself as I waxed on, self-importantly, "everything 'post modern' – I mean after the fifties, after the advent of TV sets and after the washing machines and Donna Reed, and mushroom clouds and Sputnik, and after hula-hoops and hootenannies, after all that, some new symbols and rules took hold and it was a process that seemed to have come from nowhere. Maybe it was the Beatles, or Bob Dylan, but it was even more than music. Kennedy was President when that all took off."

He didn't get me and I wasn't sure that I knew what I was saying either.

We pulled into Beijing station an hour late, 9 AM. It was going to be another hot day. I let everyone get their bags and push out first. It was an extra five minutes, but I felt great as I stepped off the train, unhurried and back in town. I only wanted to get over to the Youyi swimming pool and cool off with about three vodka gimlets, boom, boom, boom. At some point after that I would be drunk enough to get some sleep and maybe not have to dream about chasing Zhang or being chased by a dragon or vice-versa or both.

I hadn't checked any bags so I was able to get out easily enough. I walked toward the main station entrance feeling in my pocket for cab fare. I had had enough of public transportation for one day.

"Hey! Nate!"

There she was, lugging a big backpack and dragging two suitcases. Her big brown eyes were laughing at me like the first day we met.

"I was going to surprise you."

"You did." She dropped her suitcases and I dropped mine and we did a Hollywood scene right there in the middle of Beijing station.

"Miss me?"

"Of course!" We kissed again. I was only half lying, because I was really glad to see her. She started crying.

"I've been here for at least two hours waiting for my luggage. Hong Kong, Guangzhou, I haven't slept since I flew out of Butte. It seems like weeks ago."

"What have you got...?"

"Clothes..."

"They sell clothes here..."

"I know, some books too and – but...don't give me any shit now – come here." We kissed again. I remember I had a good feeling, a feeling that things were going to change and it that it was all going to be OK. I guess I was wrong about that too.

"Come on." I picked up her bags and she grabbed mine (I travel very light) and we walked into and then out of Beijing Station.

"I want to hug you more," she said.

I did not speak. I kept looking at her. She smiled.

Finding a taxi was easy and we were on our way. We pretty much kissed all the way past Chairman Mao at Tiananmen. I made it clear to the driver where we were going, so he didn't need to bother us, but he did watch through the mirror. We ignored him.

"It's been so long," she said. "You know what I want?"

"Yeah, I have a good idea." We kissed some more. "How was the trip?"

"My mom says hi."

"Oh. She is a nice lady." She didn't say anything. She had cut her hair while she was away. And she had lost a little weight. She looked good! And felt good too.

"What about you? How you been?"

"Business has been pretty good."

"Have you saved any money?"

"Yeah." I had to think about that. "A couple of thousand dollars, almost three thousand really."

"Wow. That is great. It's in cash? Dollars, right?"

"Well – yeah – I said dollars."

"My hero!" We kissed again.

"Why were you at the train station? Did my mom wire you that I was coming?"

"No, I don't think so, at least I didn't get it. But, I spent the last four days traveling to Xian and back. I sold some software to a hotel there."

"Which hotel?"

Which hotel? Shit…"The Golden Flower."

"Oh yeah, that Swiss guy is the manager there, isn't he," she said.

"Yeah." I lit a cigarette.

She grabbed it and put it out. "Remember, we met him in Qingdao."

"Yes of course." I picked it up out of the ashtray but it was crushed beyond repair. "He wasn't there – it was his assistant, actually I think it was a business person who was just there for the summer. French guy. He was planning to take the software back with him to study. In France."

"That's weird." It is very hard to read silences in conversation when you are lying. "When did you start smoking again?"

"Oh – I don't know – in bars. You can't talk to people without a cigarette. Anyway, it was good to get out of town."

"But school starts this week, it must have been packed with students. It was awful. At Changsha at least five hundred students got on. You should have seen the crowd!"

"Yeah. I didn't think about that, bad timing."

I asked the driver to roll down his window. I gave her a warning look and lit another.

"Did you get any hash in Xian?" she asked. "I want to get stoned and fuck your brains out. Oh. We need to get condoms! I got some new pills, but I haven't started them yet."

"Uh…we can stop off…" I gave Gang all my hash for his glaucoma and of course I still had rubbers. Why couldn't it be the opposite?

"The Youyi dispensary has them."

"Really?" I asked.

"Yeah, I've seen them there," she said smiling. I smiled back. Molly and I hadn't used rubbers since we started dating back in the States.

"Yeah, let's stop there first."

Part 3

Chapter Twenty-One

"So, will you see her again?" asked Mikku. "She is your true love, you know."

"Who?" Mikku looked slightly bemused and dumbfounded by my answer. I smiled at her and she smiled back.

She looked at me, waiting for the answer. I didn't know what to say.

"All of 'em," said Gregor after quite a pause. "Women are so wonderful, don't you think, Nate?"

"Yes," I said. I leaned over and kissed Mikku right on the lips. She didn't pull away and we stayed planted for one long Tokyo minute right there in that Beijing luncheonette.

"What will you miss the most when you leave?" She was one inch from my face.

I looked at her for what seemed an Alabama hour. "Teaching," I said finally. "I should never have given up teaching. I am good at it, I like it, and money is overrated anyway. I screwed up badly."

"Then why did you quit? Why didn't you just wait until the software sales job came through?" She stayed planted right in front of me, not retreating even one eyelash.

Last month, just before I gave my notice to the school that I would be resigning, I taught a class that almost caused me to change my mind. We discussed a silly story in a language workbook about renting an apartment in America. Talked about first and last month's deposits and meeting new friends, locking your door and long-distance telephone calls during inexpensive hours, and the class was laughing and joking about it the whole time, in English of course. People that didn't get it had their hands up and the class was teaching itself. Left nobody behind, everyone was closely engaged, yet we drove mercilessly ahead. I had been assigning mountains of homework that they took as a challenge to their ability to suffer and persevere, a challenge the Chinese think they can never lose, a quality of character to which hundreds of proverbs attest. I focused on every student and they focused back and I was exhausted.

Came home and ate lunch, looked over homework requiring at least two but probably four hours correcting and marking and commenting. Every mark I made on each student's paper, I knew, I absolutely knew, would be discussed and parsed around dormitory beds, with this faction saying it means that and that faction saying it means this, staying up late into the night, mature mid-career Chinese manager/ intellectuals examining my scribblings like they were English characters on crumbling Egyptian papyrus.

But I was exhausted and realized I can't run an international software business doing this every day. I had made one sale in the last two weeks and what was worse, I hadn't developed any prospects.

Maybe I am making a mistake, I thought. But I am thirty-six and I am making the equivalent of $120 a month. After a certain point this will be it, unless I make a change. I have to quit teaching.

But, to make it even worse, I don't have any reason or energy to go down to the office today. I decided to make a cold call on Preston. I needed a telephone! Since I didn't think I would need my computer, I rode my bike over to the Youyi.

The ghost lady, Mrs. Newhouse, answered the door with a tight smile, invited me in and asked me to have a seat in one of her straight backed pseudo-Colonial American "antique" style chairs. This whole fucking apartment gave me the creeps. I must have disturbed Preston's nap and what was even stranger the Ghost Lady didn't try to screen me. I sat for about five minutes in their dusty living room listening to whispering. Their voices modulated as though they were arguing, but I couldn't quite make out about what.

Finally Preston came out looking half asleep and disheveled. I apologized for coming unannounced but since I hadn't seen him in a couple of weeks I was just wondering, "... Since we installed the software, I haven't heard from you. Are Paul and Hanna learning how to use Quick Rabbit? Have you produced any documents for your business yet?"

"We have, Nathaniel, thank you for asking." Nathaniel? Come to think of it, this apartment reminds me of the *House of the Seven Gables*. "Yes, we are using your product. Although business has been slow. Yes. Things have been slower." He paused here to gather his thoughts. It isn't nice to wake an old man from a nap, but he should pay his bills.

"I might have been a bit too optimistic as to how fast we would move," he said. "But we will succeed; there is no doubt about that."

"I've been slow too," I said. "Things are cyclical, I guess."

"Yes," He was laboring as he breathed and I was a little concerned. "Cyclical. It is cyclical."

"I just thought..."

"You know Nathaniel, most of my organization's focus has been devoted to finding that sacred stone that we talked about. My sources tell me that it has been stolen."

"Stolen from whom?"

"Well – it has changed hands several times. In fact, it has been here in Beijing, maybe even here in the Northwest part of the city. We actually almost had it. But something happened and...and we lost it."

"You mean you were going to steal it?"

"Well – no. I don't know any of the details. I am not involved with that end of the operation! But it was at the train station not long ago. Imagine right downtown." He paused and looked up for a minute. "Something happened, some kind of scuffle on the platform and it was left unwatched and we lost it."

"Oh." Naturally what else can he be talking about? Scuffle on the platform? When the East Germans grabbed me? There was nothing in his voice or eyes that indicated he thought I was the "scuffler."

"We think it has been taken by foreigners."

"Foreigners?" My eyes went Buckwheat-wide.

"Yes – non-Chinese. Probably Eastern Europeans, Communists." He said that last word ominously. How much did he know? I really couldn't tell, but he didn't give me any suspicious looks. "Anyway I'll keep in touch about the rest of that order. Keep an ear and an eye out for the sacred tablet. It might be a ruse. I think it never left Beijing."

"Why?"

"It is what I feel when in prayer."

"Really?"

He nodded, and gave me a deep pregnant look. I was pretty sure that his informant was somebody other than God. "Others say it is on a train heading across Russia. I believe the train was a ruse. If we can pinpoint who has it we still might be able to get our hands on it."

He stopped and I said, "Wow."

"There will be a lot of money changing hands if we find it." He tried to work his eyebrows up and down roguishly, eyebrows too bushy to move, so it looked like he was just twitching. At that point I wanted to impress upon him that theological arguments were not working with me, so I cut to the cash.

"Speaking of money, Preston, you owe my company $700."

"Yes, of course." I caught him unawares with that, and he stood up red in the face and it looked like he was in pain. After a couple of seconds to catch his breath he limped over to his roll-top desk (another phony piece of Americana oddly out of place in this hemisphere) and wrote out a check from the First Liberty Bank of Bartlesville, Oklahoma. I did a double-take. It was made out for the whole amount, $3500.

"Thank you," I said. He post-dated it by almost a week.

"I made it out for next Monday because I have to take care of a few technical issues on the transfer."

"No problem. I'll get the other units to you by next week." It was more than I expected. "Thanks. Let me know if you need any technical help with your computers. I'll be glad to help out."

"And I'll listen for word about the stele."

"That is wonderful. We'll keep in touch."

Fuck you, I thought as I left. It wasn't so bad really, although – could he be part of some organization that would be thinking about heisting a Chinese train? Is this what Dagmar was transporting, what they were loading onto that refrigerated box car? Shit, how dumb can I be? They will figure out that I was involved with Dagmar. It was me on the platform; how can they not know that?

He's either fucking with me or someone is fucking with him. The second possibility worried me more.

Dexter. Maybe none of them could add two and two. Them? I am them! And I seem to be even stupider than any of them.

Anyway, as with most situations after 4 PM, it called for a drink, so, since I was at the Youyi compound anyway, I headed over to the downstairs bar.

Harold, the fat PhD from England, was there as usual with Gregor and Rennie and some older guy I didn't recognize. They hadn't seen me yet...

"Nate, my friend, come over!" Gregor stood up and walked toward me to make sure I didn't get away, even though I was already around the corner when he spoke.

"See! I knew you always avoid me! Why?" It was a good question. "Have I ever stolen from you? Or betrayed a confidence?"

"No. I'm just shy, Gregor. That's all." He looked hurt, but Gregor was always on stage.

"I think it is something else," he said. "But I don't know what." I shrugged.

"So what happened?" asked Mikku.

"Well, Gregor will remember this, but I'll repeat it for you, Mikku."

"Come and join us," said Harold. He had a dissipated, pessimistic, droll style that was almost too stereotypical to take seriously. The English need to be sure of their place in the world, I guess, particularly when they are abroad. Harold told funny, horrible stories about being stuck in an oppressive, English "public" school, where he lost his lower class cockney accent along with his cherry asshole no doubt. Erika had once told Molly that Harold led a monastic life, but someone else (Was it you, Gregor?) said that he had a "hot" Chinese boyfriend. I really don't want to know any of this shit. I am not a sophisticated "café intellectual" who likes to trade secrets and gossip. I'm kind of dull when I think about it, happy to read a book by myself.

Anyway, I had nothing else to do that afternoon, and looked forward to a beer, so I joined the table.

"Nate, this is Jorgen," said Rennie. "He's from Norway and is working on a geologic survey in Western China." We exchanged pleasantries and I told him, "I work for a company that makes software that models mineral mining and earthquake probabilities, International Tectonic Measurement Systems."

No visible recognition. In fact, Jorgen looked really loaded. So much for a sales pitch. I just felt lucky with Preston's check in my pocket so I thought I'd ask.

"I specialize in the top," he said.

"The top of what?" I asked. I looked at Harold and wondered if he was the "bottom."

"Surface rocks, geologic history." He paused. "Do the girls who work here, are they…"

"No," Gregor said.

"Not the ones in uniform anyway," I said. "I'd stay away from them."

Harold looked at me, half annoyed as if I were hijacking his mark. "Yes, anyway, this fellow came in last year and started flirting with one of the girls here," he said. "Real innocent at first, but the Chinese they don't know how to say no – really NOO!" Harold put on his schoolmaster's face. "Believe me, I know about flirting in secret." He fell into a brief faux-swoon. "But this man – he kept at it and at it and soon, the police came. They took him to an office around here somewhere and he didn't come back."

"Do you think he is in the Gulag?" Jorgen asked, suddenly a little more sober.

"No. No. He just got a talking to. But…that must have been unpleasant. I wish that was all I had to worry about. I would get much worse than a talking to!" Harold gave a little pantomime phony-fainting.

"So how did you meet these losers, Jorgen?" I indicated the present company.

"Harold and I go way back."

"You know I was here five years ago for the Pierre Trudeau visit. I stayed on to sight-see and we met up near Xining (西宁) wasn't it?"

"Yes. It's a small country if you're not Chinese," said Harold.

"Xining is in Tibet," I said.

"That's what I meant about it being a small country." We all laughed. "Jorgen has an interesting story. Tell them what you told me," said Harold.

"I am just afraid I'll get a talking to." Jorgen was pouting a little, sneaking a look at the vapid young barmaid in the over-sized doorman's uniform.

"No, we are all comrades. Right, Nate," said Gregor.

"Waiguoren," I said.

"What," asked Jorgen. "Oh – Waiguoren – foreigners of course." Jorgen looked as though someone slapped him.

"Speaking of foreigners," said Rennie. "Isn't that the guy who was dancing with your wife the other night?"

"Well, she's not actually..." I turned around and there was Dexter, pretending he didn't see us – or me.

"Yes – that was the guy," said Gregor, laughing, "The American James Bond."

"Yeah. Or maybe Matt Helm. It was pretty weird wasn't? Anyway Mikku -"

He looked over and "saw" us, so I waved him over.

"Dexter! Are you moving your office over to the fun part of town now?"

"Hello, Nate." He looked very embarrassed to see me. "What's going on?"

"We're just sitting around shitting bulls – You?"

"Oh...Nothing really...I am...I hear there is a great gift shop around here somewhere."

Dexter's handsome, blank face struggled mostly successfully against the urge to express any interior feelings. No surprise to see me, yet his cheeks did redden for just a second. I knew then, I knew I was losing her to him.

"I want to get an authentic Chinese seal for a friend."

Friend?

"I was told they sell very good quality seals here – at the Friendship Hotel, I mean." He was shaking his head, agreeing with himself.

Harold stood up. "I know just what you are looking for. Let me show you where the shop is. It is in the back in another building actually."

"Yeah, it's behind the pool. But Dexter, why don't you join us for a drink first?" I said. He looked uncomfortable and I wanted to enjoy it.

"No – no. Thank you. No, I can find it."

"Please!" Harold insisted. "It will be my pleasure – I've been sitting in this bar for the last four hours. I need to stretch my legs. Sometimes, it can all be so boring. I've heard all of the stories anyway."

I thought, is he kidding? I know Harold just wants to pump Dexter for details of how he was cuckolding me – or would be if Molly was actually my wife. I knew he would live on those stories for the rest of the semester.

"Thanks, I appreciate it." Dexter looked over at me, very sheepishly. "Well – say hi to Molly for me, Nate."

"Yeah, of course I will. But you probably see her as much as I do now that she is working at the American Embassy."

"Oh I don't get to see her that much. She is teaching and…"

You fucking prick!

"Well, say hi to Molly when you run into her," I said sarcastically. Gregor snickered.

"Dexter – Is that right? American embassy – how fascinating! I am Harold, of course we met the other night up on the rooftop bar I think. Let's go find the shop. I actually know quite a bit about seals. Are you looking for Qing or something older…" Harold led him away.

"What a creep," exclaimed Rennie.

"Do you think so?" I looked at Rennie and worked very hard not to look at him the way Dexter was looking at me. Gregor was a rock for a change.

"Who's Molly? Will I get in trouble if I talk to her too?" said Jorgen. We all laughed.

"She is Nate's wife," said Gregor. "She is the most beautiful woman in Beijing." He said it with a tone of Slavic awe, like when Serbs talk about the Battle of Kosovo.

"Fuck you and your 'Slavic Awe'," sputtered Gregor. "When Serbs talk about Kosovo, my left nut gets a tingle. That's Slavic Awe."

"Give me a break," I said.

Jorgen was amused by all of this, even as he watched me catch Rennie give me a look of pity and saw how calmly I took that.

"I tried to give you the pity look too," Gregor said while trying to hold in a laugh.

"You have an interesting story, Jorgen?" I was desperately trying to change the subject.

"I just got back from the west – Muslim country – Xinjiang. There are uranium deposits up where I was, almost right on the Russian border. It is wild and where I was there were no people. But on the old maps, there are villages where now – nothing…We had no detailed maps, current maps anyway, certainly nothing geologic, and so our first task was to survey the area."

He took another drink. I couldn't tell what his state of mind was at this point, but he had seen something and it scared him.

"We spent about six weeks surveying. I had a local team who only spoke Chinese, but they were very good surveyors and flashing numbers is all you need to survey actually. We had hand signals that worked well for that. We all slept in the back of a pickup truck, in sleeping bags, under the stars, way out there. It was cold at night."

Jorgen took a drink and looked around at us as if wondering about something. He continued.

"After a few days it was pretty clear what I was seeing, but still, I didn't want to jump to conclusions. The ground was burnt. The pattern was jumbled at first. But as I mapped it out, it became clear that the burns were concentric and the center point was burnt the worse, in fact it was covered with modules of melted sand, little balls of glass. The burns went out from that point for almost a kilometer. That focal point was a huge uranium ore deposit."

"So did the uranium blow up?" asked Rennie.

"Uranium doesn't 'blow up.'" Jorgen was laughing and Rennie looked annoyed and then Gregor suddenly smiled.

"KABOOM! - hey, Molly – come in, come in." Gregor got up like a Central European gentleman. "POW! Molly, we are pretending to fire big bombs. Would like to join us?" I turned around and there she was. She smiled painfully as she walked over.

"Hey." She looked like she was trying to compose herself. "You never come over here in the afternoon," she said almost accusingly. I shrugged.

"Gregor, I think you might be right," said Jorgen.

"I told you. Molly, this is Jorgen," said Gregor.

Molly looked at Jorgen and said, "Hello." She stood next to our table, making no move to sit, like she was trying to remember something. "Bombs! Jesus! Did you hear about the bombing on the Trans-Siberian?" We all looked blankly at her. "It happened a few days ago, right after the train left Irkutsk. Apparently it was a robbery or something."

"Which train? When did it leave Beijing?" asked Rennie.

"I don't know." The bottom fell out of my stomach.

"How did you find out?"

"Oh, somebody at the Embassy told me."

"Please join us, Molly," Jorgen said.

"No. No. Thank you, I have to..." She turned to me. "I wanted to get some corn and tomatoes. We have to start eating healthy again." She looked at me like she was telling me the most important secret of her life. "The market across the street has a better selection than ours does sometimes. I took a cab today Nate. I just could not face the bus."

"You're making money, honey. Enjoy it," I said.

"Bring me another Bloody Mary," said Jorgen.

"Here," Gregor grabbed Jorgen's money. "Let me go get them – the service is so slow. Molly, are you sure you won't join us? I can get you something?"

"No, no thanks. I know, it's just...it isn't the money. It is the people at the embassy. Some of them have never been on a bus in China. They are afraid of China. I don't want to be like them. I hate it all sometimes." She rubbed my cheek.

I think that moment was the last time Molly and I really loved each other. We really were a good fit. But we were both beginning to realize it was too late.

"Not everybody is that way," said Rennie, our man of the people! "It is just the bureaucrats." Even if Rennie was a little dumb, he had his moments.

"No. No...no more taxis, no more crappy food." She looked at me. I looked back at her. I think we were both scared of something at that moment, mainly because for that brief moment we both knew we had something to lose. "You'll be home for dinner?"

"Yeah – I got my bike – it's parked right in front. Why don't you take it? I'll jog home. I'll be there in an hour or so." We continued to stare at each other.

She moved close to me and whispered, "Don't let me become like them, Nate. Please?" She kissed me on my cheek and left.

"Is everything alright?" asked Rennie.

"Yeah, fine," I said. Gregor returned with the drinks.

"Anyway, as I was saying…" Jorgen took a long drink of his fortified tomato juice. "Um, that's good. She is very beautiful, Nate." He toasted me. "I actually found a villager who spoke English. I couldn't believe it. You know how primitive a Chinese peasant can look. I mean beaten down, bags for clothes, almost no teeth, wrinkles the size of canyons even when they are in their twenties."

"Yes – almost as bad as Albanians," Gregor said.

"I did not say that!"
"Yes you did. Yes you did."
"Maybe, I did. I read too much Serb propaganda."

"Well – this one looked worse than that. He said he learned English during the Cultural Revolution. They sent a teacher out there from the city. What a shitty assignment that must have been. He spoke pretty well; at least he knew a lot of words. He said that in the early 1970s, there was a surface mine at the center of 'the burnings.' He didn't know what kind of mine, but obviously…"

"Yes. Uranium," said Gregor.

"Well, according to what I could fathom from his story, because the details seemed foggy to him, and of course his English a bizarre mix of Russian, Chinese, and Turkish, (along with English of course). Anyway the Russians moved some troops in and took over the mine. It was just a big hole in the ground, dug with picks and shovels. They had been carrying the ore out with donkey carts. The Russians forced all the Chinese workers out and said that it was in Soviet Territory."

Nobody blinked, as he sipped his drink.

"So Mao brought up a division and surrounded the Russians." He took another drink. "The Russians had done their homework because they dropped paratroopers all around the Chinese and had them trapped. Inside – out. Cut off and surrounded on all sides. No way out for the Chinese."

No one said anything.

"Mao – Lin Biao (林彪) – I don't know. When did Lin die?"

"Who is Lin Biao?" asked Rennie.

"'71 or '72. '72 I think," I said. I looked around – shrugs – no one was sure. "He was a Chinese general who revolted against Mao, Rennie."

"Mao or somebody dropped an atomic bomb in the middle of it. It killed all the Russians and all the Chinese. But he got his mine back. It was contaminated so he couldn't use it. They are thinking about using it again. World Bank is paying for it and for me…so drink up." He lifted his glass.

We didn't say anything for a while.

"It makes sense," I said. "Maybe that's why Nixon went to China. To congratulate Mao."

"Do you really think the Americans know?" Rennie asked.

"You mean does the United States Government know? More to the point, did Nixon and Kissinger know?" said Jorgen.

"And when did they know it!" Rennie smiled at me. "It's Watergate all over again," he said excitedly.

"That would be pretty hard to hide," I said.

"But satellites weren't as good back then," said Jorgen. "Who knows – who knows? Glitches? Still, it seems unlikely that it could have stayed secret."

"Well, we're all set," said Harold. Dexter walked behind him carrying a wrapped box. "Your friend will really like it. It is in the Song style and that is really the high point in Chinese calligraphy and art."

"Well, thank you. It was nice of you to take the time."

"It was no problem."

"Oh, Dexter. Molly was just here."

"Oh, really?" His face remained stone, even as it lost a bit of color.

"You just missed her," I said. "I forgot to say hi. I'll tell her tonight."

Chapter Twenty-Two

"So that's what this is all about," said Gregor. "You son of a bitch! You've been playing all of us!"

"What are you talking about? You were there. This is an old rumor. We've all heard it."

"The A-bomb? No, not that! So what? The Russian and Chinese throw nukes at each other out in the middle of the desert. Nobody cares." Gregor smiled but Mikku stared blankly off. "No, I am talking about the stele! That's what the fucking American Jesus missionary tried to steal at the train station. You screwed up a lot of plans that day! No wonder he doesn't pay you."

I looked at Mikku. I don't know why I just started talking like that. I guess it was her Nipponese "Truth Grip" that got it out of me.

"I don't know where it is. I don't know anything about it really. That American, the old man who lives on the north side, I met him because I was trying to sell him software and he just brought it up. I guess his missionary friends want it," I said.

"I see." Gregor looked at me and smiled. "Let's not tell anybody."

"You couldn't keep a secret if your life depended on it," I said.

"You are wrong. We still don't know where the stele is, do we? Am I right?"

"You are right," I said, technically not lying.

"Maybe one of us find! Whoever find we split equally – what do you think?" Gregor was smiling much too happily.

"Are you going back to the Youyi from here?" I asked, making it clear I wanted no deal.

***

"Well," said Mikku, "Where do you want to do?" Where do I want to do? That was a cute little slip. We had left Gregor at a bus stop that connected right to the Friendship Hotel. He was unhappy that I didn't take him all the way home in the cab, but mostly because I didn't agree to split the stele with him. Since I was already pretty sure I knew where it was, (or at least who had it) I didn't really need him. Mostly though, I didn't trust the Croat to keep quiet. Although why I mentioned it in front of him, I'll never know, other than trying to impress Mikku.

To shine him on, I asked him what he planned to do. Gregor said he was going to figure out who was talking to Preston. He would show me, he said, that he could be valuable to me in many ways. Gregor had contacts – and it was certain that not everybody Preston dealt with was dealing with him straight. That bothered me a little, but Gregor said he would keep it quiet, for me not to worry, that he knew how to keep a secret.

But Mikku's question – "Where do I want to do?" – was another fork in the road that I would be sorry about, no matter what I chose. Stop at the PLO Embassy and let Mikku off or invite her to come over to the PLO Mission apartment where I was staying just down the block. Where to do? To do or not to do. Where's the doobie, doobie do! I didn't see Ibrahim's staff car where it was usually parked in the semi-circular driveway on the side of the Mission. Women always want me to decide this stuff. I decided to get out there with her and come into the Embassy.

The reception desk was empty as usual as we walked into the foyer. This was actually the worst possible decision, because I could see Mikku was pissed and since I was in the Mission Proper, I couldn't just flop on the sofa and snooze, and certainly the two of us sneaking into a bedroom was not a good idea either. I never get it right; something is wrong with me and I can't figure out what it is.

We sat stiffly on the couch, separated by all of the space available. She offered me a hard candy from a jar on the coffee table. The clock in the hallway was awfully loud.

"You have definitely lost your job with the Canadian company?"

"Definitely," I said.

She looked at me, a little blankly and impatiently as if to say, if you are not going to talk, then why did you come in here in the first place? So I told her how I lost my job, three weeks ago.

Fucking garlic chopping again! I turned and there she was lying next to me. I didn't even hear her come in, and I know I didn't fall asleep for a couple of hours after I got home. I shook Molly.

"What?" She woke quickly and looked scared.

"What time did you get home last night?"

"Late – what do you care?" She lay facing away and slapped my hand away from her pajama-covered ass.

"Well, what were you doing?" I asked her.

"I was with some people from the embassy. Americans. I don't know if you remember but we're Americans. At least I am. That means..." She turned toward me and when I saw the look in her eyes I realized she was – gone mostly.

"Fuck you," I said, morosely.

"No. FUCK YOU!! I am sick of living in your little 'Hero of the Third World' fantasy. Why don't you start wearing your little button that the Party gave you in Louyang?"

They did give me a button – a gold-trimmed lapel pin – Renmin Laoshi (人民老师, People's Teacher). I was kind of proud of it.

"...These are just poor people who want to come to America...every one of them – don't you understand? The only thing you have that is worth anything is your passport. You are living in a dream world."

I didn't say anything.

"Why don't you go fuck one of them if you are so unhappy?" She stared at me and her eyes burned with tears.

I felt as if I were in free fall. It must have shown.

"Oh – I'm sorry." She gave me her coldest smile. "I am sure you already have. How is that going for you?"

"What are you talking about..." She looked at me and I stared back for what seemed like a long time, then she turned back over.

"Let me sleep," she said.

I lay there with my eyes open. There was a knock and I got up to answer the door.

"Who is that?" she yelled from the bed.

"I'll get it!"

It was Pan. "I came by bus this time. Can I come in the door?" She was sluttishly dressed, with heavy dark eye make-up, a see-through yellow blouse and very tight pair of jeans that rode up both in front and back. As I stood there she gave me her sad, Taiwan-soap-opera bedroom eyes and I tied my robe tighter and I nodded toward the bedroom. She gave me a look of pleased surprise and then something like hatred as she realized I meant, "There is someone in there." I guided her into the living room.

"We have a new boss and he wants to see everyone right away," she said, quickly recovering her composure.

Pan looked worried now. I asked, "Why did you take the bus?"

"No more car. Lin is gone too."

Oh shit. "Let me get dressed." I turned around and there was Molly. "Oh Pan, this is Molly, ah, my wi...ah...girlfriend."

"Oh, hello," said Molly, yawning and not looking at Pan. "How do you know Nate?"

"I am the secretary at the ITMS joint venture," Pan said proudly.

Molly looked at Pan, who was dressed like a not-so-prosperous Hong Kong prostitute and then at me.

"I have to go to the Embassy today. I've got some paperwork I have to finish," she said.

"It's Saturday," I said, thinking, *you teach third grade, you don't work in the Embassy either.*

"Is it? It won't be very hard work then, will it? I'm going to go take a shower." She grabbed her towel, flip-flops and shampoo and headed across the courtyard to the public shower.

I wanted to get out of there before she came back, so I left her a note saying I had to do some paperwork as well, at my office. I knew she would think I was just playing tit for twat, but I was pretty scared suddenly about the whole thing down the drain, my job, visa, and probably girlfriend. I'd been in China so long I had begun to take it for granted that I could stay forever. I threw on some clothes and Pan and I headed out the door. We got out to the front of the school just as the bus was arriving. It wasn't full for a change.

"I've never met your girlfriend before," said Pan. "She is pretty." She looked for a reaction, but I gave her none.

"What is going on at the office?" I asked.

"Oh. New boss. He is Indian."

"What happened to Tai?"

"I think he resign – something bad in Canada."

We got there and like she said, there was an Indian man in Tai's office looking at the ledgers. He had brought his own assistant, a Chinese woman from Hong Kong who would not speak Mandarin. All she said to everyone (in English) was "Continue with your work. Ravi will be here through next week."

I tried to insist to her that I talk to him, because I was in a bit of a bind for housing and I needed some decisions.

"I am sorry," was all she said.

I tried to grab him as he left for lunch but all he said was "I understand your problem. We will settle it all on Monday." Then he left. His assistant left word that everyone was to leave immediately and that the office was to be closed for the rest of the day and absolutely no one was to enter until Monday morning.

Ling Ye was not anywhere to be seen.

The next morning, Molly and I had sex, one of those roll over and mount up before she had time to think about it jobs. At first she just lay there looking off over my shoulder. But she became enthused as we went along. She wasn't enthused with me, though, I knew that. But I knew she was enjoying getting fucked. It was a relief for me too. She even smiled afterward for the first time in a while. Later, in her goodbye note, she would call it rape.

Molly and I talked or at least I tried to her and that was a mistake. I tried to explain that things were up in the air at ITMS, that there was a new boss and I couldn't get him to talk about the "situation." She was very pissed.

"You mean he was right there and you let him tell you nothing about what is going on? How could you do that?" She jumped up and I looked for something to use as a shield against whatever was coming.

I was too ashamed to tell her that I felt that things were so tenuous that if I insisted on an answer he might give me the one I didn't want. I was afraid to say that the Indian's mood was so negative that I didn't dare push him, that he had already fired my boss Tai, and Lin the driver and others. There were fewer people in the office. I didn't see Ling there at all yesterday.

I wanted to pack but I didn't know what I was packing for. Molly and I could move into a hotel, but we only had enough money to last two, maybe three weeks, living reasonably, and still make it to Hong Kong and home. There are some cheaper hotels south of town. But then there were visas and hotels aren't supposed to let you stay there without one. The school stamped us an extension that runs out at the end of October, but we had to be out of the apartment by Monday.

It was early afternoon and I was thinking it would be nice to watch a football game on TV. Somebody knocked again. I didn't have a shirt on and hadn't combed my hair but I didn't care, so I opened the door.

Rou Ming, one of my colleagues from the English Training Center, stood there looking like a prison chaplain doing his grimmest duty. Behind him stood an American married couple, evident from the perky "Hi!" they said in unison. Rou stepped back behind them like a shamed informer.

The couple wore big smiles of relief that screamed out, "Finally a white face!" They looked as though they expected me to hug them. They seemed to think that they were the rescue mission that had finally arrived in the nick of time. I just stood there and didn't invite them in.

"We just wanted to meet you. I'm Kathy and this is Mark. We are staying at the Friendship Hotel -"

"Boy, there is a misnomer!" said Mark.

Kathy laughed on cue. "I guess we are moving in here next week." She tried to look past me and was smiling tightly.

"So you are going back huh?" Mark said. "You must be excited. How long have you been here?"

"Um…"

"We just wanted to see the apartment. We want to make sure it is OK, in case we have to make any changes," Kathy said.

"I've talked to some people and they said you have to get things done right away…" Mark stepped up, *basso profundo*, speaking very candidly, man to man, seeming sure that we intuitively understood each other, "…because if you put things off, they will pretend not to understand you and you will get the run-around. You have to let them know you mean business from the beginning." Mark was treating Rou Ming like a dumb porter and not a member of the English language faculty who could understand exactly what he was implying.

Molly came to the door and greeted them. She was completely dressed and her hair was combed. She even wore lipstick and eyeliner. How is that possible so fast? She was very happy to meet them and invited them in and showed them around and took them to lunch. I stayed home and took a nap.

The next morning, I wanted to get to work when the doors opened, so I was at the Minzu Hotel having breakfast at 7:30. I only had one decent white shirt, jacket and tie, so I paid almost 20 kuai (块) to have them laundered and dry cleaned at the Youyi yesterday, extra for quick delivery. I didn't have any decent slacks so I took a chance and went for the cowboy businessman's look and wore blue jeans. I knew I looked like a sleaze-ball, but that can be a good look in Beijing. Someone left a copy of the *South China Morning Post* on their table so I snatched it before the waiter could clear it off.

Something drew me to the business section and I looked up ITMS's closing price for last Friday. Fifty cents! Holy shit it was more than twelve dollars a couple of weeks ago.

This was not good.

Shit.

"Hello, Nate."

It was Serena. The Minzu Hotel was the home of the Kone office, and I was still on great terms with the wait staff there, from my time with working as Serena's "buffer".

"Serena!" I said, a bit too enthusiastically, but she gave me a wide, almost sexy smile anyway. "How's business?" I tried to put on a bluff, hale and hearty face while I got up and pulled a chair out for her. "Do you have a minute to sit? Let me get you some coffee."

"No, no, well only for a minute." She sat down and looked at me carefully. "Business is slow. I had to let Andy go."

"Really? That's too bad," I said. She looked at me and smiled. That ended any inquiries about a job.

"I heard about the trouble at ITMS. Has it affected you?"

Trouble? "Well my boss, Tai Sengxian, who hired me, has been replaced. In fact, I've got a meeting with the new boss this morning."

"Oh." She looked me up and down. I never dressed this well when I worked for her, yet I still looked like a small town used car salesman. "You don't know, do you?"

"Know what?"

"Your boss was arrested for fraud in Vancouver last week. Apparently his techniques for raising capital were so egregious that even the Vancouver Stock Exchange was ashamed and that is the most lax securities market in the world."

I just sat there looking dumb.

"It is really stupid because he did a lot of crooked things, but the most obvious thing according to the press was getting caught trying to pass off 'entertainment' expenses as capital investment. It was in the *Post* last week. Apparently it involved prostitution."

"Really?" Tao Yuan, I thought.

"What are you trading at today?" she asked.

"Point five," I said.

"Ouch! You didn't know, did you?" I could see deep disappointment in her eyes that I was so ignorant of something so important to me. I really wasn't cut out for business, I guess. She stood up. "Well, good luck."

"Listen if you need anybody to clean up your data or…"

"As I said, we are a little slow. But keep in touch. Let me know where you land."

***

I walked into the Fuxing office at 9 AM. The Indian guy, Rav something, and his Hong Kong girl Friday waited in Tai's office. Pan was wearing old People's Liberation Comradette work clothes (set off by iridescent cherry-colored lipstick), and Ling was in an old Mao suit that fit his pudgy body like a bulky leotard. They were moving files up the stairs from the storage closet on the first floor. They ignored me.

"Hello," I said.

"Yes. We've been waiting for the last hour. Is this when you usually come to work?"

"The office doesn't open until nine," I said. "Does it?"

"Um huh. I understood you were to provide some leadership here. That is what Tai said in his report."

"Well Ling Ye is the..."

"I know who he is." He shook his head at his assistant. She handed him a file. "Is this your customer?" I took the file. Right on the top was a photostat of a check that Preston wrote for $3500. It had been returned by the Oklahoma bank. It was stamped "Insufficient funds."

"It bounced?"

"Yes. Bounced." His lip curled as he took the file back. "Where is your leads list?"

Leads? "I have a meeting with a Mr. Qu from Digital Equipment – oh – and Chuck Yeager Jr. – He runs the Rockwell office here. I met him in the Jiangguo bar and we...but now that I think about it, we left it open..."

"What about Chinese firms?"

"Chinese firms?" Shit, I thought, Tai said for me to concentrate on foreign firms. "Don't you think we would need to adjust the price point when we began to target the local companies?"

"I see." He looked at his desk for what seemed to be forever, moving paper around. "We have had some financial setbacks in the company. We need to make cuts. I'm sorry, but you could make this easier by offering your resignation."

"In other words, I am one of the cuts." I took a breath and said "fuck" quietly to myself. "I have made plans. I quit another job on the expectation that I had this one. I have a wife."

"I am sorry. Business..."

"It is not right!"

"Please don't raise your voice. I will make sure you get a good reference."

As I left his office Ling pulled me aside. We walked out into the vestibule, which stunk of turpentine, and old paint. He had a proposal for me.

"You can work as my cousin's agent," he said. "Sell 'Red Tassels.' Here." He handed me a blurry mimeographed spec sheet which was too technical for me to read (even if it was in English). But it had a fuzzy black and white picture of a hand-held surface to air missile.

"You sell to 'Arab friends.' My cousin works for Liberation Army factory. Excess capacity. Big commission." Ling gave me his card – which of course was identical to mine except it had his name on it.

I told Ling I would think about it.

Pan looked at me. Her heavy eye make-up was running.

"What is the matter?" I asked.

"I am afraid I'll never see you again." Pan handed me two letters on my way out and ran into the bathroom.

> Mon Sept 7
> Dear Darling Nathan,
>
> I am in Irkutsk on Lake Baikal. I dream about you every night, and even more so now that I am in the most romantic place in the world. The nights are cold already here and I dream of piling the quilts up and...you know what I dream!
>
> I never thought that I would fall in love with a place. I never thought that a lake could completely enchant me but it has happened. You know we Germans are nature lovers at heart, but I have never experienced anything like Lake Baikal. I hope that it takes a month to fix my train. I suppose that I could have them unseal it and transfer the contents to another car, but it will only be trouble for me if I do. For once I will follow orders and sit by the lakeside as the summer draws to a close, drink vodka and dream of our time together, Nate.

An American woman has just arrived and has been very curious about me and my train car. At first I liked her, she was very nice. But she continues to stay here, when she could have taken any one of the trains that come through every day. She has bought me dinner twice and I don't want to eat with her anymore. I have made a pact with one of the Siberians here, an old man who looks like he was alive during Genghis Khan's time. (The Mongolian king is supposed to be buried on one of the islands in the Lake.) The old man warns me when she is on the porch overlooking the lake. When she goes to her room, then I go out. I don't answer my door unless I get the secret knock – (Beethoven's fifth of course) – He won't take money from me. It is too bad he is so old no? Thanks to him I have avoided her.

Next day

The train is fixed and we leave tomorrow. The American woman is coming? I don't know, now she is hiding from me. And more unusual, how many outfits did she pack? I never saw her in the same clothes. Last time I saw her she was reading the black book at lunch yesterday. Perhaps it is a Bible, or perhaps a fashion manual for Lucifer's wife. I'll write again as we get closer to Moscow.

Dag

Sept 20 Omsk

My Glorious Lover!

Greetings from the great prison town of Omsk. The Czar sent Dostoyevski here after commuting his death sentence. I know he is your hero, so I walked around breathing the air he breathed. Still, it is a dreary town and we stopped for only a day.

The big news is the train was robbed and most of what I was carrying in the freight car was stolen. They fired a bomb under the lokomotive. It knocked the train off the tracks. I was sleeping and I fell from my bed. I hit my head and it is only today that my headache has ended.

The bandits came into our car. They searched me and threatened to kill if I didn't tell them where "It" was. I didn't know what "It" was I told them. They were supposed to be local tribesmen but I knew they were more than that – too many blue eyes wearing clean turbans. I think my bump on the head saved me. I really did understand what they wanted, but I was so confused from my bump and they either believed me or thought perhaps I was too strong to break. (Don't laugh, look how long I held out from you!) They didn't have much time and didn't have control of their own soldiers. They took money from people with random and left – no one was killed although the engineer was badly hurt from the bomb.

So now I am here with nothing to escort. I have been filling out paperwork saying yes I was transporting this and that and no it was not mine. I only told them what I had to and nothing more. It is all officially stolen!

So I am done. I don't know what to do. I will go on to Katrinburg – there I will choose. The railways go north or south from there.

It is so difficult to write you. I don't believe you will ever read this for one thing. But I know you were OK, that my country's agents didn't hurt you. A Mongolian working on the train watched it all and told me. Still sometimes I think I will never see you again even if I decide not to return to Berlin.

But the train robbery has freed me. (Either that or the bump on my head has made me a crazy woman!)

I wish you were lying next to me tonight,

Dag

Chapter Twenty-Three

"You can stay here as long as you want, my friend," said Ibrahim. He had walked in, catching Mikku and me sitting together, closely, as she read Dagmar's letter over my shoulder. The way he said it though, like he was answering a question I didn't ask, made me very uneasy.

Recent events suddenly overwhelmed me. I almost started sobbing, but quickly pulled myself out of it.

"I mean it, Nate. You can stay here. You don't have to leave China. You have been a source of strength to so many people, even if you don't know it..."

"I know it's trouble to have an American here..." I was fighting back tears again. Yasir Arafat's smiling face looked down from the wall. I was hideously embarrassed but I couldn't help it.

"Nonsense! We love America. Our only hope is that you will see the injustice that has been done. Americans are always welcome in Palestine." He put his big hands on my shoulders and turned me toward him to make sure I understood him. "You've never seen my pictures of the Chairman, have you? Here look at this. I will get some tea for us."

He put a big, thick, overflowing photo album on my lap and went into the kitchen. Ibrahim is a little fat now but when he was younger he looked like a tiger. There were pictures of him and his unit, in the Bekka Valley, standing on Roman ruins, and another lying behind a sand hill looking through binoculars. There were pictures in cities, in Beirut and Tunis and one standing over a sitting Arafat, who was looking at a map. Then we came to a series of marriage ceremony photos. It was his wedding pictures to a beautiful girl, a Christian obviously from the Church. She was still in Damascus, he told me, a kind of prisoner there or even a hostage perhaps. Arafat is standing off to the side in their wedding picture. There's him and the Chairman hugging and more with the Chairman at a meeting of some kind. Another meeting with Arafat and Ibrahim is starting to gain weight. A waving Arafat getting off a plane at the Beijing airport and then another, and then right in the middle of it – the bodies from Sabra and Shatila.

"When you are a soldier and you can't protect your own people, it is the greatest humiliation possible. I have been living with humiliation for a very long time," said Ibrahim as he gave me the tea.

Ibrahim was angry, but he took a deep breath and laughed. "I tell you the truth – to both of you. I have been afraid that you would be encouraged by Molly to leave me for another. Mikku – I have even been dieting, can't you tell? Don't I look like a movie star?" Ibrahim posed like an Indian film star, trying to make a joke, and we both tried to laugh but it only came out as lopsided grins.

"Yes," I said, "this can be contagious. Women are like lemmings, they tend to follow one another's folly," I said. Mikku rolled her eyes.

"What are you going to do?"

"This summer I had several offers to teach in other universities," I said. "Even the school for Politics and Diplomacy offered me a job. But now, that is all over, I think I am finished in China. I was greedy and it was my fault. I'll probably have to return to the US."

"It could be worse," Ibrahim said, glancing at the open photo album.

"I know."

We drank tea and reminisced about the past year. We talked about where I might find another teaching job and I tried not to obsess about the investigation, but that was all I could think about. Erika and Sandor were dead.

And Molly was gone, with another man. At first I thought it would be the sex I would miss, but now it was her friendship, our team of two that was no more. I told myself it was doomed from the start, foretold not to be. She'll get her ranch and a good life, and she will be happy. Or not. But that was no longer my story.

So it really is over.

"The US stock market crashed last week," said Mikku. "I didn't even realize it until today."

"I did," I said. "I was going to start looking for a job next week. They are already calling it 'The Crash of 1987,' in October just like 1929." I was beginning to wonder if I should go back at all – whether I should go someplace other than home.

"You will have no trouble – America will not be depressed." said Ibrahim, distracted, as he sorted the Embassy's mail. He handed me an envelope. "Someone in a black Hongqi brought this to the door earlier."

> Oct 12, 1987
> Dear Nate,
> I am in Yekaterinburg – you must know that place – where the Czar's family was killed – and I feel the same dread that Anastasia must have felt. The Soviets call the city Sverdlovsk but nobody else does – not even the people who live here!
> I am afraid again, Nate.
> I decided to abandon the train and am staying here in a very shabby hotel. I had the money for bribing, and I am keeping it. Let them figure out what to do with the empty freight car in Moscow. Someone is mad because they have nothing to sell in Switzerland. I want nothing to do with it. I am giving up my DDR citizenship. Remember we talked about where we would go? Tonight I leave on a truck. I have met a Turk. He is a good man, I think. I don't know but I can't stand this anymore.

> *I'm heading south – to Uzbekistan or Kyrgyzstan or*
> *maybe Tajikistan – I don't know. Some place where I can*
> *wear a burnoose and hide.*
>   *Nate – I'll wait for you.*
>   *Dag*

We didn't talk for quite a while. I put the letter in my pocket and neither of them asked about it. Mikku brought out the hot water and cups and the tray with four different containers of different teas. I poured hot water over the red tea into three cups while Mikku served it and Ibrahim sat silently, seemingly in no more of a mood to talk than I was. Mikku excused herself and left the room.

"Is he dead?"

He didn't answer me. He stood up and looked out the window at the gray day.

"Remember, I told you we should go to a nightclub? I think we should go – tonight."

I laughed, but Ibrahim didn't. I realized at that moment that I was in no position to argue. It occurred to me that I knew things that Ibrahim probably wished I did not know. I had been thinking about that too, but I had pushed it back. I didn't doubt his friendship, but I also knew that he was first of all a soldier.

"You said that it's out by the Great Wall?"

"Yes, I am surprised you remember after all that has happened."

"Sure," I said. I felt that now, this had to play out.

**

I walked back to the apartment and waved to Abdul, who was at his post next to the Mission's green Toyota Celica. He spoke neither English nor Chinese, so that was the extent of our relationship, which was more than fine with me.

I noticed the weather was changing – it was starting to get chilly. I took a deep breath and tried to relax. I wanted to change my clothes. If something is to happen, I want to be clean and look presentable, and not be caught with dirty or torn underwear. I decided to shower too. Unlike at the Institute, they have hot water all the time over here on Embassy Row, even for the auxiliary apartments.

For only being a mission, the PLO had a lot of pull with the Chinese. Ibrahim seemed pretty sure he could straighten out my problems if that is what I wanted. At least that is what he said. I got dressed. I was very careful in choosing my clothes. I had clean clothes that I had intended to save for my trip home, which I guess I was planning to make in the next couple of days. Maybe not.

Anyway I decided to wear them that night. I thought about walking back to Erika's apartment that night.

Oct 18

"Zev! Hey, when did you get back?" At that moment I was glad to see him. I thought, great, just what the party needs tonight! Zev was wearing a very large black hooded sweatshirt. The hood was up even though it was a warm evening.

"Hey, mate." He looked at me with puppy dog eyes that suddenly turned reptilian.

"What's the matter, Zev?"

"Sorry, Nathan." He pulled a Luger from inside his front pocket and very quickly got right up against me. "In there." He pushed me into the shower room.

"What are you doing?" He kept pushing me, past the woman's dressing room and into the shower itself.

"Turn around." Suddenly everything went slow motion and I vaguely began to see he wasn't fucking around and realized that I was about to die. I just looked at him. He is going to kill me, I thought. Without taking his eyes off of me, he slowly put down his suitcase and tote bag, and then pushed the gun into my face.

"I said turn around!" He hit me sharply on the side of the head with the butt of his gun. As I turned around to face the wall, I saw him out of the corner of my eye take a short, metal pipe out of his pocket and start to screw it on to the end of the gun. I made a grab for the gun but he punched me in the solar plexus and I went down on my knees, trying to breathe. "Don't look

up at me again." But I kept looking at him so he shrugged and pulled the hood back off of his head. He had no problem looking at me as he checked the clip and slapped it back in.

He spun me around and pushed me square with the wall and I heard the bolt on his gun click. My mind was completely blank. Then I heard a loud thump. I froze wondering if I was dying. I stayed still and so did time. I felt a chill on my neck.

"Kuai! Bang wo! (快! 帮我!) Quick! Help me!"

I turned around. Rashid was kneeling on Zev's back, using one hand to try and pull away the gun and the other to hold his face down. Zev wasn't letting go, so Rashid lifted up his arm and came down on Zev's head with what looked like a sock. I heard the same thump as before.

Rashid looked up at me as he pulled the gun out of Zev's hand. He seemed slightly annoyed at me as he stood up and handed me the gun.

"Kan ta! (看他!) Watch him."

He turned and walked quickly out of the shower room.

I looked at the gun. I didn't know if it was ready to fire. The little slide button on the side, the safety, is it on or off? I had heard the click before the thump so I assumed it was ready to fire. I aimed it at Zev.

Zev wasn't moving. I stood behind him so he would have to turn around if he tried to lunge at me. But then I thought about having my back to the door. I moved around above his head and pointed the gun at the top of his skull.

He was breathing. His hand moved. He opened his eyes and looked down at his feet. He didn't see me yet. He bent forward slowly groaning, reaching for the suitcase that was still standing up right where he left it.

"Don't move!"

He stopped and took a deep breath. He lifted his head and looked at me and then started to pull himself up. I kicked him in the head straight on, and my toe caught him right in the ear.

"I said don't move." I don't think he heard me. I was shaking so much that I didn't think I could hit him with a pistol shot from this range.

I heard a car just outside the door. Rashid looked around the corner and then both he and Ibrahim walked up quickly.

"I kicked him in the head (我踢了他的头)," I said.

"Good," said Ibrahim. Rashid began to pinion his hands with tape while Ibrahim searched him. Rashid finished with his hands, then he wrapped up his feet and connected them to the bound hands. Then he wrapped the electric tape around his head several times covering his mouth.

Ibrahim took the gun from me and Rashid searched his pockets and removed a wallet, some keys and a pocket knife.

He handed them to Ibrahim.

"That reminds me. Here," said Rashid. He smiled. It was my wallet. "It fell out of your pocket in the car. I was coming to give it to you when I saw the Zionist push you in here."

"Thank God I'm so careless," I said.

"Yes, praise him." Ibrahim picked up the suitcase.

"Erika," I said. I looked at Zev and his eyes widened. He shook his head, like he knew something.

"What's he saying?" Zev was gagged, and I bent down toward him.

"Never mind! Go see if the German woman is alright," said Ibrahim. "If not, just let the Chinese try and figure out what happened. But none of this happened. Understand? It is very important that you understand that!"

I nodded. Rashid and Ibrahim picked up Zev like a trussed-up goat. As they did, Zev looked at me, but I could not tell what his eyes said. Was it sadness, or fear or hate or was he trying to tell me something different? I wanted to take his gag off – but this was all beyond me now. They moved quickly. Zev and I kept looking at each other as they carried him out of the cement shower building. Ibrahim had backed the car right up to the entrance and they put him in the truck like an old rolled up rug and slammed it shut.

"Forget about this," Ibrahim said. "Tell no one. No one! You must understand that!"

"I am going to check on Erika," I said.

"Yes, do that. Take her to the Youyi. You never saw him. Don't drink too much."

They drove off.

As the car pulled away, I walked back into the shower and moved into the back and sat down against the wall. I had never been in here except in the early morning. It was usually very busy then. Empty now, the cement was cold and I was shivering even though the weather was pretty balmy. My gut hurt where Zev had hit me and the adrenaline was wearing off. I was gasping for breath. Everything that had just happened replayed in my head in slow motion. Even though I knew I should be dead, I felt strangely sad that I had kicked Zev so hard. I actually felt him go limp through my foot as it landed on his head.

This was all merely to prepare myself for what I would find in Erika's apartment. Ibrahim hadn't seen Zev's eyes like I did. Something was wrong. I pulled myself up and walked to the door and noticed my shoe was untied. As I bent down to tie it on the unfinished cement block set just inside the shower entrance, a bald white guy was just walking past. It was the teacher they hired to replace me! I stayed perfectly still. Now I remember him. Mark. Mark and Kathy, the teachers living in my old apartment. He looked toward me, but it was getting dark, so I guess he didn't recognize me. I remember standing up from tying my shoes and being particularly depressed as I watched Mark the American walk past me. He must have seen me, although I am sure he didn't realize I was a "foreigner," like him. He just missed witnessing an international kidnapping by about two minutes. I thought to call to him, but decided against it. I felt very lonely at that moment for some reason. I turned and started toward Erika's apartment. I remember I didn't walk the shortest way...

Chapter Twenty-Four

Showered and dressed in relatively clean clothes, I walked back to the main embassy building. I kept breathing deep and slow, and sat down on the sofa in the main reception room. Mikku came out and poured me some more tea. We didn't speak.

Then the door opened. Ibrahim came back in carrying an old beat-up leather suitcase, the same one that Zev had been carrying that night. I moved the tea cup, spilling some in the saucer, and Ibrahim set the suitcase carefully on the table. He took a key out of his pocket and opened it.

He removed a custom-fitted foam pad and there it was. I was surprised how small it was, a rough piece of stone about an inch and a half thick and maybe fifteen inches long and eight inches wide. The very old characters had been cut into the stone and were barely visible. They looked to be written in Great Seal style, like those on the ceremonial cauldrons they found in old tombs. I couldn't make heads or tails out of it other than recognize it as ancient Chinese. It was very irregular along all the edges, as though it was a fragment from the middle of a larger tablet.

"It looks like Zhou dynasty, but there have never been any steles from that period," said Ibrahim.

I had learned recently to never be surprised by what Ibrahim knew. He seemed to read my thoughts. "I've been reading about steles. The Syrian Embassy has a great library. I have a friend there."

"What does it say?"

"Something about a king, and a brother or some brothers and a river. It is very hard to follow and the characters are...the meaning seems very confusing. I never studied old Chinese."

"According to the old man at the Youyi, the missing stele fragment might tell something of Genesis," I said cryptically.

Ibrahim looked at me. "Possibly. But I don't really know."

"Why did he kill them for it?"

Ibrahim looked away in thought for a moment, seemingly about something else. "He was only interested in money, I'm sure. But..."

"You mean, he wasn't working for..."

"The Israelis? I don't think so," he said, "I think he is who he said he was. When I met him again that night at the Youyi Bingguan, I was sure he was Mossad, but now I don't think so."

"So, Erika had it?"

He looked at me hard. "Don't you know?"

"No. Well, yes. She hinted she had something from Dagmar. And this letter from Dagmar confirms it sort of." I showed him the letter. "I knew that the East Germans were trying to steal artifacts and smuggle them out of the country." I didn't mention that I saw Sandor walk away with the suitcase at the train station.

"Zev didn't need to kill you, did he? He could have lied to you and said she wasn't home and he could have escaped. By the time you found out they were dead, he would have been long gone, right?" He looked at me. "Unless he thought you knew."

"Thought I knew? Look - you know about the missionary Preston, who had heard something about it. Dagmar told me she was transporting rare antiquities, but she wasn't specific. Zev left for western China after Dagmar left. He told us he was going to work on a movie out in Xinjiang (新疆). The fucker! He probably blew up Dagmar's train too. I think she is OK. I hope you made him suffer when you..." I stopped and looked at the letter Ibrahim had given me. "It took Dagmar so long to get to Omsk. Her train was sabotaged then robbed. I don't know for sure he did it, but..."

Ibrahim smiled and put the stele down into the suitcase, looked at me and shook his head with wonder or disgust, which I wasn't sure. "This is yours. Your visa is up soon. When you leave here, please take it."

"What! And do what with it? What can I do with it?"

"People will kill for this; they will do much worse than that. The PLO wants nothing to do with it. It doesn't matter to me. I know where my grandfather's orange orchard is. It is not in China. I advise you to return it to the Chinese, but it's up to you. If you want to sell it, good luck."

He closed up the suitcase carefully.

"Let's go." It was already dark when we left the compound. Rashid had the car ready. Ibrahim put the suitcase in the backseat and the three of us took off.

We went north on the Eastern Ring road and soon we were out of the city. There wasn't much traffic once we got on the two-lane black top highway toward Badaling (八达岭), the Great Wall gate town about eighty kilometers north, and we drove mostly in silence.

"We should have brought Mikku," I said. Ibrahim didn't answer. I looked at Rashid and he nodded silently in agreement with me.

After a minute Ibrahim said, "Tonight we are going to meet interesting people. You will be very popular."

"Why? Because I'm an English teacher?" I said laughing.

"Yes. That is right," he said laughing too. "Would you rather be a movie star?" He did his little pose.

This time I didn't answer him.

We came around the bend and suddenly there was a building that looked like a motel you might find off an American road before the interstate highways. It had a circular driveway right off the road, and a lobby that was lit up and visible from a half a mile away. We drove in and a party hack-valet in a clean and ironed white shirt and creased black pants met us.

"Here." Ibrahim reached behind the driver's seat and grabbed something. "Do you want to bring this in?" Ibrahim handed me the suitcase with the stone.

"Can Rashid carry it? It will be less conspicuous."

Rashid shrugged and Ibrahim had no reaction. Ibrahim gave his card and the keys to the valet and we went in.

We walked into the main lobby, which led to a banquet hall. The tables were arranged around the outside and there was food and drinks, very expensive looking bottles of sparkling wine and other spirits. Nobody was sitting at the tables. The middle space was where everyone was crowded, talking intently.

At first, I thought it was a Japanese party. I had never seen such stylish, such well-tailored clothes, such sparkling jewelry, or women's hair done with such precision, or such perfect make-up on mainland Chinese people. It looked like Asians had taken over the TV show *Dynasty*. It was an exclusive gathering, one I had never seen mentioned or that had been shown in any TV show or society gossip magazines. The two anchors of the National TV news were there. The famous actors, men and women, from the TV soap operas, a couple of movie stars, the host of a popular "investigative" talk show. Those were just the people that I recognized.

"That is Zhao Ziyang's niece, and that is Li Peng's nephew, that is..." Ibrahim went on for a bit. These were the Young Lions of Communist China. "And the ones who are here that we don't recognize or have never heard of are the real rulers. Or will be in twenty years. Most of them are graduate students at the Political University."

"Welcome to our party." A young woman, not beautiful but with very good English, came up and introduced herself. "Hello, Ibrahim," she said. "Is this the man you were telling me about?"

"Yes. Yang, this is Nate."

"How do you do, Mr. Schuett? Did I say that right?"

"Yes. It is difficult for Americans to say correctly."

"Thank you." She blushed with a little pride. "I understand you were teaching at the Foreign Language Institute recently."

"Yes."

"China certainly needs good teachers. It is most unfortunate to hear about the deaths of the two foreigners at the school recently. I am very sorry. It must have caused you a great pain."

"Yes. I was friends with both of them."

"Yes." She paused for a bit. "I understand you speak very good Chinese as well?"

"Not very well – so-so." I looked at Ibrahim and he nodded toward Rashid. He wanted me to give up the suitcase, here.

I looked around. People looked at me and smiled. I looked for Gong Li, the actress, the most beautiful woman in the world. If she was here, I would give it to her. I'd do anything for her. I would do anything for a woman that beautiful, but I didn't see her. The rest of them, maybe not bad people, but this stone, that "proves" that they are all Jews – I started laughing.

Ibrahim said it was mine, that it was my decision.

I shook my head at Ibrahim, laughing. He smiled. "Sorry," I said. I nodded to Rashid, who had made himself at home, off to the side, eating and talking to one of the hostesses. I walked over to him and waited. He looked at me sideways with a question in his eyes. "Put it in the car," I said.

"Hao (好)." Chinese for OK, good. He walked out with the suitcase without looking at Ibrahim for approval.

"It belongs to China," I said to Ibrahim. "But not to them."

He shrugged. "I just thought this might be easier for you here. When you know what to do, you will do it. It must be soon though, promise me?"

"I can promise that."

The young woman came back to us, "Chen tells me that you understand China in a very special way and are a very special teacher." She gave me a slight leer. "What does she mean by that?"

"Chen?" But of course. There she was, Gregor's girlfriend and witness to many of my best and worst moments. "Hello, Chen." She came over. "I am not sure what Chen means by "very special teacher". Perhaps I have a good reputation as a teacher? Is that what you mean?"

Chen shrugged. "Ye xu (也许) Perhaps...?" Still pretending not to know English...

"I don't believe I am a very good teacher. I just tell jokes – I don't know if anyone really learns."

Chen looked at me with her catbird grin. "Nate has made me welcome at so many gatherings of our foreign friends. It is so nice to have a chance to have you join us at one of our parties." She looked at our host. "I know one of his students, and she has told me how much she has learned..." All I could do was feign modesty.

I was completely at ease now. Ibrahim and I stayed for another couple of hours. We talked to nearly everyone. I sipped the same glass of champagne throughout the evening. I actually had fun and was sober. At the end when we were leaving, Yang, who seemed to speak for the gathering, shook my hand.

"If you decide to stay in China, I can help you. Just let me know." She handed me a card. It merely had her name and phone number on it. "Whatever you need, just call." She gave me that look again.

We left and got in the car and headed back to town.

Ibrahim and I didn't speak for quite a while once we got under way.

"You never answered my question. Did you kill him?"

Ibrahim kept his eyes on the road.

"No," he said finally. "He's not dead."

"Why not?" I asked.

"He didn't do it. He didn't kill them."

"Is that what he told you? He could have been lying."

"Yes. I might be too. He could be buried in that field, right out there." He pointed out into the dark.

I said nothing.

"But he's not. He's on a freighter that leaves Tianjin tomorrow afternoon, sailing to Timor. We have friends in the Indonesian merchant fleet. They will release him on Timor and from there he can get to Australia easy enough. He probably still has a bad headache. He told me to compliment you on your kick."

"Then why did he try to kill me?"

"Maybe he found her dead first and thought you killed them?" I looked at him like he was stupid and he shrugged. "Anyway, maybe he wasn't going to kill you. He denied to us that he would have hurt you, that he only he wanted to scare you, to find out what you knew and..."

"That is ridiculous!"

"Perhaps. Zev found a note in her apartment." He pulled a scrap of paper out of his jacket pocket.

I turned on the overhead light and read.

It was in German.

"I'll translate it to Chinese for you," said Rashid.

> Erika,
>   If you are able to get it, be careful. It will be stored in the refrigerated car. There will be a distraction and perhaps a chance to grab it. But only if it is safe. The Stasi is pretty smart and very mean.
>   Dag

It was in her handwriting. No date, nothing else. "Was there an envelope?"

"I don't know. It was in the suitcase lying on top of the stone. Zev thinks it was the East Germans who killed them. I don't think so though. The Democratic Germans here in China are not of the same quality as their comrades in Europe."

"They might have been mad for losing their treasure at the train station."

"Perhaps." Ibrahim didn't take his eyes off the road. "Also Zev knew about you and the American missionary. A Chinese man, pretending to be a Christian, pretending to be Chinese security police, who was looking for some money told him about you meeting the missionary. People like him and Zev tend to find each other. I think Gregor might have introduced them."

Gregor! He had a guy tapped into Preston's operation. No wonder he was so confident he could take him out.

"Zev figured you for a treasure hunter too and that Erika and Dagmar were trying to cut you out and you found out about it. So he said he suspected you too. I explained to him that it would have been very difficult for you to kill them since I knew where you were for the whole day...remember we ate together at the Korean restaurant on the other side of town. But still, it got me thinking, why would he think that you might have killed them?" He looked at me smiling.

"Zev and I met in a strange place," I said. The foggy memory of the Peach Orchard – the only tangible evidence of that night was that my dick was sore the next day. "It isn't really important. But then, who killed them?"

"What do you think?"

"Sandor shot her? And then killed himself?" It was the theory of least resistance.

"Perhaps. Jews and Germans – you know..." Ibrahim was nodding his head like a professor trying to be respectful to an unprepared student.

"Dexter – the Americans? He and Molly went missing the day before the murder. Maybe Molly did it because she thought I was fucking Erika." Ibrahim shook his head.

"The North Koreans? They were angry because they lost the romantic attentions of Erika to Zev. She was their Great White Sex Goddess. That must have made them crazy after a life of listening to the Great Leader of Pyongyang." Ibrahim nodded and shrugged.

"The Russians? The East Germans? Revenge for messing up their shipment? Or maybe my Chinese friend who wants to be a Jew? Bing? I hear that he has gone missing." The more I thought about it the more confused I got. "I don't know." Occam's razor seemed very dull.

"I really don't know either," said Ibrahim. "Zev could have been lying. We didn't torture him, not that it would have done any good. He convinced us, but then, as you say, maybe he was a very good liar. Maybe we should have killed him. We still can as far as that goes."

I just let it drop. It could be the Koreans I suppose. It wasn't me.

"What's the name of the ship?"

Ibrahim looked at me hard and I looked back. It was a no bullshit moment.

"The *Atlatas Supraman*."

Chapter Twenty-Five

The next morning I took a cab to my old work unit office on Fuxing Lu. It was cold and wet. I came in and everything looked the same, except Ling was the only one there. Ling was in his office neatly dressed in his "good" Mao suit, the one that fit appropriately bulky, as if business was as usual. He still acted as though he were running a busy shop, greeting me warmly and acting very sympathetic to my plight. "India is our enemy; this man will never help China!" But there was clearly nothing he could do. The Party wasn't going to get involved for fear that the money would completely dry up. ITMS had run out of money for the time being and he needed to play ball in hopes that their fortunes would reverse.

He told me his cousin, who works for a Liberation Army missile factory, can deliver immediately. Swiss bank accounts, wire exchanges, no problem. Ling had done that before – all he needed were the numbers and the go-ahead, $10,000 apiece, very cheap for the "Red Tassel," a shoulder-fired surface to air missile. It's not as fast or accurate as the American Stinger but it works well on low-flying helicopters, very high impact. "You are a good salesman. Software, missiles, what is the difference?"

Lately I had been thinking I couldn't fall any farther, but then I suddenly looked at where I was and thought that I was free. I was alive and healthy. How much higher is there than that? I told him no. I wouldn't sell arms.

Pan came into Ling's office. She looked at me. "Where is Lin?" I asked her. "I need him. I can pay." She smiled, as if of course, I knew you would come back. She made a call.

"Ten minutes," she says.

We sat close, across from each other and she told me how the rest of the staff was moonlighting at other work units for almost nothing, because all of the extra money had dried up, so nothing was really being done. The software engineers didn't bother coming in even though they were supposed to. No one was afraid of her father anymore and she thought that was funny. She said it wasn't much fun anymore though. She missed Tai, her Taiwan boss. She blamed Ling Ye for Tai's fall. Somehow Ling had not produced enough. I told her it was nobody's fault here; it was completely outside anyone's control. She blamed me too; I could see that, even though she didn't say so. We talked all in English. I gave her the best English lesson I could for the next ten minutes. Her eyes looked very hurt when I left.

Lin was sitting in his car. Pan told me that the joint venture had stopped paying him, but they couldn't take the car away. It wasn't his car of course, but it might as well have been. He was still being supported indirectly by the Canadian company, through the contracted fees that they had to pay just to stay open. So his job was just to sit in the work unit square, drinking tea, playing Go or dominoes or polishing his car.

I gave him fifty US dollars.

"What's this?"

"I never paid you for all the driving you did for me when I was working here.

"I never took you anywhere."

"Oh – yeah that's right." We looked at one another. "If you drive me to Tianjin (天津) and back then we are even – OK? I will buy the gas."

"That's OK. Let the Work Unit pay for the gas."

***

I sat in Lin's Hongqi parked along one of the more rundown piers in Tanggu (塘沽), the port of Tianjin. Lin was very glad to see me today

320

and to show off what he had done to the Hongqi (红旗). He had fixed it up with new upholstery, a tape player, even a little snack bar filled with warm beer and peanuts. Help yourself, he said. He was listening to some high-pitched Beijing Opera. It was great to get out of Beijing, he said, and I agreed with that. The place was starting to close in on me and I needed to get out for even a day. But I needed to get out without being noticed and what better way than in an old Hongqi, polished up and flying the Chinese flag off of the front aerial.

Security at Chinese merchant docks is very military. In the States, the Mafia watches the docks. But I had a pass from the PLO mission, countersigned by some Chinese Party guy Ibrahim knew, and of course I was in the backseat of a tricked-out Hongqi. I let Lin do the talking, while I tried to look pissed off and important. We made it in, and Lin parked next to the Indonesian freighter *Atlatas Supraman*.

A couple of dark-skinned sailors in baggy lightweight pants and collarless shirts accompanied a light-skinned guy with gleaming sky-blue eyes in jeans and a polo shirt. They were walking toward the car. I breathed easy.

"I'll try not to be long," I said to Lin as I got out. "If I'm not back in two hours then go back to Beijing without me. I am with a friend so don't worry." I handed him an envelope. Lin nodded and waved his hand, indicating he would wait. I joined Rashid and the two Indonesians.

The gangway was all rope, a single thick line for a foot path, and two thinner ones for hand rails. The two sailors went up it like squirrels. Rashid and I went a little slower. Unceremoniously aboard, I followed Rashid down stairs next to the hatch. At the bottom, a tough looking sailor wearing a Nehru "Good Humor man" hat sat on a stool, running a pipe cleaner through the barrel of a Tec-9 machine pistol. He fished out the keys and let us into the room and locked the door behind us.

Zev was lying on a cot reading today's *International Herald Tribune*. I had to squat down because the ceiling was so low with pipes crisscrossing it like jungle vines. I could hear water lapping right behind Zev's head.

"Hey mate, did you bring me the Peach Orchard lovely that I ordered?"

I had to smile.

He sat up and made space for me to sit down. "You should have known to bring her without being told," he said, reaching over to shake my hand like an old frat brother.

"I will leave you two to talk," Rashid said in Chinese, as he closed the door.

"What'd he say?"

"He said that if you hurt me, they will sew your balls in your mouth," I said.

"Um. Figures they'd have a quaint expression for that. Nobody has told me anything. Who'd they pin the murders on?"

I just looked at him.

"Did you tell them you saw me?" I laughed for some reason. "Look." He took a deep breath and looked at me blankly. "You don't have any idea when it comes to interrogating, OK? Let's knock off the shit. Tell me what you know, and I'll do the same. You wouldn't be here if you didn't want something." His accent was different now, no more Australian lingo, almost middle European.

"They don't know about me seeing you that night. One detective thinks its murder, but he doesn't know how. He thinks I know."

"Do you?"

"You did it."

"Why?"

"You stole the stele and didn't want any partners." He was quiet and looked at me for an uncomfortable moment.

"Apparently we sail tonight. Ibrahim says they'll let me out in Timor. I can get home from there. I guess you're wondering why I'm still alive?"

"You guys knew each other back during one of your wars."

"That's right. Abe was a PLO sapper in '67. He couldn't have been more than fourteen or fifteen years old. A couple of my guys caught him and another boy after they blew up a jeep right in middle of Jerusalem. Killed a friend of mine." He paused for just a second. "There was something about him. I made sure we kept him around, said I wanted to interrogate him. And I did. Got nothing of course, but he was such a balls-up, fearless joker. Can't help but like him."

"What happened to the other kid?"

"I don't really know. He was a bit of a dumb shit. Sent him to POW land. Some of our boys wanted to just shoot him. We did that sometimes, everybody does in war. I don't know why I saved him. He killed my friend. To be honest, I wasn't the same after that."

"Were you going to kill me that night in the shower?"

"I don't know, probably not. I swore to Ibrahim I was only trying to scare you. And in the end another body would not have helped me at all. I just wanted to get out of there and was afraid you were going to slow me down. Could have gone either way. Nothing personal."

"You mean after you killed Sandor and Erika you needed to get out of the city and out of the country. So one more body wouldn't matter, right?"

"Do you think I could have killed her? Do you really think I am an animal?"

"She was a bitch," I said.

"Well, yes, yes." He scratched his forehead. "She was much, much worse than that." He smiled. "But, in a strange way, I was fond of her."

I wanted a cigarette. He saw me reaching and produced an open pack.

"The movie I was supposed to be in out west didn't work out. Remember the last time I saw you?"

"Yeah," I said. "You were leaving campus to go off to work on that movie, if that was what it was." I paused and he didn't blink. "I ran into Erika right after you left. She didn't have anything good to say about you that day and she was pissed at me because the school offered me a promotion..."

"OK, here's the story." Zev had lost weight since the summer, but looked older. He was sitting on the bed comfortably in the lotus position with a very blank look and no internal struggles on his face. "I didn't tell this to Ibrahim. Professional pride you understand. But I owe him, so you can tell him the truth after I'm gone. OK?"

All I thought was just listen.

After I got back from Vietnam, I had some trouble finding good work in Australia. I hung around with a lot of strange people in Sydney. Bikers, Messianic types of various denominations and persuasions, nut jobs of various sorts. Straight-up types bore me. I was painting houses and that's no fun. So I kept my ears open for some unorthodox employment that might pay better and be interesting. All I really know is soldiering, so I thought I'd look for mercenary work.

I got in touch with some old friends. I kept in touch with the past, let's just leave it at that. Through that I meet this crazy housewifely American woman, a real wacky Jesus freak. A great fuck as long as you were willing to pray with her first. She gives me a check from an Oklahoma bank to go look for this, Chinese Ten Commandments rock. I don't know. Said something about Genesis and lost tribes, I think sometimes maybe I'm the lost tribe, the last of a long lost tribe. She says the stone tablet is in Beijing. She gave me a plane ticket to HK plus expenses. If I found it, my cut was to be two hundred K US.

Drinkwell? I asked. That got his attention. Preston? Zev is looking at me with a little more respect now. Didn't mean to hit me the other night, he said.

Erika never had the tablet. Not until that day, in fact. I was practically living with her. Don't you think I'd have known? You know where it was? It was in Sandy's room. The room he shared with three other students, who he barely knew. After he grabbed it at the station, he just left it in the same suitcase under his bed for the next two months. Erika imagined it was hidden in some remote place. She thought it was in a false stone in the Great Wall or buried by the ruins of the old Summer Palace. Very imaginative, the girl could be sometimes. I usually think the most obvious and convenient place is where you start looking, but even I didn't think it would be there. I had him followed for over a month. I could have grabbed it and been out of here long ago if I'd have just stopped and thought about it.

Anyway, it's just as well. Drinkwell and Preston owed me about five K expenses and kept shining me on. I got back from Xinjiang illegally, and it is hard to stay here like that without money. I was on my way over to the Youyi to deliver it to the old man, when I ran into you. I really was going to kill that fucking old man and his dingbat wife if he didn't have my cash in US dollars.

"He'd have written you a check."

So do me a favor, don't leave Beijing without hurting that fucker.

So anyway, I lived with her for almost two months, and didn't hear hide nor hair of it. I was pretty sure you had something to do with it but, watching you – if you did, you were one cool customer! I followed you to the Peach Orchard of course, but I ended up talking to that asshole boss of yours.

When I couldn't find it, Plan B was that it was on the train after all. You can't believe what we went through to delay it. Had a little help with that, thanks to your friend Dexter. He was working with Drinkwell, which made me a little nervous, to be honest. The train was delayed for weeks in Mongolia and Siberia. That seemed an easier answer to the problem, since no one gave a shit once it got out of China. Money can buy anything along the Trans-Siberian.

By the time I got out there, I was just part of the entourage. Nancy and I had a nice reunion and we finally searched the train in Siberia. Nothing but old coins and some stinking black eggs. And that sassy East German girl, we got nothing out of her. So I went AWOL and snuck back into the country. I hung around, mostly hiding out south of town for almost two weeks trying to decide where I would go. I didn't know who was more likely to come through with my back pay so I had them all watched, Erika, Sandor, and that old fuck Preston over at the Youyi.

"Was Gregor helping you?"

What, the Yugo? Nah, he's a blabbermouth, Erika would tell him a secret in the afternoon and by the evening everyone up on the roof would be talking about it. I would have watched you too, except you had moved away from the campus with Abe. I didn't know what that was about. You meet Hanna? She was my spy. So I knew what you were up to with the missionaries.

"How did you recruit her?" I asked.

Money, or the promise of it anyway, and she took a fancy to me, if you catch my drift. Hell, he wasn't paying her, why not? Eager and grateful, my favorite type.

That afternoon Erika had that lunch to say goodbye, sentimental bitch, I hung out at the little café and when everybody left I came over the wall in the back and up to her patio. She had no idea I was coming back. She never locked that back door when she was home, so I thought I'd surprise her. I was even counting on a little welcome home party if you know what I mean. I was kind of curious to see if she had taken up with Sandy. They really did belong together; other than the ol' pendulum poke, she and I didn't have much in common."

"So you guys, you and Erika, were for real?

"What do you mean?" Zev looked disturbed by the question.

"I mean it wasn't just a business arrangement between you two?

"I was like the Koreans to her. She like to get fucked by exotic men. Its pretty common. Most women grow out of it when the baby bells go off."

I thought about my red hair. I knew what he meant.

"You're right, it was weird I guess, because Sandy and her were two peas in a pod. They'd have been much better suited together."

Anyway they were having this argument and I'm on the porch listening. She wanted to go to Hong Kong, he was saying it would be safer to fly to Germany direct, just one plane to get on and off. Here it was, the day they were planning on leaving and they haven't even figured out the escape route. That kind of stupidity is not long for the world. At that point I was still thinking I was going to cut her in, but I didn't know what to do about Sandor. It was clear from their conversation that the stone was there, in her apartment. I knew I couldn't spend much more time on the porch, even though I was lying down, listening with my chin on the floor and my ear to the door.

Chapter Twenty-Six

"You want a drink?"

Zev pulled a bottle cheap Chinese brandy from under his pillow. It tasted like cleaning fluid, but it hit the spot.

"Anyway, I'm listening to them argue and they are getting loud, and in another minute or so I was afraid someone would see me out there and call the guards, when I hear, faintly – pop!" Zev took the bottle from me and hoisted down a big gulp. "I look in and Sandy is lying on the ground with the side of his head blown in. I pulled out my little Glock 9, slid open the door and rushed her, got the drop on her and grabbed the gun."

"What did you tell Ibrahim?" I asked. "You didn't tell him..."

"Only that I didn't do it. I cashed my chit with him, no bull, even-Steven, end of story. But he believed me."

"Rashid work you over?"

"Not that much," Zev smiled.

"So what happened next?"

"Well," Zev took another pull on the bottle, and thought for a bit. "She was blubbering, saying how Sandy raped her and how he wanted to take the tablet to Israel rather than sell it and how happy she was to see me. Looking at him on the floor took away some of my desire for her. I pushed her away and she sat on the couch crying. I packed my Glock, and put her gun on a chair by the door while I looked at Sandy but it was clear he was gone. Even though they had been arguing, I think she completely surprised him. She was crying hysterically, still claiming he raped her, which I knew was a lie without a doubt. I – I couldn't imagine Sandor – could you?"

I shook my head.

"So it looked to me like he had delivered the stone and she had eliminated him. I was trying to figure out what to do, when over the patio and into the room came Bing. He must have been watching me. I came in so fast that I didn't bother locking behind me. Now things are a real mess. He's blubbering about how much he loved Sandy. He just picked up Erika's gun, a Type 64 Chinese job. I can't believe how stupid I was. He just held it but didn't threaten me. I held out my hand and he just handed it to me. I stuck it in my back pocket."

"OK, wait a minute," I said. "You said 'pop,' but that gun didn't have a silencer on it. The whole apartment building would have heard the shots."

"It's a Type 64, numb-nut. Chinese standard issue. They made the gun with the silencer built in. Didn't you notice how thick the barrel was?"

"Yeah, but I don't know much about guns. The cops said it was a seven point something semi-automatic."

"That's what a Type 64 is! It just has a silencer on it. The fat barrel."

"Yeah." Shit, I thought it looked like a super-soaker squirt gun. "I did notice that but I didn't put it together. Where did she get it?"

"I asked her that. She said the Croat."

"Was he cut in on the stele?"

"No. She kept her mouth shut about that but gave him three hundred dollars for the gun. Said it was for her trip. She didn't like traveling on trains unprotected. She had money you know. Her daddy had been sending her checks every month."

"OK, walk me through this." I took a pull and the brandy tasted like a blend of Lysol and Listerine.

"I asked Bing to sit down on the chair across from her on the sofa. Erika had on a short party dress, in fact, the same one she wore that night we went to the Youyi, last summer. It seemed strange to want to travel dressed like that this time of year. I guess she figured she might have to do some charming, if you catch my drift. If she was giving me the eye, I wasn't in the mood to notice it.

"Sandy is way past caring for, so I'm squatting down looking at the stone. Bing stood behind me and I felt him grab the gun, and by the time I turned he had taken the safety off like a pro and gets the drop on me. And her." He laughed without humor. "He got the gun, then he gave it back to me and I completely let my guard down. I guess he just started thinking. After he came in behind me like that I should have known he was primed for anything. I am just getting old. Should never have let Rashid surprise me either." He took the bottle back and pulled back enough to make me gag just watching him.

"Bing was waving the gun at me and her – he was ranting and threatening, half crying, about Germans killing Jews again, about being the lost tribe caught up in the genetic ocean of the Chinese. How Chin somebody destroyed all the books and turned them into irreligious heathens, shit I don't know what he was blabbering about. It was bizarre getting lectured by a Chinaman about Germans killing Jews. I just listened to him, wondering what he was talking about."

Zev took another pull off the brandy and handed it to me.

"Then he turned and shot her. And I just watched him. He knew how to handle a gun because bang. You saw her, right?"

"Yeah."

"Right in the cross hairs."

"I think he had some practice during the Cultural Revolution," I said.

"Then he handed me the gun. Again. And said – can you believe this? 'I am a Jew. And so are you. She killed one of our people. Do what you like.'"

I said nothing.

"I asked him what he would do if I let him walk out of there. He said he had already planned his escape. He had an open-ended plane ticket to Frankfurt, a passport and visa – and said he could leave that night. So I let him walk away." Zev gave me the "I know you don't believe me" look and shrugged.

"Then what?" I asked.

"I took off their clothes and set them up on the couch. I just figured that would make it more plausible, you know, kinky suicide pact kind of thing. I cleaned up the mess on the floor. Sandy got some blood on his shirt, so I had to deal with that. I mean, if they were naked when he shot himself, how would the shirt get bloody? Erika's dress was clean, so I just left it there on the chair. I put the gun in Sandy's hand and had his finger shoot into a book, the only thick thing I could find, so he'd have nitrates on his arm. I think the bullet went through though, and the hole was in the couch, so I didn't bother digging it out. Left the gun in Sandy's hand, cleaned fingerprints and waited until dark. Packed up Sandy's shirt and the stele and then left. Then I met you in the shower. You scared me. But I swear I was just going to scare you. If Rashid hadn't hit me, I'd have just tried to put the fear of Mossad in you."

"So you are Mossad."

"If you think so. I wouldn't make a fuss about it, if I were you."

"But why did you tell Ibrahim that you thought I had killed them?"

"It seemed a lot simpler than telling the truth. He's fucking PLO for shit's sake."

Chapter Twenty-Seven

Wed Oct 21

"What if I am followed when I leave the embassy?" I asked Ibrahim.

"We will test first." It was 9 AM. "Take a walk, and carry a bag with you. Rashid will know if you are being followed. He is very good at this sort of thing."

I needed a razor and I wanted a cheese omelet. I decided to walk to the Friendship Store. The weather was beautiful and the day was peaceful. The Embassy neighborhood around Guanghua Lu (光华路) was deserted as I walked past the Temple of the Sun (Ritan, 日坛). A few people were walking around the grounds of Ritan but otherwise it too was unusually empty.

As I got closer to the Friendship Store (友谊商店), the streets became more and more crowded until the corner itself was jammed with people, mostly round-eyed foreigners! I walked into the Friendship Store, more foreigners! I felt edgy being around so many white people, or even the two or three well-dressed Africans also shopping there. The people pushing their carts through this little supermarket gave me the chills. What is wrong with me? I got an allergic reaction just being there. I kept my head down, because I didn't want to get in any conversations. I bought some cheese to cook an omelet when I got back to the Mission. I also bought a pack of Gillette disposables.

I walked back thinking about my omelet, onions, lots of fried onions, sliced tomatoes, then maybe a little fried pork, cooked thick like Canadian bacon, and a big hunk of Swiss cheese. I thought about the smell as the cheese and eggs melded together, but still a little runny. I couldn't wait.

Rashid must have sent somebody to see if I was being followed, but I didn't see anyone.

I turned onto Guanghua Lu and I was back to the seemingly peaceful morning on the somewhat hidden street. The trees were beginning to turn yellow and orange, and leaves were falling. Every morning old Chinese ladies were out at dawn sweeping the streets with big hand-made straw brooms. Every cigarette butt, every loose blade of grass, every leaf was swept and carted away. You can eat off of the street. The embassy lawns on the other side of the walls were stately and serene. It was all too tranquil.

Then a black Mercedes with tinted windows slowly drove by. It continued past me and pulled up at the end of the block just at the corner.

They want me to catch up with them, I thought. They think I have the stone and they want to make a deal. Or...

The two blond hunks. Hadn't seen them since the train station. They quickly moved to stand against the wall. I moved behind the tree and although they must have seen me as they passed, they didn't look back at me. They were about twenty meters ahead of me.

She came around the corner and still had on her black leather jacket. The East German Hag was with Monique, the French girl from school. The hunks were quickly on one side and then the other and they frog-marched the Hag to the car, pushed her in the back seat and were gone in thirty seconds.

I came from behind the tree and started walking. Monique was standing there with a look as if she had forgotten something. As I approached she looked at me as if she didn't recognize me.

"Zao (早)," I said. Good morning. I kept on walking, didn't have time for her drama. She had a look in her eyes like Zev had the night Rashid threw him in the trunk.

****

"I have something for you." I handed Zhang the suitcase. The sun reflected off of the lake at Beihai Park (北海公园), making me squint, and I was mad that I didn't buy sunglasses at the Friendship store earlier that morning. "It is a stele that I think was found near Xianyang (咸阳). I believe it was stolen from your country recently. Please return it to someone who will protect it better."

She had cut her hair short and looked like a little peasant girl. She had her Madame Mao Zedong clear half-frame glasses on. It got chilly that afternoon and was windy and she was bundled a bit. She looked at me as if she were waiting for something. "You know a way to return it, I am sure. Let them think you were given it in Xian or Chongqing. You've been there recently. I don't care. Tell them the truth if you need to. It belongs in a museum and should be studied by Chinese archaeologists. Your country has to figure out what it is. Please, take it." I said.

She took the suitcase. "Did you kill those two foreigners?"

"No." Strangely I wasn't hurt that she would ask me that. We were past all that now. Her matter-of-fact manner was comforting to me. It allowed me to get through this without breaking down, even as I knew so many dreams were ending right in front of me. She seemed happy too that that was all I wanted from her, to act as a courier, with no please-come-to-America-with-me scenes. This was easy by comparison. As long as I stopped myself from saying something like, "I'll never forget..." it would be easy.

"I will think of something to say," she said. We walked along the edge of the lake. She said that she was going to marry Quan. Other than skipping my heart, it was no problem. I wished her good luck, I really meant it too and she knew that. She didn't ask me what I was going to do, because she could see that I didn't know. I don't know what else she saw because I had trouble looking at her. I was so happy right then just being with her, and I didn't think about her and me. I didn't talk about Xian or our brief time together. She didn't either. I told her I was leaving in a week. She said we will meet again before I go, that I had to hear her duet with Gang. She made me promise I would come and listen to it before I left. We could say goodbye then, she said. After returning the stone she would contact me. I told her the number of the Embassy.

I walked back. The weight of the stone was off me and I think I was relieved for more reasons than just that. That must have been why I was laughing. Or crying, I forgot which.

Fri Oct 23

I rode my bike across town for the last time. I would need money eventually, so I thought I would sell my bike at the Youyi and take the bus back. I rode north behind Beihai. I went past Zhou's hutong and it was gone! All of the houses had been flattened by a bulldozer. The skeleton of a high rise was looming over what had once been a vibrant little neighborhood of alleyways and connected courtyards. I thought of how different everyone's life would be that lived there. I was glad that Zhou was leaving all that now, because I knew she would miss her hutong. It was a good time to leave, not just for Zhou.

I rode past the Exhibition Hall and the Zoo. I was sleep-riding. Nothing seemed to register as I cycled by, even while I was aware that I was seeing it all for the last time.

It was still early for a late afternoon, so I decided to stop at the school and see if Bing's family knew where he was. I rode past the guards, who didn't seem to notice me.

I only saw one of the idle workers, one of the fellows who waited every morning to watch Molly walk to the shower building in her robe. He was sitting outside his unfinished building.

"What are you building here anyway?" It struck me how foolish I was that in all the time I lived here I never knew what it was they were working on, and never bothered to ask.

"It is a New Party headquarters for the school," he said. "We will never finish."

"Why?"

"We live like emperors here. We eat three times, every day. If we finish, it all will end. Where is your wife?"

"Gone."

"All of them?" He laughed. I shrugged and laughed too. I guess they were all gone.

I parked my bike in the vestibule, in my old spot. I looked at my old door. It looked like Mark and Kathy, the new Americans, must have installed a new lock.

I walked up the stairs and passed the Liu apartment on the second floor. I hadn't seen Mr. Liu since the summer and part of me wanted to stop by and say goodbye. But I didn't have time and it would be rude if I didn't stay for at least an hour. I walked up one more flight to Bing's door and knocked.

His sister answered. The apartment was unrecognizable from the doorway. The dark, depressing death chamber was gone. A huge TV was located in the corner where Bing's father's chair used to be, a bright green rug was on the floor and a red couch was against the newly plastered and painted yellow wall.

At first she pretended not to know me, but I pleaded friendship with Bing. She knew that he had very few friends, so she relented.

"He left."

"When?"

"He left yesterday," she said.

"Yesterday?" He must have had some help. How could he have waited that long after the murders? Yesterday? Zev said he left right after he killed...Forget it, Jake. He had been here all this time? And he just walked out and left the country? She didn't have any contact information for him. I thanked her and left.

I rode back over to the Youyi and parked the bike in front and didn't bother locking it. If someone stole it, then that would be one less decision later. It was getting dark and cold.

Gregor and Harold were in the downstairs bar. Gregor, the tough cynical Croat, was talking about the bodies. Were they still in the morgue? Have you ever seen a Chinese morgue, he wondered. What would happen to them? He saw me and they both stood up. Harold hugged me. Then Gregor hugged me too and now was crying, and Harold seemed to be trying to cry as well, but I don't think he could, because his Englishness won out over any sloppy sentimentality he might have felt. I didn't cry; I was still too numb. Because of the investigation, none of us had really come to terms with the fact that two of our friends were dead and gone. It was clear from looking around that everybody felt that way. We were finally having the wake.

Gregor ordered some spare ribs and I picked at them. I hadn't eaten much lately and I was vaguely hungry but drinking a glass of water seemed to fill me up.

"Is the upstairs open?"

Harold went to ask.

"How are you?" asked Gregor.

"OK."

"Do you need money?"

"No." I never thought Gregor would ever ask me that, but he was probably flusher than I was. "I'm fine. I have money. Well, not a lot, but enough. I have a ticket from Hong Kong back to the States, if I want to use it."

"That bastard who didn't pay you for your computer program, he is the reason you lose your job. I can get him for you."

"It isn't worth it."

"I know his room number – I know everything about him! I know he is leaving China soon, maybe tomorrow. I will deal with this. I'll put him forever in a wheel chair! Don't tell me you want him to go free because he is an American?"

For the first time ever, Gregor frightened me. "He is an old man who has failed. That is enough revenge for me."

"You have no understanding of the real world," he said angrily. I shrugged.

"Upstairs is closed," said Harold returning. "They say it is too cold and no one wants to work up there tonight."

"Just as well," I said.

"Molly came by earlier," said Gregor.

"What?" I woke suddenly. "Is she still in town?" I was suddenly angry.

"Two hours ago everyone was here. She said she talked to Erika that afternoon for a long time, much longer than what she told the Chinese police. It makes me wonder if perhaps..." I wasn't sure what Gregor was driving at, "It is funny because Erika was mad at her and she was mad back. Molly said, 'Erika messed with the wrong people and then the wrong people messed with her.'"

"Did she?" Now Gregor was starting the conspiracy mongering, and he was pissing me off. "Why did you sell her the gun? You know that it was the gun that killed them? You know that, don't you? Can they trace it to you?"

Gregor looked around and then at me and as he lowered his voice, and pulled me aside. "How do you know?"

"Why did you sell it to her?"

"Money! US dollars! I needed the money. Why didn't you let me help you in your business?" He asked it as if it was entirely my fault.

"Where did you get the gun?"

"Friends, friends."

"Does she know?" I meant Chen and he knew it.

He didn't say anything.

"I am not understanding what you are saying, Gregor. Molly and Dexter left her apartment late that afternoon and then that evening I find Erika and Sandor dead. How late? When did they leave?" I paused and looked at him. "I know they had been dead for a few hours at least." He gave me his best stone face. "What are you saying?" I asked him. I never did pin Zev down on the time. It takes two or three hours for any rigor to set in.

"Sandor did not kill her," Gregor said. "You knew him. It could not be murder-suicide. He was not capable of it. It could not happen."

"Well it wouldn't have happened if you hadn't sold her that gun," I said.

Gregor looked away. He was pissed at me but I didn't care. "Whoever killed them would have found another gun." Harold, who had pretended to ignore us, now rejoined us.

"Molly said something else that afternoon at Erika's apartment," said Harold. "She said that she and Dexter were going to open a Buddhist monastery in Mountania or Black Mountain, I don't remember. Isn't that in your country, Gregor?"

"Montana, the state. Molly is from there." I said.

I couldn't tell if Harold was putting us on or not. Buddhist monastery, right. He knows where Montana is too. I looked at Harold, but he would not look at me. Not him too? I left them. I was pissed at Gregor. I thought about Ling asking me to sell Chinese Stingers. Had I actually considered it?

I wondered, though, what would they have argued about? Did Molly accuse her of sleeping with me? Did Molly have Dexter do it? Did Zev lie to me? He didn't tell me everything. The CIA was mixed up with this and that is Dexter. Would Mossad cover for the CIA? Or the other way around? No, what am I thinking?

Rennie and Zhou came into the bar. It is funny after all that has happened, I think in some ways he had managed the best of us. He looked at Zhou like a dog looks at its owner, deep, deep in puppy love. Rennie is rich though and doesn't have to worry about money. All of my problems were because I wanted more money. He is on the other hand happy. I envied him at that moment. He hadn't made a mess out of his life. Does he know too about me and his woman, Zhou? Like Molly knew? Was I some village idiot whom everyone forgave because I was not responsible?

"You need some drink with us. Rennie, you, me, Nate, here we drink." Boris and Yevgeny had just arrived. Gregor seeing me talking to the Russians, smelling a fight or free booze, joined us with a big smile, apparently completely self-absolved from his weapons dealing, at least in his own conscience. Harold was talking to the barkeep again.

"No. I have to stop drinking for a while," I said.

"When do you leave?"

"Today is Friday right? Sunday morning," I said.

"Then drink with us!"

"I have to stop. It is not good."

"It is good. You can still be like Russian. We teach you." Boris put his arm around me.

"I am sorry about saying the bad thing about Dagmar," said Yevgeny. "You know, I love her too. She made me crazy. Women make all of us crazy. We love the other German too, the one Hungarian Jew kill."

"He didn't kill her. You probably did," said Gregor.

"Stop. Gregor, stop. We are all very sad, right?"

"Yes."

"Yes, yes, yes."

"I'll drink. I'll drink to Erika and to Sandor. We will all drink to them."

"Erika and Sandor," we all said.

I fell over and lost consciousness.

I vaguely remember being carried and woke up on the roof. The cool air felt so sweet as I breathed it. There was a little wind and I looked up and the clouds were swirling. Rennie, the Russians and Gregor had carried me up. The barkeep had agreed to stay up with us and open the bar but only for soda, glasses and such, no liquor. He didn't feel like taking money tonight.

The Russians of course brought their own, two liter bottles of Stolichnaya. It was chilly but I didn't notice. I felt like I was on my death bed and was being sent off like an Irishman before his time.

Zhou sat next to me very close. "I moved in with Rennie. We live together and it is wonderful. He said you told him to make me do it. Thank you." She kissed me, openly. "We go to Delaware in December and will have a Christmas wedding. I don't know what a Christmas wedding is like in Delaware. I am going to be fat then. Because..." At that moment she looked like the purest woman who ever lived. I could actually see her glowing and I was happy for her. I looked at Rennie, who was watching us. I smiled, and he smiled back.

"Because why?"

"Because in May I will have a baby."

She looked at me blankly, with no outward emotion or meaning that I could discern. Inscrutable. I was inscrutable too and then I looked over at Chen. She gave me that look of hers, very scrutable.

Gregor was holding forth on the future of the world with the Russians.

"It is ending soon," he said. They didn't argue, in fact for once they seemed to agree. "These are the last days of Socialism."

"I think you are right," Boris said. "But it won't be like America. No one wants that. I know that in my bones."

"When it falls," said Yevgeny, "I don't want it to fall on me."

"There will be blood everywhere soon."

"Especially in your country, Croat," said Yevgeny.

"My country! Serbs make it like a giant toilet. We Croats want it flushed." He was off recounting the many wrongs his fellow Croats had suffered at the hands of the nefarious Serbs and, by the way, from the Muslims too and the Hungarians had to be pushed back across the Danube where they belong...

I sat up, and felt better. I signaled Chen over to talk to her. "What will they do?"

"What do you think?"

I knew her father, from the shadows, would be one of the final judges in lieu of conclusive evidence.

"Not the Koreans?"

"No."

"I didn't think so." I said.

"But they remain suspects. They could have done this. We know that. All of them have been trained in the craft. Three of them admitted having relations with the West German woman, as recently as this summer. They admitted that they were very jealous of the Australian, and then later of Sandor. Only one of them has an alibi that doesn't involve another Korean. They will continue to be questioned."

"So they weren't sent back to Pyongyang."

"No. They are still here."

"The East Germans?"

"They would not have dared to do this. They don't have that many friends. They know we know about the freight car. Some Chinese have been arrested. The East Germans are cooperating. They have arrested people too."

I didn't tell her I saw the Hag rounded up.

"Americans?"

"You mean that spy who stole your wife?" Chen laughed slightly. "You know more than they do about what is going on – the Americans seem very foolish sometimes. I am surprised they don't try to hire you to work for them. You would be a good spy. Look how much I trust you!"

I laughed, but it was true. Molly left me for a fool.

"She wasn't really my wife anyway," I said. "Did you know the school was going to fire Erika in December? She wasn't a good teacher," I said.

"So, you think we Chinese killed her so that we don't have to fire her?"

"Chinese don't like confrontations."

"That is true. We prefer indirect methods. Murder is not indirect."

"Why do you stay with Gregor?"

"You like him, don't you?"

"Yes I do. I can't help it. I do like him." We smiled at each other. I decided not to bring the gun up with her.

"We know the Australian returned illegally from the Soviet Union." She was thinking about it hard, not looking at me. I needed to be on guard here. "He never had his passport stamped in China. There is a witness on campus who says they saw a big foreigner in the German woman's apartment earlier. It wasn't you, was it?" Full bore right in the face. I knew it was coming.

"No. I was across town all day. I told the inspector. The Korean Restaurant..." I gave no startled looks of outrage or bewilderment. Full bore right back at her. My alibi was tight.

"Have you seen him since he left?"

"No," I lied.

"Until we find him it does not make sense to pursue it. It was probably one of the Koreans. Jealous. But until we know for sure it will have to be murder-suicide." She relaxed.

"Why don't you think it is murder-suicide? I can't imagine Sandor doing that, but I really don't know. I can't honestly say I am sure he didn't do it." I wasn't lying.

"No one hears the shots, there was no silencer in the apartment. Erika had been dead for five hours. Sandor had been dead for maybe only four hours. The tests show the Hungarian fired the gun. Three shots. One shot we found in the couch, one in Erika's forehead and one in the side of Sandor's head." No silencer? Doesn't she know it was a Type-64? Did they test Erika to see if SHE fired the gun? The autopsy sounds like bullshit. For once in my life I kept my mouth shut.

"So Sandor or someone else killed Erika first. Maybe two different people with two different motives did it?" Now I was very confused. Erika killed an hour before Sandor? I saw the gun! I know it was silenced! "Are you sure about the times? Are you sure that Erika was killed an hour before Sandor?"

"Why do you ask?"

Why the fuck can't I keep my mouth shut! "It's just," I tried to explain, "if Sandor did it then why did he wait around the apartment for an hour before killing himself? That doesn't make sense? Did he undress her? Are you sure about the times?"

Chen smiled and shrugged.

"With the same gun?"

"Yes," said Chen. "Perhaps."

"Did she have sex?" I asked.

"No." She paused. "Did you have sex with her?"

"No."

"I mean ever?"

"No."

"Your wife seemed to think you did." So wherever she is, she had been questioned separately.

"She was wrong. And she wasn't my wife." I could tell Chen knew where she was or where she went. I didn't care.

She smiled at me. "Then it was probably as you say. But you knew them and you are not sure he did not do it. I trust your instincts. If you are not sure he didn't do it, then you think he could have done it?"

"I didn't know him that well."

"So, he killed her, then an hour later killed himself. Right? The rumors that foreigners spread are very dangerous. This place where we come to meet – this special relationship we all have here in China – if the rumors don't stop then this will end."

I shrugged. "I am leaving," I said.

"Someone could have done it and made it look like a murder then suicide. But who and how? And more important – why? I don't think the Hungarian killed her. But I didn't know him as well as you. Didn't the Germans kill his family?"

"That happened before he was born. No. That is not a motive. That is crazy. He was not crazy." Why does she steer my away from the possibility that Erika shot first?

"But there is something else."

"What?"

She smiled at me.

"A most valuable piece of the stolen archaeological treasure has been recovered. Gregor has mumbled in his sleep that he thinks you know about it. But clearly you don't because it was returned to a famous erhu player by the Weiwuer tribesmen who robbed the train in Siberia. He said it was repayment for an old and honorable debt. So who knows?" She looked at me as if my face was changing color. "He of course is unchallengeable because he is a true Chinese treasure himself. He has suddenly become very famous again..." She paused now and it was my turn to stare hard at her. "The Weiwuers are a strange people, a very strange people. Our history with them is very long and not always friendly. So the story sounds strange."

"Is the erhu player suspected...?" I started to ask.

"No. no. Although he has a helper, a Beijing woman. But she is beyond reproach." Chen stopped and looked at me again, and smiled. "His story is welcomed because, after all, in the end the archaeological treasure has been recovered. It makes it clear that the rumor that this murder was about an archaeological artifact obviously false. The artifact was outside of China this whole time. So that leaves jealousy as the most likely motive, which of course points back to a murder then a suicide."

Zhou looked over at us and smiled as she gave me a little wave with just her fingertips.

"Is it my baby?"

"Who will be able to tell? You both look so much alike."

Chapter Twenty-Eight

I told myself, again – "forget it Jake..." Somebody's lying. But the dead are dead and will stay that way. So far I am the only foreigner who seems to know Chen's story, although I am sure Gregor does too. This chronology stinks. Someone saw Bing leaving the apartment, maybe they needed to move the time of death so it didn't get pinned on him. I don't think Zev lied.

Like a storm moving off shore, Bing was "safely out to sea."

I gave my bike to Gregor. He had broken his and will, no doubt, break this one, but nothing lasts forever.

Then just as I was ready to go, something happened that was almost miraculous for me anyway. Three of my students from the foreign language school just showed up at the Youyi rooftop bar. I knew them only as well as a teacher can after just a month of teaching, but they somehow found out I was leaving and came to say goodbye.

The barkeep that had opened for us suddenly became very angry. "What are you doing here! This is off limits. I'll call the police! Get out of here. You will all go to jail!"

All that my students said was, "It is our country. We are free in our country." Actually, as everyone knew, they weren't. The Youyi was off-limits to Chinese without explicit permission. But they were firm about it and I didn't interfere. The barkeep looked at us foreigners for help. Chinese can't come here freely, his look said. I didn't say – "Let them stay for me, they are saying goodbye," which would have made it easier and saved face for all concerned. But sometimes it's best not to be so quick to smooth things over. They could speak for themselves just fine.

The barkeep looked blankly at the wall and said. "I am closing now. Please put the chairs up on the table when you leave." He left.

It was a subdued goodbye. My students were colleagues now and I spoke for a while in English to each of them. "The new teachers are boring," one of them said. "We miss you." After I had left them so shamefully, I was humbled almost to tears by the honor they showed me.

Finally enough. I shook everyone's hand. I hugged Zhou, but not too tightly. My stomach rubbed against hers and...I didn't want to think any more about it.

I walked out alone and took the bus back to the PLO compound.

One other thing happened. It was very late. I am pretty sure I just caught the last bus to Tiyuchang (体育场), the Worker's stadium, near the PLO Mission. There were only two passengers, an old lady and myself. The conductor asked me where I was going and I said, "Daodi de difang (道底的地方)." I meant "the last stop." It also can mean, I suppose, the final destination - you know - death I guess. The old lady looked at me with deep compassion and she repeated what I said under her breath. "Daodi de difang." She looked hard out into the night and kept any further thoughts she had to herself.

Sun Oct 25

Tonight I'll go to Tiananmen Square and hear Gang and Zhang play their erhu duet. Then, I am off, leaving Beijing by train. I guess this is the end of my time in China.

> *October 27, 1987*
> *Beijing Train Station*
> *Dear Dad,*
> *I am writing this fast, just to let you know I am OK. I am leaving Beijing in couple of hours. I'm heading west – not sure where yet. Possibly to a place called the Kirghiz Light, a fire that always stays lit out in the middle of the Asian*

Steppes, a place steeped in legend, a place that may well be the very center of the earth. It is a place where it is said that you can find your destiny. It may not be a real place at all. But it's kind of what I am after.

I am writing this so that you won't worry (I don't think I am doing a good job here). We Americans have spent so much time pursuing something somewhere, sea to shining sea, mountains, prairies and all that, that I think we forget the great undiscovered place, for us anyway, the middle of Eurasia itself. It is that big sweep of land that Ghengis Khan rode over, that Marco Polo crossed, that Alexander almost conquered, the land that goes on like the Pacific, almost endlessly, not just along the Trans-Siberian Railroad, but in its endless lost paths.

I know you are worried about me (and I know the more I write the worse it gets!) and I am telling you, don't worry. If I am ever going to be happy, then I have to do this. You want the truth? I'm chasing a woman, OK? Don't laugh. You are laughing anyway.

I used to dream about going to sea with you, particularly right after you went back, after the business failed. I was only 13 then and I suddenly hated life. Well I don't hate life now. I cherish every minute of it and live each day as if it is my last. (I guess that doesn't make you feel better either does it?)

Little League filled me with big league dreams but when we moved from our small backwater Jersey shore town to the suburbs outside New York, I suddenly hated baseball, in fact I hated everything. I hated the days that never seemed to end, and the nights that never brought sleep. I started dreaming in my half-awake world of other places and I hated you because you got to go and I had to stay. I read everything I could, and I got through that time, not always of "sound mind," and I thought in the end, I'd just end up a regular

349

guy somehow, with a wife and a job, a guy that came home every night.

But I don't think that it is going to be that way for me.

Who knows? Maybe I'll find the woman I'm chasing, and who knows? That could change everything.

I spent last night in Tiananmen with my Chinese friends. Tiananmen is a special place in China. It was the outer courtyard of the Emperor's palace. My Chinese friends are like the earth itself, so very solid with such a clear understanding of what is important. They understand the meaning of friendship in a way that I never did. One of those friends is a beautiful woman, like a fresh wild flower, with a heart as pure as gold, although if I told you everything you would smile at that description.

An old man and a young woman played their Chinese musical instruments, erhus, in the shimmering silence of the vast stone-covered square. I sat on the steps of the People's Heroes Monument and listened to the most beautiful, personal music you can imagine. It was the first time the piece had ever been performed and it was one of the most emotional experiences of my life. It was so silent otherwise, in the middle of the heart and center of the "Middle Country," Zhongguo, China's name for itself, the oldest civilization. I only now have begun to know how little I understand it.

And there were others as well, neighbors, students, colleagues. For an hour, maybe longer, all of us sat there in the moon shadow of the Monument to the People's Heroes. I can't tell you what it meant to me. They have helped me and loved me and I have given them nothing. They came to honor me and fill my spirit with hope and determination to live and be happy and that makes me sure that I will come out of this. They helped me regain my faith in people, and that is the most important faith in the world. Nothing like this has ever happened to me and I suspect nothing like it ever will again.

You see, Dad, you don't need to worry. We didn't have enough time together when I was young because you had to leave to make a living. But now I think of you and Mom first and I think of my friends here. I know that I have to thrive. Make a family someday maybe and make my children strong the way you made me strong.

So don't worry. I'll go find the Kirghiz Light and come back. I might bring someone back with me too, we'll see.

By the way – The Chinese curse about living in interesting times is false – there is no such curse. We all should live in interesting times. It would be very dreary otherwise.

Nate

CPSIA information can be obtained
at www.ICGtesting.com
Printed in the USA
BVOW09s1343030817
490983BV00001B/20/P